"Real vampires, real fun, real sexy!"
—Kerrelyn Sparks, *New York Times* bestselling author

Real Vampires Know Hips Happen

"I love this series . . . The humorous writing style mixed with the steam . . . makes this worth reading." —*USA Today*

"Ms. Bartlett keeps each book fresh." —*Night Owl Reviews*

Real Vampires Hate Skinny Jeans

"*Real Vampires Hate Skinny Jeans* . . . contains the fast-paced and funny entertainment expected from the series. Glory is hysterical; her relationships with her shoe-shopping friends and her male paranormal beaus are heartwarming and clever." —*Fresh Fiction*

"I am completely enamored of Glory St. Clair and enjoy seeing what she gets herself into through each new book." —*Once Upon a Romance*

Real Vampires Don't Wear Size Six

"This has to be one of the best series I have ever read. Even after seven books, Ms. Bartlett keeps the story and her characters fresh and never boring . . . Ms. Bartlett is an auto-buy." —*Night Owl Reviews*

continued . . .

"Every time a new Gerry Bartlett Real Vampires story comes out, I know I'm going to get a fantastically funny and highly enjoyable read, and this story was no exception." —*TwoLips Reviews*

Real Vampires Have More to Love

"A book that you can reread again and again. I have been with Glory from the start and can't wait to see what happens next. Each book is like coming home and catching up with old friends."
—*Night Owl Reviews*

"Fans will learn new and interesting tidbits about familiar characters and meet some fascinating new ones, making this addition to Bartlett's vampire series an entertaining read."
—*RT Book Reviews*

Real Vampires Hate Their Thighs

"Laugh-out-loud fun . . . *Real Vampires Hate Their Thighs* has a reserved spot on my keeper shelf!" —*Fresh Fiction*

"The chemistry between Glory and Jerry is explosive. But when you add in the secondary characters, the result is nonstop laughter!"
—*The Romance Readers Connection*

Real Vampires Don't Diet

"An engaging urban fantasy filled with action and amusing chicklit asides. Glory is terrific." —*Midwest Book Review*

"Another must-have . . . *Real Vampires Don't Diet* is honestly a tasty treat that's sure to please even the most discerning palates."
—*Romance Reviews Today*

Real Vampires Get Lucky

"Gerry Bartlett delivers another winner . . . Fans rejoice—this one's a keeper!"
—*Fresh Fiction*

"Fun, fast-moving and introduces some wonderful new characters, along with having plenty of familiar faces."
—*RT Book Reviews*

Real Vampires Live Large

"Fans of lighthearted paranormal romps will enjoy Gerry Bartlett's fun tale."
—*Midwest Book Review*

"Glory gives girl power a whole new meaning, especially in the undead way. What a fun read!"
—*All About Romance*

Real Vampires Have Curves

"A sharp, sassy, sexy read. Gerry Bartlett creates a vampire to die for in this sizzling new series."
—Kimberly Raye, *USA Today* bestselling author of *The Devil's in the Details*

"Hot and hilarious. Glory is Everywoman with fangs."
—Nina Bangs, *USA Today* bestselling author of *Wicked Memories*

"Full-figured vampire Glory bursts from the page in this lively, fun and engaging spin on the vampire mythology."
—Julie Kenner, *USA Today* bestselling author of *Turned*

Real Vampires
Know Size Matters

GERRY BARTLETT

B

BERKLEY BOOKS, NEW YORK

THE BERKLEY PUBLISHING GROUP
Published by the Penguin Group
Penguin Group (USA) LLC
375 Hudson Street, New York, New York 10014

USA • Canada • UK • Ireland • Australia • New Zealand • India • South Africa • China

penguin.com

A Penguin Random House Company

This book is an original publication of The Berkley Publishing Group.

Library of Congress Cataloging-in-Publication Data

Bartlett, Gerry.
Real vampires know size matters / Gerry Bartlett. — Berkley trade paperback edition.
pages cm.
ISBN 978-0-425-26703-5 (pbk.)
1. Saint Clair, Glory (Fictitious character)—Fiction. 2. Vampires—Fiction.
3. Overweight women—Fiction. 4. Paranormal romance stories. I. Title.
PS3602.A83945R4367 2013
813'.6—dc23
2013031381

PUBLISHING HISTORY
Berkley trade paperback edition / December 2013

PRINTED IN THE UNITED STATES OF AMERICA

10 9 8 7 6 5 4 3 2 1

Cover art by Chris Long / CWC International.
Cover design by George Long.
Interior text design by Kristin del Rosario.

This book owes its name to a genius with titles:
Tracy Dittrich.

Thanks, Tracy,
for being such a loyal friend to the series.

Acknowledgments

Size doesn't matter to Glory, but in the book business, it can be a factor. I owe so much to the size of my fantastic street team, whose members are out there spreading the good news about the Real Vampires series both online and in the trenches every day. You know who you are. Thanks so much!

Also, I have a sizeable support system in place and couldn't have gotten this book done without it. My wonderful editor, Kate Seaver, has always believed in this series, and I really appreciate that. The team at Berkley does such a super job, from the illustrator Chris Long, who cooked up such a fun cover this time, to my copy editor, Mary Pell, who knows my series better than I do. What a great experience I've had here!

My superstar agent, Kimberly Whalen, always has my back. I'm so glad she understands contracts and fine print, because I'd sure hate to tackle them.

Finally, my awesome critique partners suffer with me through every step of creating a book. Thanks to Nina Bangs and Donna Maloy for the long lunches and shopping orgies necessary to keep my writing muse fed. You guys are priceless and irreplaceable.

One

We'd been invaded.

You can do this. Suck it up. Attack. Use your powers. Instead I leaped up on the sweater table, shaking and screaming along with the mortals in the shop. *No. Get down, Gloriana St. Clair, and face the enemy.*

Weapons, I needed weapons and I sure as hell wasn't using my fangs this time. I glanced around. The two women perched on the chair next to the dressing room were no help. Their shrieks could have broken glass. Three more women crouched on the counter in front of the cash register. More mortals, totally useless, though one swung an umbrella at the horde. Impressive compared to me.

I tossed a sweater at one. Stupid. Didn't even slow it down. I was a failure. A wimp. I couldn't quit shaking and couldn't force myself to get off the table. If a god from Olympus attacked, I'd be right in his face, toe-to-toe. Or another vamp. Bring him on. But whoever had planned this had found my weakness. I thought I heard one right there, on the table, and moaned, horrified.

Mice! Dozens of them. Even Achilles had his heel thing. Glory St. Clair has hers. I don't like anything that's creepy or crawly. Now my reputation and the business I'd built from nothing were in shreds along with my pride. Would you shop where you saw mice? I'd have joined the stampede for the door myself if there'd been time.

My clerk Lacy, a were-cat, was running around like a starving woman at an all-you-can-eat buffet in kitty heaven. She whipped past me with a smile on her face, making sounds too gross to think about.

"Oh, God, there's another one!" The brave soul on the counter with the vintage umbrella slashed at the floor, knocking a mouse toward the door. That got the logjam there cleared with a chorus of screams.

I heard a smack near my feet. "Lacy, what the hell are you doing?" I gagged and realized I was going to have to whammy every mortal in the place.

"Glory, relax. I've got this under control." She held up a brown bag that rustled ominously. "There must be dozens of them. I wonder who sent them. An early birthday present from Mom?" She scrambled after a dark shadow that streaked across the floor. "Naw. She knows a stunt like this could get me fired." She glanced at me.

"She'd be right." I didn't want to know what had made that smudge on her cheek. Lacy was a natural beauty, red hair, porcelain skin. She dressed in the vintage clothes we sold here and looked like a model in them. Tonight the seventies bell-bottoms and tie-dyed tee were taking a beating.

"Well, not Mom. These are the pet store variety. Feeders. For snakes, that sort of thing. Someone brought them in here. Planted them. There goes another one." She dove and disappeared under a dress rack.

I heard a crash and a mannequin bit the dust. The women who'd been balanced on the chair had made a run for the door but were tangled up in a dress display.

"My God! My God! Get it off of me!" Loud sobs then the sounds of my mannequin being used as a sledgehammer.

Obviously I had to suck it up or we'd have mass hysteria on our hands.

"Ladies, please, calm down." At least I wore boots as I jumped in front of them, staring into first a pair of brown eyes, then blue. I had them mesmerized in a second. "You are fine, the store is fine. There are no mice, just a little game we're playing with discount coupons." I shivered as a mouse ran by and I kicked it toward Lacy. "Here's a twenty-five percent off coupon for your next visit. We're closing for some minor repairs. Mugs and Muffins next door has great coffee if you want to wait. We'll reopen in about thirty minutes." I snatched coupons from behind the counter then tugged them both to the door, dodging even more mice. These things had been planted. I had a feeling I knew who'd done it.

I got those two women out then went back for the three hugging their knees near the register. Ignoring Lacy's crows of triumph as she claimed more victims, I got the last customers whammied and out of the shop, coupons in hand. Finally, I hopped on the counter myself and waited for Lacy to finish.

"Whew. That was amazing. I bagged at least three dozen." Lacy grinned, her mouth still smeared with something I didn't want to think about. "Whoever pulled this stunt must have cleaned out a pet supply store." She stapled the wiggling bag closed then pulled out a wet wipe from the container under the counter and cleaned off her hands and face. Lacy glanced at me. "You okay?"

"Not really." I sighed. "Had your dinner break?"

"Um, yeah. Sorry about that. I got a little carried away. I need to clean up the floor too." She laughed. "Hey, I'm a predator. Think how you'd act if someone came in and offered you that negative blood type you love."

"I get it." I swallowed, not sure I wasn't going to hurl. "Thanks. You saved the shop."

"No problem. But I can sniff out a mouse a mile away." She wiggled her nose. "They weren't here yesterday. I wonder who . . ."

The phone rang before I could answer her. "Vintage Vamp's Emporium, the best store on Austin's Sixth Street."

"Really? Is it? I heard it just closed." The female voice was full of satisfaction. "Mice infestation. Disgusting."

"Who is this?" I jumped off the counter, pretty sure I already knew.

"Is this the owner? Gloriana St. Clair?"

"Yes. And is this the woman who thinks she can win Jeremiah Campbell back? Mel?"

"How did you like my little gift?" There was a throaty chuckle. "Did you scream? Of course you did."

I bit my lip, refusing to answer. Had she been in here? Seen me make a fool of myself? Damn it, if I'd known . . . What could I have done differently? Dematerialized and damn the consequences.

"Give him up, Gloriana. Or I'll run you out of business. Leave town and leave him to me. It's the smart play." The line went dead.

I stared at the receiver, tempted to throw the cordless across the room. "Are you kidding me?"

"What?" Lacy had a mop in her hand. "Who was it?"

"A woman Jerry used to be with." I carefully set the phone back where it belonged. Killing it wouldn't help. It was the woman I wanted to tear into pieces. "Clean up and I'll reopen. I'm not going to let that bitch ruin my business."

"It'll take a minute." Lacy didn't move. "Tell me about this woman. Mr. Blade has an old flame? What's going on? She sent in the mice?" She dipped the mop into a bucket of sudsy water that reeked of pine cleaner. "I might want to write her a thank-you note."

"If you do, send it from the unemployment line." I shook my head. There was no reason to take my bad mood out on Lacy. "Sorry. I know you're kidding. Jerry knew her in Miami, thought it was ancient history. But the woman doesn't see it that way. You know he's been having issues with his hotel there, making trips to deal with them. It's been her, causing trouble, trying to get his attention. Now she's brought her game here and found out I'm the competition. She wants Jerry back and thinks running me out of business and out of town will do it. This was just her latest trick. I'm surprised she didn't use magic." I quit breathing. I hated that pine smell. "If she were a mere mortal, this would be a nonstarter. Unfortunately, she's a voodoo priestess, Lacy, with some nasty tricks up her sleeve. Have you seen anyone in here who looks like she might be into that stuff?"

"Voodoo? Don't know. How do they look? Would she be wearing a caftan and a turban, have a scary vibe? Carry around a bottle of Love Potion Number Nine?" Lacy shook her head and began mopping. "That would be too easy, Glo."

"You're right. All I know is that Jerry says she's beautiful"—I made a face—"with dark skin, black hair and unusual gray green eyes."

"Bet you loved that description." Lacy leaned against the mop. "You know her name? I'll watch for her credit card."

"Good idea. Melisandra Du Monde." I sighed. "Of course

she's beautiful. I need more info on her. I'm calling Jer right now. This mouse thing is just her latest in the war on Glory."

"Latest? What else has she done?"

"There have been a few accidents." I headed over to turn on the ceiling fans to air the place out and dry the floors faster. "I realize now that they were her work. Remember, I told you that big shelf in the back room fell on me?"

"You think that was voodoo?" Lacy's eyes widened. "Crap. Maybe we should get out the holy water again."

I smiled. "Couldn't hurt. But that loaded shelf sure did. It weighed a ton and went over for no reason that I could see. Luckily I have good reflexes and dove under the table back there to avoid the worst of it." I had actually broken my arm, but it had healed with a good night's sleep and lots of synthetic blood.

"That woman's crazy if she thinks you'll just give up your business after a few setbacks. We've gone through plenty before, even been firebombed. But we reopened, better than ever. And you and Mr. Blade have gone through a lot. Yet you two have been together for hundreds of years." Lacy finished and headed back to the storeroom. "I'd better take my to-go bag and scoot. Shift's over. Will you be okay until the night crew gets here?"

"Sure. I expect Megan in a little while. Please get that bag out of here. Are you sure all the mice are gone?" I righted the mannequin and straightened her dress.

Lacy sniffed. "All clear. Open the doors. We're good to go. And be careful. If she really wants Mr. Blade back, she'll go for you harder next time."

"I'd like to see her try. A mortal? Bring it on." I headed for the door, surprised that most of the customers had stuck around. But we were close to Halloween and my shop had great vintage clothing and costumes. I flipped the lock.

"Come in, everyone. We're having a sale. All furs, twenty percent off." That got a reaction, especially since we were having a cold spell. The crowd surged inside. I couldn't believe I had actually laughed about the crazy woman who'd sworn to get Jeremy Blade back as her lover. A voodoo priestess? Okay, maybe I could buy that. Though I'd never actually seen her, I'd smelled the evil spirits she carried with her.

But I could deal with evil. I'd even fought Lucifer and won. You'd think a mortal would be easy compared to him. Right? Wrong. First, Luc and I were both fairly reasonable people. Who knew? But the angel of darkness actually admired my spunk. Melisandra didn't admire anything about me. She just wanted me gone. In her warped worldview, I was an annoying speed bump on her fast track to bliss with Jerry.

Obviously she thought that once I was out of the way he would realize she was the one for him. She'd tuned out when he'd told her to take a hike. He had even changed his address and name to get away from her. Mel wanted Jerry and would do anything to get him, even if it meant chaining him in a mausoleum somewhere until he felt the love. I shuddered just thinking about it.

Of course picturing Jerry as a victim was ridiculous. My guy was strong, an ancient vampire. But I was more than a little aggravated that he'd hooked up with a voodoo queen in the first place. What had he been thinking? More accurately, what had he been thinking *with*? Men.

Despite his faults, I loved him. And I wasn't about to quit seeing Jerry. Jeremiah Campbell aka Jeremy Blade and I had been through way too much lately for me to call a halt while

Mel moved in on him. Instead, I was going to show her just how not scared I was after her little trick.

"Gloriana, you've got that look again. What are you thinking?" Jerry arrived less than an hour later. We were going to our favorite club for a little dancing, even meeting friends there. Did you expect us to keep a low profile? That would feel too much like giving in to the wicked witch.

"That I've got to do something about Mel." I told him about the mouse invasion.

"I'm sorry." He put his arm around me. "What can I do? I've tried to talk to her, but my seeking her out makes her happy, no matter the reason for it."

"You sure you've made it clear you're done?" I could read his mind and he knew it. But I didn't even try. We had to trust each other now. I'd come to terms with the fact that this was the man I wanted to be with forever. Not an easy decision. But this complication from his past was ruining what should have been a special time for us. I knew I'd made some big mistakes with my choice of hookups in the past, but a wacko like this?

"I said, 'Go away, I don't want you.' Is that clear enough?" He held on to my shoulders, his eyes meeting mine.

"Ouch. Now you're making me feel sorry for the bitch." I sighed and leaned against him. "No wonder she's acting out."

"I made it clear that she's not to hurt you or your business." Jerry rubbed my back. "She swore she'd back off." He stared down at me. "Are you sure she's responsible—"

"Damn it, Jerry. Are you under a spell or something? She called to gloat. And then what about this gift box?" I tapped a present I'd received the day before. A voodoo doll. Cliché much? Of course it looked like me, though she'd padded the hips until I looked deformed. It was riddled with pins. Bitch. "Did I send it to myself?"

"No, of course not. But she laughs at those things. Calls them tourist trinkets. She's just pulling your chain. Don't let her play mind games with you." He pulled me close again. "Come on. Let's go. Try to have some fun. And I won't meet with her again. Obviously her word means nothing. I'm not sure I can think straight when I'm around her now because I'm so damned sick of her and her tricks. She infuriates me, thinking she can just force me to take her back. I'm surprised I haven't already put an end to her."

I stiffened and pushed back staring into his dark eyes. He meant what he said. If Jerry hadn't been able to act on his homicidal impulses, then Mel must be working some kind of magic to keep him under control. I wasn't about to tell Jer I thought he was being handled by a woman with superior skills. But I knew I had powers and experience with evil that he didn't have. "That cinches it. I want a face-to-face with her."

"Glory, you and Mel in the same room? A recipe for disaster. She won't back down and you'll probably lose it." Jerry pulled me close again. "You aren't the kind of person who can just rip out a throat and walk away."

"She'd probably taste like raw sewage anyway." I'd had a whiff of her when she'd spied on Jerry and me, lurked in the bushes outside his house. Stalker. She'd smelled like burnt sugar, evil left too long on the stove. I really didn't want to get close enough to her to touch her. Why didn't she just crawl back to Miami and pick a man who wanted her? I wasn't giving up on the idea of a meeting but figured Jerry was never going to like the idea.

"Let's go. Our friends are probably already at the club. Your pal Israel Caine and Sienna Star are supposed to sing their new duet tonight." Jerry tugged me toward the back door.

"How do you know that? Are you actually communicating with Ray or Rafe?" I rested my hand on Jerry's chest. This was unlikely. Jerry was jealous of both guys because he knew I'd had a special relationship with each of them. They were still my friends, but had been more than that in the past. I'd made it clear to both of them that I was with Jerry now.

"Richard told me. He and Flo get a newsletter from the club with the coming attractions. I'm surprised you didn't get it." Jerry pulled open the back door, pausing to check out the security like he always did. "Come on. We don't have much time. Caine doesn't float my boat, but I know he does yours."

"You got that right." I laughed when I saw his face. "Oh, come on. We both enjoy good music. I'm way behind on e-mail or I'd have seen the newsletter myself and dragged you there." I grabbed his hand and we hurried down the alley toward N-V, the club my former bodyguard Rafe now owned. It wasn't far and the shifter stationed at the door waved us in ahead of the line at the door. We settled at a table with my best bud, Florence da Vinci, and her husband, Richard Mainwaring. Then we ordered synthetic blood with alcohol, stocked here for us by Rafe, and settled back to watch the show.

"*Amica*, how are you doing? Any more *disastros* in your shop?" Flo leaned in to whisper.

"Nightly. That bitch won't give up." I told her about the mice and she shuddered.

"That could ruin your business. I know I would never go back to a place where I saw *topi*." Flo patted my shoulder.

"Me either." I sniffed the air. "What perfume are you wearing, Flo?"

"Nothing. Ricardo says it destroys his defense. He needs to smell the enemy coming." She stroked her husband's arm. "He takes very good care of me."

"I bet she's lurking around here right now. Following us." I glanced around. If he were a woman, Jerry would have pictures of her on his phone, but I'd never seen him snap a photo. Too bad.

"No!" Flo grabbed Richard. "Ricardo! Glory says the bitch is here."

"Where?" He leaned forward. "Blade, do you see her?"

Jerry stood and scanned the crowded balcony. "Not up here." He sniffed the air. "There's a faint whiff . . . I'm going downstairs to check it out. Richard, you stay here with the ladies."

"No, we're all going." I got up.

"Here? *Puttana!*" Flo glanced around the narrow balcony. "We will make that creature sorry she bothers our Glory."

"Don't taunt her, Flo." I squeezed Flo's hand. "She's got some mean tricks up her sleeve. I told you."

"Mice, falling shelves. Child's play." Flo's eyes gleamed. "I say we can take whatever she dishes out. *Ti credi?*"

"Sure." I smiled at her, feeling better than I had in days. The band was taking the stage, the people on the dance floor surging forward as we headed for the stairs. It was Ray's band and I knew the guys from a time when I'd pretended to be engaged to the rocker. Publicity stunt. I'd been Ray's mentor right after he'd been turned vampire. Had even been his date to the Grammys. It had been a magical night. I could use another one about now.

"I heard Ray and Sienna are a couple now." Flo studied me for a reaction as we stopped on the stairs.

"I'm glad. He needed someone." I saw Jerry and Richard waiting for us.

"No sign of her." Jerry held out his hand. "Let's just enjoy the show. I can get us closer to the stage. Follow me." He rubbed the back of my neck. "Are you okay?"

"Sure. Did you know Ray and Sienna are together and not just to sing?" I stayed close to him as we eased around the crowd and the lights dimmed.

"Glad to hear it. Keeps him away from you." Jerry kissed my cheek. "But he's stupid to pick a mortal. He'll screw it up, mark my words."

"Hush, Jer, they're getting ready to start." Very afraid he was right, I slipped my arm around his waist as we found a spot close to the stage. Ray was reckless, impulsive and a fairly new vampire. Sleeping with a mortal could have consequences and none of them were good. The house went dark except for spotlights on Ray at the piano and Sienna leaning against it. They started singing and you could have heard a mouse squeak in the huge club. The song was beautiful, the lyrics haunting. The way the two sang to each other, it was clear this love song had meaning for both of them.

Jerry turned me into his arms and we danced, making the song ours too. I was sure all the lovers in the audience felt the same way. He held me against him, his hands sliding down to rest on my butt as we moved slowly. I laid my cheek on his chest, my fingers delving into his hair while I breathed him in. We were together and no bitch from hell was going to pull us apart. If Mel was nearby, she could just watch and see how much we loved each other. I was sorry when the song ended.

"Wow. *Meraviglioso!* It makes me want to take you home and ravish you, Ricardo." Next to us, Flo kissed Richard on the lips. "What do you think, Glory?"

"Oh, yeah." I sighed, struggling to come back to earth. For a few moments it had been great just to dance and forget everyone but Jerry. I squeezed his hand. Ray and Sienna jumped up to sing together again. They put their arms around each other, bumping hips as they danced, and sang a rock song this time, Ray's band backing them up. It was high energy and fun.

"You okay?" Jerry said softly into my ear.

"Sure." I turned and ran my hand over his jaw. "Flo's right. That song put me in the mood to make love to you. What do you think?"

"I could handle that." He grinned and pulled me toward the door. "We're out of here." He nodded to Richard.

"Right behind you." Richard hauled a giggling Flo up into his arms and followed us. "Caine has a hit on his hands."

"Ricardo, put me down." She hit his shoulder. "You're embarrassing me."

"These kids think it's funny. Look at them." He grinned and nodded. Sure enough, his stunt helped clear a path for us to the front door. Once I thought I caught a whiff of that sweet, nasty smell again but I never saw anyone fitting Mel's description. Then we were outside, the fresh October air a welcome relief after the crowd inside.

"See you later." Richard set Flo on her feet then hurried her toward his car, ignoring her protests about manners. He had a look that promised a passionate night for them both.

"Well, now what?" I grinned at Jerry. "You know I have a roommate." And she was a terror. No way was I dragging my man home to that.

"Come home with me. They don't need you in the shop again tonight, do they?" He pulled me toward his car parked down the street.

"Not unless Mel unleashes another invasion. Roaches maybe?" I shuddered then patted my pocket. "I've got my cell."

"Let's go." He glanced around. "If that woman knows

what's good for her, she'll leave you alone. This isn't the way to win my heart." He helped me into his convertible, then settled in, hitting a button to let the top down before steering into traffic. The cool air felt good and I let the wind blow my worries away.

"I still don't understand how you ever got involved with a woman like Melisandra Du Monde." My comment made Jerry's hands tighten on the steering wheel. We were stopped at a red light.

"She's a strong woman and there is something about her . . ." He punched a button and the CD player came on. Trying to distract me? I punched it back off.

"Come on, Jerry, try to explain. This is important to me." I twisted under my seat belt to face him.

"Right. So can you explain why Israel Caine has your panties in a twist every time you see him?" He gave me a knowing nod, like he'd made a point, before he stepped on the gas.

"I guess so. He has musical talent and I'm a sucker for that. He's handsome, tall, has those piercing blue eyes that make a woman feel—"

"Enough. I really don't want to hear a catalog of Caine's fine qualities. Mel got to me. She has a way of looking at a man that makes him feel powerful. Like he's a sex god."

"I swear you're blushing." And I swear I was getting pissed. Well, I'd asked for it.

"You make me feel that way too, Gloriana." He reached out and snagged my hand. "I've always wanted to protect you because you make me feel like I'm invincible. It's something a man needs—to be wanted, looked up to." He kissed my knuckles. "You and Mel have more in common than you know. But you're two sides of a coin. You're the good side. I discovered too late that she's the bad one."

"Oh, gosh, Jer." I glanced around and realized we were in his neighborhood, almost to his house. "This is bizarre and yet I understand what you're saying. It's like when a man makes me feel that I'm the most desirable woman in the world." I pulled our joined hands to my lips and ran my tongue across his knuckles. "You always do that to me."

"But I don't just see you as a sex object. I hope you know that." He pulled the car up in front of the garage and hit a button on the remote. He turned to face me as we waited for the door to open. "You are much more to me than a way to get my rocks off."

"Back at you." I smiled and popped off my seat belt, leaning over to kiss him. I crawled right over the console to make sure I could reach his mouth and give it my full attention. The steering wheel cut into my back but I didn't care.

"Let's put the car away and go upstairs." He gently lifted me off of him and drove the car into the garage.

I let him pull me out of the car and then followed him to the house. The garage door came down and we stepped into the kitchen. The house was quiet and smelled faintly of the cleaning supplies his housekeeper used. It was reassuring. At least Mel hadn't managed to come inside his home yet.

Jerry lifted me into his arms and was about to carry me upstairs to his bedroom when my cell phone buzzed in my pocket.

"Oh, no!"

"Ignore it." He leaned down to kiss me then strode toward the staircase.

The buzzing was insistent before the call went to voice mail. I gently shoved at Jerry's chest when he stopped at the bottom of the stairs. "Let me check the message. I told them not to call unless it was an emergency in the shop."

"Go ahead." He set me on my feet. "I'll be upstairs in my office checking e-mail. Come and get me when you're done."

"Count on it." I jerked my phone out of my pocket. The voice mail was from a number I didn't recognize. I hit play and pulled the phone to my ear.

"If you want our lover to live, you will meet me tonight. Be in the alley behind your shop in thirty minutes. Believe me, I would rather put a stake through his heart than see him with you forevermore."

I recognized the voice instantly, smooth yet determined. So I'd finally get a face-to-face with Melisandra. If I was lucky, I could finish this once and for all. Either she saw the light, realized he was never going to be hers, or she was going down. Permanently. One problem. What was I going to tell Jerry? He'd never let me meet her alone if he knew about it. I looked up the stairs toward his office. Damn. I really wanted to forget this woman's demands and enjoy an evening in Jerry's arms. But she was just crazy enough to kill him rather than let me have him.

Did I really believe my man couldn't handle her? I leaned against the banister, suddenly weak in the knees. Maybe he could, but I wasn't willing to take that chance. I'd almost lost Jerry recently and it had been the worst time of my life. No way was I going to risk that again. Who knew what kind of tricks a voodoo priestess could pull?

So I put on my game face and headed up. I hadn't told Jerry, but in the nights before the voodoo doll had arrived I'd had strange pains in my body in the exact spots where those pins had been in it. He'd still been in Miami then and I hadn't known about Mel yet. Only hindsight made me realize the pains and the pins went together. Obviously this woman was more powerful than we realized.

Lying to Jerry was nothing new, even though I hated it. I invented a problem in the shop then kissed him good-bye until he was ready to carry me to bed anyway. Laughing, I promised him a date later. I just hoped that wasn't another lie.

I was on high alert when I flew into the alley behind my shop. The smell hit me immediately. It was bad enough that Mugs and Muffins was baking at this time of night, but added to the sugary muffin scent was that overpowering reek of evil. Melisandra was waiting for me.

"You must be Gloriana St. Clair." The husky voice came out of the darkness near my parked car. I heard the click of high heels as a woman strolled into the light. A breeze brought the unmistakable evidence that she was mortal. She trailed her hand over the trunk, the smile on her face making me shiver.

"I don't have to ask who you are, skulking here in the dark." I'd hoped Jerry had been exaggerating, but she *was* beautiful, her dusky skin the color of milk chocolate. Her long black hair tumbled to her shoulders, and her unusual gray green eyes, framed by long lashes, examined me like she could see right down to my soul. I straightened my own shoulders when all I wanted to do was shift again and head back to Jerry's arms.

"Yes, I am Melisandra Du Monde. I've been wanting to meet you for a long time, Gloriana. Gloriana. Ah, yes, the most interesting Gloriana." My name had become a chant. She gestured with her right hand, her scarlet nails gathering air around her.

I stepped back before I could stop myself when that air swirled and darkened around her. Magic. I recognized it and quit breathing, sure inhaling it would sear my lungs and either muddle my senses or make me pass out. I glanced around,

almost expecting some familiar demons to leap out from behind the cars to sing backup for her.

Hey, I was no ordinary vampire. I could take her. Malicious
tricks or not, she could die. *I* couldn't. I smiled.

"I've seen your handiwork in my shop, Mel. Do you really
think those stunts are going to help your cause with Jerry? So
far you've just pissed him off on my behalf." I couldn't help
noticing her voluptuous figure under a sharp black business
suit that came from a well-known designer. She would have fit
right in at a conference table in any Fortune 500 company. She
was just Jerry's type with full breasts and generous hips. Only
her eyes betrayed the crazy beneath her professional demeanor.
"He really doesn't like to see me upset."

"Ah. Were you? Upset?" She blew on her palm and dust
peppered my face, making my eyes burn. "That makes me very
happy."

"Didn't you hear me?" I blinked to clear my vision, refusing
to rub my eyes which stung like a son of a bitch. "Your dirty
tricks are alienating Jerry."

"He'll get over it." She smiled. "When we're back together,
Jeremiah will forget all about you. I have ways to ensure it. I
know what he likes, you see."

"Get a grip on reality. He kicked you to the curb a long time
ago. Where's your pride, woman?" Taunting her probably
wasn't my best move, but I really didn't like being reminded
that she'd had Jerry in her bed. I was trying not to lose my cool
and jump her, rip out that beautiful hair and pound her head
against the concrete. That would make me feel better but would
probably give her the out-of-control reaction she was hoping
for. I drew on every reserve I had and stared at her, trying for
cold and disdainful.

"Did he tell you how we met, Gloriana?" She leaned against my car, drawing a line with her nail on the trunk.

"No." I wanted to hear this.

"I had rented a ballroom at his hotel in Miami. It was a sellout. People pay small fortunes to hear me speak, get motivated." She smiled, her red lipstick perfect. All of her makeup was perfect. Damn.

"I can't imagine. What do they say? A sucker is born every minute?"

"I am worth every penny. As a life coach. People hear me speak and they are reborn. They leave my seminars and become successful, do great things." She flicked a disdainful look at the back door to my shop. "Some people are satisfied with a little life. My clients are not. Check out my Web site. Read the testimonials."

"You know nothing about me or my life." Why didn't I just rip out her throat now? But that would make me as evil as she was. And then there was that cold, malignant wall surrounding her. I'd be stained by it, my soul tarnished, if I gave in to my urge to kill her.

"You have worked your vampire wiles on my Jeremiah. But I will put an end to that. Then he will realize that I am his soul mate. The only woman to make him truly happy." She ran a fingertip down her throat. "You should see him when he drinks my blood, Gloriana. The pleasure, the passion—"

"Shut the hell up!" I vibrated with the need to tear her apart. Her smile was so sure, triumphant. Had Jerry actually kissed that mouth? I wanted to retch, or launch myself across the alley and obliterate her face so that she'd never kiss anyone, ever again.

No.

I forced a laugh. "Seriously? Don't you realize vampires will do and say anything to get mortal blood? Jerry played you, bitch. Used you as a donor and then moved on." I took a step toward her. "You were handy when he was in Miami, but that's over. He's lusty, I can attest to that. Obviously you were easy." I gave her my own cold smile. She didn't take it well, her teeth snapping together. If she'd been a vampire, she would have been snarling, her fangs down. "Now he's got his number-one lover back. Me. You are old news, Mel. He's throwing you out with the trash."

"Old news? I'm not the one with hundreds of years invested in a failed relationship, Gloriana. *Pobresita*." The air around her swirled and pushed at me, frigid and menacing. "You are a bad habit that Jeremiah needs to break. But once you are gone, he will be all mine."

"Get a grip. Jerry's not some trophy you can pass around, the prize in your pissing contest. He's a man who knows what he wants and it's not you. Now, why don't you go back where you came from? Find some other man to terrorize." I shoved at her creepy air and met resistance. I hated that I was even arguing with her, sounding desperate. Damn it.

"You'd like that, wouldn't you? For me to just leave him to you?" She raised her arms and howling creatures appeared around her. Spirits? Ghosts? Whatever, they gave me the creeps. "As long as you are between me and happiness, Gloriana St. Clair, you will never have peace of your own. This I vow." She muttered an incantation and the restless things around her wailed louder, rising and falling as she got more agitated. They zipped past me, tearing at my hair and snatching at my clothes.

Okay, I admit it. I hit at them like they were real and got nothing but air. It was all I could do not to dematerialize, just vanish the hell out of there. I reminded myself that I was dealing with nothing more than a mortal playing with the dead. Yeah, dead. How much could they really hurt me? The ghosts I'd dealt with before had been benign, helpful. But the chilled air brushing against me when one of those howling creatures darted past made me jump in spite of myself.

"All right, you want to play hardball? It's on." I showed fang. "I don't think you know who you're messing with."

"We will see." She threw her arms wide and my ears rang as her followers screeched a final time, twirling into some kind of otherworldly dust devil before they disappeared. "He will be mine, Gloriana. It is decided."

Decided? I couldn't stand it. I threw myself at her, finally giving in to my hatred. I landed on empty concrete. She'd disappeared, just poofed. I jumped up and took a quick look around. She must have had an escape route figured out because she was really gone, nothing left of her but that stench of bad news.

I leaned against the back door into the shop, my stomach doing a pitch and roll as I hit the code for security and practically fell into the storeroom. I needed a bottle of synthetic blood. The first gulp helped, the second felt even better. A voodoo priestess. What next? I should know better than to ask that question.

Two

My phone buzzed in my pocket. I was almost afraid to answer it. Here it came. Cosmic payback. Caller ID made me feel a little better.

"Ray? That duet tonight was amazing." I smiled as I said it. A good memory to wipe out the bad.

"Glory, babe. I'm in a shitload of trouble here." Ray's voice shook and I could have sworn he sobbed. I sank down in my one chair in the back room.

"What is it?"

"It's Sienna. We came back to my place after the concert. Hit the sheets, had some fun and then I did the whammy on her so I could drink her blood. You know, my idea of a nightcap these days." He sniffed.

"Ray, what the hell happened?" I gripped my phone so hard the pink sparkles on the case cut into my palm.

"I drank too much blood, Glo. I can't wake up Sienna. I think, I think she's dead. Come out here, Glory. Quick. Help me." He took a shuddery breath. "I might be able to save her if I turn her vampire but I can't do it alone."

"I'm on my way." I stuck my phone in my pocket and threw open the back door, barely taking the time to lock it again. If Sienna was already dead, we were too late. If she had a little life left in her . . . I shifted and flew into the night sky. Either way, Ray and I were in a hell of a mess. And I'd thought voodoo was my biggest problem.

I landed next to Ray's front door. One of his bodyguards, Will, met me and let me in immediately. I knew all of them, thanks to my history with the rocker. Will Kilpatrick was a Scot, and knew me better than most.

"He's really shook up, Glory. They're in the master bedroom. I tried to help him, but he insisted we wait for you." Will stayed right on my heels as I ran through the house.

"What do you think? Is there hope for her?" I hesitated in front of the closed door, dread making my stomach churn.

"Maybe. But you never know. We should have done something right away. But Ray wouldn't hear of it. Had to call you." Will reached around me and opened the door. "Good luck. You need me, give a shout. I don't have to tell you what this means if the girl doesn't make it, do I?"

"Either way, Ray's really screwed up this time." I took a breath of courage and ran into the room. It was bathed in moonlight, the centerpiece of the large room a king-size bed with black satin sheets in a tangle, the dark comforter in a heap on the floor at the foot. Ray jumped up, his eyes wild as he dragged me over to where Sienna lay in the middle of the bed.

"I think she's got a faint pulse but I can't rouse her." He

jammed my finger against her pale throat. "Feel. Isn't there a heartbeat?"

"Ray, calm down." I could see that she wasn't breathing but that didn't mean she was dead. I concentrated, listening for that subtle thump that meant her heart still beat. Yes, she was in there somewhere but didn't have long.

"God, Glory, I never meant for this to happen." He hovered over me, his hand on my back as I leaned closer, trying to feel for a whisper of breath.

"Bring me a mirror, Ray. I think she may be breathing after all. Hurry." I reached out and he slapped a silver hand mirror into it. Sienna's. Ray would never own a feminine piece like this. I held it over her nose and got just a bit of cloud. "Good news. She's not gone yet, but there's no way to avoid it. We have to give her blood."

"Can we take her to the hospital? Or give her some synthetic? Or is this it? Will we have to turn her?" Ray sagged onto the side of the bed, his shoulders drooping. "I swore I'd never do this. Never turn another person. Not after what was done to me."

"We don't have a choice, Ray. Look at her. I can almost see her soul leaving her body." I leaned down and put my head to her chest. "Her heart's starting to skip beats. We can't take the time to get her to the hospital for a real transfusion, and synthetic won't save her."

"How do you know?" He picked up Sienna's hand then shuddered. "She's so damned cold."

"Synthetic isn't real blood. It can keep us going, but a human's not equipped to metabolize it." I was quoting one of the vampire doctors I knew. "You want me to do it?"

"Please. I'm sorry, but I just can't." He wouldn't let go of her hand. "Save her, Glory. I hope to hell this is the right thing to do."

"Me too. Right or wrong, I don't see an alternative." I picked up her other wrist. First step, drain her completely. I'd done this once before, when I'd come across a woman bleeding out in my alley. It had turned out I'd have been doing myself, Ray and the world in general a favor if I'd left Lucky Carver to die. Instead I'd played Good Samaritan and saved her skinny ass. At least I knew Sienna for a decent person who deserved to live.

But how would she feel about waking up a vampire? Ray had been horrified, waking up with fangs, and still hated some aspects of being a vampire. I guess we'd find out what Sienna thought about this deal when—oh, God, *if*—she woke up. I fought back a wave of nausea and tried to remember I was the old pro here. Ray and Sienna were counting on me.

"Stand by, Ray. Watch what I do. You never know when you might need to know this." I said a quick prayer, then set about making my second vampire. Saving Sienna's life or not, this was so permanent. There would be no going back.

First, I bit into her wrist, sucking on her vein. There was pitifully little blood, a sign that we really *didn't* have a choice. No reaction, not even a moan, as I drained her. Ray? He was beside himself, cursing and pacing around the bed.

Once I was satisfied that she was empty, I sat up and bit into my own wrist. It hurt like hell, but I didn't have a choice. This next step was important.

"Hold up her head, Ray. I've got to get her to drink from me." I ran my bleeding wrist across her lips which were now almost blue. No reaction, of course. Mortals don't have a natural hunger for our blood. A vampire would have gone for it instantly. Even Ray's fangs were down and the idiot had already drunk his fill tonight. He sat behind Sienna and settled her head in his lap, tenderly stroking her short hair back from her forehead.

I had already noticed that he wore nothing but his trademark black silk boxers and had to remind myself that I wasn't here to appreciate his beautiful body or remember . . .

"How will you get her to drink?" Ray didn't spare me a glance. He couldn't look away from Sienna's pale face.

"Open her mouth, force it open if you have to. I'm going to drip it down her throat and make her swallow. Once we get enough in her, she'll come alive, vampire style, and begin to drink on her own. Or at least that's what happened with Lucky, when I turned her." I watched while Ray jammed a finger into her mouth and pried open her teeth. It was like working on a doll. Sienna was still lifeless.

"That's right, you did turn that skank. At least it gave you the experience to help Sienna." He kept brushing Sienna's hair back from her face. Rock star. Sienna had gone for platinum with pink stripes this year. "We've got to save her."

"I know, Ray. Just keep her mouth open." I squeezed my wrist to increase the amount of blood that dripped into her mouth. Then I rubbed her throat until I saw her swallow. She coughed and gagged.

"Hold her mouth closed now, we can't let her lose that." I watched her carefully. She settled down but was still unconscious. "Okay, open it again, I'm giving her some more." I couldn't remember how much blood I'd had to give Lucky back then. I'd been crazy with fear, caught off guard and forced by circumstances to turn a human I didn't even know into a vampire. This was different.

I felt almost clinical, like a doctor myself, detached, watching for signs, waiting to see if this worked. It was a freaky feeling and I didn't like it. I should be more upset, like Ray was, shaking and calling Sienna's name as he cradled her head between his thighs.

"Are you feeling woozy? You don't look so hot, Glory." Ray finally spared me a glance. "Will, get in here!" he shouted as I swayed over Sienna. "Bring Glory a bottle of the premium synthetic. Quick!"

"Yeah. Good idea. I can't keep giving her blood and not get some to replace it." I'd been standing, leaning over Sienna. Now I sat down on the bed, hard. No wonder I hadn't felt much about this. It had been almost like an out-of-body experience.

Will showed up on the run, a bottle of AB negative in his hand. He twisted off the top and handed it to me. "How's it going?"

"She's still not coming around." Ray glanced from me to Will. "Maybe Will should take over. Give her his blood."

"No, I think that might confuse her. I'm going to be her sire." I wasn't sure about that. Frankly I wasn't thinking straight. But it seemed like the sire blood bond was kind of important. More important than any of us vampires wanted to admit. Switching donors in mid-transition didn't seem like a good idea.

"I'm okay." I drained the bottle. It really helped and gave me the energy to continue.

"She looks better to me. You guys probably don't see it, but I think there's a tinge of pink in her cheeks already." Will stayed near the foot of the bed. "A little more should take care of it, Glory."

"I hope you're right." I bit into my other wrist this time and pressed it to Sienna's lips. Ray held her mouth open enough to allow another few ounces to dribble in. We all watched and waited as I rubbed her throat until she swallowed. Sienna should begin to drink on her own soon. If this was working. If she didn't, then we'd been too late and it was time to admit she was dead, Will's pink cheeks wishful thinking.

I felt a tickle against my wrist then pressure as her lips pressed against my wrist. Suction! "She's drinking!" I blinked, startled to realize I was actually crying with relief.

Sure enough, Sienna suddenly grabbed my wrist with both hands and latched on, a growl of pleasure rumbling up from her chest. She took a deep pull, starving. It was the same reaction I'd gotten from Lucky. I remembered it now. I had to be careful. Too much and I'd end up a victim and she'd be more vampire than she needed to be at first. Wild, out of control.

Of course it was important that we watch her for the next night or two. The transition wasn't easy. And she didn't have a clue that vampires even existed. Or did she?

"Ray, does Sienna know you're a vampire?" I nodded toward Will and he helped me break Sienna's hold on my wrist. She opened her eyes and stared into mine. I caught her gaze and talked to her calmly. "Sleep now, Sienna. It's almost dawn." I relaxed when I saw her blink, close her eyes with a sigh then settle into sleep. "Ray? I asked you a question."

"No. Hell, no. I told you I mesmerized her to drink. I was working up to tell her, even hinted at it, but she always laughed off that stuff. She likes to read fantasy stuff, you know, books about vamps and shifters. But she never bought into it for real. I finally decided it wasn't a good idea. Not like how it went with Nate." Ray eased out from under Sienna and covered her with a sheet. No one had commented on the fact that the woman had been wearing nothing at all. Will was smart enough to look everywhere but at his boss's lady friend.

"Well, I guess that means I stay here tonight and help you

tomorrow night. Because we're going to have to explain our life to her. And it's not a laughing matter." I sat on the foot of the bed. "I could use another bottle of that premium."

"You got it." Will raced out of the room, obviously eager to get out of the way.

"She's going to take it badly. Like I did." Ray collapsed next to me. "Shit. I can't believe I did this."

"It's done. No good will come from beating yourself up about it. We'll do the best we can to help her with the transition. She'll probably be mad at you, not want to be with you at first." I put my hand on his shoulder. "I may have to take her home with me."

"You'd do that?" Ray kissed my cheek. "Damn, girl, there's just no end to your generosity, is there?"

"Oh, yes, there's an end. You do this again and I'm going to make you sorry you ever got that pair of fangs, Israel Caine." I gave him a hard look. "I can turn you to a statue and leave you there until the sun comes up. Make you fry."

"Tough talk, Glory." He grinned and ran a finger down my arm. "But you know you love me, sweet thing. And this has taught me a hard lesson." He lost his smile. "I'm done with mortals. I like Sienna. But I'm not in love with her, not like I was with you. Now I've ruined her life. And it was just so I could enjoy a drink at her fountain." He jumped up and stared at the night sky, visible through the glass doors that led out to his terrace.

"I don't know if you *ruined* it, Ray." I didn't like where this was going. Ray was volatile at the best of times. As an alcoholic, recovering now, he was always close to falling off the wagon again.

He faced the bed once more. "I know what I am. A selfish bastard. I've got to stop using people. I *will* stop. Helping

Sienna . . . Well, maybe that's something I have to do to learn what's important in my life." He watched me, obviously hoping for approval.

"I wish you meant that, Ray. But instead I feel like I'm listening to one of your song lyrics." I was tired, drained, and I'd heard his vows of change before. "I'm going to bed. Good night."

I left him standing there with his mouth hanging open, for once realizing his charm had deserted him. Good. I met Will in the hall, where he handed me another bottle of the good stuff.

"It's almost dawn. There's a guest room right here." He led me to it. "Anything you need?"

"To call Jerry. I won't tell him about this yet. It will just reinforce his poor opinion of Ray. But he had been expecting me to come back to his house." I opened the door to a neat bedroom with a queen-size bed. It must be nice to be rich enough to hire paranormals to clean your house while you slept.

"Do you think we should notify the vampire council about this?" Will stood in the doorway as I kicked off my shoes.

"It was an emergency. I know they have rules about making new vampires, but this was life or death. Of course Ray made a mistake, no getting around that. Dumbass." I sat on the foot of the bed and drank my synthetic. "I'll call Damian myself tomorrow night and explain things. First, let's see how Sienna takes the news that she now has fangs."

"Odds are she won't be thrilled. Only those of us who grew up in families of vampires knew what we were getting into." Will was from a Highland clan, neighbor to Jerry's Clan Campbell. Their parents were "made" vampires, who then turned their adult children when they chose to become vampire.

"You're probably right, Will. I'm not looking forward to it." I sighed and pulled out my cell phone.

"You did a fine job tonight, Glory. Saved her life. Now we'll see whether she's going to thank you for it." He smiled and closed the door, leaving me to my bed and death sleep as dawn drew closer.

Would she? Thank me? And did I want to take her home with me if she needed to get away from Ray? Too many questions for my tired brain. I stripped and crawled into bed, called Jerry and made up a story about shop complications, then cratered. Tomorrow was soon enough to worry about all of that.

I woke up to peace and quiet. Okay, either Sienna still slept or Ray hadn't told her the news. Was he waiting for me to do it? I wouldn't be surprised. I glanced at the bedside clock and realized I'd slept past sunset. Unusual for me, but then I'd lost a lot of blood last night. Not even two bottles of synthetic could make up for how exhausting the stress and blood loss had been.

My cell phone rang and I picked it up off the nightstand. I saw at a glance that this wasn't the first call I'd received. Two voice mails waited for me. I just answered.

"Jerry? Sorry, I overslept."

"Where are you? I'm at your apartment and Aggie says you didn't sleep here last night."

Aggie was my roommate. She didn't know when to keep her mouth shut. In more ways than one. More about that later. "I'm at Ray's. He almost killed Sienna. Drank too much of her blood. I . . . I had to turn her vampire, Jerry." I suddenly choked up, the reality of what I'd done hitting me.

"Are you all right? Gloriana, are you still there? At Caine's?"

"Yes. I had to sleep in his guest room. So I'd be here when she woke up." I sniffled, getting myself under control. "I'm her sire, Jerry. I have to check on her, help explain to her about vampires. She doesn't even know we exist."

"I'm coming out there. You sound like you need me."

"I do. Thanks." I ended the call. I'm usually strong but for some reason this was getting to me and I liked the idea of Jerry beside me. I pulled on my clothes, wishing desperately for some clean underwear, and washed my face in the adjoining bathroom. I hated to be seen without makeup. Maybe if Sienna still slept I could borrow some of hers. A hairbrush would be nice too. I did find a new toothbrush and toothpaste in a drawer though.

Feeling almost presentable, I opened the bedroom door and walked down the hall toward the master bedroom. At the last moment I changed my mind and headed to the kitchen instead. I needed some of Ray's premium synthetic first. I still felt a little weak. Or was that fluttery feeling in my stomach dread? I wouldn't be surprised.

"Good evening." Will sat on a bar stool, sipping from a mug of synthetic. Obviously he'd heated his in the microwave. I liked mine cold.

"Nothing from the new vampire yet?" I opened the fridge and helped myself, twisting off the cap and taking a deep swallow.

"Not a peep. I figure Ray is up and just watching her." He gestured with his mug. "I can nuke that for you."

"No, I'm fine." I drank some more. "Guess I'd better go see what's happening." I glanced up at a rap on the French doors that led to the deck outside. "It's Jerry. That was fast."

"And one of the guards." Will grinned and walked over to unlock the door. He spoke to the guard who stood back but didn't leave. "Are you here in peace or do I send you on your way again, Jeremiah?"

"I'm just here to see Gloriana." Jerry frowned at Will. They were old friends but Will knew Jerry was not one of Ray's fans. "I'll not bother your boss as long as he doesn't bother me."

"He has much more on his mind tonight than you or your lady, Jeremiah." Will nodded and the other guard took off. "Come in. I'd count it as a courtesy if you'd leave your knives here in the kitchen before you go with Glory back to see Caine."

"You have to be kidding." Jerry glanced at me. "Gloriana?"

"Humor him, Jer. He's just doing his job. Surely you can respect that." I walked up to him and put my arms around his waist, coming away with the knife he always kept at the small of his back. "Here's one, Will." I set it on the counter.

"Damn it, Gloriana." Jerry scowled but leaned over and pulled a knife from his boot and set it beside the other one.

"Give me the one under your arm as well." Will grinned. "Come on, you know Ray is going to say or do something that will make you go for his throat, it's his way. I can't have you tossing one of your knives into the mix."

"You're right about Caine. He's an aggravating bastard." Jerry pulled the knife from the sheath under his arm and set it on the counter. "There. Satisfied?"

"Good job, Will. I like to see Blade without his toys." Ray strolled into the kitchen in jeans and a black T-shirt. He was barefoot of course. He stopped next to me and slung his arm over my shoulders. "Glory here saved Sienna last night. I hope you're not going to cause a dustup over that."

"No, I'm glad she could help." Jerry shook his head. "Too bad you can't control your urges though, Caine. What's the woman going to say when she wakes up vampire?"

"What the hell are you guys talking about?" Sienna wandered into the kitchen dressed in one of Ray's black silk shirts and nothing else. She rubbed her eyes. "Ray? You let me sleep all day again."

"Yeah, sorry about that, babe." Ray shot Jerry a look that said *shut up*, then took her hand.

"What's to eat? I'm hungry. Any of that pizza left?" She headed for the fridge and pulled open the door. "Yeah. I just love cold pizza for breakfast. Anyone else?" She pulled out the box and set it on the counter then looked around.

The four of us just stared at her then each other. I knew this was on me.

"Sienna, I don't think you really want pizza." I pulled a fresh bottle of synthetic out of the fridge and twisted off the cap. Hot or cold? I dumped it into a mug and Will grabbed it, setting it into the microwave.

"Sure I do. Look, it's pepperoni and mushroom, my favorite." She flipped open the top and pulled out a slice.

"Don't put that in your mouth." I grabbed it before she could take a bite. "I guarantee it will make you sick."

"It didn't yesterday. It was delicious." She frowned at me.

"Tonight it will." The microwave beeped and Will handed me the mug. "Here, try this. You'll be surprised how good this tastes. It's just what you need."

"If that's the shit Ray drinks all the time, I want no part of it. I've tasted it when he was in the shower. It's gross." She made a face and wouldn't touch the mug.

"Trust me. You will have a whole new appreciation for it now." I took her hand and wrapped it around the mug. "One sip. That's all I'm asking you to take."

"Why are you all staring at me?" Sienna looked around the room. "Okay, I know I've got great legs." She glanced down. "And maybe I should have buttoned a few more buttons, but

I'm getting a different vibe than male appreciation here." She sniffed the mug. "It does smell pretty good." She took a cautious sip. "Wow. It does taste good. This must be a different brand or something." She took a deep swallow. "I could get used to this."

"I hope so." Ray slipped his arm around her waist. "Because you'll have to."

"What do you mean, Ray?" Sienna leaned against him. "You know, I'm feeling a little funny. Wobbly."

"That's natural. It'll take a while to adjust to this."

"Adjust to what?" She sipped some more. "I'd like some coffee too. Will? Did you make some?"

"No, no need now. I only made it for you, Sienna."

"Well, I'm still here." She smiled at him. "So?"

"So, he doesn't need to make you coffee anymore. You're on the wagon now." Ray kissed her cheek. "Something happened last night. You don't remember because I did something to make you forget."

"What the hell, Ray?" She jerked away from him. "I told you from the get-go that I'm over drugs. I went through rehab and I'm not going there again. It was hell. I thought you understood. We have that in common. Right?"

"It wasn't drugs." Ray sighed and looked at me.

"Sienna, maybe you should sit down." She looked pale, not surprising, considering. And I knew my news was going to knock her off her feet.

"Why, Glory? If Ray didn't drug me, why can't I remember something from last night? And why are you all here staring at me?" Sienna's voice was rising and her mug was shaking. "Damn it, what's going on?"

"We're vampires, Sienna." I glanced around the room and we all were suddenly showing her our fangs.

"Oh, God!" She dropped her mug and ran out of the room. "Get away from me!"

"No, you don't understand, baby." Ray ran after her. "We're not going to drink from you. Not anymore." He caught her in the hall. "Come back. Let Glory tell you what happened."

"Not anymore?" Sienna hit Ray on his chest as he carried her into the kitchen and thrust her onto a bar stool. "What the hell? Did you drink my blood? Ray? Is that why you slept with me? So you could drink my blood?" She slapped his face, tears running down her cheeks. "How long has this been going on?"

"Baby, please. Listen to me. I never meant—" Ray didn't defend himself, just let her keep hitting and slapping him. "I'm sorry. I was an asshole."

"He sure was," Jerry muttered.

I gave him a quelling look. Not helping.

"Sienna, what Ray did was wrong. And it had consequences." Consequences I knew she'd hate. I struggled for the right words. "We can't turn back the clock. If we could, he never would have used you like that. I'm sure." I stared at him, his cue to apologize again.

"No, of course not." Ray shook his head. "I lost control. Stupid of me. But you were so fine."

"Shut up!" Sienna lunged for one of Jerry's knives on the counter and stabbed Ray in the arm. "Vampire? I can't freaking believe it!"

"Damn it!" Ray backed away while Will, bodyguard that he was, wrestled the knife from Sienna and tossed it to Jerry. Jer, of course, instantly made sure his other two knives were back where they belonged, on his body.

I handed Ray a kitchen towel to press against what was essentially a minor wound and grabbed Sienna's hands while Will kept her pinned to the bar stool.

"Calm down, Sienna. I know you are upset."

"Upset? Are you fucking kidding me?" She stared at me, her eyes wild. "I saw your fangs, Glory. All of you have fangs. This is a nightmare. What the hell is this? A coven?"

"No, we don't have those. We're just, um, friends." I glanced at Jerry's scowling face. "Some of us anyway. I'll mentor you, help you figure this out."

"What the hell does that mean? You going to tell me why I can't eat pizza?" Sienna tried to jerk her hands away and I let her go. Will glanced at me and I nodded. She jumped to her feet, swaying for a moment before grabbing the counter.

"Tell me the truth, Glory. What happened last night? Why did you make me drink that red stuff? Is it blood?" She grabbed her mouth. "Oh, holy fuck, I have fangs!"

Three

"Explain. How did this happen?" Sienna collapsed on the long leather sofa in Ray's living room. I'd managed to get her there during her freak-out. I figured the kitchen wasn't exactly the best place for this. Too many sharp objects.

Ray sat beside her and started to pick up her hand. "I—"

"Get away from me!" She shoved him, hard. "You think I haven't figured out this is all on you?" She hit him again and again. "What the hell is wrong with you?"

He didn't try to defend himself, just took it. "I deserve whatever you want to dish out. Stab me again. Blade, give her one of your knives."

"No." Jerry leaned against the cold fireplace. He was just observing. Not exactly enjoying the show, none of us were. Seeing a mortal come to terms with our world wasn't exactly a treat. It made me want to cry for all she'd have to face. The losses . . .

"Sienna, it was an accident." I managed to speak calmly, trying to keep things from going off the rails even more. "Ray made a mistake. He'll take care of you now. He owes you that. Definitely. But *I'm* the one who made you vampire." I sat across from her, in one of the big overstuffed chairs Ray favored, and leaned forward. It would help if she'd quit using Ray as a punching bag. "Look at me and listen."

"*You?*" She finally sagged back, her hands falling into her lap. "Why? This is nuts. Hell." Tears glittered on her eyelashes. Fakes. I'd bet my last dollar on it. I wish I could afford such a gorgeous set.

"You're right. I wouldn't have done it if there had been any other way to save you. You almost died, Sienna. Ray had just about drained all the blood out of you before he called me." I had plenty of time to analyze Sienna's makeup while she sobbed into her clenched fists. It was a good distraction from my churning stomach, a cross between guilt and pride. Hey, I *had* saved her. So I admired her tattooed eyeliner and eyebrows with those piercings she was famous for. Flawless skin even without any other makeup. Me? I didn't fare well with the fresh-scrubbed look, especially with three hot men staring at me along with Sienna.

Okay, the waterworks were now occasional sniffles and I had to get down to business. Sienna finally looked up at me, her eyes glittering like her trademark sapphire on the side of her nose.

"You were a heartbeat away from meeting your maker. Turning you was the only way to save your life. Ray called me because he knew I could do it." I got up and sent Ray a mental message to move. He jumped up and got out of the way and I took his place at her side. "I used my blood to bring you back."

"Drained me? Wait a minute. Ray? What the fuck?" She shot Ray a narrow-eyed look.

"Ray got carried away and drank too much of your blood."

I grabbed her when she lunged for him again. "Yes, he's a jerk. A selfish asshole. We all agree on that." I glanced around the room and everyone nodded, even Ray. "If it makes you feel any better, he'll have to go in front of a vampire council and defend himself. They don't like us making new vampires. It's against the rules here to drain mortals like he did. He was careless and he could be killed because of his mistake with you."

"Killed?" That took some of the steam out of her. "That's a little harsh."

"An eye for an eye, Sienna. You're not alive now. You're what some people call undead." I patted her knee. "Your life is over as you knew it. Everything is changed."

"That's crazy. I don't feel all that different. What do you mean?" She looked around. "Explain. Pizza. I can't eat it?" She glanced back toward the kitchen. "Or drink coffee?"

This had been the hardest part for me. Giving up mortal food and drink. Depending on her priorities, it could be for Sienna too. I knew Ray hadn't missed food. He'd mourned the sunshine and booze more.

I tried for a sympathetic smile. "Blood will be your only menu option now. That was a synthetic blood you drank earlier."

She was on her feet before I could stop her. "But Ray, he wasn't satisfied with a fake, was he? He just had to have the real deal. Right from the source. Me." She poked him in his healing stab wound and he winced. "Is that right, lover boy? Was your seduction, the invitation to come here and make another record, all of that just an excuse to get to my blood?" She was shouting now, and her pokes had turned into shoves until Ray was pinned against the wall. "What the hell, Ray?"

"God, I'm sorry, babe. But you've got to know you mean more to me than just a blood donor."

"Do I? Really? When every word out of your mouth is a lie?

Your sleep schedule. Your energy drink." She sobbed, bit on her fist then screamed when her fangs must have pierced it.

"We do make good music together, Sin, don't we? The label loves us." Ray tried out a smile. He knew better than to reach for her, holding his hands out to his sides in a mock surrender.

"Bastard! User! Yeah, I helped you win a Grammy after you hit a dry spell." She wiped tears off her cheeks. "What I want to know is how the hell you did it. Drank my blood and I didn't have a clue you were doing it." She whirled and we all got a flash of her bare butt. She really needed to go put on some clothes. "Glory, how could he do that?"

"I call it the whammy. He mesmerized you, Sienna. Stared into your eyes and made you go into a kind of trance. He could erase your memory of the things he did to you. Or you two did together. Even put you to sleep." I took her arm, easing her away from Ray. "Why don't you and I go to the bedroom and you can shower, get dressed and I'll answer all your questions? We don't need to do this in front of an audience. Especially not with Ray watching. Right?"

"No kidding." She strode toward the hallway. "I don't care if I ever see that jerk-off again." She stopped and turned around to glare at him one more time. "You could make me forget things we did together?" Her voice rose. "What else, Ray? What other perverted shit did you do to me besides take my blood while I was in la-la land?"

"Nothing, Sin, I swear it. Please believe me. Just your blood. I didn't need . . ." He glanced at the two other men. "You know, we had fun. I wouldn't have to—"

"Just shut the fuck up." Sienna turned on her heel and kept going toward the bedroom.

"Don't believe I'd have said that, Caine," I heard Jerry say as I headed down the hall. I couldn't have agreed more. Dumbass.

I heard the shower start and decided to leave her alone to clean up and clear away at least the smell of her last night with Ray with soap and shampoo. Her stash of makeup sat on the dressing table next to the walk-in closet and I helped myself after I shut the bedroom door. Putting on my face did a lot for my own attitude, that and using a hairbrush.

"That's better, darling." My mother appeared next to me as I brushed on some pink blush.

The brush landed on my nose and I reached for a tissue to wipe off the streak. "Seriously, Mother? Here? Now? Can't you see I have my hands full?"

"Yes, of course. And I have a feeling you're going to offer to take her home with you. Don't you think it's already a little crowded in your tiny apartment?" My mother, a goddess from Olympus no less, strolled around the room, kicking aside Ray's discarded boxers with a knowing look. "That was quite a show you put on last night, saving the girl. Not surprising that you'd run to the rescue. You have the urge to play hero. You inherited that from me." She settled on the foot of the bed and crossed her legs.

Tonight she wore an expensive dress that matched her blue eyes, eyes the same color as mine. Of course her dress was about four sizes smaller than anything I'd ever fit into. It didn't help that I wore the dress I'd had on the night before that still seemed to have a stench of evil on it. As usual Mother made me feel dowdy and in need of a makeover.

"You play hero? I've never seen evidence of that. You want a chance to be *my* hero? Get rid of Aggie for me. She's the reason my apartment is too crowded. Are you getting your jollies spying on me? Watching me lose my mind with that woman in my extra bedroom?" I can't tell you how much I hated the fact that my mother did spy, eavesdrop and in general insert herself into my life whenever she felt like it. But come when called, actually help me? I wished.

"Spying is such an ugly word." She admired her designer shoes and I paused in my tirade to do the same. The woman had exquisite and expensive taste. "I came by to compliment you and offer to help you out. We could make a run up to Olympus right now, meet your grandfather and perhaps solve the Aggie problem for you." She smiled sweetly.

"Give it up, Mother. I've told you before. I'm not going up there. You'll figure out some way to trap me and I'd never see the human plane again." I sighed and sat at the dressing table. "Come on. I'm sure you could get hold of that Siren treasure if you really tried." You think I was being mean to my mother? We'd only met recently. Blame it on the fact that she'd hidden me away in a Siren harem for a thousand years or so under the power of the Storm God. When I'd showed a lack of killer instinct, that creep had cast me out into the mortal world to die, wiping my memory of the whole deal. Where had Mom been then? Oh, she'd forgotten she had a daughter.

Jerry had saved me, turning me vampire and giving me immortality. Now Mother was suddenly back in my life, a few hundred years too late, wanting a "relationship." I wasn't so keen on the idea. She hated vampires, wanted me to dump Jerry and relocate permanently to Olympus. Need I say more?

"Gloriana, I've explained this. If you want to get rid of your roommate, I know she has a debt to pay. To get the Siren treasure for her, you'll have to go to your grandfather personally and ask for it." Mother frowned down at her nails and stood. "I need a manicure. Let me know when you're ready to be reasonable. Take this new vampire home with you. Try living with two difficult women for a while. I'm sure you'll be calling for me soon, eager to go to Olympus." She patted my cheek. "Your grandfather will adore you." Then she vanished.

I rolled my eyes. Grandfather. Yeah right. When Granddad was the head honcho of Olympus, you didn't just drop by for a visit, ask for treasure and then return to your normal life. Who was she kidding?

"Who was that? And did she just disappear, like a magic trick?" Sienna swayed in the bathroom doorway. She had a towel around her body and a towel turban on her head.

"Here, sit before you fall down. Yes, she disappeared. Welcome to the paranormal world. That was my mother." I did my best to explain what she was.

"And your grandfather?" Sienna stared at me, obviously seeing the resemblance now that she knew our relationship. My mother and I did look something alike, though I was a blow-up version.

"Zeus. Can you believe it?" I didn't need to see her stunned expression to know she wasn't buying it. "Neither can I, but I've felt the lightning bolts from up there as proof that Olympus is real, Sienna. I've got some strange powers too. Cool powers. I'll give you a demo sometime. Mom and I have basically just met. Long story." I knew information overload was a danger in a new vampire. "Get dressed and then ask any questions you have."

"Yeah, I have plenty." She got up and wandered into the closet, a glazed look in her eyes. In a few moments she came out in a pair of jeans and a T-shirt. She walked over to the dressing table, picked up a brush, looked into the mirror and burst into tears. "Where the hell am I?"

I put my arm around her. "I'm sorry. I should have warned

you. Mirrors don't work for us. Here, let me." I gently took the brush from her and ran it through her short hair, slicking it behind her ears. "You'll figure this out. You can use a computer video cam as a mirror. We do show up in pictures. I have a nice setup at my apartment." I tossed down the brush. "I handle my hair and makeup just by feel. But then I'm pretty ancient. They didn't have computers or even cameras when I was turned."

"How old are you?" She leaned back to stare at me.

"A little over four hundred, give or take a decade." I tried not to smile when she gasped. I left off the thousand years as a Siren. She was already shocked enough. "Don't look it, do I?"

"This is surreal." She shoved away from me then collapsed on the bed.

"How are you feeling?" I sat beside her. "Are you dizzy? Weak?"

"Tired. Confused. Overwhelmed. But strong." She lifted her hands and flexed her fingers. "Does this vampire thing make you strong, Glory?"

"Yes, it does. We'll test it later." I didn't want to start breaking things yet, though trashing Ray's bedroom would probably make Sienna feel better.

"You look early twenties. Will I always look this age, right now?" She pushed herself into a sitting position. "Am I, uh, immortal?"

"Yes and yes. That's pretty good news, isn't it?" I smiled as she processed that.

"I'll say. Periods?"

"Gone. Sorry but you'll never have children now." I held my breath. Was I crushing a dream?

"Oh, well, I'd already decided I wasn't cut out for that trip anyway. So I won't have to worry about birth control. Cool."

She plumped up a pillow and leaned back on it. "What about disease, illness? Can I catch anything?"

"It's pretty rare. There are a few vampire doctors but they are mostly engaged in research, working on drugs to help vamps see daylight, eat solid food, stuff like that."

"Daylight?" She glanced at the French doors which had automatic shades that closed at sunrise. They were open now and we could see the terrace with its steps down to the lake and Ray's boat dock. The moon was shrouded in clouds so it was dark except for deck lights.

"We sleep all day, wake up at sunset."

Surprisingly, Sienna took that news without much reaction. Then she jumped up and faced me. "Why did Ray call *you*, Glory? You two still have something going?"

Was Sienna jealous? Hard to believe. "No, Jerry is my boyfriend. I'm Ray's mentor. I helped him right after he was turned. So naturally he called me for advice when he saw he was in trouble. You would have died otherwise. He did the right thing."

"Forgive me if I'm not grateful to the bastard." She paced around the bed, finally jerking the sheets off and tossing them out the sliding glass doors onto the deck. "I'm so mad I could kill him. Vampire! Can I go back? Be normal again?"

"No. This is it." I put a hand on her shoulder but she shrugged it away. She grabbed a crystal vase and threw it at the mirror over the dressing table.

"Won't be needing that, will we?" Her laugh gave me chills.

"Calm down, Sienna."

"Why? Why the hell should I? I'm vampire. And you are going to tell me what I can and can't do. Thanks a heap, Glory." She stomped out to the deck and took a breath. "Shit. I don't think I can even breathe the same. Though I can smell everything, even the bird shit on that rock over there." She pointed to a spot yards away.

"You don't have to. Breathe. But your enhanced senses are cool. Enjoy them." I stayed a few feet away from her. I saw the men standing around in the living room and knew they could hear us from here through the open terrace doors.

"Not breathe? That's just plain creepy." She faced me, her eyes full of tears. "You meant it. Undead."

"Afraid so."

"How do you keep it a secret? This vampire thing." Sienna reached for me, squeezing my arm. "I had no idea and I was, um, surrounded by you guys."

"It's not easy. We use the whammy. If a mortal sees something he or she shouldn't, we make them forget it. Like Ray did with you." I hated to remind her. Of course that had her looking back at the living room. At Ray. The tears were gone, her mouth a hard line. I kept talking.

"I'll teach you how to do that. You'll have to deal with mortals constantly if you continue your singing career. You'll have to be careful, Sienna."

"What the hell do you mean, *if* I continue my career?" Now she glared at me, her eyes blazing. "I'm on top, my records are hitting the charts and I'm about to go on tour. I've got—" I could see when her new reality hit her. "Oh, God. Radio interviews, talk shows. Can I stay awake but inside out of the sun?" Her squeeze became a painful clutch.

"No. When sunrise hits, you're dead, out like a light. You can't function at all." I covered her hand with mine. "I'm sorry, Sienna. But Ray has managed to keep his career going. Much as you hate to deal with him, he can give you good advice. Or his manager can. Nathan knows about us and our world. Ray clued him in as soon as he was turned."

Before I knew what she was going to do, she ran inside and landed on top of Ray, taking him down to the floor. Her new fangs tore into his neck and she sank them into his jugular.

"Guess she figured out how to feed on her own." Jerry just stood there, watching.

"Think I should pull her off?" Will, as bodyguard, had a duty, but Ray waved him off.

"If she takes too much, we'll have to do something." I stopped in the doorway. Sienna was crying and drinking, making an ugly mess of Ray's throat. Her bloodlust had kicked in and her anger had taken her straight to Ray to satisfy it. He had his head back, eyes closed while he stroked her back. I was silently counting, making sure this didn't go on too long.

"Okay, Will, pull her off now. Killing Ray might make her feel better but I'm not letting it happen." I knelt down and touched Sienna's cheek. "Let go, Sienna, you've had enough."

She shook her head and held on. I could see the ragged wounds she'd torn into his neck. Luckily Ray would heal fast or there could be ugly scars.

"Pinch her jaw, Glory. That'll get them open. I've got her shoulders." Will knelt on her other side.

Strong pressure and her fangs popped loose. Then we heaved her up and off.

"Selfish bastard. You ruined my life. My career." She kicked at Ray, connecting with his ribs. "We wrote that love song together. Did that mean anything to you?" Tears ran down her cheeks to mix with the blood that smeared around her mouth.

"I'm sorry. That's all I can say. Your career will be fine. I'll help you." Ray propped himself up on one elbow with a wince.

"Damn right you will. Vampire!" She struggled against Will's arm around her waist. "I hope that council ties you to a tree and lets the sun fry you."

"Okay, I've heard enough. Let's get out of here." I glanced at Jerry. "Sienna, do you have a car?"

"Yeah, let's go. My rental's out front. I can't wait to get away from this asshole." She gave Ray one more kick then rushed back to the bedroom.

"Where are you taking her?" Ray struggled to his feet with Will's help.

"Where else? Home with me. Someone has to keep an eye on her and it's not going to be you." I saw that the wound on his neck had already stopped bleeding. "Jerry, why don't you meet us out front? Will, can you show him which car is Sienna's rental? We'll be out in a minute. Ray, do us both a favor and disappear now." I glanced back down the hall.

"Call Damian and order whatever synthetic you need for her. Tell him to put it on my tab." Ray sighed and started toward the kitchen. "Tell her I'm sorry."

"She's not ready to hear that." I knew Sienna would be out any moment. "Remember how you felt when this was done to you?"

"Yeah, too well. I took away her future." He ran his hand over his eyes. "Damn it, if the council decides to end me, they'll be doing me a favor."

"Ray." Sienna stood in the doorway. "I really don't want to watch your pity party right now." She stomped over to face him. "You can't fix this so now I expect you to make amends. We both know that's part of a twelve-step program. You'll be doing some big-time making up to me. Understand?" She pressed a black-painted fingernail to his chest, drawing blood.

"Yeah. Sure. If that's what you want." He straightened his shoulders, smart enough not to grab her hand.

"No, it's what you owe me. First, from what Glory is telling me, I may need a new manager. Seems like Nathan is the only one who knows the vampire scene. Talk to him, persuade him to take me on because obviously I'm going to have to let mine go." She took a shaky breath, tears glittering on those long and beautiful fake lashes. "Damn, I hate this. But I can't put Ethan through this. Canceling shit for what he'll think are arbitrary reasons. And he'd never get this vampire thing." She covered her eyes for a minute. "*I* don't get it."

"Babe . . ." Ray obviously couldn't stand it and tried to take her hand. Sienna sprang back, startling herself when she landed across the room, near me.

"I'm not your babe." She looked down. "How far did I just jump?"

"About eight feet." I settled my hand on her shoulder. "A new manager. That's a good idea. Make Nate go along with it, Ray. Get busy. Make some calls. If you're already helping Sienna, the council will be impressed. I hope." I could feel Sienna shaking, her surprise at her new physical prowess obviously more upsetting than she let on. "Ready to go, Sienna?"

"Yeah. I have three bags in the closet. Will, can you get them?" She picked up her tote. "Let's jet." She stepped aside when Ray reached for her. "Touch me and die, Ray. I will never forgive you."

"Sorry." He moved when Will appeared with Sienna's bags and followed us outside. The car was a small convertible. By the time we got Sienna's stuff crammed inside, Jerry had decided to fly to the apartment and meet us there.

"What? He can fly?" Sienna had overheard our discussion.

"Not in my human form like Superman. I shape-shift. We'll teach you how." Jerry kept his arm around me. "Gloriana had a hard time with it at first but it's really a simple process." He kissed me on the cheek. "Watch." He transformed into a blackbird and took off.

"Oh. My. God." Sienna leaned against the car. "This is getting weirder and weirder. What else can you guys do? Can you turn into other stuff?"

"Sure." Will did the bat thing then easily became a dog before turning back into his human form.

"I think I'm going to be sick." Sienna rushed over to the bushes and we heard her retch.

"Guess I should have saved some of that for another time." Will grinned and strolled over to pat her on the back and offer her a handkerchief.

"Damned show-off." Ray had stayed near his front door.

"You got it, flaunt it. Sienna, you'll have fun with that once you try it. Don't be a wuss like I was." I helped her climb into the car, taking her keys and settling into the driver's seat myself. She was pale and shaky, our reality still too much for her. I could see that she couldn't imagine "fun" and "vampire" ever going together. "Are you okay enough for me to start the car?"

"Let's go. I asked Will for water and he said I couldn't even drink that." Sienna's eyes filled. "This is too much. Maybe the fresh air will clear my head. Just drive, Glory." She leaned back against the seat and closed her eyes.

"You could have rinsed out your mouth." I glared at Will. It wouldn't have killed him to fetch her a bottle of water. "I'm sorry, Sienna. The first few days are the roughest. Take some breaths and try to relax." I started the car and took off. It had been so long since I'd been turned I couldn't remember that early adjustment period. But Sienna had a lot more to lose than I'd had back in 1604. I'd been an actress of sorts and no one had missed me when I'd stayed with Jerry instead of returning to the theater. Sienna was going to have to do plenty to make her career stay on track despite her new lifestyle.

Her display of bloodlust had reminded me that she'd have a

raging thirst these first few days. But I'd have to make sure there were no more uncontrolled feedings. As soon as we got to my place, I'd have to give her a lesson in drinking from a vein. Fun and games. Because you know whose vein it would have to be.

When we arrived in the alley behind my apartment and the shop, the lights were working and Jerry leaned against my car. No sign of you know who. Of course not. She'd never let Jerry see her threaten me. Probably played innocent around him, though it wouldn't help her cause. Jerry grabbed Sienna's bags while I helped her out of the car. She was fading fast and sniffing the air. I knew I was going to have to feed her as soon as we got upstairs.

At the door to the apartment, we could all hear the TV blaring. Obviously Aggie was home and watching one of her favorite shows. She'd given up *Judge Judy* after losing an important court case in her own life. Now she was hooked on other reality shows. If there was a *Real Housewives* on the air, she was there watching. I unlocked the door and saw she was riveted by a hair-pulling fight next to a pool. Looked like either Miami or Los Angeles. Seriously? These "housewives" in bikinis with spray tans had had enough plastic surgeries between them to finance a clinic.

"Who's this?" Aggie set a bag of rice cakes on the coffee table. She was supposedly on a serious diet these days though a Snickers wrapper peeked from under the couch cushion. "Suitcases? Is she planning to stay here? Where is she going to sleep?"

"Sienna Star meet Aggie . . . Did you decide on a last name?" I helped Sienna into a chair.

"Not yet. Maybe I'll be like Cher. One name's enough." She glared when I snorted. "Hey, Star. Rock star Sienna Star.

Didn't you do a guest appearance on *Real Housewives of Malibu*?" Aggie was interested now.

"A lifetime ago." Sienna collapsed in a chair.

"What's the matter? You look pale. Glory? What's up? Is she a vampire?" Aggie glared when I nodded. "Let's get something straight right now, lady. Famous chick or not, I'm off the menu. Glory, you tell her." Aggie grabbed her rice cakes and a diet soda and clicked off the TV. "I'm going to bed. The DVR is set so I can watch this when I get home from work tomorrow. Maybe you should get a pullout couch, Glory, if you're going to bring home strays. Speaking of. I fed your cat." She made a face, then headed down the hall. We could hear her muttering about bloodsuckers.

"Thanks, Aggie." I looked for Boogie, but he was probably hiding. He did that when we had company. I'd inherited him when a fledgling I'd mentored had moved to California to enter med school.

"What a bitch." Sienna sighed as she leaned back. "What did I do to her?"

"Nothing. She's always like that these days. She tried to sue an ex-lover and lost. Now she has to clean his house every day as part of a settlement. Wouldn't that put a kink in your tail?"

"Yeah. I'll try to cut her some slack. She did smell pretty good though." Sienna covered her mouth with one hand. "These fangs are going to be a problem if they just pop out whenever I'm around a, whatcha call 'em, mortal."

"Give it time. You'll gain more control." I sat on the couch, smiling when Jerry settled next to me. "We've been working on a way to get her out of here, but so far no luck."

"How much does she owe?" Sienna's head wobbled. "No, don't tell me. I'm not paying off anyone's debts. I have no idea how I'm going to be able to work with this new life I've got, so money may be tight for me too." She sighed and let her head drop until it rested on the back of the chair. "Glory, I don't feel so hot. I need to lie down."

"I know. Here, stretch out on the couch." I jumped up and grabbed one of her arms, Jerry the other. Soon we had her stretched out on the couch. "You need blood and this time I'm going to show you how to drink properly. You need some ancient vampire blood. What you got from Ray held you for a while, but he's a fairly new vampire. My blood is a lot stronger. It will give you strength."

"No, Gloriana. You turned her last night and are still fairly weak. Go get a bottle of synthetic for yourself. I'll feed her." Jerry sat beside her on the couch. "Now here's what you do, Sienna. You remember me, don't you?"

"Sure, though you seem to have a couple of names. Is it Jerry or Jeremiah or Blade?" She stared up at him, her face paper white.

"I go by Jeremy Blade this century. We change our names if we think we've used the same one too long. When you live for hundreds of years, it's sometimes necessary." He glanced at me where I stood in the kitchen doorway. "Now I want you to take my hand and pull my wrist to your mouth. Smell it and see what happens."

"Smell?" She tentatively took his hand. "This is weird. My senses are totally out of whack. Like I'm hyped up on something. Just like Glory told me they would be." She glanced around. "Is there chocolate here somewhere?"

I walked over and pulled out that Snickers wrapper. It left a smear on my upholstery. Damn Aggie. One name? She'd be lucky to have that when I got through with her.

"Here's what you smelled. But concentrate. Lean in, toward Jerry's wrist. Smell something else?"

She closed her eyes and pulled his arm toward her. "Oh, geez, my teeth are shifting again. Your blood!" Her eyes popped open. "I smell it, Jerry. And it's, um, delicious. Better than the chocolate. Though I never would have thought . . ." She wrinkled her nose. "Wow. I can actually hear your pulse too. It's like a drumbeat. Bu-bump, bu-bump, bu-bump. Singing 'Drink me,' clear as can be." She grinned and there were her fangs. She ran her tongue over them. "Damn, my teeth are sharp."

"That's so you can bite into my vein there, in my wrist. Go ahead, pierce it carefully. We don't rip into skin like you did Caine."

"Guess that was pretty harsh. But the bastard deserved it. Am I right?" She looked at me for validation. I nodded.

"He'll heal and not even scar. I'm sure it hurt. But you don't want to act like an animal when you drink. For one thing, you'll lose some of the blood you're after." I leaned over the back of the sofa and pointed to the blue vein that we could all see clearly in Jerry's wrist. I had my own thirst to contend with and took a deep swallow of synthetic then pointed. "There. Position your mouth like you're going to give him a hickey, but your fangs will sink in. When his blood begins to fill your mouth, suck."

"Oh, man." She frowned at me. "You won't mind? This is your boyfriend I'm getting groovy with."

"It's feeding, not sexual. At least not like this." I ran my hands through Jerry's hair. "Trust me, when you are with your lover and feeding is part of it, it can be quite a turn-on. You'll have to find your own man to experience that with."

"Got it. It sure won't be Ray again. Bastard. You think drinking my blood while I was unconscious turned him on?" She pulled Jerry's wrist closer and inhaled. I could see her hands shaking. "Probably did, the perv."

"Go on and drink. My blood is vintage, about five hundred

years old, even older than Glory's." Jerry reached for me with his other hand. "Don't worry about hurting me. I'm a warrior. I can take the little pain your bite will cause me."

"You sure? I . . ." She licked his arm. "Oh, sorry. That was icky of me."

"No, that was right. Instinctual. You just anaesthetized the area. Our saliva does that. It'll help dull the pain. Go ahead. Bite. I want you to feel better. It pleases me to help you. Because you are Glory's child."

"Oh, geez. That's bizarre. Here goes." She closed her eyes, took a deep breath, her nostrils flaring. Then she sank her fangs into Jerry's skin. He winced. Obviously this newbie had no finesse.

I slid an arm around him, my cheek against his. "Thanks. You're being awfully cool about this. I wonder what I could possibly do to make it up to you."

"I'll figure out something." He turned his head and kissed me. His mouth on mine always made me realize how right we were for each other, his taste the perfect completion that I always searched for.

I pulled back with a sigh. "Don't let her take too much."

"I won't. I'm timing her." He rested his free hand on her hair, then gently pressed on her forehead. "Enough, Sienna. That's enough."

"Mmm." She gripped his arm with both hands, refusing to let go.

I walked around behind her and grabbed her shoulders. Together, Jerry and I managed to wrench her free.

"Oh, gosh. I'm sorry. I was so into that." She was flushed and wiped her mouth with the back of her hand. When she saw the blood there, she shrieked. "Oh, shit. What have I become? Glory, am I some kind of mindless animal?"

"No, calm down." I took Jerry's place next to her on the couch. "Look. It will take time for you to learn control. But you *will* learn it. You've only been a vampire for twenty-four hours. Like he said, Jerry's blood is really ancient. Premium stuff." I smiled up at him. "I have a hard time pulling away from him myself." I took a cloth Jerry handed me, wiped her face and cleaned off her hand. "Now relax. Do you feel better?"

"Yes. Jazzed. Almost high." She sat up. "It's hours until daylight. We should do something. Go out."

"I'd rather you not be around mortals just yet." I frowned down the hall. We had a mortal pretty close. "Aggie is right. She's not on the menu. When you smell her blood, it will tempt you. Don't give in."

"Why would I? She's not very nice." Sienna got up and walked around the room, scowling at my Israel Caine shrine. I had one of her CDs there too.

"Nice has nothing to do with bloodlust. You want to go out, let's head downstairs to my shop. Now you know why my store is open twenty-four hours a day. As a vampire, I wanted to be able to work all night. I hire shape-shifters to work it during the day. This time of night there won't be many people there who aren't paranormal, no one Jerry and I can't help you handle."

"Shape-shifters? Like Will? No, he was a vampire who could change into other stuff. Jerry too. So what are those? More paranormals?" Sienna grabbed her purse like she was ready to go.

"Yes, you have a lot of things you need to know. Gloriana, we should stay up here." Jerry frowned, clearly not happy about a field trip with a new vampire.

"I'm too hyped to stay here. And I sure can't stay in this tiny apartment all the time." Sienna smiled at me. "No offense,

Glory. Just a few minutes, Jerry? I'll behave and maybe buy something in the shop."

I knew Jerry was right, but couldn't turn down the chance for the business. The mice fiasco had to have hurt sales. Sienna had shopped in Vintage Vamp's before and spent a bundle.

"Okay, just for a while, but you're going to run out of steam soon, Sienna. This burst of energy won't last." I was desperate to change clothes. "I'm taking a quick shower first. Jerry, will you wait?"

"Of course." He reached for the remote and settled on the couch. He soon found a European soccer match.

"Okay, I need to fix my makeup. You never know when the paparazzi will try to snap a picture. Glory, you said you had one of those computer setups here so I can see myself. Can I use it?" Sienna dropped her purse and grabbed her tote from by the door.

"Sure. It's in the bedroom. Follow me." I led the way, then snatched clean underwear and a robe before I headed for the bathroom. "You can figure it out. It's there on my dresser."

She sat on the foot of the bed. "Thanks for this, Glory."

I sighed. What had I gotten myself into? "No problem. Just remember that there will be temptations down there. It's important for you to use self-control."

"Hey, I've been stalked by fans, paparazzi, you name it, and never killed one of them yet. I think I can handle myself around, what do you call them?" She grinned. "Mortals." She rummaged in her tote.

"She has the confidence of the innocent." Jerry stood in the doorway and pulled me close.

"Yes. Be prepared to use the whammy down there. I figure she'll get close to a mortal and show her fangs. I just hope no one gets a picture of it." I pulled him back into the living room, where the noise of the game would drown out our conversation.

"She's a public figure. This is going to be about as bad as it was with Israel Caine."

"At least she isn't an alcoholic." I ran my hand up his chest. "But, Jer, when are we ever going to be alone again?" I'd just pulled his head down to kiss him when we heard shrieks coming from my bedroom. What now?

Four

We ran into my bedroom to find Sienna with my comforter draped over her head, swatting frantically at . . . bees?

"Get them off of me!" She flailed her arms, a quilted butterfly on steroids. "I'm highly allergic. Look in my purse for my EpiPen." She sobbed and threw herself facedown on the bed, covered from head to toe.

Jerry ran to my window and jerked up the black-out shade then the window itself. "Where the hell could these have come from?"

"I have a pretty good idea." I swatted at the bees—there had to be dozens—using a hardback book from my dresser. I'm always interested in self-help. This one focused on inner peace. I wish. Right now I'd take peace anywhere I could find it.

Jerry grabbed my hair spray and attacked them with that. It seemed to do the trick and most of them flew toward the fresh air coming in from the open window. With my fanning and Jerry's spraying, we soon had all but a few out of there. He smacked one with his bare hand when it landed on my arm.

"Sorry about that." He brushed it off. "Check on Sienna, I'll grab her purse." He strode to the living room.

"Sienna, can you talk?" I lifted the edge of the cover. She peered up at me, her face swollen and covered with stings.

"Oh, God, don't look at me." She jerked the quilted spread back over herself. "Bring me my pen before my throat closes."

"It may not. You're a vampire now. You're already healing. Look at the bites on your arms. Are they as bad as usual?" I sat beside her. Jerry dropped her purse next to us.

"I'm not about to go purse diving. You look for it." He shook his head. "How is she?"

"She looks terrible but she's still able to talk. I think she's already on the mend. Aren't you, Sienna?"

She sat up, cautiously looked around, then threw back the cover. "You know, it's a freaking miracle, but you're right. I'd be dead if I were still a, um, mortal." She examined the backs of her hands which were covered with angry red dots but weren't as swollen as they'd been even a minute ago. "I can't believe it."

"You just fed. So you're healing very fast. It helped that Jerry's blood was ancient." I leaned back against him. "Your face already looks a thousand times better."

"Thank God. I freaked when I opened your computer mirror thing and suddenly all those bees swarmed out." She glared at the laptop still open on my dresser. "What the hell? Has this happened before?"

"No, of course not." I looked back at Jerry. "I think we had a visitor today, while no one was home. Sabotage and meant for me, of course."

"Who would do such a thing?" Sienna sighed and climbed off the bed. She grabbed my book and slammed it onto a stray bee that dared land next to the laptop. "Got it."

"Jerry has an old girlfriend who wants him back. I'm pretty

sure she did this. She wants me to give him up so he'll turn to her."

"You're jumping to conclusions, Gloriana." Jerry sat next to me on the bed.

"Are you kidding me right now?" I felt my jaw drop. "How else do you think we suddenly have a beehive in my laptop, Jerry? Obviously, Mel got in here and planted them while Aggie was at work and I was at Ray's." The very idea of that woman in my home during the day made me sick. No, terrified. If I'd been dead to the world here when she'd come in . . . All it would take is a stake to the heart.

"She doesn't have your key or the code to security here." Jerry clutched my hand. I could see the implications weren't lost on him either. "This building is supposed to be safe from intruders during the day."

"Are you defending her?" I jumped up. "Aggie forgets to set the security system half the time and the woman practices voodoo. I imagine she has some kind of 'Open Sesame' spell to crack through any defense, any place she chooses." I jumped up. "Oh, my God! Boogie! Here, kitty!" I fell to the floor and looked under the bed, his favorite hiding place. I managed to scoop him into my arms. "He seems to be okay." He purred against my chest. "When I think what could have happened . . ." My breath hitched.

"Calm down, Gloriana." Jerry reached out and stroked the cat's head. That was Boogie's signal to leap down and race for his food bowl in the kitchen. "First, we'll make sure Aggie never forgets again. That's intolerable. Second, I doubt Mel is that strong. A spell like that? I've never seen her do anything more than make a few things disappear. Parlor tricks."

"You and I both have smelled the evil around her. She's much more than a trickster. But if you saw her in Miami on business a while back, I suppose it's possible she got hold of your keys there while you were in your death sleep and had copies made. For future use." I walked over to stand next to Sienna, brushing a dead bee off the laptop.

"I didn't see her. Not like you think." Jerry followed me. "She tried to start up again. I shut her down."

"Guess she didn't want to hear that. Maybe she hung around after sunrise and slipped past your security. Clearly she's obsessed with you, Jer." I couldn't look at him, still shaking from the idea that the woman had been in my bedroom during the day. "But why bees? Surely she knows vampires heal from stings in minutes."

"If Mel did this, she wanted to irritate you. Make it inconvenient for you to keep seeing me. Obviously she's miscalculated. You and I both know this kind of nonsense isn't going to pull us apart." He slipped his arms around me, actually smiling. "Seriously, Gloriana, I've told Mel to leave you alone. That none of her tricks will bring me back to her. This might have been her last final desperate act."

"You're assuming she's rational, Jerry. And coming here during the day isn't nonsense. It's a death threat." I glanced at Sienna. "What's the matter? Are you all right?" She was staring into the computer screen, her eyes welling.

"You said I'd heal. But look at me. Everywhere one of those bees stung me, I have a blue dot. Blue! And they aren't going away." She whirled around, her eyes wild. "Do you have any idea what this could mean to my career? How can I go out in public like this?"

"Relax, Sienna. Whatever it is, death sleep usually heals everything. Tomorrow night you should be as good as new." Of course I'd had some problems in the past that had managed to hang on past a good day's sleep. When I stepped closer and took her chin in my hand I could see that the bites *had* turned blue. And she was covered with them. There were at least ten on each cheek and a pattern resembling the Big Dipper decorated her forehead. No way could we pass this off as a fashion statement, and it would take a dump truck full of concealer to hide them. The fact that she had more blue dots on her neck, arms and chest made it worse.

"This is nuts. And you're right, Gloriana. Sneaking in here during the day *was* a death threat." Jerry stomped to the bedroom door. "I'm finding Mel and making her stop this vendetta against you once and for all. She'll fix this, Sienna, or she'll never draw another breath."

"Thanks, Jerry." Sienna brushed tears off her cheeks. They weren't swollen now, just decorated. We winced when the front door slammed behind him. "Will he really kill her? He's got to make her take care of this first."

"I have no idea. The woman has put a spell on him. He's told her many times he's done with her but if he gets a whiff of her blood . . . ?" I sank down on the foot of the bed. "I don't want to think about it, but I have a feeling he drank her blood the last time he saw her. Jer hates synthetics and has always preferred mortal donors." I saw that I had at least three blue dots on my arms too. "He won't admit it but he's a sucker, pardon the pun, for her flavor."

"That's kind of cheating, isn't it?" Sienna sagged down next to me. "Maybe you should break up with him."

"You have no idea what we've been through together. I won't let that witch tear us apart." I got up and rummaged in my dresser drawer, coming up with a stick concealer that had always worked wonders for me. "Let's see if we can make you presentable enough to go downstairs. If we hide up here, Mel has won."

"I wouldn't want that." She grabbed the concealer and started rubbing it on. "This is pretty good stuff. I'll just have to stay away from close-ups." She shook her head. "Voodoo is real too?"

"Afraid so. Ghosts, were-cats, even werewolves."

"I feel like I've fallen down the rabbit hole." Sienna kept working on her spots. "But that's okay. I'm cool with it. As long as these blue things go away. If I'm living forever, I'll be damned if it's looking like a polka-dotted freak."

"Like I said, our death sleep usually finishes any healing we need to do. With luck, you'll wake up tomorrow after sunset good as new." I left Sienna to her face painting and finally got the shower I was desperate for. It made me feel marginally better but I was furious with Mel. Not happy with Jerry either. He'd tried to make light of the woman's behavior. More and more it seemed he *was* under a spell of some kind. I needed advice. And it had to come from someone who knew the voodoo world. I remembered that Flo had gotten help for me once from a priestess in New Orleans. I had to call my best friend right away and get that expert's number.

Just explaining Mel's latest trick took a while, then Flo had to arrange to call me back after she'd dug for that number. She didn't want to let Richard know what she was up to. He didn't approve of the dark arts and she'd never admitted to her husband that she'd consulted a voodoo priestess when they'd been in the Crescent City.

I got dressed in a long-sleeved sweater and matching navy pants, then found Sienna in the kitchen staring at the bottles of synthetic blood I kept in the refrigerator.

"Ready to go?" I grabbed a bottle of B positive and twisted off the cap.

"In a minute." Sienna slammed the fridge shut without selecting anything. I doubted if she was really thirsty after drinking from Jerry. "Why'd you pick that, um, flavor?"

"It's cheap, tastes pretty good, and I'm in a hurry. I save the negative stuff for special occasions." I smiled at her. "You have a tasty blood type. You don't want to hear this, but Ray got carried away with you because you have blood that is like fine wine to us."

"A negative." Sienna looked thoughtful. "Good to know. But no excuse for Ray. I'm going to get even with him somehow. Wait and see."

"Oh, you should. The man deserves some serious payback." I finished my bottle, rinsed it out and tossed it into the recycle bin. "Be sure to put your empties in here. Save the planet. Ray's arranging to send over some expensive stuff. You'll like it better than what I stock."

"It's the least he can do. You drink it too. Putting me up like this is a favor to him *and* me. And recycling? Sure. Guess that's important when you know you'll be around a long, long time." She smiled. "I can't wrap my mind around that yet. Live forever, look twenty-five forever and I'm in the best shape of my life thanks to that last stint in rehab." She gave me the once-over. It didn't take mind reading to know she felt bad for me, stuck in a less than perfect body.

"Yes, you're lucky. I didn't have a clue when Jerry turned me." I smacked my butt in pants that had the spandex I loved. "He stuffed me like a Christmas goose before my big V-day. I'd been close to starving before then. A widow with no skills." I sighed, remembering. "After I became vampire I found out too late that I should have fasted or something beforehand."

"If he likes you the way you are, that's all that matters. And you know how to dress to look good." Sienna leaned against the kitchen counter.

"Thanks, Sienna. I know my figure's not in style, but lots of ancient males like a little padding on their women. Lucky for me." I pulled open a drawer and found an extra set of keys. "Here's the key to the door here and the one downstairs. Though now I'm thinking I should get the locks changed on this door." I shared the security code to the building.

"Am I safe here? I heard you say that woman sneaked in here and planted those bees during the day and that she could have killed you while you slept. It's scary to think what would have happened if Ray hadn't called you over to help with me last night." She shuddered. "Does that happen a lot? People coming after you while you're, um, dead?"

"It's always a possibility. Usually we're okay with normal security and black-out shades." I put my arm around her shoulders while she slipped her feet into platform sandals. She'd changed clothes, and her whole outfit, from the nude long-sleeved silk T-shirt with a logo from an Italian designer to brown leggings, screamed casual rocker with a killer body. "Try not to freak out about it, Sienna. We'll figure out a way to stay safe."

She sat on my couch with a sigh. "You want to tell me the whole story? About this bitch who can do magic?"

"I will. Later. Obviously I need better daylight security again until we put her out of commission. I used to have a bodyguard, a shifter who stayed with me twenty-four/seven. Jerry paid for it. I finally cut the guy loose and have been counting on the building security to do the job ever since. Guess that isn't enough right now." My knees turned to water and I grabbed the back of the couch while the reality of what had happened hit me hard. Aggie left us every day not long after daylight and was gone most of the day. That gave Mel hours to come in and . . . I had a horror movie going in my head that made me want to scream.

"Glory? You think we need a bodyguard again? What do you want to do?" Sienna got up and touched my arm. "I can pay the freight. I usually travel with a posse anyway. I know I griped about money, but it's really not an issue. I don't blow it like some rockers do, and I have plenty socked away. I've always known my singing days are limited." She touched her wild hair and wrinkled her pierced nose. "Can you see this when I'm forty? Sixty? I'm not planning to be one of those geriatric rockers who doesn't know when to call it quits."

"You'll never look geriatric now, Sienna." I touched her shoulder. "But you'll have to face a different issue with your looks later. When you don't age. That's years away. Something you can figure out when the time comes. As to the guard? We could split it, I suppose. That might make it easier on both of us. And it sure would make me feel better." I tried to run calculations in my head but knew I really couldn't afford to pay for even half of top-notch security. As long as Sienna was staying here though . . .

Hey, maybe she shouldn't. If I put her in danger . . . I sat down again. Overwhelmed.

"So where do we go for this help? Obviously not my usual sources." Sienna frowned and pulled out her cell. "I need a whole new contact list."

"I know who to call. Jerry won't like it, but I know who always made me feel safe during the day." I pulled my own phone out of my purse. His number was third on my speed dial, right after Jerry and Flo. He answered on the second ring.

"Glory. What's up?"

"Nothing good, Rafe. Can you meet me in the shop? Soon?"

"Sure. We're closing right now. Give me thirty minutes. Is that okay?" His voice was deep and comforting. I felt better already.

"Thanks, Rafe. I knew I could count on you." I ended the call. "Let's go on down to the shop. You can see what's new."

"Good. I love your store. I have a gig on Halloween night and a party afterward. Maybe I can pick up a costume." Sienna jumped up, purse on her arm.

"Sure, costumes are one of our specialties." I followed Sienna down the stairs and watched her try out the security code. She had a good memory and we were soon out on the street. Luckily there were no paparazzi around and we ducked into my shop unnoticed.

"Who's Rafe?" Sienna stopped in front of a rack of costumes and fingered the fringe on a flapper dress.

"My ex-bodyguard. He and I . . . Well, we got pretty close for a while. That's why Jerry won't be too keen on the idea. You know Rafe. He's the owner of N-V, where you sang the other night."

"Valdez! Sure. He's hot, Glory. So you two hooked up." Sienna gave me a high five. "Nice work. But no wonder Jerry won't like him hanging around. Will Rafe have time for a bodyguard assignment?"

"I don't know. But he can always recommend someone. He's a shape-shifter and knows a network of them. Most of the people who work at N-V are paranormals." I pulled out a two-piece genie costume that would show off Sienna's perfect figure. "You'd look hot in this. Make Ray wish he'd behaved himself."

"Yes, I like it. I'll try both of these on." She headed for the dressing room. "I never would have guessed . . ." She shut up when two more customers came into the shop. We'd been alone except for my clerk Megan until then. "What about here? Mortal or . . . ?"

"Not. It's just good policy to hire people like us. When you're not, um, normal, it's nice to help each other out. I struggled for a lot of years, trying to find work that would allow for my crazy sleep pattern." I glanced back at Megan, who was unlocking the jewelry case for the new customers, and lowered my voice. "Megan is my day manager's cousin, a were-cat."

"Oh, wow. I just can't imagine." Sienna stepped into the dressing room. "This world is crazy freaky. If the tabloids only knew . . ." She grinned and closed the door.

I turned away. There was something about her grin that made me uneasy. No, I was freaked because of Mel and her tricks, that was all. And worried that there could be more mice. Though I was sure Megan would have ferreted out any strays and made short work of them. I shuddered at the thought.

Sienna came out and modeled the flapper costume, not short enough. The blue dots on her arms showed and we both decided to take her business to the back room before a customer noticed. She was already getting looks, recognized. I was surprised she hadn't been approached for an autograph yet. She was getting into the genie outfit in my bathroom when Rafe showed up. I couldn't help myself. I ran into his arms.

"I am so glad to see you." I let his warmth surround me with safety. It was tempting to linger. Finally I pushed back with a sigh.

"Okay, now tell me what's up. You're obviously upset about something."

I dragged him to the back room, shut the door and told him the whole story. I let him know about Melisandra and her tricks, her determination to have Jerry for herself and our confrontation. When I got to the bee invasion Rafe grabbed my arms.

"She got into your apartment during the day?" He said it so loudly I was afraid the customers up front could hear him through the door.

"Yes. That's why I called you. Do you know someone I can hire to watch over us while we sleep?" I covered his hands. His concern made it clear to me that he still had some work to do before he was totally over what we'd had. And me? Just being this close, looking up into those warm brown eyes so full of caring, made me remember how he always made me feel. Safe, cherished, respected.

"Know someone? As if I'd trust anyone else. And who is *us*? Blade going to be there?" He let go and stepped back.

"No. Sienna Star. Ray had an accident and she's now a vampire. I had to turn her to save her life." I saw his face harden. Okay, so he and Ray weren't buddies. And having to ask about Jerry hadn't been easy for him either.

"You're shittin' me. An accident? Don't excuse him, Glory. What an idiot. And now that sweet young thing is stuck as a vampire." He glanced at the door into the shop. "I thought I smelled her as I came in. You know she's been at the club, rehearsing, performing. Caine just made that go all to hell, didn't he?"

"No, he didn't. Not if I have anything to say about it." Sienna opened the bathroom door and stepped into the room, proving that men dream of genies because they are hot, hot, hot.

"Sienna." Rafe finally managed to pull his tongue back into his mouth and speak. "Looking good." Understatement, if the way his eyes swept up and down her body was any indication.

"Thanks. So can you find us someone to hire? To do the bodyguard gig?" Sienna leaned against my worktable.

I tried not to stare. The costume fit perfectly, if cramming D-cup breasts into a B-cup bra was perfect. Rafe obviously thought so. He couldn't look away. The sheer harem pants clung low, well below her navel, and I saw that Sienna had a piercing there, a ring with a diamond. It was a nice touch. She'd kept her feet bare, her turquoise polish matching the trim on the gold outfit. The top had sheer long sleeves which helped disguise her blue dots and she must have brought along the concealer because the dots on her chest were barely noticeable.

"I can't hand this off to someone else. I'll figure out a way to do it myself." Rafe tore his gaze from Sienna long enough to take a breath and stare at a spot between us.

"You have a club to run. And, frankly, I can't afford your rates." I knew he was expensive, I'd seen the bill he'd sent to Jerry.

"As if I'd charge you, Glory." He grabbed my hand before I could stop him. "Seriously, this is messed up. How Blade got involved with a nut-job like this woman is bad enough, but to put you in danger . . ." He squeezed my fingers, focused on me now. "I'm going to have a talk with him."

"No, Rafe. You two don't talk and you know it. That conversation will end up in a fight." I laid my other hand on his chest. His heart was thumping, fast. And he was so warm, shifter warm.

"I'll leave you two to thrash this out, but, Rafe?" Sienna stopped with her hand on the doorknob. "I can afford to pay you. We need security. Whether this woman is an issue or not. I'll need it when I go out on the road again too. Maybe you can hook me up with some guys you trust to be my new security team." She looked down at her toes, curled under. "I'm still figuring things out but I'm not letting Ray take my career away from me. I'll be back onstage no matter what I have to do."

"Good for you." Rafe smiled at her. "Glory can help. She's figured out how to live among mortals for centuries. Blending, she calls it. It'll be tougher for you because you're a public figure, but even that asshole Ray Caine has managed it for the past year. That should show you it's possible."

"Yeah. If he can do it, I can. I can't believe we sang together at the Grammys." Sienna glanced at me. "He was vampire then, Glory?"

"Sure was. And you didn't have a clue, did you?"

"No, just got pissed because of his weird rehearsal schedule. And you know the label went along with it. Is Chip?" She shook her head. "Naw. Now I'm thinking everyone, even the label's owner, is a vampire. How stupid is that?" She looked down at herself. "What do you think, Rafe? Is this the costume I should wear on Halloween? We're singing at your club. Or we're supposed to. Ray and I. Not sure I can stand to be onstage with him again."

"Publicity has gone out. You're committed. I've got your signed contract. Of course you can do it." Rafe let go of my hand and stepped toward her. "And wear that costume. Let Caine see what he lost by being a stupid jerk. Used you as his blood donor, didn't he?"

"Yeah. And lost control. Typical addict behavior." She shuddered. "Damn, I'm going to have to watch myself. Stay away from mortal boyfriends." Her eyes filled and Rafe settled his hands on her narrow shoulders. I thought for a moment that he was going to pull her close and my stomach did a three-sixty. Stupid. I had no right to be jealous.

"If you learned nothing else from this fiasco, it's that mortal bedmates are the wrong play. Look what happened to you. Stick to paranormals who can hold their own around you." He nodded toward me. "Have a long talk with Glory about the joys of paranormal sex." He grinned and winked. "Hard to beat, right, sweetheart?"

"Shut up, Rafe." I felt my cheeks go hot. "Sienna, you look great. Buy it. I'll give you a discount."

"Thanks." She winked at me. "Paranormal sex. Oh, yeah. I want all the details." She brushed a fingertip down Rafe's black tee with the red N-V logo. "But a demo would be even better."

Rafe cleared his throat. "Slow down, Sin." He glanced at me. "How long you been a vampire?"

"Twenty-four hours, more or less." She smiled. "And I'm not a fan of slow unless it's—" She leaned close and whispered in his ear.

Rafe actually flushed. "Oh, yeah, I hear you. If I hadn't just told my girlfriend I was all in, I'd be up for that." He stepped back from her with a grin. "But just now the timing's off." He turned to me. "Guarding you again, Glory. Not sure how that's going to go over with my girl either. But I'll handle it."

"Oh, no, Rafe! Maybe you shouldn't—" I knew Lacy *wouldn't* be happy that he was riding to my rescue again. Of course he'd be there when I was dead. Lights out. Maybe Lacy would be cool with that.

"It's okay. She lives across the hall from you. She can keep me company when you're out during the day." Rafe shrugged. "If she can't handle that, then maybe we aren't meant to be, you know?"

"No, I don't. I can talk to her." I really didn't want to make his love life fall apart. I'd caused him enough pain in the past. And Lacy was my day manager. I didn't want to alienate her either. This had been a bad idea all the way around.

"Stay out of it. I'm doing this, no arguments." He didn't smile, suddenly all business. "Now, Sienna, get dressed. Glory, does Blade know you called me?"

"Um, no." I pulled my cell out of my pocket, dreading the

conversation. "He was going to see Mel. To try to get her to back off."

"Well, how's that worked so far?" He watched Sienna strut into the bathroom with a twitch of her hips then shook his head as she shut the door with a finger wave.

"It hasn't. I'm calling him now." I tried and my call went straight to voice mail.

"I don't like it, Rafe. Jer always answers."

He frowned. "Has it occurred to you that this woman may get tired of Blade's rejection?" He put his hand on top of mine that was holding the phone.

"Seriously? Oh, God. Maybe Jerry is the one who needs the bodyguard." I looked down at the phone and tried his number again. No answer. A woman scorned. Maybe I wasn't her only target.

Five

"We'll worry about Blade later." Rafe glanced at his watch when Sienna emerged from the bathroom back in her own clothes. "Wind up this transaction then let's head up to your place. I want to look around. See if there are signs of a break-in. You said she got in yesterday, during the day?"

"Yes. I think so. Otherwise how could she manage to tamper with my laptop camera, the one I use for a mirror? Fill it with freakin' bees?" I followed Sienna out to the register. "Megan, give Miss Star a twenty percent discount on this outfit."

"Sure." Megan took the two pieces and carefully wrapped them in tissue paper. She gushed over Sienna, running her credit card then asking for an autograph after she signed the receipt.

"Do we have to hurry back upstairs?" Sienna glanced around. "I see a few other things I might want to buy. My mother collects vintage jewelry. It's never too early to shop for

Christmas." She grabbed my arm. "Oh, my God. My mom and dad. I'll have to tell . . ." She squeezed until I yelped.

"Hey, you're hurting me. Relax. We'll figure things out."

"I don't think so. I'll never get old and they will." Tears filled her eyes. "How can I handle that?"

"Sienna, I honestly don't know." I patted her hand, realizing she was right to be upset and I didn't know how to make her feel better. I'd been through this with Ray but it wasn't any easier the second time around. "Take this change one step at a time. You can come back here tomorrow night. Shop some more. And we'll talk. About what to tell your family. Right now Rafe's right. We need to go back up and let him assess the situation. Dawn is only a couple of hours away." Which worried me. Why wasn't Jerry answering his phone? Had he found Mel? What were they doing? Or worse, what was she doing to him?

"I know I'm freaking out, but I can't seem to relax." She glanced out the plate glass window. "And check it, paparazzi. Those people who were here earlier must have taken a picture and posted it online. That's all it takes to get those creeps to crawl out from under their rocks."

"We'll go out the back. The door into the apartments is just a few steps from there." Rafe grabbed Sienna's bag and hustled us toward the storeroom. "Hurry and we can beat them there."

"Maybe I should face them, say something." Sienna held on to the counter, halting our progress.

"Like what, Sienna?" I again had that feeling, my instincts warning me that she was up to something I wouldn't like.

"Give them a scoop. Tell them Ray isn't what he seems, the bastard. That would teach him to suck a woman's blood when she's basically unconscious." Her eyes flashed and her fangs were down.

I darted glances everywhere. No customers inside but I saw flashes that meant the photographers outside were trying to get a picture through the window. Luckily my new Halloween displays, spiderwebs and all, and the lighting would keep them from getting a clear shot.

"Stop it! Are you crazy?" I dragged her into the back room, Rafe helping. "You will not start rumors that could out all of us. We fly under the radar and it's going to stay that way."

"Why? I think it's cool that we're superstrong and run and jump better than Olympic athletes. And that shape-shifting thing? Totally awesome." She jerked her arm out of my grip. "We could rule the world, Glo. Staying hidden in the shadows is nuts. Think of the lost opportunities. Why I'd have millions more fans who'd come hear me sing just on the off chance that I'd show fang or jump off the stage and bite one of them." She laughed. Laughed!

"Shut the hell up. You have no idea what you're saying. I've been on the sharp end of a stake, stalked by a vampire hunter. Trust me, there's no way we're going public." When she started to argue, there was no help for it. I grabbed her chin and looked into her eyes. In a moment she was mesmerized and staring into space.

"She's going to be trouble." Rafe picked her up and heaved her over his shoulder. He bumped into a chair which fell over with a crash.

"No kidding." I flinched when Megan stepped into the storeroom to see what the commotion was about. She stared wide-eyed and speechless at Sienna, a limp accessory that Rafe adjusted as he reached for the back doorknob. I shrugged, not ready to explain too much though I was sure she'd heard everything. Damned paranormal hearing.

"It's a shame, Megan. These rock stars. Blame Sienna's

erratic behavior on something she must have taken. I hope she hasn't fallen off the wagon again." I knew Megan could smell her, had figured out Sienna was now vampire. But this raving about letting vampires be known to the world was the worst kind of betrayal of our kind.

"Glory, are you sure? I heard her. Rule the world? That's crazy talk." Megan followed us to the door that led to the alley. "You *are* going to nip this in the bud, aren't you? Because first it's the vamps, then the shifters can't be far behind. I'll report her to the vampire council myself if I think she's a danger."

"No, no, I've got this. Sienna's staying with me. I'm mentoring her and giving her the four-one-one on the life. Trust me. She's still really new but I'll get her under control." I tried for a confident smile. "I know you'll keep her crazy outburst our secret. She had no idea what she was saying. When she understands how outnumbered we are, she'll cool it with the going public thing."

Megan held the door while Rafe checked the alley then made a beeline for the door into the apartments and hit the code to open it.

"She'd better. You've had enough trouble with the few vampire hunters who have figured out you guys exist. I remember how it was when that fellow Westwood was after you. Nightmare." Megan shivered, wrapping her arms around herself. "Thank God the cats are still a secret. But make vamps common knowledge and there'd be stake kiosks popping up in malls everywhere before you know it."

"Thanks for that image, Megan." I hurried after Rafe. "Lock this door behind us. If anyone asks, Sienna shopped and left, going out the back to avoid the paparazzi. You have no idea where she's staying."

"Got it. Just take care of this. None of us, my cat family,

the other paranormals, want to go public. We like our life in the shadows. It's the only safe place." She jumped when car lights appeared at the end of the alley. "Hurry, you may have company."

"Call if you need me." I darted inside and locked the door into the apartments behind me, arming the security system with a shaking finger. First Jerry was out of pocket and now Sienna had gone off the rails. How much more could I take? My phone rang. A number I didn't recognize. I couldn't afford to ignore any calls.

"Hello?"

"Glory, it's Cait. Bart and I are sitting outside Jeremiah's house. He's not answering his phone and the house is dark. Do you know where he is? Is he with you?"

Cait, Caitlin Campbell, Jerry's sister. I'd forgotten she and her new boyfriend, Dr. Bartholomew O'Connor, were arriving from Scotland tonight. They'd arranged to pick up a rental car at the airport and meet us at Jerry's house. But with everything going on . . .

"No. I'm sorry. Of course you're supposed to stay with Jerry. He keeps a key in the birdhouse, behind the garage."

"I see it. You've got to be kidding me. I have to shift or climb that pole?" Cait said a few choice words in one of the many foreign languages she knew.

"It seemed like a good idea at the time." I laughed at the idea of Cait shimmying up the pole. "Do the bird thing then push it out to Bart on the ground with your beak."

"Oh, thanks. Like I couldn't figure that out. Stay on the line. I'm making Bart shift because he just laughed at me."

"I'm sorry, Cait. Let yourself in the back door. I'm sure Jerry'll be sorry he missed you, but make yourself at home. Hopefully he'll be there soon." I trudged up the stairs and saw my apartment door standing open. Guess Rafe still had one of my keys and had let himself in. He'd dumped Sienna on the couch, where she stared vacant-eyed at the ceiling.

"Cait?"

"I've got it. Bart pushed it out but it's got bird poop on it. Oh, but my brother's never going to hear the end of this. Where did you say he went?"

"I didn't. He took off, said he had an errand, and that's the last I heard from him. I'd say come over here but I have a full house at the moment." I tried not to groan at the thought of cramming two more into my tiny apartment. Vamps don't like to use hotels, problems with housekeeping during the daily death sleep.

"Is something wrong, Glory? You don't sound right. You did say Jerry got his memory back, didn't you?" Cait sounded distracted and I heard water running. Washing bird poop off that key I guess.

"Oh, his memory's fine and he was looking forward to your visit." I gestured when Rafe glanced at me with a question in his eyes. He finally just sat in a chair and waited for me to get off the phone. "There *are* some things going on though, Cait. I'll explain tomorrow night. I imagine you and Bart would like to get settled. Rest up after your flight. I heard Bart flew you here in his own plane."

"Yes, that's right. We had a layover in Miami, did a bit of sightseeing, then came on here. He's an excellent pilot. Okay, we're going in."

"Great. Explore Jer's house. He has a couple of guest rooms. Pick out one or two, however many you need, and unpack. Hopefully he'll get there before dawn." I sighed. "If I hear from him, I'll have him call you. Okay?"

"Wait a minute. You said there are things going on. Glory,

I don't like the sound of that." Cait murmured something to Bart. "Is Jeremiah in danger, Glory?"

"He may be. Look, it's a woman who wants him for herself. She's being a pain but I doubt she'd hurt him. It's me she's after." I realized Rafe had moved closer and laid his hand on my back, comforting me. "But I *am* worried about him. He took off earlier, looking for her. To tell her to quit hassling me. I expected to hear from him before now, to tell me how she took that ultimatum. Not well, I'm sure. She's extremely jealous but, like I said, I can't believe she'd hurt him."

"Well, she should be jealous. Of course Jeremiah is in love with you. I can't imagine him with another woman." Cait said something to Bart. "What do you need? We want to help. We can search, stay here and call if he shows up, whatever you think best. Just tell us what to do."

"Thanks, Caitie." Tears filled my eyes. I did count her as a good friend. "Thank Bart too. Just stay there and make Jerry call me when he shows up. I'm worried sick. This woman is into voodoo. I have no idea what she might be doing to him when she hears what he has to say. He was determined to break it off with her."

"Glory, it's Bart. Voodoo? I know something about that. I studied in the Caribbean for a while. It's an interesting practice but can be dangerous in the wrong hands." Bart had taken Cait's phone. Vamp hearing. Of course he'd been listening to our conversation. "Do you have any idea if she's used any spells on Jerry?"

"He doesn't think so, but then he seems almost addicted to her blood. He doesn't have a problem when he's not around her, but when he's near . . . I don't know. She's done some things to his hotel in Miami, caused problems, accidents. To get him to go there. That's her base of operations. He won't tell me details but he can't seem to stay away from her when he gets close enough to smell her blood." I gripped the phone hard, my hand hurting from the crystal case that bit into my palm. I kept seeing Jerry at Mel's vein. Such an intimate act. Sexual with the right person.

"Glory, you still there?"

"Barely. Does that sound like a spell to you, Bart?"

"Certainly could be. Have you met her? What can you tell me about her?"

I told him all I knew, even about the recent break-in during the day. He was as horrified as I'd been.

"This woman sounds very proficient in the arts. You're right to take her threats seriously. It's possible Jerry *is* under a spell of some kind. Let me do some research. What's her name?"

I could almost visualize Bart taking out his ever-present notebook. He was old school, preferring pen and paper to a tablet computer.

"Melisandra Du Monde." The very name made me sick and I finally sat in a chair, taking the bottle of synthetic Rafe handed me. "If she's put Jerry under some kind of spell . . . Oh, God. I don't want to think about that. Thanks, Bart. I could use some help. I'm also reaching out to a voodoo queen in New Orleans. I'm hoping she has some ideas about how to shut this woman down."

"It's worth a try, though there are different kinds of voodoo. I'll see what I can dig up on Ms. Du Monde. Maybe I can find out which practice she's likely to use. Don't give up, Glory. Cait and I are here for you. Now she wants to talk to you again."

"Glory, Bart's right. We've got your back. You need anything, call or text. Okay?"

"Thanks. Now I've got something going on here. Talk to

you tomorrow night." I ended the call and took a deep swallow of my drink.

"Blade's sister is here?" Rafe sat in the chair opposite me.

"Yes, with her boyfriend, a doctor. Smart man, and I just found out he knows about voodoo. That'll come in handy. Bart tried to help Jerry in Scotland when Jer first got amnesia."

"Good to know." Rafe glanced at Sienna. "First things first. What are we going to do about *her*?"

"I'll wake her up and then she's going to have to get a freaking clue." I leaned forward. "Damn it, Rafe. I don't need this right now. I'm worried about Jerry, about myself for that matter, and now she thinks we ought to go public? No way in hell."

"Relax, Glory. You can handle her. Wake her up." Rafe took my empty bottle then sat back to watch.

"Glad one of us is confident." I snapped my fingers in front of Sienna's eyes. "Wake up, Sienna. We need to talk."

She sat up, her eyes wild. "What the hell did you do to me?"

"Mesmerized you. It's a handy skill, the same one Ray used when he drank your blood. But it's one I won't be teaching you just yet. You have to earn the privilege." I sat in my chair again. "That stunt you pulled in the shop pissed me off."

"Stunt? What did I do?" She brushed back her hair with one hand and swung her legs down from the couch to sit facing me.

"You raved about making vampires public. That's never going to happen. Never. If you start that kind of talk again, I may let the vampire council have you. They'll lock you in a coffin in the council leader's basement until you come to your senses. Learn to behave like a proper vampire."

"Wait a damn minute." She jumped to her feet. "No one locks me up. No one. For one thing I'm claustrophobic. I'd go crazy. For another, I'm a public figure. Don't you think people will notice if I just disappear?"

"Rehab. Again. We can put out the story and no one will doubt it. Poor Sienna Star just can't stay off the pills, booze, whatever your drug of choice is these days. You've been hustled off to a secret location to dry out." I watched her pace the room.

"Don't you dare. I worked too damned hard for my sobriety." She pulled a coin out of her pocket. "Three hundred and sixty seven days and counting. I'll never go back."

"Good for you. But the public will believe anything we tell them." I frowned. "That's the problem. You start spouting stories about vampires being real and there'll be a panic. Sure, the movies are cool, the idea of vampires is sexy. But the reality of fanged monsters in alleys, wanting to drink mortal blood? Scary as hell. We'll become targets and innocent people will be killed."

"Innocent? Are you telling me you're innocent?" Sienna collapsed on the couch again. "Come on, in four hundred years have you always been satisfied with sipping bottled juice or taking an occasional drink from a mortal? And tell me, Glory, did you always leave that mortal able to walk away in good shape after you quenched your thirst? Look at what Ray did to me. I almost died. Are you telling me you never had one of those little accidents back in the day?" She stared at me, probing my mind. Fast learner.

"I'm not telling you anything. My past is my business. What I am making clear is that *you* will never kill anyone. You'll drink synthetic or find a mortal now and then who'll give you blood willingly. Cautiously, not with a shout-out to the tabloids. Maybe this mortal'll do it out of love or for money."

"Hey, I heard that." Aggie stood in the doorway. Her nightgown was right out of my shop, a vintage piece that, if I'd known she'd taken it, I would have ripped right out of her greedy hands. It was damned expensive and way too revealing to wear in front of Rafe. He was noticing of course, one eyebrow raised.

"Aggie, go back to bed or put on more clothes." I didn't need this right now.

"No, I heard what you said. Sienna can pay a mortal for her blood?" Aggie trailed a finger along her jugular. "Ian always told me I had delicious blood. I'll be happy to donate. For a price."

I jumped up and got a robe from my bedroom. "Put this on." I wasn't going to stop the negotiations. If this helped Aggie pay off her debts so she could get out of my apartment sooner, she could sell her entire body to Sienna if she wanted to. Consenting adults. I could care less.

"Seriously? You'd let me bite you? For money?" Sienna got up and strolled over to sniff Aggie. She leaned in, putting her nose close to Aggie's neck. "It does smell really good. And you're clean, though I could do without that perfume. Lose it if you become my donor." She sneezed then glanced at me. "You seem to be calling the shots here, Glory. Am I allowed to pay this woman for her blood?"

"Why not? I'll have to teach you how to count, so you won't take too much blood at a time. We're not taking a chance on another incident like Ray's."

"No, I don't want to be responsible . . ." Sienna kept eying Aggie. "I'd probably prefer a hot guy but I guess if we do it at the wrist . . . Really? Can I do this?"

"I guess so. Aggie needs the money and you can do it here, in the apartment. At least until I think it's okay for you to be on your own. It's a pretty safe arrangement." I glanced at Aggie. Of course she hadn't closed that robe, still flashing Rafe. Aggie was always about impressing men and hadn't given up the idea of finding a rich man to support her. Rafe was doing well, but wasn't nearly rich enough to afford the former Siren.

"I'm game." Aggie plopped down on the couch. "Glory's right. I need the cash."

"Name your terms, Aggie." I wondered how much she'd ask for.

"Five hundred bucks a pop." Aggie leaned back and crossed her legs. "Seems reasonable to me. I'm like takeout. Right here, curb service, so to speak. Feel free to leave a tip."

Sienna narrowed her gaze. "Three. I think you're trying to rip me off."

Of course Aggie was, but it surprised me that Sienna was into negotiating. By the time they were done, Aggie was getting four hundred and some perks to be named later. I had a feeling Sienna would regret that last part. But at least we weren't still arguing about the vampire publicity issue.

Rafe had been prowling around the apartment, checking windows, the door, all the locks. Now he pulled me into the kitchen while Sienna took her first drink from Aggie's wrist. I had told her how to count but wanted to watch the time myself and to keep an eye on them.

"You have a pretty tight situation here. I'm not sure how this woman got in. She must've used her powers." He was serious.

"I hate to hear that. How do we fight it?" I was counting in my head, ready to stop Sienna if she drank too long.

"I want to use the element of surprise. Much as I hate to do it, we'll lure her in. Make her think you're unprotected during the day."

"Sienna, that's enough. Pull out." I was relieved when she actually did, using a paper towel I'd left on the coffee table to wipe her mouth. "Lick the puncture wounds closed. It makes them disappear."

"Do I have to? That seems, um, icky." Sienna jumped up from the couch where Aggie lay, moaning, like she'd suffered great pain.

"Really? You want to leave me scarred too? I think a rabid dog would bite with more finesse than you just did." Aggie waved her arm in the air. "Check it out, Glory. This newbie gnawed me like an old bone. I'm mangled. Don't you think she should kick in a bonus for pain and suffering?"

"Give it up, Aggie. You knew donating wasn't going to be a joyride. You're already charging plenty for this. Go ahead, Sienna. We never leave evidence of a feeding on a mortal." I crossed my arms, giving the rocker a stern look.

"Fine, whatever, but no bonus." Sienna licked her finger and swiped it across the puncture marks on Aggie's wrist.

"I hope you get better at the biting. Glory, give her some lessons. Make her bite her own wrist till she gets it right." Aggie yawned and stretched, showing us all that the robe had slipped off and her gown was sheer.

"No pain, no gain. Deal with it." Sienna pulled her checkbook out of her purse, her cheeks flushed from feeding. I moved aside when Aggie got up and headed for the fridge. She picked out a pineapple yogurt and grabbed a spoon.

"You don't have to be a bitch about it. Now I'm hungry." Aggie swallowed a spoonful then suddenly grinned. "Hey, this blood donor thing might help with my diet. You vampires don't know how lucky you are, stuck in your bodies. Oh, except for Glory, of course. Glo, you should sue Jerry for turning you on one of your fat days." She tossed the lid in the trash. "I'm going back to bed. I'll take a check or cash, Sin. No credit cards. You can leave it on the kitchen table. I have to get up early tomorrow. Did Glory tell you? I have to clean my former lover's house. Bastard. I'm getting my own little revenge, though. Washed his sheets in a detergent that's sure to make him itch. Underwear and socks too." She cackled, stopping in the door to the hall to take another bite of yogurt. "And the glasses he uses to drink his synthetic blood from? Washed them in the toilet. Hah!" She strutted down the hall with a wave of her spoon. "Night all."

"Bitch." Sienna and I said it together, then exchanged looks.

"Yes, she is. Long story to explain why I'm stuck with her here. I'm seriously wondering if I've lost my mind. She's one more cutting remark away from being tossed out on her butt."

"Who would blame you? I sure wouldn't want to be on her bad side though." Sienna grabbed her tote. "I'm going to shower. Okay?"

"Sure. And you're right. I've been there. On Aggie's bad side. Of course that was before she was mortal. She goes too far around me now and I can definitely make her regret it." Rafe and I slapped palms. "How was the blood, Sienna? Worth it?"

"Totally. So much better than synthetic." Sienna dropped a check on the kitchen table then started toward the bathroom. She stopped in the doorway. "How often should I feed from her? This could get expensive."

"You can supplement with synthetic. Try once a week, twice if you just can't stand the synthetic after the real deal. The bloodlust hits new vamps pretty hard. Luckily, the older you get, the less often you have to feed. The main thing is to not let yourself get too thirsty. It can make you lose control and do something you might regret." I had to admit I envied her the funds that allowed her to have a mortal donor like that. The real thing *was* better, but I wasn't about to stalk hapless victims like a lot of vamps did, including Jerry. It was a subject he and I didn't discuss since he knew I disapproved of his drinking habit.

"You mean like attack an innocent bystander. Taking down one of those assholes with a camera wouldn't be a bad idea." Sienna laughed when I started to squawk. "Kidding. I *have* been listening to you, Glory. And the last person I'd drink from would be a member of the paparazzi. Bunch of user losers." Sienna scowled and disappeared into the bathroom.

"Finally, a few minutes of alone time. Tell me quick, Rafe, about this plan of yours. How are you going to give the illusion that we are unprotected?" I settled onto the couch.

"Do the dog thing again. Valdez back in action." He grinned and shifted. Now he was a black Labradoodle, cute with curly fur and dark eyes that were the same as they'd been for five years while he'd guarded me, employed by Jerry.

"Oh, no, you can't do that to yourself. You hated it." I shook my head as he jumped on the couch. "Seriously?"

Back then he'd communicated in my mind, especially when we were in public. This time he just spoke using his mouth, which looked freaky in a dog but was something I could handle. "I figure that if she tries to come after you and sees you asleep in your bed with only a dog to protect you, she'll try something, figure she can stake you. I can take her, I know it."

"Yes, you could if she were a mere mortal. But, Rafe, if she's using voodoo spells . . . ?" I ran my hand over his head and tugged one ear. So soft. "This is dangerous. We need to find out more about her powers. Have some magical weapons of our own. Flo is getting me the phone number of a voodoo priestess down in New Orleans. Even if it's a different kind of voodoo, maybe we can get some spells of our own to throw at Mel."

"I heard you tell Bart that. That's good. But in the meantime, I'll be here during the day today. And Blade certainly can't object if I'm in my dog persona. You know how he can be." He lay down, his head in my lap. Trust Rafe to get close while he had the chance. I couldn't push him away.

"Is that why you're doing it, the dog thing? To keep things cool between Jerry and me?" I rubbed his ears. "I know he's been jealous in the past, but I think we've worked through that."

"Good. But staying in dog form can't hurt. I'm mainly doing it to trick the bitch who came after you. She invaded your space when you would've been defenseless. I'm scared for you." He raised his head and bumped my chin.

"Thanks, Rafe."

"What's this? Where'd the dog come from?" Sienna emerged from the bathroom in a tank and boxers. Obviously she was ready for bed. She was going to have to sleep on the couch and we were sitting on it. Which was a problem. If Mel came into the apartment, the first vampire she'd encounter would be Sienna. Would she attack her? Just because she hated vampires who weren't Jerry? I couldn't run that risk.

"Take my bed for today, Sienna. I'll sleep out here. We're dead during the day so it really doesn't matter where we land and Rafe wants to be close to the door."

"But where is he? And what about the dog? Where'd he come from? I thought Rafe was supposed to be protecting us." She had scrubbed off her makeup and I was glad to see that her recent feeding had done some good, fading those blue spots on her face and arms.

"Rafe's here." I patted his back. "This is how he protected me when he was my bodyguard. Cute, isn't he?"

"You are shittin' me." Sienna moved closer. "Yes, he's a cute dog, but I can't believe . . . Say something, Rafe. So I know it's true."

"It's true. And Glory's right. We'll sleep out here. Close to the door in case anyone tries to bother you guys during the day. If they do, I can be in human form in a heartbeat and take them down." Rafe woofed for good measure when Sienna squealed.

"That is so freaking amazing. Shape-shifter. Holy crap. I remember you now, the cute Labradoodle hanging around Glory when I first met her. I had no idea . . . I wouldn't have believed this if I hadn't seen it with my own eyes." She yawned. "Must be close to dawn. I can hardly keep my eyes open. Thanks for the bed, Glory. Night." She smiled before she headed into the bedroom. "And thanks for guarding us, Rafe. Appreciate it."

I pushed Rafe off my lap and got up to get bedding out of the linen closet. It was no problem to make up the bed. I could feel the dawn too but worry about Jerry made me resist the pull. I tried his cell one more time. No answer. Where could he be? Had Mel done something to him? I headed into the bathroom to wash and change into a sexless sleep shirt, my Snoopy one, to razz Rafe.

Just before I passed out, I tried Jerry once more. Voice mail. I didn't bother leaving a fourth message. If he had his phone, he knew I was worried and looking for him. Obviously he couldn't call me or he would have. Dawn edged even closer and I prayed he was where daylight couldn't touch him. Surely Mel wouldn't hurt him. Unless she finally got the message that he didn't want her. I needed to check out her Web site, but dawn hit before I could reach for my laptop.

Six

I woke up with a start at sunset. The worry I'd gone to bed with was still there. I smelled coffee and knew that Rafe must have morphed back into his human form and was fixing breakfast for himself. In the bad old days, when he'd been forced to stay in dog form twenty-four/seven, he'd subsisted on Twinkies, his favorite snack, and rare steaks when I'd cook for him.

I tried Jerry's cell again. No answer. So I got dressed and took my laptop into the living room before I found Mel's Web site. She had quite a professional setup. And there was a place to contact her. I composed a message. But when I found myself begging her to let Jerry go, I deleted it. I had no way of knowing if Jerry was even with her. Maybe he'd lost his phone and had arrived home just before dawn. I ran through various scenarios in my mind but kept coming up with no real excuse for him not to call me back unless he was hurt . . . No, impossible. Mel claimed to love him. She would never hurt him.

So I scrolled through the woman's Web site. No wonder she was so successful. Even I got sucked in by her inspiring message.

"Be the master of your own fate. Take control of your life. You can own the world. The only thing limiting your reach is your own fear." Her words resonated and if I hadn't met the bitch I'd be tempted to sign up for one of her seminars. In fact, she was holding one here in Austin this weekend, at a hotel downtown. I gasped when I saw the price she was charging. Yeah, I bet she owned *her* world. Unbelievable. The large ballroom was almost sold out.

"What's doing?" Rafe stood behind me, reading over my shoulder. "She actually gets that price?"

"Apparently. Look, only three spots left."

"We should go. It'll be nice to get our minds off the vampire drama." Sienna had joined Rafe and read the description too. "I'll buy the tickets. The woman sounds fabulous. Look, Glory, you could take your shop to a whole new level. End up with a string of Vintage Vamp's Emporiums all over the world." She patted me on the shoulder. "I want to thank you for mentoring me. Let's go to this. It sounds good." She bumped against Rafe's shoulder. "And the bodyguard can come. In human form. I doubt they'd let the dog in. Even though your Labradoodle thing is cute."

"I'd do it again if that's what she needed to stay safe." Rafe wasn't taking Sienna up on the flirting. Guess he was serious about Lacy.

"You have no idea why I'm looking at this Web site, Sienna. And take you to a ballroom full of mortals? Not a good idea." We'd never mentioned Jerry's stalker chick by name other than Mel. Her picture here showed a professional woman who looked nothing like a voodoo priestess.

"So I'll fill up before I go. Come on, Glory. You hit this site for a reason. You going to deny she's got something you want?" Sienna flashed me a smile.

The bitch's head on a plate. But I didn't say that. Instead, I took a breath. Did I want to hear Mel speak? Definitely. Even if it was only to get a better idea of the enemy I faced. What would she do if I walked into one of her seminars? Probably smile smugly and go right on with her spiel.

"I'm guessing you want more out of life than a small boutique. Not that it isn't great. I love your little shop. It's cool and you have great taste. But it could use more marketing. Expansion." She glanced around my tiny apartment with its used furniture. The only new piece was the massive coffee table Jerry and Rafe had bought after they'd destroyed my old one during a fight. "Seems like you need to increase your income. This seminar could be a good thing for you."

I exchanged glances with Rafe, who'd moved around the couch to settle into the chair across from me. He'd made himself an egg sandwich. Now he took a bite and raised an eyebrow. Okay, he was thinking this might not be a bad move. I decided then and there that Sienna didn't need to know the truth about this woman's identity.

"You're right. I've got a small life, that's what this woman calls it, and I've been satisfied with it. But maybe it's time to think bigger. Going to this seminar might give me some ideas. Thanks, Sienna, I'll take you up on the offer. You handle the tickets. Do you have a name you use when you don't want to be recognized?"

"Yeah, sure. And a special credit card for just that purpose. I'll put the tickets on that one." She snatched her purse off the kitchen table. "I'd better hurry before they're sold out."

"Good." I patted the seat next to me then handed her the laptop.

"If it wasn't at night, we wouldn't be able to do this. I still can't wrap my head around all the limitations . . . Well, you don't want to get me started on that." She pulled her credit card out of her wallet and began typing. "I need this distraction so I won't go over to Ray's and try to kill him again. This night out will be nice. The three of us going somewhere together. I'll be in disguise of course. I have a long black wig and sunglasses that I wear when I'm hiding from the paparazzi. You'll see. No one will have a clue I'm there."

"Maybe I'll wear a disguise too. Just for fun." I winked at Rafe. "Why not go? It couldn't hurt to hear some new ideas. I would definitely like to increase my cash flow." I glanced around my apartment too. Why *had* I been satisfied with such a subpar lifestyle? I hated to admit that Mel's words were getting to me. *Live large. Go for it. Don't be satisfied with less than the best.*

Since I'd refused to let the men in my life help me and I lacked a formal education, my life had always been a struggle. Well, I was tired of living hand to mouth, never knowing if I'd have enough money to pay my bills at the end of the month. Mel hated me but I wasn't above using her. If I could just hear from Jerry, be assured he was safe, I could almost get excited about this seminar on Saturday night. Almost.

My phone rang just as Sienna shouted, "Score!" and got a confirmation number for our tickets.

"Jerry, where the hell have you been?" I know, not the most loving greeting, but he'd left me worrying and waiting for hours.

"I don't know, Gloriana. I had a, um, blackout." He sounded tentative. Not like the Jerry I knew at all. "I'm afraid it might be a residual effect from my amnesia."

"Oh, God, no!" Then I thought about it. "Wait. How can that be, Jerry? You were cured. It was a sorcerer's spell that took your memory and you got it all back thanks to another sorcerer. Were you with Mel when your blackout started?"

"I think so. When I finally got her on the phone last night, she insisted on a face-to-face. In her room at her hotel."

"Of course. Then I bet she put the moves on you. Do you remember that?" I'd lost all sympathy for him. Going to her hotel room when she snapped her fingers. Surely he could have figured out a better meeting place.

"I remember her opening the door. After that . . . nothing."

"What was she wearing when she opened the door?" Hell, did I have to drag every last detail out of him? Apparently.

"Gloriana, is that relevant? I'm telling you I'm losing my mind. If my amnesia is coming back again, I don't know what I'll do. The last thing I recall is seeing her in her hotel room. Then I woke up in my car in the garage this evening right after sunset."

"Oh, God, Jerry." I could hear how upset he was so I didn't press him. But since he wasn't sharing, I just bet Mel had greeted him wearing the skimpiest thing Victoria's Secret carried in an extra large. "Didn't Bart or Cait hear you come in last night?"

"Apparently not. Look. I'm weak and have to feed. I got your messages, knew you were worried so I called first thing. Now I've got to go. I'll talk to you later." He ended the call abruptly.

I stared at the phone in my hand. Excuse me? He'd sounded almost angry at the end of that call. What had I done? Amnesia? He wasn't angry at me, of course. Just scared. I didn't blame him. I looked up, hoping my mother would pop in for a visit. She'd caused the last memory loss. I needed to know if she'd had any part in this one. No answer. Of course not. She only came on her own schedule.

I found Cait's number. She answered on the first ring.

"I thought I'd be hearing from you, Glory. I don't know what's going on with Jerry." She sighed.

"Does Bart think he could be having some kind of flashback? Going through the amnesia thing again?"

"Let me put him on. Jerry's gone out. You know my brother. He wants to find a mortal to feed from. Jerk. We can talk freely."

"Glory, it's Bart. My first thought was that Jerry had been drugged. He's the one who assumes his amnesia was coming back. I explained about flashbacks. That it was possible he could have some brief episodes . . . That was all it took. Now he's convinced this is the start of something bad even though he's just missing a few hours." Bart swore. "You know how the amnesia made him feel. I couldn't reason with him. If he thinks he's losing his mind again, I don't know what he'll do."

"Oh, God." I closed my eyes. Mel must have done something to erase his memory of their time together. Did she have any idea how horrific that would be for him? It was like tapping into his worst fear. Maybe she did know and this was his punishment for trying to dump her.

"I got him to give me a blood sample. I called Ian MacDonald and I'm headed over to his place to use his lab and run a test. I'm going to find out if Jerry *was* drugged. I'm pretty sure that's what it must have been. There are several common substances that can erase a few hours. The date rape drug for one, though I'd be surprised if it worked on a vampire. The woman probably drove him home herself then did her vanishing act. You did say she could do that, didn't you?"

"I thought so, but now I'm wondering if it wasn't more of a magic trick. She *is* mortal, you know. I'll just bet it was all smoke and mirrors. But then again I don't know a damned thing about voodoo." Date rape drug? I barely held on to my temper. If I showed up at Ms. Own-the-World's room, would she manage to dose me too? I was on my feet, pacing. I really needed to know more. Fury rode me hard and I had to stuff it back down and try to think things through, rationally. "She could have help, Bart. Backup to drive her away after she left him there."

"Of course. You're right. I looked at her Web site. She's bound to travel with a few flunkies, people to help her set up for her seminars and so on. Apparently she's quite charismatic. They'd do whatever she told them. Even help her move an unconscious man." Bart was a scientist and always the voice of reason.

"What gets me is that the bitch claims to love Jerry. If she drugged him and then . . ." I had to stop and clear my throat. "Thanks, Bart. If you can prove she did such a horrible thing, then that should convince Jerry to stay away from her. Or to take some reinforcements the next time he sees her."

"She's definitely an evil woman. I sure wouldn't want to be on her to-do list. Cait asks if you're coming over. She'd like to see you, but doesn't want to leave until Jerry comes back."

"I'd like to see her too. And to check on Jerry of course." I glanced at Rafe. "But I have a new vampire I'm mentoring. Let me try to make some arrangements. I'll call Cait before I come if I can swing it."

"Fine. And I'll let you know what I find out at MacDonald's lab."

"Thanks, Bart." I ended the call then met Rafe's interested gaze. "That bitch made Jerry forget half of last night. You have any idea how that made him feel?"

"Like he's losing his mind?" Rafe got serious. "That's cold."

"Are you talking about the woman who's stalking Jerry?" Sienna was interested.

"Yes." I really didn't feel like sharing with her. She was now a problem I had to handle. "You wanted to do some more shopping tonight? Rafe, can you stay with her down there in the store while I go visit with Cait and check on Jerry?"

"I'm supposed to be protecting *you*." He wasn't happy with the assignment.

"Please do this. It will really help me out. I promise I'll shift and jet straight over there. Once I'm in Jerry's house, I'm sure I'll be okay. What mortal would take on a vampire when she's awake and alert?"

"Seems like that mortal handled Blade last night." Rafe followed me when I got up and headed into my bedroom. Wardrobe. I wanted to look tough because it helped me feel that way. I pulled out black leather pants and a black satin blouse. My leather jacket was vintage and would help me blend into the night. Perfect.

"Glory, the woman probably drugged Blade and he was at her mercy for hours he can't remember. You know I could hear your phone conversation, right?" Rafe had Sienna on his heels.

"I don't need a babysitter. If you want Rafe to be with you, take him." She pouted, then got distracted. "Cool jacket. I love the look. Got anything like that downstairs?"

"Yes, I do. Ask Megan to show you. There's one in the back room I haven't priced yet. If you like it, tell her to call me for a price check." I pulled open a drawer and collected clean underwear. Rafe raised an eyebrow at the sight of a black thong and pushup bra. So what? He'd seen me in less. I headed for the bathroom but stopped to pin both of them with a stern look.

"Don't give me a hard time about this. Sienna, you're too new to be left alone. Rafe, I need this favor. I can't have my new vamp around mortals unsupervised. I'll be fine. I hope I do run into Mel. I'll rip her throat out and we'll be done." I smiled, full fang, ignoring the fact that I hadn't been able to get near her the last time we'd met. "Jerry's mistake is that he tried to reason with her. I won't bother."

"Gee, Glory. I've never see you like this." Sienna shivered. "You'd really *kill* her?"

"No, she probably wouldn't. For all her tough talk, Glory's not like that. Which is what worries me. Let me call someone else to stick with Sienna so I can go with you, Blondie."

"No, I don't have time for that. And I can kill if I have to. Quit underestimating me, Rafe. I'm into my powers now and I'm not letting this woman get the best of me." I tempered my message with a smile. "I know where you're coming from."

"Yeah, years of watching over you." He shook his head. "You've changed. That's good. But don't get cocky. This voodoo thing is a new threat. You don't know what you're up against."

"You're right." I touched his cheek. So dear. How did I get so lucky? To have this strong man care . . . "I'm on it. Flo's connecting me with a voodoo expert. I'm going to find out what I need to know so I'll have even more weapons to work with. In the meantime . . ."

"Be careful." He pulled me close. "I mean it. Watch your back since I won't be there to do it."

"Thanks, Rafe. I will." I gave him a brief hug then pushed him away gently. "Now run along. Get shopping." I headed into the bathroom, refusing to listen to Sienna's questions or Rafe's answers about our relationship. I tried to tune into Mel's message. Yeah, I wanted to own the world and I was starting tonight. Taking charge of my universe and the people who were important to me. Too bad for Mel if she got in my way.

My phone rang as I was about to leave the blessedly empty apartment. Flo, coming through for me.

"*Amica*, I'm worried. Are you sure you want to deal with a

sacerdotessa vudù?" Flo always lapsed into Italian when she was nervous. "Those people scare me."

"Relax, Flo. The last time we used your contact's help, it worked. Remember when we got that demon out of me? We used love. It was great. Not scary at all." I smiled at the memory. "Or at least not as scary as that demon was."

"You're right about that. Okay, I give. But be careful, my friend. This stuff is nothing to play with."

"I know. Mel means business. You won't believe what she did to Jerry just last night." I told her, sinking down on the couch as I did. I hoped he was there when I got to his place. I wanted to hold him, comfort him. If Bart found a drug in his blood, surely that would make Jerry feel better about his memory loss. At least convince him that his amnesia wasn't returning.

"This is *terribile*! That *strega cattiva*! Call the woman in New Orleans. I hope she can help you get rid of this creature permanently."

"Thanks, pal." I glanced down at the paper where I'd written the number. "I'll let you know what happens." I hung up then dialed. The woman who answered the phone had a soft Creole accent that convinced me I had the right number.

"Is this Madame—"

"Do not say my name. Who told you to call me, *chère*?"

Hmm. Paranoid much? "Florence da Vinci. She used you a few months ago. For a sensitive problem with one of her friends. I'm that friend."

"Yes, I remember. I assume you have another problem, *chère*. Tell me."

"Well, um, there's a woman, a practitioner of voodoo, who is determined to trap a man and keep him. He's told her he wants to be with another woman, but she won't let him go. Now she's doing all kinds of things, including drugging him, I think, to make him stay with her. I'm his girlfriend and she's threatened me. Wants me to give him up. What—"

"Where is this woman from?"

"Miami."

"Her name?"

Uh-oh. That question made me think there might be a history here. "Melisandra Du Monde. Have you heard of her? Can you help me?"

"Child, you are in trouble. Yes, you are. This is one powerful *sorcière*. She uses Haitian magic. And she's dealing with the dark arts. I work with the light. The dark can bring much bad luck to the one who deals with it. A *malheur*, curse, on one of them . . . Well, I hope that is not what you have come to me for." She muttered something, an incantation, a prayer?

"She's evil, Madame. I can smell it on her. I am way too familiar with the stench. I was possessed by a demon, have had dealings with Lucifer himself." I heard her exclaim. "But I triumphed over him. I'm a good person. I swear it. Worthy of your help. And I'll pay. I have a credit card ready right here, if you have something to offer me, something that will help break her hold on my man."

"That will be very difficult, child. She is strong. And to face a powerful *sorcière* . . . Are you sure you want to risk it? Is this man of yours really worth it?"

"Yes! He's the love of my life. You have no idea what we've been through. I have to do this. Whatever it takes."

"Then I will send you a book. It will have a recipe for a special potion. Follow it exactly with every ingredient as listed, no substitutions. It will be powerful, strong. You can use it to poison this woman's mind. It will taint her thoughts and send her screaming into the night, away from your man and your place. Does this sound like something you want?"

"Yes." It actually sounded perfect. "But I've tried to reach her, Madame. I am . . ." I hesitated. Okay, go for broke. "I'm vampire. I thought if I could just jump her, tear out her throat, I could end this. But I can't get near her. She's shielded somehow."

I heard her muttering prayers this time, a Hail Mary? Not sure. Anyway there was a long silence. Finally she came back on the line, her voice hard but determined.

"Vampire. Of course. I should have guessed. Your friend was one also. There are so many of you. I try not to think about it. You will remember that I helped you. In case I need a favor? In the future?"

"Yes, sure. But what about this potion?" I was getting desperate. If this woman didn't want to help a vampire, I was wasting my time.

"You must somehow lull her into trusting you. Better yet, get the man to do this. My potion will kill her love for him and make her go away."

"Do you throw it on her or does she have to drink it?" I had visions of Mel dissolving like the Wicked Witch in Oz, only her expensive high heels left afterward. I'd sell those in the shop of course. If I was going to own a chain of Vintage Vamp's shops someday, I couldn't miss a trick.

"Instructions are in the book. As long as I know we are committed to helping each other . . ." She paused.

"Yes, yes. I promise. A favor in the future. You have my word." Easy to promise when I doubted I'd ever cross paths with a voodoo woman from New Orleans again.

"Fine. It's a deal. I'll even give you a discount." She quoted a price that still put a good dent in my credit limit. I read her my card number and expiration date then gave her my shipping information. She promised to overnight the package.

"Let me know how this goes, *chère*. I've heard of some

of Du Monde's tricks. She gives all of us a bad name. It would not break my heart to hear that she has lost something this time."

I smiled. Good to know. "Certainly, Madame. And thank you. I'm sure you will mark the right page? This whole thing is new to me, I wouldn't want to screw it up."

"Of course. Just don't try anything else in the book. In the wrong hands some of the other potions can be dangerous."

"No worries, Madame. This is a one-shot deal. I'll be very careful. Thanks again." We ended the call.

"You're into voodoo now?" Aggie smiled at me from the doorway. I can't believe I hadn't heard her come in.

"No, not really. I'm just desperate enough to try anything. With Jerry being hassled by a voodoo priestess, I figured why not use the same weapons." I stuck my phone in my bra since I was going to shift to Jerry's.

"I get it. Good move. Where's Sienna? Surely you didn't let her go out on her own." Aggie dug into a pint of Ben & Jerry's.

"She's downstairs shopping. Rafe's keeping an eye on her. Why? It's too soon for her to drink from you again if that's what you're thinking. And what's with the ice cream? I thought you were dieting." I walked to the door.

"Flo's coming over. She's decided to be my trainer. I have been dieting but I'm not losing. That diet book I got from your shop sucks. I think it's out of date."

"Of course it is. I sell vintage books, Aggie." I was in a hurry to leave and check on Jerry. "Why is Flo helping you?"

"She feels sorry for me." Aggie looked me over. "Nice outfit. Going all black is slimming. Not that I can afford leather anything. Ian only lets me keep a few bucks a week for myself, the rest goes toward what I owe him. That pittance barely covers food and hair spray."

"Well, you could buy the store brands instead of—" I opened the door.

"Blasphemy!" Aggie waved her spoon. "*You* can't taste this, but there's no comparison. Store brands don't have half the nuts, the cherries, the everything!"

"Pah! Look at you, stuffing your face with calories." Flo practically flew into the room and snatched the carton out of Aggie's hands and dumped it into the kitchen garbage can.

"No!" Aggie actually tried to dig it out. "Damn it, who put coffee grounds in here?"

"Rafe. Flo, thanks for the phone number. Madame in New Orleans is coming through for me."

"Good, but be careful. This is creepy stuff, no?" She stalked over to where Aggie was leaning over the trash can and swatted her on the butt. "Go! Put on workout clothes. You're running tonight. I have it all planned."

"Yes, creepy." I stepped out of Aggie's way when she flung coffee grounds at both of us. Her language would do a rock star proud. No, I think even Ray might blush at one combo.

"My tennis shoes are from Goodwill. I doubt they can take much running. You know I'm not good on dry land." Aggie glared at Flo.

"You're not a Siren now. You'll run or I drag you." Flo herself looked cute in a designer jogging suit and matching Nikes that had to be fresh out of a box.

"Are you actually running too?" I smiled at the idea.

"Me? You must be kidding. No, I drive, Aggie runs alongside. I have the top down on the convertible. I'll shout words of encouragement like 'Move your lazy ass.'" Flo grinned. "You know how we hate that bitch."

I laughed and hugged Flo. "Got to go. Have fun."

"Where are you headed?" Flo got serious. "Be careful. You said that woman is after you. She hasn't given up, has she?"

"I'm shifting to Jerry's. I don't think Mel can fly. If she can, I'll take her down. Surely a vampire can take a voodoo woman in a fight."

"Wait. I want to hear about the voodoo." Aggie appeared dressed in loose gray jogging pants and a sweatshirt with the University of Texas logo on it that made her look twice as big as she really was. The shoes were neon pink and had obviously been donated because they matched nothing, certainly not the burnt orange UT logo.

"I'll tell you. After the run." Flo looked at me for permission. "Just a little?"

"Sure, why not? Ian's already getting an earful so why not Aggie too?" I shrugged. "We're using Ian's lab to see if Jerry was drugged last night. Just keep the woman's name a secret for now. Okay, Flo?"

"Got it. Come on, Aggie. Move your butt." She dragged a griping Aggie toward the door and down the stairs. Then up again. Then down. By the third time, I just laughed and headed up toward the roof, Aggie's colorful curses ringing in my ears.

Once on the flat rooftop, I gazed up at the clear night sky. The stars were beautiful and it was cold and crisp. I took a deep breath and caught a whiff of something really bad. Dead. Worse than dead, coming from the alley. I glanced down and saw two figures lurking near the Dumpster in back of the shop. I had to check it out so I shifted into bird form and landed on the light pole above them.

The smell was almost unbearably strong this close, so I quit breathing. The two were dressed in business suits. The woman had on what had once been a high-quality pants outfit in navy.

The blouse under the jacket had dirt stains. And a trip to the edge of the Dumpster showed me why. I could see her face or the ruin of it, and her matted hair. Zombie. The walking dead.

Her partner was a man, older, but dressed much as she was in what had been an expensive suit. His gray hair was cut close but grass stained. And I could see that his eyes were vacant and staring. What the hell? While I watched, Mel came out of the shadows at the end of the alley.

"You are to stay here and wait. If she comes out, take her down. Do you understand?" She stared at first the woman, then the man.

Their grunts must have satisfied her because she smiled and stalked off down the alley. I sat there, trying to decide whether to pursue her or just to fly to Jerry's. Zombies. How were they supposed to take me down? By killing me with their smell? A worker came out of the back door of Mugs and Muffins and one of the zombies moaned and started forward. The woman shrieked and dropped her garbage bag, running back inside.

Okay, this was going to be a problem and not just for me. Diana Marchand, the owner of Mugs and Muffins and a fellow vampire, peeked outside her back door and gagged.

"What the ever lovin' hell is this? I'm gonna have to do some serious mind erasin' tonight." She stared at the zombies, almost as if she was waiting for them to make a move, and one did start to shuffle forward again, raising its arms. "You'd better not come after me or my people, you creeps. I've got a blowtorch inside that will turn you into ashes before you can say, 'Hello, Lucifer.'" That stopped the man in his tracks. Diana looked around. "Glory? Are you around, hon? You in trouble with demons and such again? 'Cause you're the only one I know hereabouts who gets into these kinds of jams."

I chirped, then sent her a mental message to look up. I waved my wings then sent a second message to meet me out front. She nodded and headed back inside. It didn't take me long to fly to the end of the alley and shift then walk to the front of our shops, which are next door to each other.

"What the devil is goin' on, Glory?" Diana was waiting for me, hands on her hips. "I had to calm Louisa down then convince her she'd seen a homeless couple doin' the nasty by the Dumpster."

I gave her a quick summary of my situation. "I don't know how long they're going to be camped out there. I'm the target, but it looks like they're too far gone to recognize me versus anyone else. You have any experience with, uh"—I glanced around, there were mortals nearby on the sidewalk—"these things?"

"I hate to say it, but yes. I've seen them a time or two. That's how I knew about the blowtorch. Guess you heard my threat. Actually, it's just a little acetylene thing I use to brown meringues, but they don't know that. Those creatures can't handle fire. It's the only sure way of taking them out." Diana grabbed my arm and steered me into my shop.

"Good to know." I had visions of a zombie roast, the stench would be unbearable. I sure didn't want it behind my shop.

"You warn your people to stay out of that alley. I'm pretty sure they won't know the difference between one woman and another. Either that or you and I can go torch those suckers right now. You got a broomstick and newspaper handy?"

"Uh, not on me." I had a new admiration for this delicate southern flower. "But I'll definitely give the staff a heads-up. Thanks, Diana." I smiled. "Sorry about this. I'm working on ending the threat. Will let you know when it's safe to resume normal activities."

"Make it fast. My store produces a lot of garbage. We need

the Dumpster back there." She tapped her foot. "Though they're after you, so I guess they won't be there during the day. Fine. All garbage will go out in daylight from now on. Tell your staff the same. The Dumpster's emptied in the mornings anyway." She smiled and gave me a hug. "Good luck with this. Fight for your man. That's my motto."

We parted on those words, with me having to take a few minutes to warn Megan and my other clerk before I slipped over to the park across the street. There I was finally able to relax and shift again. I settled just feet from Jerry's walkway and changed into human form. Then I inhaled again. Was there evil on the wind? I heard footsteps and turned quickly, ready for fight or flight. What I saw didn't reassure me.

Seven

Jerry's face was grim. "What are you doing out here alone? Don't you know how dangerous Mel can be?"

"Jerry!" I ran into his arms and held on to him. "How are you feeling?"

He pushed me away. "Like shit. Come inside." He hustled me into the house then locked the door behind us. "Cait! Gloriana's here." He practically shoved me toward the kitchen. Cait sat at the bar with a glass of synthetic in front of her.

"Hi, Cait." I hurried over to give her a hug and a questioning look. "Everything okay?"

"Sure, if you can stand being around sourpuss here."

"That's enough, Caitie." Jerry stomped into the living room and collapsed onto the leather couch. "If I'm not all smiles, who can blame me? I think I'm losing my mind. Not exactly cause for celebration."

I grabbed a bottle of synthetic out of the fridge and carried it into the living room. I was boycotting the couch, visions of Jer's daughter and a couple of guys playing a scene straight out of a "Shades" novel there forever seared on my brain. So I sat in a chair across from Jerry and twisted off the cap. I took a swallow while Cait sat next to her brother and patted his knee.

"This is nothing like what happened in Scotland. You recognized Glory. You can drive a car, work the TV remote, hell, even troll the Internet looking up your symptoms. Does that sound like amnesia to you, Jeremiah?" Cait exchanged glances with me.

"Yeah. When I can't remember hours last night." He stared at me. "I know Bart is blaming a drug, but how'd Mel manage to drug me? She never offers me a synthetic. And I sure as hell wasn't going to drink her blood."

"I don't know, Jer. This voodoo thing is way over my head." I caved and skirted his coffee table to claim a spot on his lap. He looked so lost. "But maybe her drug can be passed on by touch, like the substance on that knife you were stabbed with when you got amnesia in Scotland." Boy, did I hate bringing that up. My own mother had orchestrated the fiasco. But it was a viable option and couldn't be ignored.

"You're right, Gloriana." Jerry pulled me against him. "All right then. She grabbed my hand and pulled me into her room. Maybe that's when she transferred some kind of drug to my skin."

"And you don't remember anything that happened after that?"

Jerry dropped his head to the back of the sofa and stared up at the ceiling. "Not a bloody thing." He sat up, his eyes hard. "But I know what was in my heart. I was there to tell her, Gloriana, to leave you the hell alone. That I loved you, only you. That I would never touch her again, no matter what she did. No matter what games she played." He ran his fingers through his hair. "Sometimes, when she'd cut herself, the smell of her blood . . . You know how I am about mortal blood. But I made it clear. I was done. I wasn't drinking from her again."

"I bet she didn't take that well." Cait leaned forward. "This woman used to be your mistress, Jeremiah? How in hell did you get involved with a voodoo priestess in the first place?"

"She's also a motivational speaker, Caitie. When I met her, it wasn't obvious what else she was into. By the time I realized . . ." He looked at me. "No excuses, but I think she did something. She's into spells. I had to have her blood. It became an addiction that I had to fight my way out of. It was one reason I moved to Austin. Not the main one. Gloriana drew me here of course."

"Of course." I jumped off of his lap, twisting away from his hold. I couldn't get the image out of my mind of Jerry with Mel. The intimacies they'd shared. I fell back onto the chair, a gulf between us much wider than his chrome and glass coffee table. "I wish you'd never gone near her last night."

"You see how you hurt her?" Cait slapped his thigh. "Damn it, Jeremiah. Next time send a text message to the bitch. Obviously you can't get close to that Mel woman without complications."

"You're right. And I hope to God nothing happened during those hours I've lost. But I was sure I could handle her last night, Gloriana. I certainly wasn't there to drink from her. Your blood is like home to me." Jerry's gaze burned as he stared at me, willing me to believe him. "After centuries, it is the one source that means the most to me. Yet I can be near you, Gloriana, and not feel consumed by the need to feed from you. Not like it was with Mel."

"Good to know." If I slapped him, would he shut the hell up?

"Don't be mad, Glory, I heard a sweet compliment in there.

Go on, Jeremiah." Cait rubbed his thigh where she'd hit him pretty hard.

"It *was* a compliment. I'm trying to explain how it was with Melisandra. When I was around her in Miami, my thirst was out of control. I could barely think about anything but having her blood. It had to be some kind of voodoo spell she'd worked on me. Then, when we were close . . ." He stared down at his boots. "Well, I finally refused to fuck her again. I won't call it making love. She'd always tried to turn my feeding into something sexual. Then she showed up here, wanting to start up again. I still had that unnatural thirst, but I managed to fight it. I guess her spell was wearing off."

"This isn't helping, Jerry." I dug my nails into the arms of the chair to keep from leaping across the room and wrapping my hands around his neck. Jerry was a wonderful, powerful lover. I had a picture now of his body against Mel's, his mouth on her . . . everywhere.

It was all I could do not to scream my pain, turn Jerry to stone, or toss his precious coffee table around the room until glass rained over us and the chrome was a twist of metal that I used to castrate him.

Cait obviously saw my evil smile at that idea and didn't like it. "Now, now. Let's get this straight. Miami? I gather this was when you and Glory were taking a break?" Cait was trying to soothe troubled waters. Obviously I looked pretty scary. "Come on, Glory, you know you've had other men when you two were apart. Cut him some slack."

"Oh, I have. Cut him slack and had other men." I finally threw off my jacket, leaned back and crossed my legs. I moved my arms so that the satin stretched over my breasts. Jerry took note of course. He liked me in satin. Tough shit.

"I'll tell you all about them sometime, Caitie." I showed

just the tip of my fangs and licked my lips to bug Jerry. "But we're done with our extracurricular activities now. Since this bitch has threatened me, we're supposed to be working together to get rid of her. What do you say, Jerry? Are you on board with that? Or has she got you under her spell again?" The devil made me do it? Lame but possible.

Jerry jumped up. "God damn it. I want her gone for good. That's the only reason I confronted her last night. I had my knives ready, fully prepared to kill her if I had to. You know that, Gloriana. How the hell things went so wrong . . ." He ran his hands through his hair. "This memory thing is driving me mad."

"She drugged you." Bart stood in the door from the kitchen. "I hope you don't mind, but I kept that extra key and let myself in the back door."

"Doctor." Jerry turned, clearly jumpy. "Seriously? It was a drug. Not—"

"Not amnesia. Or at least not a recurrence of your old problem." Bart came into the room and kissed Cait on the cheek. "Gloriana, you look, um, dangerous tonight."

I nodded. "Thanks, Bart. That's exactly the look I was going for."

"A drug, you say. Any idea what kind?" Jerry sat again, clearly relieved.

"You don't want to discuss this now." Bart glanced at me.

"Oh, yes, he does." I leaned forward. "Was it the date rape drug? Did that voodoo vixen make Jerry have sex with her under the influence?"

"What the hell?" Jerry shot to his feet again, one of his knives in his hand. "No one can force me to do that."

"Want to bet?" Bart faced him. "Sorry, Jerry, but this drug makes you lose track of time, forget what happened, and does a number on your libido. While you were under its influence you *had* to have sex, were wild for it. It scrambles your brain, makes you lose touch with reality and of course wipes out your memory. While you were drugged you might have even imagined you were with another lover. Gloriana for example." Bart glanced at me. "If you said her name during the act, I'm sure that would make the woman who drugged you hate Glory even more."

"God, I need a shower." Jerry looked sick and staggered away, holding on to the banister when he headed up the stairs.

"Bart! Surely there's been a mistake." I felt like crying, my urge to talk tough vanishing. "You really think Jerry might have had sex with Mel and not realized who or what he was doing?"

"Exactly." Bart sat in Jerry's spot and pulled Cait against him. "It's a hell of a drug. The bitch was clever. Ian and I are still trying to figure out how she got it into Jerry." He spouted some scientific jargon that went right over my head.

"He didn't want to drink from her. He wanted to kill her." I looked toward the stairs. I wanted to go to Jerry, console him somehow. But the idea that he'd been intimate with that woman . . . My stomach churned.

"Ian is all over it. He's fascinated by the voodoo connection. We're wondering if she mesmerized Jerry somehow, then made him drink a tainted blood. I don't know." Bart kissed the top of Cait's hair. "I can't imagine how you feel, Glory. Knowing how she used Jerry."

"How *do* you feel, Glory?" Cait's eyes filled with tears. "Are you furious, hurt, ready to give up on my brother?"

"Mad at Mel of course. But I can't abandon Jerry now. You heard him. He loves me. He was trying to protect *me*." I stood.

"Don't blame yourself, for God's sake." Bart was on his

feet. "But I'm sure he could use your support right now. She made a fool of him. He's a proud Scot. We can't stand to be exploited."

"No, it's the worst kind of humiliation. If I abandon Jerry now, she's won, hasn't she? No way in hell I'm giving her my man." I stalked to the stairs and ran up them. When I got to Jerry's bedroom door I heard the shower running. Steam filled the bathroom but I could see Jerry through the glass shower doors. He was leaning against the tile, the hot water hitting his back, his head bowed, the picture of despair. I couldn't stand it. I stripped off my clothes, piling them on a chair in the bedroom before I slid the glass shower door open.

"Gloriana. How can you want to be with me now?" He didn't reach for me. His eyes were bleak when he looked over his shoulder. "I don't think I'll ever feel clean again."

"Then let me help you." I grabbed the bar of soap and a washcloth. "And of course I want to be with you. You're my lover, my best friend, Jerry." I smiled, kissed the spot under his right shoulder blade where he had an old scar, then ran the cloth over his broad back. "Relax and let me take care of you. This is just another battle wound. It will heal."

"I don't deserve you." He turned to me, letting me soap his chest and his earth brown nipples as the water hit us both.

"Quit talking, Jerry." I shook my head. "I can't believe I just said that. How many times have I begged you to communicate, to share your feelings? But this moment is too important. I know you don't want to hear it, but you were Mel's victim."

"By God!" Jerry's fists clenched.

"That's right, you should be livid, not up here feeling sorry for yourself. You're a virile, dynamic man who always makes my knees weak when you look at me, touch me." I gave his body a good checking out, my heart pounding as I saw how aroused he was. I ran that soapy washcloth down to scrub away any hint of voodoo priestess from his cock. I couldn't bear the thought that she'd taken him inside her.

"If that woman were here now, I'd break her neck with my bare hands." He pressed his fist against the tile wall and I could see his muscles jump. "Gloriana, you are the only woman I want. I hope you believe that." Jerry pulled me against him, our bodies slick and warm, easily finding our fit from years, no, centuries of practice.

"Prove it." I wrapped one leg around his, his hard cock nudging my inner thigh. "You're mine, Jeremiah. Take me with your eyes wide open. Know you're with me every minute. I don't need to cast some lame-ass spell to have you, do I?"

He lifted me, wrapping both my legs around his waist as he pushed into me. He pressed my back against the tile, the warm water cascading around us. Feeling him inside me, I thought about what he'd said. That my blood was home to him. Sweet words. And so very true for me as well.

"Drink from me, Jerry. Get more of her poison out of your system. Drink until you can't remember what in hell she tasted like."

He growled and leaned forward, striking hard, his mouth rough at my jugular. I'd stoked the anger simmering inside him. I wanted him in fighting form, not moping around like a wounded little boy. As he began his rhythm, coaxing an answering arousal in me with a clever finger, I had proof again that he was far from an inexperienced child. Jerry knew all my pleasure points and easily brought me to a screaming crest. Then he turned off the water and wrapped me in a towel.

On his bed, he stripped away the cover to stare down at me.

"My beauty. Let me love you."

"Have at it." I smiled and held out my arms. He fell into them, kissing me breathless before he rolled me over to lick a path from my shoulder blades to behind my knees with stops in between. I moaned when he pressed open my legs and pulled me up to kiss me intimately. His clever tongue made me call his name and beg him to come inside me again. He did, mounting me and riding me like he was the bull in a barnyard. He held my hips, his arms strong, his cock filling me and making me gasp as he surged into me time after time.

He said my name over and over, as if to reassure himself that he was with me, only me. I came apart, crying out his name, my heart demanding it. When he rolled me over to face him, I felt loose-limbed, replete.

"Drink from me, Gloriana. Or are you afraid my blood might be infected by that creature?"

My answer was to pull him down so I could sink my fangs into his vein. I tasted his blood and couldn't help the questions that haunted me. Did it taste different? Contaminated by Mel's evil? I didn't stop for long, his sweet familiarity reassuring. I drank until satisfied, licking the punctures closed with a sigh.

"I love you, Jeremiah." I snuggled against his shoulder.

"And I love you, Gloriana. Will you forgive me?" He kissed my wet hair.

"What did *you* do? That bitch tricked you. Scared the hell out of you with her mind games. Let's forget it ever happened. We need to plan what we'll do next. I'm going to try to use voodoo against her. I've even got a book coming, with a recipe for a potion in it."

"You think you can cook up something to send her away?" His voice was skeptical. "Since when do you know voodoo?"

"I called an expert. Hang loose for a few days. Avoid her and let's wait for the book." I rubbed my hand over his chest, thinking about maybe going another round.

"What if I left town? I still have that management problem in Miami and I thought I could do some investigating. Maybe I can find out more about Melisandra's background if I go back there and ask some questions. There might be something I could find out that could help us." Jerry had caught on to my idea of another round and slid his hand down my waist to the curve of my hip.

"Not such a bad idea. I know Mel's stuck here all weekend because I saw an ad for her seminar in Austin Saturday night." I sat up. "But you've known her for years, Jer. Didn't you have a pretty good idea of her background then? Meet some of her friends and family?"

"Not really." Jerry actually flushed. "It was a hot and heavy affair, Gloriana. We would meet at my hotel and, you know, get together. I have no idea if she has anyone important in her life. So this is worth a shot. Maybe I can find out if she has any vulnerabilities."

I lifted his hand off my hip. Counted. Put it back. Okay, I couldn't be mad at him for an affair he'd had when we'd been apart. I'd had my own, two actually. One when Jer and I had kind of been together. Anyway, it was an area we didn't need to explore right now. Instead we had naked bodies and healthy appetites that deserved exploration.

Shallow? Sure. Too much introspection can lead to short and sad relationships. That's one reason Jerry and I had lasted for centuries. We skirted deep issues, kept things light. It helped that he was usually all action and did very little talking. Now he proved he was still that way, rolling me under him and kissing me silent.

Finally, he pulled back and stared into my eyes. "Are we okay?"

"I suppose. Go to Miami. Get the dirt on Mel. Give me time to get that picture of you two being 'hot and heavy' out of my head. In the meantime, a demo of 'hot and heavy' here and now might help." I tugged on his hair, just to show him I was semiserious.

"Gloriana, she's mortal. There's no comparison. I was making do until I could be with the woman who takes 'hot and heavy' to a whole new level." He grinned and rolled until I sat astride him. "Look at you, perfect, tasty and able to read my mind. What more could I ask for?"

What more indeed? I leaned down to kiss him, shoving my old insecurities into the dark corner of my mind where they usually skulked. Perfect? Not hardly. But he didn't seem to mind my extra pounds or the way my ass dimpled. So I put a little extra enthusiasm into my lovemaking, to give him something to remember while he was in Miami. With luck, he might even find something useful there.

"This book came while you were at Jerry's." Aggie tossed it at me when I walked into the apartment after sunset the next night. "Pretty creepy stuff if you ask me."

"I didn't ask you. What are you doing opening my mail?" I frowned. It was an old book and Aggie's rough handling hadn't helped it any.

"I thought it might be something I ordered online. A new diet book. I figured you owed me. Nice that you've got a credit card on file at Amazon." Aggie groaned when she settled on the couch. "Flo is killing me. I swear my thighs are paralyzed."

"No pain, no— Hey! How did you get my password

anyway?" I grabbed my laptop. Sure enough, it didn't take me long to see she'd ordered a book and a couple of other things. Candy? How did that fit on her diet? I started to change my password.

"Please. You used your cat's name. Boogie. How easy was that?"

I stopped typing. I'd been about to change it to something equally easy, the name of my shop. I smiled and typed in Aggie's name. She'd never guess that. I closed the computer.

"Stay off the Internet. Don't use my credit card. Are we clear?"

"Desperate times." Aggie frowned when Sienna came in wearing a vintage leather jacket. She'd had Megan call for the price and had ended up buying it in the shop. "Look. Everyone is shopping but me."

"Goodwill has leather jackets. Check it out." I smiled at Sienna. "Looks good."

"Yes, I think so. Thanks for the great deal. I also bought some early Christmas presents but I can't imagine how I'm going to handle giving them out." Sienna's eyes filled with tears. "Guess I'll tell the family I have to be in the studio, recording, so I can't come home like I usually do. I'll just mail the gifts."

"This first Christmas it would probably be for the best." I patted the couch next to me. "By next year you'll be able to work out a way to be with them only at night and not arouse suspicion."

"I can't tell them I'm a vampire? Seriously?" Sienna blew her nose. "I don't think that's a promise I can keep."

"Think about it. They'd freak if they realized vampires really exist, wouldn't they?"

"Well, my baby sister would probably be cool with it. She's

a big *Twilight* fan. But Mom and Dad?" Sienna sniffed. "No, I can't imagine it. I'm from a nice little town in Oklahoma. We have football on the weekends, you know high school games where everyone goes. I actually went back for homecoming last year and my first boyfriend got me a corsage. One of those big mums with streamers." She smiled, obviously remembering.

"Sounds . . . nice." I couldn't imagine it. It was like a movie I'd seen once.

"It *was* nice, though I didn't realize it back then. Everything's so *normal*. I was always a freak in high school. So I ran away. Which broke my folks' hearts. We've made our peace and they're over it now. Proud of me. But a vampire? No, can't see it." Sienna collapsed with a sigh.

"Your sleep cycle would give you away. If you went home, how would you explain that you conk out when the sun comes up and simply can't wake up until sunset? It's just too bizarre for 'normal' people to deal with. Forget church on Sundays." Picturing Sienna's "normal" family made me wistful. Not that I had a clue about how a real family acted. My only exposure had been TV reality shows and I hoped that wasn't how most families lived.

"You're right. The lunch after church is always a big deal. You should see the way my mom feeds me when I'm home. Cooks all my favorites. And even if I stayed in a hotel, which my folks would never allow, it wouldn't work. My mom would be pounding on the door of the Holiday Inn before noon, wanting me to drive over to the mall in the next town to shop the after Christmas sales." Sienna wiped her wet cheeks. "I love that shit. What did Ray do to me?"

"Screwed you over, hon." Aggie had microwaved a diet dinner and was busy scarfing down spaghetti and meatballs.

"I'll say." Sienna licked her lips, tears drying up fast. "God, whatever you're eating smells delicious." She turned to me. "Seriously? We can't eat anything solid?"

"There's a drug that allows eating temporarily. Ian MacDonald invented it and sells it. Costs the earth. It gave me some bad side effects, but most vampires can probably tolerate it. He also has a daylight drug. It'll give you enough time to watch a sunrise, but that's about it. I can't tell you how many thousands of dollars Ray's sunk into buying that stuff. He's addicted to it."

"Of course. Once an addict, always an addict. He's just transferred the behavior to something else. Tell me about Ian MacDonald. Vampire?" Sienna got up and took off her new jacket. The outfit underneath was pure Hollywood, the latest in skinny jeans and antique lace blouses. The blouse alone must have cost four figures.

"Yes, and a doctor. He's the one Aggie sued." I tried to keep a straight face. No one had been rooting for Aggie in that trial.

"Seriously? What's the deal?" Sienna sat across from Aggie again.

"We were in love. I was a Siren, that's a woman who lures men to her, takes their money then, um, finishes them off." Aggie waved her fork. "Don't look at me like that. Glory was one too, back in the day. At least I was a *good* Siren. Had plenty of kills to my credit. Glory sucked. Was kicked out of the sisterhood for refusing to follow through."

"Yeah, I lacked the killer instinct." I hung my head. "I'm *so* ashamed."

"I'll bet." Sienna winked at me. "Go on. This is getting good. So what about MacDonald?"

"Well, Ian and I were a couple. He's brilliant and hot. In bed . . . Well, don't get me started. So I fell hard. Decided he was worth leaving my day job for." Aggie sighed, obviously going through her personal highlight reel.

"Not much of a job. Sounds like you were a hit woman." Sienna glanced at me. "Glory was lucky to be kicked out."

"Yeah, well, I'd come to see there wasn't much future. No room for advancement. You get my drift. So I decided to give up the Siren life to become mortal." She looked down. "I had a perfect body, perfect. Didn't I, Glory?"

"Of course. It's a Siren requirement. When I was kicked out, the Storm God, the man in charge of the Sirens, played a dirty trick on me, rearranging my parts so I wouldn't be perfect anymore." I slapped my hip. "Go on, Aggie, finish this fascinating tale."

"Don't mock me, Glory. It's a tragedy." Aggie chewed her last meatball. "These things are too damned skimpy. I'm zapping another one." She got up. "Anyway, I arranged to leave the Sirens, hit the dirt as a mortal and took Ian at his word that he'd give me back my immortality by making me vampire."

"Ah, the plot thickens. Ian promised to turn you? Yet here you are, still mortal and cleaning his toilets." Sienna laughed. "This is where the lawsuit came in. Right?"

"Yes." I continued because Aggie was in the kitchen microwaving another dinner. "When Ian smelled Aggie's mortal blood, he decided to just keep her as a blood slave. Use her kind of like you're doing but without the paycheck. He also lost interest in her physically. He'd figured out, you see, that she'd done the Siren song thing to make him fall in love with her. Once she lost her Siren magic, Ian lost the love."

"The rat bastard wouldn't touch me." Aggie stood in the kitchen doorway, waiting for her dinner to finish. "So what if I used a little magic on him? We were hot together and I thought maybe we had the real deal." Big sigh. "Well, you won't find me talking about love again, that's for sure. So I was stuck, mortal, and no lover. I took Ian to the local vampire court for breach of promise but those ass-hats are all about their own. Seems they don't like Sirens. Can you believe they ended up fining *me* a hundred thousand dollars for harming *him*?"

Sienna glanced at me. "Can you do that too, Glory? Make a man love you with music? Sounds like the coolest power ever."

"It *was* cool." Aggie frowned. "Glory sings now like a frog in pain."

"Not anymore. My mother gave me my song back." I almost laughed at the look on Aggie's face. Shock to put it mildly.

"Are you kidding me? Hebe can do that?" Aggie looked up like maybe she was ready to ask my mother to do her the same favor.

"Apparently. But I wouldn't hold my breath waiting for her to do it for you, Aggie. You know Mom isn't going to give you anything without expecting a big payback." I saw her face fall. "Besides I'm not about to try to call a man to me. When Jerry thought that's how I'd made him fall in love with me when we first met, he left me. Guys hate being manipulated. I'm not risking another breakup over that Siren shit."

"You're nuts. You ought to try out your voice. At least see if it works. I'll bet you can do some kind of whammy with your vampire mojo to erase the love thing if it doesn't work out. What do you think?" Aggie leaned forward. "I mean that's a serious power."

"I want to hear you sing. Come on. Hit me with your best shot, Glory." Sienna's eyes gleamed.

"Not now. What if you fell in love with me?" I grinned. "Maybe sometime when we're not in the middle of a crisis." I wasn't about to get into that now. "Have you tried your own song, Aggie?"

"Sure. First thing. I figured a sugar daddy could be a perfect rescue from my situation. Oh, my voice is still great." Aggie preened for a moment, then sagged. "But men just look at me like I'm nuts for breaking out in song at odd times. I can't call squat." She jumped when the microwave dinged. "So I'm working off my debt to Ian the hard way."

"That's why you're so desperate for money." Sienna sat back but she kept giving me a speculative look. I felt sure this wasn't the end of her determination to hear me sing. She'd produced her last album herself. Surely she didn't think I'd be interested in a career in music. "You didn't have any savings? What about all those men you tricked out of their cash when you were a Siren?"

"Oh, we weren't allowed to keep any of it. It's all up on Olympus, in the Siren treasure chest. Glory could get hold of part of it for me, if she'd go up there. Play nice with her kinfolks." Aggie had her new dinner on a tray and she carried it back in, blowing on it to cool it off. "Chicken in peanut sauce. Not sure about this one."

"That's right, darling. A quick trip to Olympus with *moi* and Aggie would have enough cash to pay off Ian and get a place of her own. Even leave town. Where would you like to go, Aggie?" My mother shimmered into view and sat on the other end of the couch.

"I've always been fond of the Amalfi Coast. I speak Italian, of course. And the water there is beautiful." Aggie grinned. "Looking good, Hebe."

Sienna had jumped when Mom had popped into the picture. Now she stared openmouthed. Mom did look good. She wore the traditional Olympus garb tonight, which fit her figure perfectly. Her diamond pin at the shoulder gleamed and her blond hair was shining as it tumbled in waves down her back.

"Mother. I see you decided to join us. I called you the other night. Didn't you hear me?" I kept a grim face. I wasn't about to take off for Olympus now.

"Oh, dear. No, I guess I didn't. What did you want?" She looked innocent as she studied her silver nail polish.

"Never mind. I had a question. It's been answered." I thought about asking for help with the Mel problem. No, like I'd told Aggie, my mother didn't do favors without asking for serious payback and she didn't want me to be with Jerry at all. Of course if I told her I was in danger . . . I'd wait and see if my recipe for a stay-away spell worked first. I'd make Mom my contingency plan.

"Nice to know you actually wanted to see me for a change. Now about the fortune. Have you given it any thought? Look at poor Aggie, suffering because you're too selfish to take a little trip to get the money she needs." My mother glanced at Aggie shoveling chicken and some kind of noodles into her mouth. When a noodle landed on her robe, Aggie picked it up with her fingers and sucked it in. Mother wrinkled her nose. She didn't need to say "disgusting," we could see it on her face.

"Hey, I *am* suffering," Aggie said after she swallowed. "I can't wear rubber gloves for everything. I've broken all my nails and can't afford a manicure. My body is completely ruined, with bulges everywhere. And I'm getting older by the day."

"You could afford to move away if you had the money." Sienna obviously saw the most important benefit to me. "But are you nuts? You want to be a vampire? How about all this food you're scarfing down? I've seen you with the Ben & Jerry's. You want to give that up on purpose?" Her eyes filled. "And give up daylight. I just don't get it. Why would anyone deliberately—"

"It's all about the immortality, hon. Mortals have ridiculously short lives. If I had money, the first thing I'd do would be to pay a rogue vampire to turn me. Then I'd be immortal again." Aggie slurped down another bite of the diet dinner. "After I get back my perfect figure, of course."

"What's this about a rogue vampire? There are such things? People who turn you vampire for a paycheck?" Sienna dragged her gaze from Aggie to me.

"Yes, and it's strictly against the council rules. You'd be in a world of trouble if you got caught soliciting any more vampires to turn you, Aggie." I ignored her one-finger salute. "Mother, thanks for dropping by but I'm in the middle of something important here. There's no chance I'm going to Olympus with you anytime soon. You want to help Aggie, give her the Siren magic back." I smiled at Aggie, who looked like she was about to choke on her chicken.

"No, I don't think so." Mom ignored Aggie's squeal of dismay. My mother picked up the book on the coffee table. "What's this? Recipes for spells. Voodoo? Oh, my dear, this is so beneath you." She tossed it back on the table. "If you need to get rid of someone, say no more. I can make anyone vanish just like that." She snapped her fingers and Aggie was gone. Poof. The only thing left was the sweet tangy odor of peanut sauce and Aggie's discarded bunny slippers on the floor in front of the couch.

I took a moment to savor it. "Where'd you put her, Mother?"

"Does it matter?" She snapped her fingers again and Aggie reappeared, cursing and shaking her head.

"What in the name of Zeus was that? Who sucked me into the black void? I was like, *gone*." Aggie narrowed her eyes on my mother and slapped her tray down on the coffee table. "Hebe, I thought we had an understanding."

"Say no more." My mother waved her hand and Aggie was frozen in her spot.

"Understanding? Now, this is interesting. Are you behind this whole thing? Aggie needing cash, staying here? I should have known you were in on this plot. It's all a ploy to get me to come to Olympus, isn't it?" I jumped to my feet. My mother had made a fool of me. Aggie had made a fool of me. Did she really need money? No doubt about it. But I just bet my mom was slipping her some cash on the side. To get her to cooperate and make my life a misery, so I'd be more open to taking that trip upstairs.

"Now, calm down, Gloriana. I didn't orchestrate all of this. Some of it just fell into my lap. Aggie fell in love on her own. Made her foolish choice to leave the Sirens on her own. If I took advantage to press my little agenda . . . ? Well, who can blame me?" Mother gestured, like she was practically a victim of circumstance.

"*I* can blame you. Have fun waiting till eternity for me to go with you to meet Zeus. Grandpa Zeus. I wonder what he would think of your manipulations." I tapped my foot. If the woman had needed a door to make her exit, I would have flung it open.

"Darling, don't be naïve. Manipulation is how we survive up there. Zeus would be proud." Mother stood and tried to put her arm around me. I darted across the room, out of reach. Sienna stared at us both, wide-eyed. No need to freeze her, she wasn't about to move and miss a reality show worthy of prime time on the Syfy channel.

"I won't go up there and that's final."

"Not even to save your man?" Mother actually smiled.

Eight

"What the hell do you mean?" I stepped closer to her.

"You think I haven't been following along? That I don't know what that voodoo person has been up to? I would never have let her hurt you, you know. Rest assured. But your Jeremiah? She can have him and good riddance." Mother flicked her fingers then just disappeared.

"What? Oh, you are the most infuriating creature I have ever had the misfortune to meet!" I kicked the wall, making a hole in it and scratching my good black boot. Damn it.

"Uh, Glory. What are you going to do about Aggie? I don't think she can move." Sienna had crept over to the couch and touched Aggie on the shoulder. Sure enough, the former Siren was still frozen.

"Maybe I should leave her like that. Serves her right, colluding with my mother." I sighed and trudged over to where Aggie sat, her fork halfway to her mouth. "Get out of the way, Sienna. She's liable to come out swinging."

"Don't thaw her yet." Sienna grinned. "It's kind of fun, seeing her like this. Speechless."

"Oh, no, you didn't say that." I shook my head. "She can still hear us, just not move. Stay back. I'll handle this." I watched Sienna scurry to the bedroom and heard her lock the door. Famous rock star, scared of Aggie. I wasn't, but then I knew how to deal with backstabbing traitors. I touched Aggie and she did come out fists flying, noodles and chicken going everywhere.

"Stop it." I grabbed her hand. "You realize you're an inch away from being homeless?"

"What the hell did *I* do?" Aggie subsided quickly. "Sienna was mean to me."

"She's your paycheck. You can take it. Now listen up. You'll behave yourself from now on or I'll kick your butt out of here. Understand?" I got right in her face, making sure she knew I meant every word. "Working with my mother? Not cool."

"She's been nice to me when no one else around here gave a rat's ass. See? My feet were cold. She bought me these slippers." Aggie stuck out the bunnies. "Passed me a few bucks at the grocery store too. I have to eat you know."

"I gave you money for food." I let her go, refusing to feel guilty. When Aggie had complained I hadn't given her enough cash, I'd ignored her, figuring she was just being greedy. Maybe prices *had* gone up since I'd shopped for steaks and snacks for Valdez.

"That pitiful amount you spotted me barely covered staples. You expect me to live on bread and water?" Aggie sniffed. "Those diet dinners don't come cheap."

"Wait a minute." I wasn't buying into this guilt trip. I stomped over to the kitchen and pulled on the freezer door.

"Staples? Since when is a premium brand of ice cream a staple?" I opened a cabinet. "Hah! There are three kinds of chips in here, even Cheetos." I whirled on her. Had someone told her I'd had a thing once for those little orange puffs?

"What? We didn't get junk food where I came from. Fancy banquets can be such a drag. I . . ." Aggie shut up at what must have been a wild look in my eyes as I pulled open a drawer.

"Look at all this candy! What did you do? Hit the Halloween treat aisle?" My mouth watered. Chocolate.

"Uh, yeah. What if we get trick-or-treaters? That's all they were talking about at the grocery store." Aggie's food tray was shaking.

"Trick-or-treaters?" My voice rose. "Are you freaking kidding me? Here? Where vampires live and there are double dead bolts on every door? You have to have a code to even get in this building, Aggie!" I ran my hands over a particularly delicious-looking bar. Dark chocolate, the label said, with coconut and almonds. The reminders of my unfair life made me whirl around and land in front of Aggie again, my vamp powers in overdrive.

"You took money from my mother and now you're torturing me." I thumped her on the shoulder with my fist. "Traitor! Ingrate! I brought you into my home. Gave you a roof over your head when you had nowhere else to go."

"Ow! That hurt!" Aggie cringed and rubbed her shoulder. "I'm sorry, Glory. I didn't think about you when I bought that stuff, I swear. Just me. I wanted it. Even though it's not on my diet."

"It's sure as hell not." I could smell that chocolate from where I stood, inches from Aggie. I jerked her stupid diet dinner from her hand and practically threw it on the coffee table. What a farce. Expensive diet dinners followed by who knew how many trips to the kitchen for snacks. No wonder she wasn't losing weight. I imagined Aggie enjoying a bag of Cheetos and snarled.

"Glory, calm down!" Aggie scooted to the other end of the couch and looked like she wanted to make a run for her bedroom.

"Stay put, we aren't done." I blocked her escape route.

She shook and held a hand to her throat. "Are you going to kill me? Over my food choices?"

"If I did kill you, it would be because you plotted against me, with my mother." I frowned down at the scratch on my boot. "Did she tell you what to buy at the store? She's probably trying to make me regret being a vampire. This would be just like her."

"I don't know. I got a craving. Hebe has the power . . ." Aggie kept staring at me. "Shit, look at your big honkin' fangs. I get it. I'm just a weak mortal now. At your mercy." A tear ran down her cheek. "Okay, I was wrong. I shouldn't have listened to Hebe. But she was the one who gave me a chance to be with Ian and she freed me from Achelous." Big tears were rolling now, dripping off the end of her chin. "Come on, Glory. Surely you can relate. I *had* to get away from that controlling son of a bitch. And you don't take a favor from a powerful goddess without expecting to pay her back."

Well, well. For once, Aggie did look scared. I realized her mortal blood had taken over in the delicious smell contest and my fangs *were* fully extended. I wasn't about to do something stupid and had never been a killer anyway. Obviously Aggie was as much a victim of my mother's plotting as I was.

"Aggie, you drive me nuts." I fell back into a chair and took a steadying breath. "I thought you had a goal. To get into Flo's size-six cast-offs."

Aggie wouldn't look at me as she wiped tears off her face. "I do. I'm desperate to lose weight. But it's so *hard*."

I could see she meant it. "I know. I'm sorry. Look. You're a good size right now. Own it, work it and quit obsessing about the stupid diet. I'll give you a few more things from the shop if you'll stop worrying about the size number in the label and concentrate on being proud of yourself now."

"I can't." Aggie's wail was straight from her heart. "Glory, size matters. I want to hook up with a guy who'll take care of me. When I was a Siren, the Storm God handled everything. If I'm little and cute, I'll stand a better chance of snagging a rich man." She sniffled. "Look at you, vampire, able to do stuff like freeze people, shape-shift, scare me shitless. I'm just an ordinary human now. You have no idea how helpless that makes me feel."

I gritted my teeth. Okay, I got it. Before I'd decided to use my powers, I'd acted like her for years, no, centuries. But I'd grown past that now. And there were plenty of mortals who managed to take charge of their lives and they didn't have power one.

If my own powers were suddenly stripped away, would I be so sure I could handle things on my own? I did a gut check. Hell, yes. I could take care of myself now. My dependent days were over.

I studied Aggie. She'd been a force to be reckoned with for centuries. I had a feeling that pushy broad was still in there somewhere.

"Get a grip, Aggie. I've never known a woman more capable of handling herself than you. Quit looking for someone else to take care of you and look inside. You have what it takes to make it on your own. You're smart, beautiful—not that that matters—and talented. You *have* skills, lady, you just need to discover them."

Aggie's mouth quivered. "Skills? I get it. You want me to turn tricks? Those are the only skills I've got and you know it. Sex. Sirens are famous for it."

"No!" I jumped up and gave her shoulders a shake. "Stop it. Sex isn't all you know. I'm thinking you must be pretty smart and I know you're manipulative. There's got to be some way to make that work for you. You can still sing too, can't you? Even though it isn't magical, it's a good skill."

Aggie firmed her mouth and I could see the wheels turning. "Hey, maybe you're right, Glory. I know I'm sick of my own whining. Part of it was to bug you. Hebe had me do it." She brushed aside my hands and slapped her fork down on her unfinished dinner on the coffee table. "Of course I have a line of fancy patter I can use when I need to. I could even wrap the Storm God around my finger from time to time. Ian admitted I was smart too. Yes, my voice *is* golden. Maybe I could get a singing gig. We're here on Sixth Street where there are a dozen clubs open every night needing entertainment." She took a deep breath, her robe rising and reminding me she had a good figure that an audience would appreciate.

"There you go. So you're not powerless." I could easily imagine her in one of the clubs, tossing her blond hair as she sang.

"Damn it, I'm going to cut my hours at that bastard Ian's house and start looking for something else. A way to make money on my own." She grinned and winked.

"Cut your hours? Won't his men tell on you?" I knew she was supposed to work a certain number a day, according to their agreement.

"Naw. His day guards are putty in my hands. I think they feel kind of sorry for me." Aggie got up and stretched.

"Really?"

"Don't sound so surprised. Like you said, I can be manipulative when I need to." Aggie polished her nails on her robe and fluttered her eyelashes. "They even let me watch my shows, the *Real Housewives* reruns, every afternoon after lunch. It's not like Ian's house is really dirty, and he won't let me touch his lab."

I had a creepy feeling that Aggie's manipulation used more than charm to get the shape-shifters who watched Ian during his death sleep to give her breaks. I started to read her mind then decided the fewer details I knew the less grossed out I'd be.

"Okay then. Maybe you'll find a second job that you can do in the evenings." I was for anything that would get her out of the house when I was awake.

"First, though, I'll do a little shopping downstairs tonight. Thanks, Glory. I figured once your mom outted me I'd be toast here." She stopped in the hall doorway. "I'm in the mood for a long soak. I hope you aren't planning to use the bathroom anytime soon."

"No, go ahead." Bathing. That reminded me. "Don't use the alley. I saw a, um, rat out there. Huge." I had to give her the warning before she disappeared into the bathroom. Sure, I'd like her out of here, but I wasn't desperate enough to make her a zombie sacrifice.

I stared down at her dirty dinner tray, then thought about what she'd said. What was wrong with me? Aggie *should* have been toast. Instead I was giving her good advice. I could almost hear my mother's laughter. And what about Mom's conviction that she'd never let Mel hurt me? Really? What if the witch came after me when Mom was "busy"? She seemed able to tune in and out of my life at will.

I picked up the book Madame had sent me and glanced at the page marked with a slip of paper. I was going ahead with this plan. Too bad there were enough ingredients to create Frankenstein's monster. And how on earth was I going to find all this stuff? Maybe my mother was right and I had no business messing with voodoo. When someone knocked on the apartment door, I jumped and ran to the peephole, careful to look before I threw the lock.

"Rafe. I wondered where you were. I thought you were supposed to stay here during the day." I opened the door.

"I was here. When I got your text that you were with Blade, I slept on the couch, but left as soon as Sienna woke up. I had a few things to do at the club before I could come tonight. Plus I wanted to go home and shower, pick up a few things." He came in with a duffel bag. "Everything okay?" He sniffed the air. "What's that smell?"

"A combo of spaghetti and peanut sauce. Aggie's diet dinners." I locked the door behind him. "I need to go down to the shop tonight. Are you sure you can spare the time away from the club?"

"No problem. But if you can see your way clear to go over to N-V for an hour or two later, it would help me out." He rummaged in the kitchen and came out with the carton of ice cream. "Is this part of Aggie's diet?"

"She's struggling. Do her a favor and finish that off. There are Cheetos and candy in there too." I sat on the couch. "I can go to the club. First I want to wait for Jerry to come by. He's leaving tonight for Miami, to do some checking on the voodoo woman. He had a bad encounter with her last night and we decided it might be best for him to leave town for a while." I told Rafe about the drug, leaving out the date rape. I knew Jerry wouldn't appreciate Rafe knowing that detail.

"No way. She made him forget the whole night? That's harsh." Rafe spooned up chocolate ice cream. "Yeah, leaving town is a good idea. We know Mel's stuck here and we can scope her out at that seminar. Did that book come?"

"Yes, but look at these ingredients." I picked up the book and opened the page. "New leaves from a baobob tree. Three legs of a Peruvian cave whip scorpion. A feather from a pileated woodpecker." I moaned. "I could go on and on. It could take forever even if I could find a place to order this stuff from on the Internet and not be put on a terrorist watch list."

"Yeah, sounds pretty dicey. Let me see that." Rafe scraped the last bite out of the pint and walked into the kitchen to dump the empty carton into the garbage can. When I heard him rinsing off his spoon, I had to smile. He did make a nice roommate. Aggie's dirty dish still sat in the middle of the coffee table.

"Do I hear Rafe?" Sienna came out of the bedroom. "Hey, glad you got here. Are we going to N-V? I got a text from Ray. We need to rehearse tonight. I don't want to go to his house so I thought we could practice in that soundproof room you've got above the club."

"I'm supposed to stick close to Glory. She needs to go to the shop." Rafe was leafing through the voodoo spell book. "Glo, can we drop Sienna off at the club first, then do our thing at your shop? You trust her alone with Ray and the band?"

I was about to answer when there was another knock on the door. What was this? Didn't anyone need the code downstairs? What had happened to ringing for entrance from the street? I inhaled though and sensed Jerry on the other side of the door. Of course. He had the code and a key. He'd knocked as a courtesy. I flung open the door.

Jerry dragged me into his arms for a long kiss then looked over my shoulder. "Valdez."

"You're not surprised he's here?" I eased out of Jerry's arms.

"No." Jerry smiled and kept his hand on my waist. "I called him and asked him to meet me here. Did you really think I could leave town with you unprotected?"

I glanced from Rafe to Jerry and back again. This was huge, Jerry asking Rafe for help. "That's nice. I guess Rafe told you—"

"That I'd be happy to arrange guard duty for you, Glory. But that I don't want to delegate it. Blade understood. That you and I have a special bond." Rafe relaxed into a chair. "So what are your plans, Blade? What do you think you can accomplish with this trip?"

"I've got a line on Mel's sister. She's in Miami and may have something to tell me that could help with this situation. Mel's business is very important to her. If I can get something that could endanger her reputation publicly, ruin her business, I think that will cool her off toward me. Problem is, it has to be something that keeps my name out of it."

"Yeah, I get that." Rafe smiled. "Good plan. Drag a skeleton out of the lady's closet. Blackmail her. She should hate you for it and back off."

"If I have to, I'll drag her sister back here. I think she may be the key to getting this done." Jerry pulled me down to the couch beside him then finally noticed my guest. "Sienna. How are you doing?"

Sienna smiled nervously. "Okay, I guess. We were just trying to figure out the night's schedule. I have to practice, Glory needs to go to her shop. It's complicated."

"Right. That's the vampire life." Jerry leaned back, his arm around me. "It doesn't get any easier. Valdez, sounds like you need backup. Can't you bring in another shifter, someone to help with the ladies?"

Valdez frowned. "Sure, I guess so. Let me get on it." He got up, pulled out his cell and strode to the kitchen. We heard him talking to someone.

"I do need my own bodyguard. I usually travel with one but had done without while I was staying with Ray. He has a whole crew." Sienna stood in the hall doorway. "I'm going to finish getting ready if I can blast Aggie out of the bathtub. I dread seeing Ray again. I'm still so mad at him." She turned and disappeared into the bedroom.

"It's a full house, isn't it?" Jerry sniffed. "Aggie in the tub, she said?"

"Yes. She's still hung up on water. It's a Siren thing." I told him about our latest fight, including my mother's manipulation.

"I hate to say it, but you might be better off in Olympus right now." Jerry stared into my eyes. "Mel is capable of anything."

"No. I'm not going to Olympus. Once my mother gets me there, I have a feeling I'd have a serious problem getting back." I sighed and snuggled up against him. I still hadn't told Jerry about the zombies. Since he hadn't mentioned them, I had to assume he'd shifted here and come in through the roof. Still, I was surprised he hadn't smelled them when he'd landed. "I hate for you to leave, Jerry."

"It's for the best. Now, if you're sure you won't go, then I had a couple of ideas to keep you safer while I'm gone. Lily's apartment is ready upstairs. Her new furniture was delivered today." Jerry pulled a key out of his pocket. "Here's the key. I told her she can't move in yet. You and Valdez can stay there until I get back. Mel won't know where you are and you'll have some peace and quiet. How does that sound?"

"Like heaven." I snatched the key. "Thanks, Jerry." I kissed him. "Lily won't get mad?" I knew his daughter had been counting the nights until she could have her own apartment.

"I'm paying the rent, so she can wait a few days." Jerry kissed me again. "I explained the situation. She understood." He pulled me to my feet when Rafe walked into the room.

"I've got a man meeting us down in the shop in twenty minutes. He'll stick with Sienna so I can take care of Glory. That work for you?"

"It's perfect." I glanced at Jerry. "You said you had a couple of ideas. What's the other one?"

"I'll tell you upstairs." He stared at Rafe. "We're going to apartment three B." He tossed Rafe a key. "Meet us there in five minutes, Valdez. We need some privacy." Jerry pulled me to the door.

"I don't take orders from you, Blade." Rafe didn't look happy.

"Did you miss the part where I said I'd pay you?" Jerry wasn't cracking a smile. "Or is this a favor to Glory?"

"It's a favor. You don't owe me jack." Rafe stepped closer.

· "Calm down, both of you. I appreciate the favor, Rafe. Jerry, you don't need to pay him but thanks for offering. Rafe is doing this out of friendship. I'd say shake hands but I know better. Now let's go, Jer." I pulled Jerry up the stairs. We stopped at the third floor and he pointed out Lily's new apartment. Privacy. I wasn't fighting it. I waited until he'd unlocked the door of 3B and we were inside the freshly painted apartment before I asked the burning question.

"Okay, Jer. What else did you do to keep me safer?"

"I called Mel. Told her you broke it off with me. That I'd come home reeking of sex with her and you didn't buy my memory-loss story." He stared down at me. "I'm lucky it didn't go that way."

"Luck had nothing to do with it." I slipped my arms around his waist. "Why did you tell her that?"

"To get her off your back. I figured she would leave you alone if she thought we weren't together anymore." He pulled me tight against him. "Trouble is though she said she wasn't buying it. I cursed her. Told her she'd ruined my life with her shit and that I never wanted to see her again."

"I'll bet that didn't go over well."

"It was the truth. Then I added that you were moving on to someone without baggage. Told her I was taking a few days in Miami to fix the mess she'd made there in my hotel." He rested his chin on my hair. "I hope that'll give her something to think about. That she'll leave you alone. She's got that seminar you mentioned right here in town so she can't follow me to Miami."

"That was a good idea." I rubbed his back. "I hate the fact that you goaded her, Jer. But if she believed you, I shouldn't be on her radar at all." I kissed his skin where his collar was open over his throat. I could see his pulse and kissed my way to it. "Don't worry about me, I'll be all right."

"There's one more thing you can do, Gloriana, while I'm gone. It should help keep you safe." He pushed me away and looked into my eyes. "I hate this like hell, but it's the best way to go."

"What?" I didn't like the way he was staring at me, so solemn. His mind was blocked too, though I really shouldn't have tried to probe it. I could have pushed through the block, but didn't.

"You and Valdez. I want you to act like a couple while I'm gone. Throw Mel off. Show her that you really *have* moved on." He smiled but it was a sad fake. "Like you did when you pretended to be with Caine. Only I don't think you have to flash a big engagement ring this time."

"I doubt she'd buy that. It's too soon, Jerry." I shook my head.

"You know Valdez won't mind the charade. Hell, he usually can't keep his hands off you anyway." Jerry rubbed my shoulders, pulling me close again. "Of course I hate like hell to imagine you two together. But there's no better way to convince her that you and I are history."

"Rafe's even willing to go back to dog form for me, Jer. To fool Mel into making a move during the day. That's how loyal he is." I wanted Jerry to know how much this would cost Rafe. "To pretend to be lovers again . . . That's really not fair to him. He'd do it, no doubt about it. But it's a cruel joke."

"I can take it, Glory. I have my own woman now. And Blade's right. It's a great way to keep Mel from making another move on you." Rafe stood in the doorway. I guess we'd left the door ajar. "You did say five minutes."

"You heard." I knew my face was red. "Sorry. Jerry had this crazy idea that Mel would back off if you and I were having a wild rebound affair."

"Works for me." Rafe grinned.

"You don't have to enjoy it too much, Valdez. Besides, I know Gloriana is committed to me. I trust her completely." Jerry had me snug against his side.

"Well, then." I was actually at a loss for words. I'd waited literally centuries to hear Jerry say those words. "So that's what we'll do. Play the game and hope Mel buys it." I walked Jerry to the stairs. "We're going to the roof, Rafe. I'll be back in a few."

"And don't come looking for her." Jerry growled as he followed me up the stairs.

"Got it." Rafe was grinning as he shut the apartment door.

"Take care of yourself. Don't fly too long." Up on the roof I held on to Jerry, wishing he didn't have to go. It hadn't been that long ago that he'd been drugged.

"I'm fine. I'll lay over in one of my safe houses. You know I've made this trip many times. I have the route well laid out." He smiled and brushed my hair back over my shoulders. "Take care. Don't leave Valdez's side. I don't particularly like the bastard but he's good at what he does. If he gets carried away with this fake relationship, you know what to do."

"I can turn him to stone in a heartbeat. But he won't push things. He takes good care of me." I pulled Jerry's head down for a final kiss. "I love you. Hurry home." I watched as he shifted into a black bird and took off. He blended into the night sky, his final squawk his own good-bye to me.

I looked over the ledge down to the alley. No sign of the zombies tonight. Did that mean Mel had believed Jerry's tale of our breakup? It was a good sign anyway. I was smiling when I found Rafe setting his duffel bag in front of Lily's door.

"Nice digs. He doesn't stint when it comes to his daughter, does he?" Rafe opened the door and stepped inside. "Two bedrooms. What does she need with two bedrooms?"

"I don't know but I'd love to foist Aggie on her. I need a plan for just that." I wandered into the kitchen and opened the refrigerator. Fully stocked with premium synthetic blood. I helped myself to my favorite flavor, AB negative. What a treat.

"Do the two women get along?" Rafe looked in vain for human snack food in the empty cupboards. "We need to go shopping."

"Does anyone get along with Aggie? Do her a favor and go shopping in my kitchen." I sat on the black and white print couch. The living room was done in a contemporary style. Black and white with touches of red. There was a fluffy white flokati rug on the refinished hardwood floor. I loved it, even though I'd always been more into antiques and the retro look. There was something about everything being brand-new that appealed to me. A fresh start. What a concept.

"Actually though, the two *are* pretty friendly. Two contrary females. I've seen them with their heads together more than once." I drank my blood, sighing with pleasure. "Make a shopping list, Rafe. We'll hit the grocery store too. Aggie made me realize I haven't been giving her enough food money. I need to see what things cost now."

"Don't let her guilt-trip you, Glory. The woman's taking advantage of you all the way around." Rafe stood by the door. "We need to go. I've got to meet that new guard, bring him up to speed on Sienna's needs and take care of some things. Remember?"

I got up reluctantly. Break over. I drained the bottle, rinsed it out and set it aside. We'd start a recycle bin up here. Lily should learn to do that. I followed Rafe out and locked the door. I had a serious case of apartment envy. My feet dragged as I headed downstairs to my noisy, cramped and tired old place.

When we got to my door, I heard singing. A duet. Somehow I had a feeling this was not going to turn out well.

Nine

When I opened the door, Sienna and Aggie glanced my way but didn't stop singing. Sienna was playing her guitar while Aggie tapped out a beat on my coffee table. It was a familiar tune, a hit that had been playing on the radio recently.

I couldn't believe it. A happy sing-along? Obviously Aggie had decided to use Sienna to launch a singing career. And Sienna? She grinned and winked when Aggie took a solo turn. Hmm. So maybe Sienna thought she could stick it to Ray if she brought Aggie along to their rehearsal. She must have heard that he hated the former Siren. Aggie had tortured Ray and me when we'd first met. She'd almost sacrificed us to save her own skin when she'd been in trouble with Circe, a goddess who hated vampires on general principle. I'd sort of moved past it. Ray never had, nursing an urge for revenge almost to the point of obsession. And what Ray despised, Sienna now loved.

The song ended and they both laughed, obviously pleased with their sound. Who wouldn't be? They both had tremendous voices, clear and powerful. The harmony had been spot-on.

Rafe clapped. "Amazing. You two sounded great together. What brought that on?"

"Just a little experiment. Aggie mentioned she used to sing for a living. I wanted to hear her. Some voice, huh?" Sienna tapped Aggie's knee. "Those men didn't stand a chance."

I just stared. Did Sienna not get that Aggie had used her song to bring men to their *deaths*? I thought we'd made it pretty clear earlier. I guess the rocker didn't care. Her recent experience with Ray must have made her so down on men that Aggie's taking out over a million men had seemed like a public service.

"Thanks, Sin. Coming from you, that's quite a compliment." Aggie managed to sound humble. "You really think I have a shot?"

"Oh, yeah. We're going to make it happen." Sienna handed her guitar to Rafe when he stuck out his hand. "You're going to the club with me tonight, Aggie."

"That'll be interesting." Rafe grinned. "What's the plan?"

"Shop first. I know Glory needs to check in down there and Aggie should have some decent clothes for her new singing career. Then I'm taking her to my practice with Ray. I think Aggie would make a great backup singer."

"Backup?" Aggie started to argue but stopped when she saw my frown. "Well, I guess it's a good place to start." She grabbed her coat. "I'm used to being a solo act, Sin. I was hoping to start checking out places on Sixth Street, trying for my own singing job. A night gig of course. I can't give up my day job at Ian's. Yet." She wrinkled her nose. "He won a judgment against me. If I default, the vamp council will lock me up in a coffin in Damian's basement. Can you believe it?"

"That's a little extreme. Are they serious, Glory?" Sienna gathered up her own coat and purse.

"As a heart attack. She's got years to go to pay off Ian

unless she comes into some big bucks." I looked around my crowded place. Aggie wasn't the only one who needed big bucks. Worn chairs, drapes, kitchen table. I'd given up on an area rug after Boogie had upchucked his fifth hair ball. Since my last fledgling vampire, Penny, had left her cat with me, I'd learned to deal with having a few kitty calamities. Any way you looked at it, compared to Lily's new place, mine was a dump.

"Don't audition anywhere else yet, Aggie. I'm going to see what I can arrange. We pay our backup singers pretty well. You could probably give this Ian whatever he says you're working off each week and still have money left over." Sienna laughed when Aggie lunged, throwing her arms around her.

"Honey, you have no idea how desperate I am to be free of that egomaniac." Aggie pushed back, tears in her eyes. "I never see him anymore, thank the goddess. Instead, he leaves me lists of things he says I do wrong every day. He wants his towels folded a certain way. I should bleach his jockey shorts." She got an evil grin. "Did that, even his black silk ones."

"Bet he loved that." I had to admit that Ian could be a real bastard.

"The latest list told me to scrub the grout in his bathroom with a toothbrush. If I did, it would be with the one he uses on his own stupid fangs." Aggie danced around the room, singing a song she must have made up on the spot. It featured four-letter words and invited Ian to shove his lists.

"I guess we'd better make this happen then. And won't it be fun, singing together?" Sienna put her hand on Rafe's when he set her guitar in its case. "Do you mind bringing that along? We may do an acoustic number. Though how Ray and I can still go on together when I don't want to see or speak to that bastard ever again is beyond me."

"Contract, Sienna." Rafe carried the guitar to the door. "Let's go, ladies. Glory, you got what you need?"

I grabbed my purse then at the last minute shoved the voodoo book and my computer into a tote and brought them along. If I had time, I'd like to get started on that list of ingredients. Even if I didn't have to worry about Mel coming after me, a stay-away potion could help Jerry. I wanted it. And maybe one of my staff would be able to help. With ancient shifters you never knew what kind of connections they had.

"Okay, I'm ready." I locked the door with my new key. A locksmith had changed the locks during the day, thanks to Jerry. He had a shifter who arranged such things for him. I'd have to pack when we got back, before sunrise. The idea of that peace and quiet upstairs put a smile on my face despite the fact that Aggie and Sienna started bickering on the way down about which musical group they thought had the best sound.

"You guys are arguing about the wrong decade." Rafe put in his two cents. He named bands from the sixties, some of which were still playing. This set off Sienna, who had strong opinions, and the commotion was pretty loud by the time we stepped into the alley. Rafe came to an abrupt halt, his arm out like he was ready to shove us all back into the building.

"What?" Sienna peered around him. "Paparazzi?"

"No. Something much worse. Use one of your new vampire senses and take a whiff." He set her guitar down inside the hallway and motioned us back. "What do you smell?"

"Candy?" She sniffed and made a face. "But there's something off. Did the muffin shop burn a batch?"

"Damn, is she here?" I had already ruled out the zombies. Aggie and Sienna scurried out of the way when I stepped to Rafe's side. "That's the smell of evil. Memorize it, Sienna. You and Aggie stay in here until we give you the all clear. I mean it. Do not come out. This is serious." I glared at both of them.

"I get it. Voooodoooo." Aggie shook her hands in the air. "Go. Run her off. I know *I'm* not interested in tangling with a psycho bitch." Aggie pulled on Sienna's sleeve. "Come on back upstairs. Glory, call us on your cell when we can safely come down again."

"Sure." Sienna snatched up her guitar. "Take care of yourselves, you two." She patted my back, gave Rafe a worried look, then rushed back up the stairs after Aggie. "Hey, wait up. I'm no hero either."

"Good. Now follow them, Glory." Rafe grabbed my arm and tried to ease me back inside.

"Not on your life. This is *my* fight. If she's planning an ambush, it's for me. I'm dying to hear what she has to say." I brushed past him, firmly taking his hand off of me. "Come out, come out, wherever you are." I taunted her and why not? I wasn't convinced I couldn't take Mel in a fair fight.

"Careful, Glory. I'm reading your mind. Just what makes you think this woman's into fighting fair?" Rafe stayed close, his eyes narrowed as he scanned the dark alley. The lights were out again.

"Who's this with you, Gloriana? Moving on already?" Mel stepped out of the darkness. No business suit tonight. Instead she wore a black silk outfit that flowed loosely around her body. A dozen necklaces sparkled in the dim moonlight. I thought I saw a bone dangling from one of them. Or was it a tooth? Did those things help her with her powers? Maybe I'd rip them all off and find out.

"That's my business, Melisandra. What do you want? Seems like you've caused enough trouble around here already.

Time to hit the road and go back where you came from." I grabbed Rafe's arm. We were supposed to be a couple now. Might as well start acting like one.

"I can't do that. I have obligations. And one of them is to make you pay for hurting Jeremiah." She stretched her long fingers toward me and I saw her creepy dead people come out to play again. Spirits, I guess you'd call them. The tiny wisps of howling creatures flew up from her fingertips to gather in a circle above her head.

"You think *I* hurt *Jerry*? What are you smoking, lady?" I let her see my fangs. I had to remind myself of the part I was supposed to play. "*He* hurt *me*, but he won't ever again. I've had it with Jeremiah Campbell and his lies. As if the Jerry I know ever had to be drugged to have sex with a woman." I brushed off my sleeve, the picture of *Don't give a damn*. Mel's face had hardened. Good, my shot had hit the target.

"Is that what he told you?" She managed to sound outraged. Nice try.

"Forget what he told me." I snuggled up to Rafe. "I've got a man now who I know won't cheat on me. Rafe and I have a history and now we're back together for good. Isn't that right, baby?" I didn't give Rafe a chance to answer before I planted a big kiss on him to show Mel I was serious. Rafe cooperated, but I could feel the tension in his body, the way his bicep flexed where I held his arm. He was still on high alert, obviously worried about the woman standing a few feet away with her ghosts and ghouls doing an aerial ballet above her head. I had a feeling they were waiting for orders.

I pulled back and quirked an eyebrow at Mel. "Still here? Why? Jeremiah's all yours. If you're sure you want him. But if my man ran around claiming he only had sex with me because I *drugged* him?" I put a hand on my hip. "Well, I can't tell you how fast *I'd* kick him to the curb." I gave her a look, up and down. "Oh. But maybe you did have to resort to a little help in that department. Seriously? Slip a little something into his blood last night, Mel?"

Mel's hands shook and her creatures became more agitated. "Shut the hell up. Of course I didn't have to drug Jeremiah. He's *crazy* about me." She laughed suddenly, her scarlet mouth reminding me of the silent scream in the mural Flo had painted on my wall inside the shop. Insanity lurked in her eyes. Oh, yeah, this woman knew crazy all right.

"If you did drug him, that would make you pretty damned pathetic, wouldn't it? Desperate." I couldn't resist. "Jerry begged me to take him back last night. Hands and knees, the whole nine yards. Even brought out an engagement ring. Now, *that* was pathetic."

Mel's eyes flashed, the spirits above her flinging themselves into a chaotic circle dance. "Liar. Jeremiah would never demean himself that way. Now who's pathetic?" She smiled, her teeth very white and even. "Does it sting to know that if you'd truly satisfied him he never would have turned to me in the first place, Gloriana?"

I tensed, desperate to throw myself at her. Rafe's strong arm clamped around my waist, holding me back.

"Jeremiah says my blood is like fine wine. He can't get enough of it." She waved her arms, clearly in the middle of building her own fantasy.

I pulled myself back from the brink of joining her in Crazyland, happy to burst her bubble. "He's a vampire, Mel. Get a clue. We suck mortal blood to survive. The man would build you a temple and worship you like a goddess if it would get him a bite at your vein, honey." And didn't I hate that fact. My don't-give-a-damn attitude was wearing thin. At least Mel didn't look too happy either. "If Jerry's so into you, where is he? Why isn't he with you now?"

The ghosts and ghoulies above Mel went wild, screaming as they darted around like lightning bugs on speed. Her dark hair rose, a nimbus around her head. The freakish squeals became so high-pitched that I wanted to cover my ears.

"That's enough." Rafe started forward.

"No, leave her alone, lover. I can take it." I kept a hand on his arm, willing him to stay safe. "Hear her howls of pain? Lost him, didn't you, Mel?" It was my turn to laugh and I managed a pretty good one.

Mel's eyes blazed and her creatures paused in mid-screech. "Last night we made love, Gloriana. Jeremiah and I. It was incredible. I'm sure he'll be back." She raised her hands and we were rushed, those ghostie things suddenly tearing at my flesh. Rafe cursed and lunged at her. I touched his back, turning him to stone. I knew he'd hate that, but I didn't want him getting into it with a voodoo woman.

"I don't give a damn if Jerry wants you or not. I'm over the unfaithful bastard." I said it one more time. I wanted to be sure she heard me and knew I meant it.

"Then you won't care what happens next." She smiled, smoke and mist filled the alley, then she and her entourage disappeared.

I released my hold on Rafe.

"Damn it, Glory. Why'd you do that? I could've taken her." Rafe stomped over to where Mel had been standing and began searching the alley. "She's gone."

"Maybe you could have handled her. Maybe not. I still don't know what she can do. Did you feel those creatures hit you?" I looked down at my arms, expecting to see blood or at least some red marks. Nothing.

"Yeah. Stung like a son of a bitch." Rafe rubbed his cheek. "But I still think . . ."

"Let it go. Looks like she's done with me. But I'm afraid she's still after Jerry. We'll see." I pulled out my cell and called upstairs, giving Sienna and Aggie the all clear to come down. "When we go to the seminar Saturday night, we'll see how she acts."

"You still want to do that?" Rafe looked at me like I'd lost my mind. Maybe I had. I either had a bad case of "Know your enemy" or I was letting Lily's fab apartment get to me.

"Why not? Sin bought those expensive tickets and I'm interested in Mel's message when she's doing her motivational thing and not channeling evil spirits. Own the world. I could get behind that. The woman may be a few ghosts short of a gaggle, but she's got plenty of confidence. And her Web site impressed me. It's about time I got ambitious, don't you think?" I heard the back door open.

"Not touching that one." Rafe shrugged. "Guess you want to spare the ladies the details of what just went down?"

"Definitely. Just another ordinary night in this alley." I laughed, relieved to have gotten through the confrontation with Mel without either of us getting hurt.

Rafe shook his head. "Let's go then. Shop first, but only for an hour. I need to get to N-V."

"Thanks, Rafe. You were awesome. Sorry about the kiss and turning you into a statue." I hugged him then kissed his cheek.

"I figured the kiss was a perk. Feel free anytime." He didn't let me go. "The freeze thing? Lose it. Makes me crazy."

"I know. I'm really sorry." I touched his cheek. "It comes so easily . . ." I kept my arms around him. Maybe Mel was still lurking close enough for a glimpse, though I couldn't smell her now.

"Yeah, well. Use it on bad guys, not your friends." He stepped back and grabbed Sienna's guitar when she handed it to him as soon as she cleared the door. Then he made up a story about a false alarm when Aggie and Sienna peppered us with questions.

We headed into my shop. Aggie couldn't quit talking about new clothes, and flashy stage clothes didn't come cheap. We were trolling through my evening wear when the candidate for Sienna's bodyguard came in.

Danny Potter was a shape-shifter who'd worked for Rafe in the club for a while but had been looking for something that paid more than bouncing out unruly college kids. Rafe vouched for him and we all liked him on sight. He was big, could look mean when he needed to, and his size was intimidating. He stood about six foot six and had a neck the size of Sienna's waist. His dark skin and eyes matched his black cotton shirt and jeans.

"Call me Danny." He shook hands with everyone except Rafe, who got a serious fist bump. Then he proceeded to stand back and watch the room. I immediately felt safer.

"Hey, Danny." Sienna called him over. "Have you met Israel Caine?"

"Sure. He's played the club several times since he moved to town. Great guy." Danny smiled.

"Wrong answer. From now on, he's on your shit list." Sienna pulled Danny to the back room, I assume to fill her guard in on why she hated Ray.

Fine by me. If she wanted to use her bodyguard to intimidate Ray, that was between them. That left me with Aggie, who had an armful of cocktail dresses and was headed for the dressing room.

"Hold it. Let me look at your choices." I grabbed the stack.

"What? You said I could shop." Aggie glanced around the store. We were fairly busy, with only a week until Halloween. I wasn't going to let her pick my best looks for herself when I might never get paid for them.

"These are going back." I took the most expensive and separated them from the pile. "Try on these two, then I'm finding you a pair of good silky black pants and a few glitzy tops to go with them. You're going to have to be practical. If you don't get a regular gig, you may have to bring this stuff back and let me resell it."

"Seriously? What are you? The fashion police?" Aggie frowned down at my choices. "These are the cheapest things you've got. And I hate black. I need color! Pizazz!"

"You need black if you're singing backup. And it's kinder on those new bulges you developed when you pigged out on Halloween candy, Aggie." I had no sympathy when all I could do was sniff the candy she'd brought home by the bag.

"Halloween candy? I hear you." A woman stopped on her way to the costumes. "I'm a sucker for candy corn."

"Candy corn?" Aggie got interested. "I haven't tried it yet."

"Pure sugar and pure heaven. No fat grams either." She looked Aggie up and down. "You look great to me. Honey, quit ragging on her." This was addressed to me with a glare. "The girl's got a nice rack. She should go low cut and the muffin top won't be noticed. Am I right?" The stranger gave Aggie a friendly elbow.

"That's what I've always said. Show off your boobs and the men never look past them." Aggie snatched back a green dress, the color of her eyes. It did have a deep vee neckline. "This one will look fantastic." She turned to her new friend. "I'm a singer. These will be my work clothes."

"No kidding? Here's my card. June Raymond, wedding

planner. If you call me, I might be able to try you out. If you're interested in another gig. We're always looking for entertainment. I'd have to hear you sing first of course." The woman slapped a gold-trimmed card into Aggie's hand. "'Wedding's by June.' Catchy, don't you think?"

Clearly Aggie didn't have a clue about that but she smiled and nodded. "I may be singing backup on Halloween at N-V for Sienna Star and Israel Caine. Come catch the show and see for yourself if I'll do for your weddings."

"Wow. Seriously? You'd have to be good to sing with those two." The woman walked with Aggie toward the dressing room. "That show's a sellout. But I heard they may be adding another one at midnight. Know anything about that?"

I felt a presence at my back. "Rafe. Are you adding a midnight show? Can I get a ticket?"

"Have you ever needed one?" He rested his hand on my shoulder. "Yes, I'm in talks with Nate about a midnight show. Agents. He's being tough with the negotiation but I think we'll have a deal. You definitely have to come. Get Flo and Richard to come too. Even Damian. I'll reserve a table for you guys. The usual spot."

"I wish Jerry . . ." I sighed. "Well, maybe he'll be back and this Mel thing will be over by then." I turned to the customer. "This is the owner of N-V. Give her the scoop, Rafe."

He smiled at June. "Midnight show is in the works. Check our Web site for ticket info. News really soon."

"Is it a costume party? Halloween night at N-V?" June looked Rafe over and clearly liked what she saw.

"Yes, there will be a contest too. Big prizes. Buy one here. This shop has the best costumes in town." He glanced at his watch. "I hate to break this up, Glory, but I need to get over there. Nate is meeting me."

"Don't you think I could just stay here?" I watched June rush over to the costume rack. She glanced back at Rafe then grabbed a naughty pirate girl outfit. I could tell from here that it was going to be too small, though maybe that was the look she was going for—too tight and skimpy.

"No, I promised Blade I'd stick close. Come with me. It should be worth it just to watch what happens when Sienna drags Aggie in there to sing with Ray and the band." Rafe grinned.

"You are so right." I looked up in time to see Aggie come out in the green dress. I had to admit, it was the right look. I nodded and she squealed and rushed over to hug me.

"Thanks, Glo. I'm wearing it to N-V right now." She handed me the tag. Obviously she'd counted on winning that decision. "Can Megan hold my old clothes behind the counter for me?" She thrust the bundle into my hands.

"Guess so. Good luck tonight. I'll see you later." I watched her scurry to the back room where Sienna and Danny waited.

"She did look good." Rafe hadn't missed the amount of cleavage she was showing.

"On my dime." I walked over to the counter and told Megan what to do with Aggie's clothing. After a brief conference to make sure the shop was in good hands, Rafe and I headed to N-V. Sienna waved us off, still interested in shopping. Now she had Danny to help her with any paparazzi who might show up, and obviously she wanted Ray to have to wait for her. More games. This night had already worn me out and I figured there was more excitement yet to come.

The club was busy of course. I was glad for Rafe's sake. He'd been able to buy out his partner recently and it was all his now. He headed for his office and I trailed along. Sienna and Aggie were supposed to stop by the office before they went up to the practice room. I wanted to go over some guidelines with Danny. The bodyguard claimed to be familiar with vampires, but had never taken on a new one before. I had to be sure he had a handle on how Sienna might react around mortals during these early nights after her transition. Rafe opened his office door and we found Nate and Ray had beat us there.

"Glory, good to see you. Valdez." Ray jumped up from where he'd been lounging in Rafe's desk chair and managed to catch me in a hug. I turned my face when he tried to kiss me.

"Not happening, Ray." I pushed him away. "Hi, Nate. How's it going?"

"All right, I guess. Ray's been telling me about what happened with Sienna. I'm sorry about that." Nate stood next to the desk and came close to hug me.

I was happy to let *him* kiss me on the cheek. Nathan Burke had been nothing but understanding since he'd found out about his best friend's "condition." If you could call being turned vampire a condition. Anyway, Nate was a brilliant manager and had helped out with the logistics of keeping Ray's career on track when everything had to be done at night. He'd also served as a mortal blood donor in an emergency. Now we were asking him to help Sienna with her career too. Was it too much?

"He's going to do it. As a favor to me." Ray stayed next to me. "Come on, Glory. You know it was an accident. Are you ever going to forgive me?"

"Give me some time, Ray. I have Sienna living with me, a constant reminder of your inability to restrain yourself. It's not a good way to forgive and forget." I pushed past him and settled into a chair. "Sienna's going to ask you to do her a favor tonight. Granting it might help my attitude toward you."

"What is it?" Ray sat in the chair next to me. We both ignored Rafe and Nathan, who had started going through some paperwork. Probably those contracts for the extra performance. I hoped the bombshell I was about to drop wouldn't affect Rafe's big Halloween special.

"You know who else I have crammed into my tiny apartment?" I spotted a fridge in the corner of Rafe's office and jumped up to check it out. Hah! Rafe had put a couple of bottles of my favorite synthetic blood in there. I glanced at Ray and he nodded so I handed him one.

"Penny's not back in town, is she?" Ray twisted off the cap and took a swallow.

"No, she'll be here for Christmas. Guess again." I opened my own drink. "Forget guessing. It's Aggie. I'm stuck with our favorite Siren."

"How'd you get so lucky?" Ray put his hand on my knee. "Kick her out. You don't need to be puttin' up with her shit."

I gave him a brief rundown of Aggie's problem with Ian. "I'm trying to get her out of there and tonight's the first step. She's been working off her debt but it will take years. Now she's got a chance to make some real money. Singing. It will make that debt disappear a lot faster." I took a drink.

"She does have a great voice. Good looks too." Ray smiled. "Pity the people who have to deal with her though."

"She can behave if she knows it will get her what she wants, Ray." I let his hand stay where it was, even though he had started rubbing my leg, his hand slipping under the edge of my dress. I'd worn a blue one, a gift from my mother, and he was eyeing the low neckline. I'd put it on for Jerry. Rafe glanced over his shoulder at the two of us and frowned.

"Ray, Glory's with Blade now." Rafe just had to say it.

"Bet that makes your tail droop, Valdez." Ray grinned. "I'm having a nice talk with our gal. Tend to your papers. Nate, I want a bonus if we go to standing room only on the extra show."

"Asshole," Rafe muttered then went back to the negotiations. Nate laughed and made a note on the papers. "Got it, bud."

"Ray, Sienna's bringing Aggie with her to the club."

"No shit. Why?" He set his bottle on the floor. "Are those two actually hitting it off? Has Sin lost her mind?"

"It's possible, Ray. You ruined her life when you made her vampire against her will. Or at least that's her take on it. Remember what that's like? How waking up vampire can mess you up?" I took a swallow of my drink. "She's lost, grasping at anything that makes her feel in control. She and Aggie sang together and liked the sound. Now Sienna's got an idea—"

"Don't tell me—" He jumped to his feet, knocking over the half-empty bottle of synthetic. The red liquid spread across the hardwood floor. Rafe cursed and grabbed a wad of paper towels from the bathroom next to his office.

"Meet your new backup singer, Ray." Sienna swept in through the door Rafe had left open.

"Over my dead body." Ray grabbed the empty bottle. Surely he wasn't thinking of using it as a weapon. I turned him to stone before he could make another move.

"That can be arranged." Sienna touched his cheek. For once Aggie showed good sense and didn't say a word. "Oh, Glory. Can you show me this trick? I kind of like Ray when he can't shoot off his mouth." She made it worse by punching him in the stomach.

"Hey. Stop it!" I glanced at Ray. Of course he couldn't even wince, still a statue. Sienna ignored me. She was in Ray's face, stabbing a black-painted fingernail into his chest.

"You have no idea how much I hate you. If I say Aggie sings with us, she sings." She poked him twice for emphasis. "Hell, if I want her to headline, she'll be front and center." Poke. "You *owe* me, Ray. And don't you forget it." One more poke then she kneed him, right in his family jewels.

"Oh, my God!" I couldn't stand it. I froze Sienna and let Ray go. I had to stop using this power whenever it was convenient. Not only was it unfair, but look what it had done. Ray dropped like a rock, moaning and holding himself as he went to the fetal position.

"Son of a bitch!" he gasped. "I don't know who to blame here. Sienna, damn it!" His fangs were down and I stepped back when he glared at me. "Glory, don't you ever, I mean *ever* do that to me again." Ray closed his eyes, his knees tucked against his chest as he cursed.

"I'm sorry, Ray. I had no idea . . ." I glanced at Rafe. He just shook his head. He and Nate looked pained, obviously members of the "guy" club and full of sympathy for Ray, who still couldn't stand.

I jumped in front of Sienna and poked *her*. "Listen to me, Sienna. What you just did was wrong on so many levels. I know you're mad at Ray, but to hit him when he can't defend himself is unfair." I stopped. Hadn't he drained her blood when she'd been unconscious? I stepped over to Ray and nudged him with my foot. "Get up."

"Man, that was fast. Sympathy gone already?" He used the chair next to him to get to his feet, though it wasn't without a moan. "What now?"

"She's right. If she wants Aggie to sing with you guys, then you have to let her." I looked toward the door, trying to communicate to the former Siren that now would be a good time to try a little humility. She actually did look embarrassed, her cheeks pink and her eyes down, like maybe she wasn't going to be her usual *I'm all that* Aggie.

"Give her a chance, Ray. Listen to her sing with Sienna. They sounded really good together at my place." I touched Sienna, hoping she'd heard me and would come out of her freeze with the right attitude.

"Jeez, but I hate that statue thing you do, Glory. Not that I don't want to learn it." Sienna brushed at her hair, sneezed and shivered.

"I can't teach it to you. It's an inherited skill. From Olympus." I was really glad few people had it. All eyes were on me and several people in the room would have turned me to stone in a heartbeat and left me there to stew for a good long while if given the chance. "Sorry." I gave them all a repentant look. No one was buying it.

"I get it. If I had it, I'd use it too. Especially around here." Sienna wheeled on Ray, who still looked ready to throw up. "Hell, I *am* sorry. I won't hit you again, Ray. But I still haven't forgiven you."

"Okay. Fine." Ray frowned at Aggie. "I still haven't forgiven Aggie either. You don't know what she put Glory and me through, Sin. Obviously Glory has the memory of a gnat or she just doesn't give a shit what people do to her. Me? I remember every bit of your torture, Aggie. You'd better sing like a fuckin' angel. That's all I'm sayin'."

"You'll let me do it?" Aggie's face lit up in a grin. "Just wait. I still have my song, Ray, my beautiful Siren's voice. It doesn't work to enchant men anymore, but it's pretty damned good, isn't it, Sin?"

"I'll say." Sienna walked over to lean against Rafe's desk. "Nate, did Ray tell you my management problem?" She wasn't smiling. "I had to call Ethan this evening and tell him I was thinking about making a change." Tears filled her eyes. "You have no idea how hard that was. The man's stuck with me through two stints in rehab. And"—she gulped—"he was so nice on the phone. Just said he'd be happy to help whoever I chose to replace him." Big sniffle. "He's such a classy guy."

"I'm sorry, Sienna." Nate put a hand on her shoulder. "Yes, Ray told me everything. I know Ethan. You're right. He's top-drawer. I'll give him a call. No need to fire him. We'll work to-gether. Coordinate. I can't take on your full load anyway. Ethan can handle most of your business and all I'll need to cover is your scheduling. Since Ray went vamp, I've gotten pretty good at figuring out how to make everything happen after dark." He smiled at Sienna. "No one will ever suspect a vampire is on their books. Not even Ethan. Leave it to me."

"Thanks, Nate. That's seriously a huge relief." Sienna headed over to the door where she linked arms with Aggie. "Now let's get upstairs and show Ray how you'll fit in with the band, Ag. Prepare to be amazed, Israel."

"Huh." Ray rolled his eyes. "Glory, come with us. I need moral support."

It was my turn to roll my eyes. "No thanks. I have my own problems to deal with. You guys go ahead." I sat back down and pulled out my phone. I needed some ingredients and had an idea where I might be able to find them. I opened my voodoo book then hit speed dial, ignoring Ray's grumbling as he left the room.

Maybe this wasn't the best idea in the world, but I was des-perate. If Mel still wanted Jerry, I had to do something to kill her interest and the potion was my best bet. If I had to deal with the devil to make that happen, so be it.

Ten

When the man answered, I got right down to business. "Hey, Ian, do you have any, um, *Periplaneta americana*? I need some. Two to be exact. Crushed. Though I guess whole ones would work and I could pound them out myself."

He laughed. I mean, big guffaws. I could picture him wiping away tears he was so overcome.

"Hey, what's so funny? Is it something gross? Tell me. Do you have it or not? I'm making a potion and that's an ingredient."

"Glory, Glory, Glory. Yes, I'm sure I could scrounge up a couple. And I'd love to watch you crush them. Need anything else?" He was still chuckling. Obviously there was a joke here I was missing.

"Yes, it's a long list."

"Then come on over." He started laughing again. "I can't wait to see what else goes into this, um, potion. What does it do? Or dare I ask?"

"Stop it. Obviously I pronounced it wrong or it's the name

of an extinct dinosaur." I had to wait while he went into another fit of hysterics at my expense. Honestly, for a usually dour Scot, Ian was being downright out of control.

"Sorry. Coming or not?" He finally settled down.

"Yes. But not tonight. I guess I should say thanks for offering despite finding me hilarious. It's late and my bodyguard has too much going on. Tomorrow night. I'll tell you more then." I saw Rafe smile with relief and go back to his papers. Nate had taken off for upstairs, muttering about signatures. Apparently their deal had been hammered out.

"Bodyguard? What kind of trouble are you in now?" Ian dropped the teasing.

"Voodoo trouble. That's why I need to make this potion. I've got a book here that has a recipe to help me get rid of someone. You ever had a run-in with voodoo?" I settled back. It would be a bonus if Ian had some experience.

"You don't want to mess with that stuff, Glory. You need to get rid of someone, tear out his or her throat. If it's a mortal, it would be for your dining pleasure."

"First, yuck. I don't kill mortals. Second, I want her to leave us alone, not die." Honestly, Ian had no conscience whatsoever.

"Fine. But forget voodoo and let me call my sorcerer again. Of course you know that comes with a price." Ian had his groove back now, definitely figuring out an agenda. "We can work together. I told you I was interested in getting to know you better. Your powers fascinate me. Especially your Olympus connection. Perhaps in exchange for my help, you'd spend some quality time with me. Just the two of us."

I heard it in his voice. Unbelievable. Ian had seduction on his mind. Apparently my goddess parentage suddenly made me desirable. I bit back the names I really wanted to call him and took a breath.

"Ian, I'm with Blade. Period. I'm not about to get cozy with a MacDonald, feud or no feud." The Campbells—Jerry's Scottish clan—and MacDonalds had called a truce but Ian's history didn't inspire trust. Too bad he was the go-to guy in Austin for all things science related when you were dealing with the weird and wacky in our world.

"Glory, you wound me. Shutting me down before you've given me a chance? Aggie always swore I was the best lover she had ever had. High praise coming from a Siren with a cast of thousands for comparison. Ask her. I'm sure she's still there sponging off of you."

"Aggie isn't singing your praises about anything, Ian. Scrubbing a man's toilet kills the love every time."

"From the looks of things around here, I doubt she's done much scrubbing. But she's been busy. I'd like to know what the hell she's done to my bed linens. They feel like cardboard, no, make that sandpaper. I think I'm developing a rash too."

It was my turn to laugh. "You're whining, Ian. Surely you didn't expect a pampered Siren to be good at housework, did you?"

"Not really. I just wanted her to suffer. Is she suffering, Glory?" His whine had disappeared. He was back to Ian as usual.

"We both are. Now about this voodoo. I *am* messing with it. The person I need to get rid of is making my life miserable. Jerry's too. I know you're already working with Bart. So will you help me too? I'll pay you for whatever ingredients you can find for me. That'll have to be the deal."

"I don't think you can afford my rates, Glory. Here's my usual fee for consulting work." Ian quoted a figure and I gasped. "Thought not. But we'll work out something. I'll see you tomorrow night. Be sure to bring the book. Voodoo. I suppose this could be interesting. But I hope you aren't getting in over your head."

"Yeah, well, so do I." I realized I hadn't sounded grateful when he was actually doing me a favor. Too bad there were always strings attached when dealing with Ian. "Thanks, Ian. Seriously. But don't expect anything more from me than a business relationship. I'll see you tomorrow night." I ended the call. Memo to Glory: Ian was a hard man and could be an even harder enemy. I needed him but I also needed to watch my back when I was around him.

"You're going to see Ian tomorrow night?" Rafe pulled me up out of my chair.

"You heard. Yes. Guess you're going to insist on being there too." I slipped the book back into my tote.

"Wouldn't miss it. Now let's head upstairs. We don't want to miss Aggie's audition either, do we?" Rafe aimed me toward the door.

"No way." I left the book and my purse in his office, which he locked, then followed him to the practice room. Even before we got to the room, which was supposed to be soundproof, we could hear the arguing. I should have known getting rid of Aggie wouldn't be that easy.

"You want me to be quieter?" Aggie's voice could probably be heard blocks away. "Maybe I should turn off the mic, or, hey, lip-sync. I could just stand back here and be stage decoration."

Rafe and I slipped inside. Ray, Sienna and Aggie were standing close to the band. Those guys saw me and waved, but their attention stayed on the argument going on beside the makeshift stage.

"Yeah, do that. 'Cause the way you're blasting away back

there, you obviously think *you're* the headliner." Ray examined her through narrowed eyes. "You may have the pipes and you're not bad window dressing, but you're disposable, Aggie. Quit stepping over my vocals. Sienna, back me up here."

"I hate to admit it, but Ray's right. Tone it down, Aggie. Are you looking at the music? You aren't supposed to sing along with us. Instead just drop in at the chorus and hit the harmonies where it says to."

"Screw it. I don't need this. I'll just go on down the street. There are half a dozen clubs where I'm sure I can talk my way into a gig." Aggie stomped away from them and shoved past Rafe, headed for the hall. I stopped her before she could escape.

"Quitting already?" I wouldn't budge, even though she slapped at my hand on her arm.

"This isn't going to work." She had tears in her eyes.

"She's right. Let her go." Ray was gleeful. "I gave her a chance and she blew it."

Sienna ran over to wave sheet music in front of Aggie. "Just look at the music, girlfriend. It tells you when to go high, low, loud, soft. Easy as pie."

Aggie shook her head. "Pie? I'd give my left tit for a piece of pie right now." She leaned her head on my shoulder and I was too stunned to do more than allow it. "Help me, Glory. I can't read music."

We all just stared at her. How was that for a news flash?

"Quit looking at me!" She jerked away. "Why would I have to learn? I can hear a tune once and pick it up. That's a good skill, isn't it?"

"Sure, Ag, it's amazing." Sienna touched Aggie's shoulder. "But it makes things tough here. There are marks on the page that indicate where you come in, when you should just hum, that kind of thing." She glanced at Ray. He wasn't looking sympathetic. "I'm sure we can walk you through it, if you've got such a great memory. That should—"

"You can't be serious." Ray wasn't in a conciliatory mood. "Aggie is trying to take over the performance. That was clear from the first note out of her mouth." Ray strolled over to my side. "She's a stage hog, Glory. People are paying to see and hear Sin and me, not some unknown." He glared at Aggie.

"Did you like her voice though?" I was relieved that Aggie had dried her tears and had her head close to Sienna's where they were going over the sheet music. Apparently the rocker was explaining the various marks. Aggie could read words at least. For a moment I'd wondered if she was illiterate. It wouldn't have surprised me. When I'd been dumped out of the Siren system way back when, I hadn't been able to read word one.

"Gloriana, you must introduce me to Israel Caine." We all turned at the sound of *that* voice.

"Mother. What are you doing here?" I wished Sienna's new bodyguard, who'd stepped forward, would bounce her right out of there. Unfortunately, when he heard me call her mother, Danny went back to his post next to the door. Mom had on her version of rocker chic—black leather pants and vest with a blue silk blouse, all of it with high-heeled boots. The result was more rocker stage mom. I smiled and sent her that mental message, earning a frown.

"Why, I came to tell your friend Israel something important since you seem reluctant to do it." My mother held out her hand. "Gloriana's told me so much about you, Mr. Caine. And I know a little about your history with my daughter." She smiled, like she was eager to begin dropping some bombshells. "Steamy."

"Mother!" It seemed like a good time to dematerialize. Of course I couldn't. My mother had a habit of disabling my powers when she was around. "Forget Mr. Caine. You and I could hit the mall, do some shopping." I grabbed her arm, desperate to get her out of there.

"Don't be ridiculous. The mall has been closed for hours." She lifted my hand off of her. "Careful, you're wrinkling my silk. Now where was I?" She glanced around the room. "Ah, yes. Mr. Caine. May I call you Israel?"

"Make it Ray. What's up?" He moved closer to me. Ray wasn't stupid and he could tell I was worried and embarrassed. Rafe had my other side. It didn't make me feel better. My mother had way too many powers for any intelligent person to relax around her.

"Ray, then." Mother was practically purring. "Did you know that I restored Gloriana's beautiful singing voice not long ago? Once I heard it had been taken from her, I had to right such a grievous wrong." She threw out her arms, like she was bestowing blessings on all of us. I almost expected twinkling stars and fairy dust.

"No kidding!" Ray's eyes lit up. "Glory? Is that true?"

"Mother, please. You sound like an actor in a bad superhero movie." I glanced meaningfully at the group of humans on the bandstand. "Yes, it's true." I gasped when Ray grabbed me, almost knocking me down.

"That's incredible!" He kissed my cheek then grinned at my mother. "You *are* a superhero."

"Mother." I nodded toward the band again. The guys had started to stare at us.

"One moment. I can take care of that." She flicked her wrist. "Now they can't hear a thing we say." Her smile was wicked. "Superhero. Yes, I can live with that. Thank you." She focused on Ray. "You attract such handsome men, darling. Well done."

"Mother, what's the point of this little visit?" I realized we were now in a virtual cocoon. The band couldn't hear us and we couldn't hear the band, which had settled down and started playing something on the other side of my mother's invisible wall. Even Nate, who'd been sitting at a table against one wall with his laptop, had gone back to work, apparently lulled by whatever spell my mother had cast.

"Gloriana. Absolutely glorious. I named her so aptly, don't you think?" She gave Rafe and Ray measuring looks before smiling at me. I was wrinkling her silk again, trying to drag her out of the room. "Patience, darling. I have this situation well thought out."

"When were you going to tell me, Glory? This is tremendous news." Ray held me close.

"I've been busy, Ray. With Sienna, Aggie, a lot of things." I dredged up a smile for him. "Sorry."

"You know how that ate at me. Your loss. I couldn't stand the fact that the Storm God . . ." He shoved back and looked over his shoulder, then seemed reassured that the band still wasn't paying attention to us and that they were making music we couldn't hear. Ray shook his head, obviously amazed that my mother could arrange such a thing. "Well, I hated what he'd taken from you. You know that."

"I do know it, Ray." I laid my hand on his cheek, the dark stubble covering it only making him more beautiful. No matter what Ray had done, I knew his love of music trumped almost everything else in his life. The loss of my song had hurt his artist's soul. "Yes, she gave me back my voice. I can sing again and not hurt your ears."

"That's fantastic, Glory." Rafe dragged me into his arms this time. His hug was fierce. "I want to hear it."

"Yes! You should all hear her." Mother was levitating she was so excited. I jerked her back to the floor.

"Calm down," I hissed.

"But it's so exciting." She focused on the men. I had a feeling it was a habit with her. "Unfortunately Gloriana doesn't have her Siren power anymore. So men won't fall at her feet." She winked. "Unless they just love her for herself, of course."

"And who doesn't?" Ray dragged me toward the band at the other end of the large room. Mother's invisible wall suddenly disappeared. "Come on, babe. I know you've got every song I've ever recorded memorized. I've even heard you mangle a few when we were pretending to be engaged and shared a hotel room." He shook his head. "You remember, Valdez. She sounded like a stomped chicken when she sang in the shower."

"No lie." Rafe was right with us. "Sing for us, Glory. I can't wait to hear you."

"No, seriously. This is embarrassing." My mother's hand landed on my back. "Mother, stop manipulating me."

"But it's what I do best, darling. Sing for the boys. It's just not right that Aggie"—Mother frowned—"should get to sing with this band and not you. Who deserves it more?"

"The two of us don't compare. Aggie needs the money." I stopped at the foot of the stage.

"And you don't?" Mother took Ray's place by my side when he began conferencing with the band, deciding what I should sing without even asking me what I wanted. "You think I don't know how you feel about your tawdry little apartment? How your friend Florence hurt your feelings when she insisted you take her gifts because she hated to see you wearing used clothes?"

"Mother, I've told you how I feel about you snooping into my thoughts and conversations." My face burned. I was mortified that she would say this in front of Rafe. Sienna and Aggie were close enough to hear her too.

"But you don't deny it." Mother glanced at the others. "If you're embarrassed, it's your own fault. It's high time you came into your own, Gloriana. If you won't come to Olympus and claim the fortune owed you, then perhaps you'll start showing off some of your other talents. Earn your own fortune here." Mother shoved me up onto the stage where Ray handed me a microphone. "You could be a star, darling. Bigger than that Sienna girl."

"Hey! I heard that." Sienna had Aggie next to her. "Let's hear what you've got, Glory. We don't have to compete, you know. You mentor me for"—she glanced at the band—"you know. So maybe I can mentor you in the music biz. Even steven."

"I, uh, I never thought . . ." My throat went dry and I caught Rafe staring at me. I'd known him for years. Sung show tunes to him when we'd driven to Texas from Las Vegas in my aging Suburban. He grinned, remembering how he'd been in his dog form then, howling to drown me out. That relaxed me a little. I could actually sing decently now and wouldn't he be blown away? He nodded, like he was eager to hear me show off. That was my friend, always in my corner.

My mother stood beside him, beaming. I wasn't about to catch her eye again or she'd toss one of her spells at me so I'd sing, ready or not.

Ray sat at the piano. "Okay, babe, you know this one. Come in when you're ready." He started playing, the tune one I knew instantly. The band joined in.

This was one of my favorites from Ray's first album. It was a love song and I closed my eyes. Jerry. I hoped he was okay and coming home soon. I kept my love for him in mind when I opened my eyes, focused somewhere on the wall above everyone and started to sing.

When the song ended there was complete silence. I felt my face get hot and quickly handed Ray the mic. So much for my "glorious" voice. Then everyone started talking at once.

"Damn, girl, that was awesome. I never knew you had it in you." Ray passed off the microphone and grabbed me around the waist to swing me in a circle. "Your mom's right. A star is born."

"No, Ray. You're not thinking straight." I wiggled my way down to my feet, sure he was exaggerating.

"He's right for once, Glory. Your voice is amazing. If I hadn't heard it, I'd never have believed it." Rafe helped me off the stage. "You should do something with it."

"It's different, nice and low. I'm so glad you weren't shrill." Sienna exchanged looks with Ray. "You wouldn't believe some of the wannabes who've pushed their way in front of us with voices that could crack glass."

"No lie. Can't see her rocking out though." Ray moved closer to Sienna. "What do you think, Sin?"

"True. I think we *could* do something cool with her though. Go retro." Sienna grabbed my arm. "I'm thinking ballads, Glory. Standards. The kind of thing Bublé does or maybe Adele. You sound like a combo of Amy Winehouse and Peggy Lee. What if you deck yourself out in fifties clothes? Do the whole look, along with the songs?" Sienna was on a roll. "Can *you* read music?"

"Yes, sure. I've picked up a few skills along the way." I thought about the guitar I had shoved way back in the corner of my closet.

"That settles it. I could arrange some tunes for her. She can do covers, then original material with that same sound." Ray unzipped a backpack and pulled out a sheaf of paper. "I wonder if I brought anything like that along . . ."

"Good idea, Ray. And I've always wanted to dig deeper into producing. I can see how this could go down. We'd do a little showcase on Halloween night. Put Glory up for a number or two to open for us."

I just stood there in a daze. Obviously the two pros had this all figured out.

"Hey, what about me? Where's *my* showcase?" Aggie wore a pout. "I have the same kind of voice."

"True enough. But you don't have the heart Glory has when you sing. Sound's there but nobody's home if you know what I mean." Sienna stared at Aggie's blank look. "Guess not. Sorry, Ag." She patted Aggie's hand. "Work on learning that material we gave you. Right now your best bet is backing up Ray and me. Maybe someday you'll have a chance to do a single."

"This sucks." Aggie stomped over to the door. "I'm out of here."

I started to follow her but my mother was still in the room, her eyes on Ray. What did she have up her sleeve, which was now part of a cute tie-dyed tee? Oh, God, had any of the mortal band members noticed her magic? She nodded to acknowledge my thoughts then waved her arm at them, probably to erase their memories of what she'd been wearing before. I felt a headache coming on while Sienna kept chattering about Ray's musical arrangements and finding someone to play the piano.

"I'll do it. Play for her." Ray slipped an arm around me. "Are you listening to this, Glory girl? Can you see it? Spotlight on you, you're sitting on my piano in one of your vintage thingies. It's a costume party anyway. 'Cause of Halloween. What do you think?"

"I, I don't know." This was moving too fast.

"Sure you do." Ray kissed my cheek. "I can pick up one of those fifties suits in your shop, match the look. We can meet and go over some musical numbers. Can you stand to work with me, Sin? For Glory?" He knew better than to lay on the charm. Ray was being all business.

"Seems like I can." Sienna grinned at me. "This is your shot, Glory. Come on. Say you'll do it."

"Gloriana, snap out of it." Mother pinched my arm.

"Ow." I guess I'd spaced, more than a little overwhelmed.

"Answer him. How do you feel about making your singing debut on Halloween night?" My mother linked her arm with mine. "I'm sure your friend Rafael will pay you. And, Nathan, is it? Can you write up a contract with advantageous terms for my daughter?" Mother had obviously been busy, introducing herself to Nate, who'd been out of the loop until I started singing. Now he hurried forward.

"Yes, sure. Glory, are you in? I have to know. Rafe, what do you say? It would certainly make for a full evening. Guarantee a big draw for that new midnight show. Glory, I'll just put you down for the one appearance, at midnight. Opening act. What do you say?" Nate pulled a legal pad out of his briefcase, ready to take notes, as if he could whip out a contract on the spot. He probably could.

"This is moving too fast." The room started to spin around me. What had I gotten into?

"Darling, take your opportunities when they appear." My mother wasn't taking no for an answer. "Of course she'll do it. Halloween. I think it's an auspicious night for a debut. Full moon if I'm not mistaken. I'll have to consult my astrologer." She smiled. "Gloriana, answer the man."

My mother had an astrologer? Oh, what the hell. I had wanted to redo my apartment. Own the world. Whatever. If singing on Halloween would help me move forward, then why not? It was one night, one performance. If I bombed, no biggie. And if I didn't . . . ?

I felt a flutter of excitement. No, not getting my hopes up. Instead, I realized I was getting way too overscheduled. Rehearsals, potion making, seminar on how to own the world, reunion with Jerry, running my shop . . . I dropped down to the edge of the stage, my head between my knees before I threw up on my mother's shiny black boots.

"Glory?" Rafe rubbed my back.

"Offer her your vein, Nate." Ray didn't care who heard him.

"Give her air." Sienna was too new to know that didn't matter.

"Everyone stand back." My mother took charge. "Gloriana, look at me."

I raised my head, her face swimming into focus. Her hand felt cool under my chin, her voice clear inside my head.

"Don't do anything you don't want to. I'm sorry if I'm bullying you." She sighed and kissed my forehead.

A calm came over me, my stomach settled, and I took her hand. She pulled me to my feet. Ridiculous to fall apart like that. This was the chance of a lifetime. Two famous rock stars were going to let me be their opening act? I'd have to be crazy to turn that down. I grinned and actually hugged my mother.

"I'll do it."

That started a chatterfest. Ray and Sienna argued about which songs I should do. Rafe and Nate headed over to the table and his laptop to discuss my compensation. My mother began an excited conversation about what I should wear. Then

I glanced at the doorway. Aggie was back. She stared at me, her mouth a straight line that made it clear I'd made a bitter enemy tonight. Was there any way to fix that?

"Aggie?" I gestured for her to come over. My mother wasn't happy with it and tried to get between us when Aggie marched over.

"I'm not stupid. I know I need to take this gig. It pays well. Nathan showed me what I could earn. I'll sing in a whisper if it'll get me away from Ian's house." She smiled at one of the band members. "Hey, Jake. While all these other people are busy, would you run through that last number with me?" She shoved past me, headed for the lead guitar player.

"Good." I needn't have bothered saying a word. Aggie had zeroed in on the newly single man who was straight, liked her cleavage and certainly could be in the market for her kind of action.

"Watch her. She isn't going to be satisfied until she has that spotlight on her." My mother dragged me toward the door. "I know her type well. Olympus is full of them. Jealous, vindictive. Next thing you know, you'll find a viper in your bed."

"No, that would be courtesy of a certain voodoo woman. If you want to interfere in my life, how about taking a run at that situation?" I stopped her in the hall. I knew Rafe would be mad if I went any further. He was taking his bodyguard role seriously and I had orders to stay close.

"No need. You handled it beautifully. You can't know how happy it made me to hear you say you were through with that Scot. Now if only you'd meant it." She frowned. "Give up this potion nonsense. I imagine your man"—she shuddered—"can take care of himself. He did go off somewhere with that intention."

"Oh, I give up." I turned to go back inside. I needed to have input if I was actually going to sing on Halloween. Obviously my mother and I were never going to agree about Jerry. "Since you're so big on snooping into my business, can you at least tell me if he's all right? If he's made it to Florida yet?"

"Gloriana, you are too funny. Why would I care where that man is? It's you I follow closely. The woman seems satisfied that you are out of the Scot's picture. That's good enough for me." Mother studied my dress. "Mall shopping. I would like that but fear they wouldn't have anything up to my standards. We should go to New York, Paris, no, Rome!" Her eyes lit up. "The spring showings are next week. What fun to take my daughter there and pick out next season's wardrobe."

"Not happening, Mother. I just committed to sing next weekend. Remember? And I'll have to wear a fifties outfit. Maybe a cute shirtwaist, cocktail dress or a poodle skirt. See what you can find and put it in my closet." I touched her shoulder. "Thanks for my voice. I felt good up there. Singing. It was an amazing gift."

"Darling." She materialized a hanky and dabbed at her eyes. "It was the least I could do. I was so proud seeing you onstage. If you'd come to Olympus, I could fix your figure too. Size six or four. Tiny waist and little butt. I know you'd love to wear some skinny jeans like that Sienna girl wears." She leaned closer. "Did you know her real last name is Starkowski?" She waved her hanky. "You will be so much greater than she is as a performer."

"Mother, Sienna and I are friends. She's going to help me. And be satisfied with the relationship you've got with me. I'm talking to you. Maybe after the dust settles we can do a little shopping together. Flo would love to join us. How's that?"

"A girl's night out. Oh, Gloriana." Mother wrapped me in

her arms and I endured it. Then she pushed back, eyeing my hips and shaking her head.

"And forget my body. I'm okay with it. I'm not going to Olympus. Just forget it. Please?" The very idea of the place terrified me. Every hint she threw out made it seem like the penthouse level of hell.

"I'll try." She looked disappointed. "Shopping though. You promised." She tapped her forehead, her brow wrinkling. "Oh, I must go. I hear Zeus calling and when my father wants me, I can't afford to ignore him." She smiled. "Not like you ignore me, you bad girl." Then she got serious. "Darling, I may have misled you just a teeny bit. I didn't actually tell Zeus about you yet. If or when he finds out . . . Well, he may insist you come. I won't be able to fight that. You may have no choice."

"Mother . . ." I tried to grab her. For an explanation. Details. Something. But of course she chose that moment to vanish. Coward.

"What's going on?" Rafe stuck his head into the hall. "Nate and I have a deal worked out. I think you'll like it. Two songs, nice compensation. Ray's jumping around like he's swallowed a grasshopper. Can you come sign this contract on Nate's tablet? If you're still up to doing this thing."

I took a breath. Up to it? "I don't know about Ray, but I think that grasshopper's doing its thing in my stomach. Give me your honest opinion, Rafe. Did I sound okay? Or will I be making a fool of myself?" I leaned against the wall, my knees suddenly Jell-O. My mother must have done a calming spell on me because now that she'd left, I was trembling again.

"Okay? Blondie, you were dynamite." Rafe put his hands on my shoulders. He stared into my eyes. "We've got no reason to lie. You've got the pipes and Sienna's right. The heart. I felt the emotion when you sang the song. Even imagined for a few beats that it was me you were singing for. Then I kicked myself. Of course it was Blade you were picturing in your head. Love song. Am I right?"

I nodded. I hated to hurt him but he knew the truth and it was old news. "Thanks, Rafe. Singing in public. I don't know. It's freaking me out. If you think I'll be okay . . ."

"More than okay, babe. Come inside and look at the songs we're talking about." Ray stepped into the hall. He took in the scene but seemed to realize there was no romantic vibe to it. "You can pick the ones you're most comfortable with. Since you said you can read music, does that mean you can play an instrument?"

"I never tried to sing for my supper, obviously, but played in a few girl bands, back when they were the thing. I can hold my own on the piano, guitar, trumpet in a pinch. But I'm really rusty. It was a long time ago. Back in the fifties actually." I laughed when Ray suddenly hauled me inside.

"Are you shittin' me? You're a *musician*?" Ray couldn't shut his mouth, gaping at me, his hand in mine as he dragged me across the floor to the stage again.

"Hey, don't look so surprised. I've had plenty of time to learn quite a few things, you know. And I love music. Always have. Since I couldn't sing, I had to do something besides just sit around and listen."

He plunked me down on his piano bench. "Show me. Here." He shoved a sheet of music in front of me. "We found some old tunes in the piano bench. Valdez says you like Broadway stuff. It's not what I'd want for the showcase, but good enough for a demo here. Play a little of that." He turned around. "Hey, Sin, come give a listen. You're not going to believe this."

I glanced at the sheet music. It was an old show tune from a Broadway hit, the fifties classic *Brigadoon*. "Almost Like Being in Love" was a song I knew very well. I didn't even have to look at the music. I'd played it often for Jerry when we'd had access to a piano. Anything Scottish did it for him. He had a great voice and he liked to sing to me. I'd been forced to sit and listen, playing his accompanist and adoring fan. What a cool surprise if I could sing it for *him* when he came home. He had a piano in his house that had come furnished. We'd been busy ever since we'd gotten to Austin. Too busy for one of our musical evenings. And wasn't that an interesting thought. I loved Austin but it seemed like I'd had a lot of problems since I'd moved here. Jerry too.

I realized the room had gone completely still when I started playing the opening notes. I did a few flourishes just because I could. Sienna and Ray grinned and high-fived each other. They settled down again when I began to sing.

I imagined how Jerry and I could sing to each other like the two lovers had done in the play I'd seen on Broadway when I'd lived in New York decades ago. I did put my heart into the song. I always had. Music meant as much to me as it did to Ray and I was glad it showed. When I finished, everyone clapped and I ducked my head, embarrassed.

I'd gotten so carried away by the music, I'd almost forgotten there was anyone else in the room. I hoped it would work that way Halloween. It would help me get through the performance in front of a crowd.

Ray laughed, sliding onto the bench next to me to go through a sheaf of other music. He was beside himself with my musical ability, talking a mile a minute about possible tunes. I wanted him to slow down and let me think. I had some ideas and needed to hit the Internet, to look up songs that might work with my own agenda. When I whispered a possible song title, Ray called Sienna over to discuss it with her, picking up his phone to find a demo on YouTube.

I glanced up and saw Aggie's sneer. She was furious. She mouthed, "Show-off." I nodded and smiled, stroking the keys in a little musical taunt. Why not? If you've got it, flaunt it. I should have known better.

Eleven

I woke up the next evening with my schedule buzzing in my brain. I would head to Ian's as soon as possible but I wasn't going to spend much time there. I had to hit my shop and check on inventory and see if I could scrounge up a costume for Halloween in case my mother didn't come through.

I didn't have time to worry about my new vampire and had left her in Danny's capable hands. He knew not to let her be alone with mortals and was strong enough to physically control her if she got a bad case of bloodlust. Still, I did need to check in on her. Of course I'd see her at rehearsals. Another piece of my double-stuffed night.

I rolled out of my comfy bed and smelled coffee. Yes, Valdez was in the apartment and making his own meal. We needed to talk. Sure, she had some creepy creatures around her, but if Mel had bought the breakup story, then I could hope she would back off with the threats. At the very least, with her reputation to think about, the woman wouldn't come at me with an audience. I could see the headlines: "Life coach melts down with own life in chaos." Talk about bad for business. Maybe Rafe didn't need to be around me as much as he thought he did. I slipped on a robe and walked into the living room. I wasn't prepared for the scene I interrupted.

Lacy and Valdez were stretched out on the couch and in each other's arms. Naked. Okay. I knew they were a couple but I really, really didn't want to see them making it. I turned on my heels and jogged back into the bedroom. Seriously, where were my bodyguard's shifter senses that he hadn't heard me wake up and come in? I could have been staked in my sleep. Voodooed to hell and gone and he'd never have noticed. I slammed the bedroom door.

"Glory?" Rafe tapped on the door a minute later.

"I'm busy." I got out my laptop. "I have some research to do. Go on about your own business. Pretend I'm not here. That's what you were doing anyway."

"Shit. I'm sorry." He opened the door. He'd pulled on a pair of jeans.

I didn't want to see his bare chest, but it was way too fine to ignore. Lacy had been all over it. At least they hadn't been in cat form. The thought made me want to puke.

"Don't be sorry. You have a life. I'm glad. Tell Lacy I'm okay with it. Go on, take care of your lady." I opened the laptop and turned it on, pulling a pillow under it for a cushion. I leaned back against the padded headboard. Nice. Maybe I'd get one similar to it. Very comfortable. If I came into some extra money, I could redecorate. This bedroom was feminine in lavender and cream. Lily must have picked out everything. I typed in my password.

"Glory, look at me." Rafe moved to the side of the bed.

"Lacy's gone. She didn't like the way I threw her across the room when I realized you saw us together."

"Gee, Rafe. That was a little extreme. Is she all right?" I looked again. How could I not? The way those jeans dipped low, the zipper not quite done up? Oh, God, but I remembered how we'd been together . . . Shifter blood is so hot. And Rafe made love so fiercely. I dragged my eyes away when I saw heat flare in his eyes.

"She's a cat. She landed on her feet." He moved around the foot of the bed. "We'll be fine. She just needs time to cool off."

"Send her flowers." I relaxed, glad I hadn't ruined things for him.

"Lacy's not into flowers. If I can get hold of some bluefin tuna, she'll forget all about that interruption." He sat beside me on the bed, making the computer slide off my lap. "You okay? I was supposed to be guarding you. Won't happen again."

"No, *I'm* sorry." I bumped my shoulder against his arm. "This bodyguard thing has put a crimp in your social life. You and I have been done for a while now. I'm glad you have someone. Lacy's nice." His hand was dark against the white sheets. I itched to pick it up. To prove I could and it wouldn't mean anything? That would be plain stupid.

"Yes, she is. I was lucky to find her. Can't say it's going anywhere long term but we're having fun." He grinned, like he was remembering that fun. Then he got serious again. "You know Blade showed me how much he loves you by swallowing his pride and feelings about us and asking me to take care of you. For the first time, I can see you two together and understand why you stick by him."

"Good. You're my best friend, Rafe. I want you two to get along."

"I'll try. But when he starts ordering me around, you know I don't take it well." He kissed the top of my head. "You and I had better get going. I'm showering while you do your research. Then I guess we hit Ian's first. Right?"

"Right." I leaned back. Rafe showering. I watched him stride to the bathroom. The bad boy dropped his jeans and kicked them away just before he hit the door. Reminding me of what I'd given up? Of course.

I sighed and fell back on the bed. Lucky Lacy. If she played her cards right, she could have Rafe forever. The girl wasn't getting any younger and her mother had been dropping by the shop regularly lately, reminding her of that fact. Not that Mom-Cat wanted her daughter hooked up with a shifter. No, she had eligible were-cat males lined up. Lacy's affair with Rafe was probably her way of sticking it to her mother. I could relate to that.

I got comfy with the computer again. Music. I was very familiar with what Ray and Sienna considered retro. I'd lived with that music. The fifties had been a fun time. I could go back a lot further but knew the rockers would be confused by it. It didn't take long for me to pick out two songs that I hoped would be crowd-pleasers on a Saturday night. I sent the links to Ray and Sin then got up and dressed, glad I'd showered the night before. By the time Rafe was ready, I was good to go, the voodoo book and my laptop in my tote again.

The ride out to Ian's was fairly quiet after we made a stop at a twenty-four-hour copy center near the University of Texas. I wasn't about to just hand over a voodoo book to Ian MacDonald. Jerry's distrust of the man and my own experiences with him made me more than reluctant to do that. I told Rafe Ian had tried to talk me out of messing with voodoo.

"He's right, Glory. I can turn around right now. Even that

book gives me the creeps." Rafe was driving his SUV. It was one of those big black powerful cars that men liked. We could probably go off road if we had to. Rafe would enjoy that.

"I want Mel to stay away from Jerry. If this potion will do the trick, then I have to try it." I'd called Sienna before we'd left and she'd told me Aggie was with her, bragging that she hadn't bothered to go to work. I wondered what Ian would say about that. I didn't have long to wonder.

Ian greeted us at the door. "Your Siren sister didn't show up today, according to my guards. Know anything about that?"

"She's not my sister. And I'm not Aggie's keeper either. I don't know what she did today." I walked in, Rafe close behind me.

"Do I have to call the vampire council and tell them she's in breach of our contract?" Ian closed the door. "They can throw her in the clink."

"The coffin, you mean." I set my tote on Ian's massive glass coffee table. "She probably didn't show because she's starting a new job that pays enough to get you off her back. Guess she decided to quit here and send you a check every week. She should have notified you though."

"That's not how our agreement works." Ian stalked over to his bar and poured a drink. It was a synthetic blood with alcohol. "Want one?" He ignored Rafe. He had always treated my bodyguard like a piece of furniture, and nothing had changed.

"Sure. Why not? Rafe? I'm sure Ian has something without blood." I was determined to nip this elitist attitude in the bud.

"Scotch if you have it." Rafe grinned, happy to goad Ian into treating him as a guest.

"Why the hell not?" Ian pulled out a bottle of good Scot's whiskey. "Seems the servants are determined to take over these days."

"Pour us all some of that, Ian. I learned in Scotland that vamps can drink it straight. As long as we don't get carried away. You're working with Bart O'Connor. He told me you two hit it off. He's done experiments to prove a little can't hurt us." I smiled, happy to teach Ian something for a change.

"Yes. Sharp guy. He didn't mention this. Good to know." Ian filled three glasses, bringing one of them to me. "Down the hatch." He clinked his glass against mine. Apparently Rafe was supposed to pick up his own from the bar. He didn't hesitate.

"Cheers." Rafe sipped. "Excellent."

"Yes, it's from my family's distillery. I just didn't think I could enjoy it again. Thanks, Gloriana." Ian took a drink, a look of satisfaction on his handsome face. "Well, now. I guess I owe you some help with this potion. Show me that book."

"You can look at it from there but I'm not about to give it to you. I've copied the page you'll need. You won't believe all the ingredients in this potion. Really weird ones too. I started a search on the Internet but finally gave up. They aren't things you'll find in a supermarket." I pulled the book out of my tote and held it up. "The recipe we need was marked with a slip of paper." I handed him the copy.

"This is ridiculous. Let me see the book, Gloriana. What do you think I'll do? Steal it?" Ian snatched the copy but stayed close.

"I don't know, Ian. Wouldn't put it past you." I stuffed the book back in my tote. "If you aren't up to this, say so. I heard there are a few Energy Vampires setting up shop out at the old site. Maybe I can connect with them."

Ian frowned and glanced at the recipe in his hand. "No, you don't want them to get hold of something like this. You'd never see it again." He sat in a leather chair and gestured for us to sit. "I'll play by your silly rules. I have to admit you intrigued me

with your phone call and here it is. *Periplaneta americana*."
He grinned and looked up at me. "Hate to burst your bubble,
Gloriana, but that's the common cockroach. You probably
have one or two on hand yourself."

"No! Gross." I leaned forward. "I should have looked that
up. I'd had such a hard time with the other stuff that I quit
before I got to that. Anything else common there?"

"Well, Old Man's Beard is commonly referred to as tree
moss. That's easy enough to find around here." Ian gestured
to the French doors that led to his deck. It had a view of the
lake and the woods surrounding it. "And I'd assume Mother
Nature's Tears to be rainwater."

"Can't believe I didn't put that together." I felt like smack-
ing my forehead. "But Ian, there are some exotic insects there
too. I did find those on the Net."

"Yes, I see. I'll have to check with my suppliers. I can have
the bugs here tomorrow night if they are in stock." He stood.
"Come to my lab and let me see if I have everything else. You
sure this keeps people away? It could be quite handy. Like a
bug zapper for people." He looked distracted as he strode
down the hall.

"Only without frying them." I hurried after him.

Rafe wasn't letting me out of his sight. "Be careful, Glory.
Remember what this guy has done in the past." He nodded to
a guard stationed next to the lab door.

"I know. He's out for himself. Always. But if you've got
something he wants, you're golden. Right now, he's interested
in me because I have Olympian powers." I smiled at Rafe before
I followed Ian. "Don't worry, I'm always alert around him."

"Son of a bitch!"

Rafe and I glanced at each other then ran into the lab.

"Sir? Has there been an intrusion?" The guard shouldered

us aside, his gun out while he did a sweep of the room. He hurried to Ian's side.

"You told me no one had been here today." Ian's face was flushed. Obviously the fact that he was holding two broken beakers in his bleeding hands had done that. The smell of his blood dripping to the floor brought my fangs down and probably flushed my face too.

"What happened, Ian?" I fought my fangs back where they belonged.

"Thompson, why don't you tell us?" Ian threw the beakers to the tile floor where they shattered. "What the hell happened here?"

"I, I don't know, sir. She said she'd left something undone here. Just stayed a minute." Thompson backed toward the door when Ian snarled.

"She. I don't have to guess who *she* is. Were you fucking Aggie, Thompson? Is that how she persuaded you to let her into my lab? You and she both know this room is off-limits. To everyone!" Ian's eyes bulged, a vein throbbed in his forehead and we all stepped back this time. I'd never seen him so out of control. I pressed against Rafe in case Ian forgot we weren't the enemy.

"No, no, sir. She came in just this once. She needed to clean up a spill, she said. Claimed you'd texted her about it. One last order before she quit." Thompson gasped when Ian grabbed his throat and threw him against the wall.

"You know I can read your stupid shifter mind, don't you?" Ian thumped the man's head against the wall, making a hole in the Sheetrock. "Idiot! She played you. I hope that blow job was worth it. You've just lost your job and are a heartbeat away from losing your life."

"Ian, calm down!" I tried to go to him but Rafe held me back. "What happened here that set you off?"

"Stay out of this, Glory." Ian didn't spare me a glance. "Obviously you have shit for brains, man, but hear me. If I find one single thing missing, you're dead. Do you understand?"

"Sir! I swear. She's a mortal and was only in here for a minute. What could she take? She didn't have on enough to hide anything." He choked, Ian's fist in his mouth.

"Out of my sight!" Ian threw him toward the door. "Don't stop until you're out of the state, the country. If I see you again, you're a dead man." Ian paced the length of the room, picking up containers and sniffing them then flinging them to the tile floor.

"Damn it to hell!" Ian ranted as he went up and down each aisle, throwing things like a wild man. The room had hardly been disturbed before. Soon it was a complete disaster and reeking of strange and very unpleasant odors.

"Ian! Tell us. What happened? What did Aggie do?" I didn't dare approach him. He finally stopped in front of a glass-fronted case filled with notebooks and glass bottles. It was locked. He sighed when he realized the lock hadn't been broken.

"That bitch contaminated every experiment I had going. Bleach. She poured common household bleach into everything." He swept his arm across a table full of test tubes in metal holders. They all crashed to the floor. The smell was so over-powering I quit breathing altogether. "You realize how much work that represented? How much *money*?" His voice rose and trembled. I swear, if he'd been a woman, he would've been sobbing. Instead, he hit the metal tabletop until his fist bled.

"Aggie hated him this much?" Rafe whispered.

"Of course she did. That cursed Siren. She knew just how

to pay me back for making her work for once in her useless life. Thank God I keep my computer locked in my office or she'd have dumped bleach on it too." Ian kicked over a table. It slid into another one and started a chain reaction. "Ellis, Desmond, Cox! Get the fuck in here!"

Three men ran into the room. Why they hadn't already come when the crashes started I couldn't imagine. Unless they were used to Ian's temper fits and had instructions to ignore loud noises until called. Whatever. They focused on Ian, who still looked totally out of his mind.

"Sir?" Ellis took the lead. "What do you need?"

"First, get a crew and have this room completely emptied and scrubbed down. I want everything replaced. Brand-new equipment. By tomorrow night. I'll have to start all my experiments over again. No one is to touch this cabinet." He pointed to the locked one behind him. "I expect you to oversee this personally. Is that clear?"

"Yes, sir. Do you have a list of what you need?" Ellis whispered to the other two men and they started carrying out the tables.

"It will be in your e-mail by the end of the night." Ian strode over to me. "I'm sorry, Gloriana. I'll work on your potion tomorrow night. I swear it. It will be a good distraction from this." He swept his arm toward the chaos he'd created. "Now I need to go."

"Wait." I grabbed his arm. "Where are you going? What are you going to do, Ian?" I was afraid I knew.

"Find that bitch and kill her. What did you think?" His fangs were down and I knew he meant it.

"Stop. No." I searched for the right words. Were there any? "She's simply not worth it." I held on to him. He was shaking with rage. "She's a mortal, suffering because she'll grow old and has no powers. Let that be her punishment. She's broke too. I'm kicking her out of my apartment tonight." I glanced around at the destruction. "This is the last straw. Yep, she's gone. As soon as I leave here. So she'll be homeless."

"The whore will find another bed. One with some unsuspecting man no doubt. Let me go, Glory. She's gone too far." Ian kicked a beaker aside. "Fuck! This is my life's work. You have no idea what she's done."

"I do. It's important work too. But she did this to get a rise out of you, Ian. Do you really want her to see how hurt you are?" I touched his shoulder. Surprise. He was trembling. Aggie had definitely found his vulnerability.

"You think I'm hurt?" Ian tried to shrug away from me but I wouldn't let go, just gripped his arm instead. He wasn't about to admit to such a weak emotion. "I'm pissed. Furious. And determined to make the bitch pay."

"Right. But if you let her see you like this, she'll revel in how she affected you." I stood between Ian and the door.

"That's all right. Mine will be the last face she sees." Ian looked like he was prepared to drag me to the door. Rafe stepped closer. I couldn't let it become a battle. Especially since the men working to clear the room were paying attention to our conversation and had only one loyalty and it wasn't to me.

"Seriously, Ian? Why not make her think this stunt didn't even make a ripple in your world? She's beneath contempt."

Ian did pull me out of the room then, but gently. He was stronger than I was, older by centuries. Rafe kept his eyes on us, ready to intervene if he thought Ian was hurting me. When we got to the living room, Ian stopped and faced me. I guess he didn't like having his bodyguards as witnesses to his pain.

"Pretend this didn't matter?" He ground his teeth. "It's not enough, Glory. My work is my life. And she betrayed me. Made me think that I loved her with her Siren magic. She made a fool of me. I'll never forgive her for that."

"But then you made a fool of *her*. Let her believe that you'd turn her vampire. Like you'd ever meant to do that." I smiled. "What did you call it? Pillow talk. She told me you were the best lover she ever had. That you talked her into your bed, promised her eternity, then used her, just like she'd planned to use you. I saw how that devastated her. How she hated working here. No wonder she acted out."

"She did hate the housekeeping. Bitched about it enough. Not to me. I wouldn't see her. But I got reports." Ian was at least listening to me now. "So she's been crying on your shoulder? How about that."

"Right. She's so desperate to get away from here, she's trying to sing for a living." I glanced at Rafe. "Ask Valdez. He was there. Aggie got the job but was humiliated. She has to work as a backup singer for a band. Backup. When she expected to be a star. Fat chance of that. The bitch can't even read music."

"Really. I'd like to see Aggie humiliated." Ian walked over to the French doors to stare out into the night.

"Good. Come with us Halloween night. She'll be singing at N-V. You can enjoy the show and let her see how little her idea of revenge affected you." I could see that he'd calmed down. He was thinking, not just reacting.

"Glory's making her stage debut too. Showing off her voice. She got it back, courtesy of her mother." Rafe finally relaxed and finished the drink Ian had poured him earlier. I picked up mine.

"Really? Hebe gave you your singing voice back?" Ian turned, looking intrigued. "I'd like to hear you, Glory. And Aggie is just doing some kind of doo-wop in the background?"

"Not for me, for Israel Caine and Sienna Star. Come to N-V

and hear for yourself. Rafe has a table reserved for vampires. If you can stand to sit with Jerry, you can be part of the party." I crossed my fingers that Jer would be back by then.

"All right, Gloriana, relax. You've talked me down. For now." Ian patted my arm. "I know what you were doing and it worked. I won't kill her. Yet. But I will have payback. You have no idea what those experiments meant to me. Years of work. With the possibility that vampires could walk in the sun for hours at a time. Eat whatever they wished." He sighed. "Shit. I may cry yet."

I squeezed his hand, actually sorry for him. "Don't cry, don't kill, get even. We'll think of something."

Ian nodded, definitely thinking and planning. Which was almost as scary as his murderous rage. Rafe and I said our good-byes and got out of there. We were in the car on our way back to the city when my cell phone rang. Jerry. Finally.

"Are you in Florida?"

"Yes. It was a long trip but I made it safely. I found Mel's sister. I'm going to talk to her later tonight." Jerry sounded tired.

"Let's hope she has some ideas about how we can make Mel give up on you." I wished I could touch him, make him feel better.

"She wouldn't say much on the phone. She wants to meet me. Meet Mel's latest crush. Apparently Mel has quite a history with the men in her life."

"Bring her back to Austin if you have to. But I'm anxious to see you again and get this whole Mel thing behind us." I tried to imagine a future without that woman and her threats hanging over us and couldn't.

"I don't know if this sister, Alexandra, is into voodoo or not. But I'll see what I can get from her to help us. Any luck with that book of spells you ordered? You know I'm not in favor of you trying your hand at any of that."

"I know. It scares me too. It's a last resort. I just left a recipe for the potion at Ian's." I told him about Aggie's latest trick and my determination to kick her out of my place.

"Good. She doesn't deserve a damn thing from you. I'm glad you finally realize that." Jerry told me a few details about his trip but I could tell he was anxious to get off the phone.

"Call me after you meet with the sister. I love you." I smiled into the phone when he said it back then ended the call.

"There was a lot you didn't tell him," Rafe said as I stuffed the phone back in my purse.

"I want the singing to be a surprise. And let's keep the seminar our secret. Hopefully we'll go, learn something and definitely convince Mel I've moved on to you for good. What could go wrong?" I shivered. I hate when I tempt fate like that.

Rafe didn't say anything but I knew he felt the same way. "Where to now? The shop or your place to see if Aggie's there?"

"Let me check." I pulled out the phone again. I called my apartment and got voice mail. "Aggie, if you're there, pick up. I need to talk to you." I waited but no answer. "I guess she's with Sienna. They probably had rehearsals. Or went down to the shop for costumes. Let's hit Vintage Vamp's. I need to do some costume shopping of my own."

"No, you don't, darling." My mother materialized in the backseat and Rafe hit the brakes.

"Shit. Was that necessary?" He looked around, checking for other cars. Luckily we were still on the back roads near Ian's and there was no traffic. "Do that in town and you'd have caused a wreck."

"Sorry." Mother clearly wasn't. "Gloriana, I've found the most darling fifties dresses for you to choose from. I brought them to your shop and put them in that back room. You can wear what you want and sell the rest. See how I think of your benefit?"

"Thanks, Mother!" I patted her hand where she gripped my seat. "That's really very thoughtful." And unusual for her. I was waiting for her ulterior motive. What did she want?

"Darling, you shouldn't be so skeptical. But I do have a plan. I was thinking. If your grandfather were to discover your existence, it would be helpful if I could prove your worth to him. He's a music lover, you see." She leaned back. "Honestly, Valdez, could you drive a little faster? I'm eager for my daughter to see those clothes. I outdid myself this time. It's not easy finding vintage designer dresses in mint condition."

"Yes, ma'am." Rafe grinned and stepped on the gas.

I grabbed the armrest between our bucket seats. "Go on, Mother. What's this plan?" I was sure there was something I wouldn't like about it.

"Oh, relax. I was just thinking that I want to make a video of it, or maybe just an audio." She sighed. "You will insist on that figure." She waved her hand. "Anyway, I'm sure he'll absolutely love your voice."

"Why, that's actually nice." I turned and smiled at her.

"I do try. You see I'm afraid he's going to be royally peeved at me for keeping you a secret all these years." She looked upward and lowered her voice. "It's been over a thousand, you know, counting your time in the Sirens. And Zeus really does hate a secret. Especially in the family. If he loses his temper . . ."

"What will he do to you?" Of course there was the question of what he'd do to *me*.

"Strip me of my powers. Make me a pariah. Sentence me to time in a really horrible place. I won't describe it. You'd have nightmares." She shuddered.

"Vampires don't dream, Mother."

"That's another thing!" She gripped my shoulder, suddenly way too close. "When he finds out a child of his blood is one of those . . . Well, I can't imagine his reaction." She rested her forehead on the seat back. "His temper is legendary. He gets a hangnail? Volcanos erupt. Stubs his toe? Earthquakes. Why do you think dinosaurs are extinct? He caught one of his favorite mistresses in bed with a hobbit." She shuddered. "You don't see those creatures around now either, do you?"

"Uh, no." I glanced at Rafe, who was fighting a grin. "I'd just as soon stay a secret from him. But it makes me wonder why you're so determined to drag me up there."

"Too many of the gods know about you already. The clock's ticking on this secret coming out. I really want to be the one to tell him. Not have him find out from someone else. If I didn't wield so much power, one of the men you met would have already tattled to him." Big dramatic slide as my mother collapsed on the leather seat. "You have no idea how tedious my life can be."

"Not a recommendation for my ever venturing up there. I'll do whatever I can to help you keep that secret." I saw that we were getting close to town. Ian lived in the boondocks because he liked his privacy.

"So glad to hear you say that, darling. I may need you to be extra nice to one of the men I'm afraid wants to cause trouble for me." Mother perked up. "Oh, we're almost there." She pulled out her compact and lipstick from a designer handbag. Tonight she was in a gray wool pencil skirt and white fuzzy sweater. She wore ropes of luminous freshwater pearls that set off the outfit perfectly. Her knee-high boots in gray suede made my mouth water.

I'd dressed casually for Ian's in black slacks and a black cashmere sweater. My vintage red leather jacket was my pop of color. I didn't look bad, just not sophisticated like my mother did. She smiled as she stroked on red lipstick.

"Gloriana, I can give you an outfit just like this one. Or at least replace those boots. You've scuffed the toe." She dropped the lipstick back into her purse. "Yes, I saw you kick that wall. I suppose you've inherited your grandfather's temper."

"No tricks now, Mother. Let's just go see what you left for me in the back room." I already owed her too much. And she'd added the worry about Zeus. Rafe pulled the car around to the alley and we all got out. No sign of Mel or her zombies. Yay!

"Really, darling. My tricks give me great pleasure. It's my way of making up for my neglect, don't you know?" She held my arm when I started to go inside. "Close your eyes, Gloriana. Valdez, would you come with me?" She smiled at him, turning on the charm. "I might need your help."

"Glory, you okay back here?" He scanned the alley.

"Sure. It seems fine. Go. I'll scream if I need you."

"Thank you, darling." My mother dragged him into the shop. "I can't wait till you see my little surprise."

I heard screaming and very unladylike curses. Doors opening and closing. "There she is. That Aggie person. I know it must be short for aggravation. Don't let her slip out the front door, Valdez." My mother stuck her head out the back. "Stay there, Gloriana. There's been a slight delay."

"What's Aggie done now?" I put my tote down on the ground. The book and computer inside made it heavy.

"You really don't want to know. I'm handling this." She grimaced, her eyes flashing. "How you have tolerated that cow in your home is beyond my understanding."

"I'm kicking her out tonight." I smiled at the thought.

"Good to know. And high time. Wait here." She darted back inside.

I tapped my foot, hummed one of the songs I planned to sing and even tried out a few bars. The echo in the alley was pretty good and I was tempted to sing out loud. No, better not. This was going to be a surprise for that night and the fewer people who heard me ahead of time, the better. I sniffed the air, relieved that it still just smelled of the muffins cooking next door and the full Dumpster a few yards away. I leaned against the door. A scuffling noise, muffled shrieks and sobbing. Finally there was silence.

The back door opened and Rafe waved me in. "All clear. Brace yourself. Your mother does know how to plan a surprise."

Have I told you how I hate surprises?

Twelve

"**What** happened?" I picked up my tote and stepped inside. The bathroom door was closed and I sensed someone in there. Aggie. Interesting. My mother stood in front of a dress rack that had been wheeled in from the shop. She was beaming.

"Voila!" She waved at the five dresses hanging on the rack.

I gasped because they were so exquisite. One of the popular fashions from the fifties had been the smart cocktail dress. My mother had found five of the smartest. The first was a black velvet number with crystal beads in a floral design that ran from the heart-shaped bodice down to the ballet-length hem. I ran my hand over the material. It was deliciously soft. Silk velvet. I didn't think they even made it anymore.

"Mother!"

"I love that one. You'd look stunning in it. But then the blue is perfect too. See? It has a little bolero jacket. And matching hat with a veil. Veils are so mysterious and sexy." My mother pulled the second dress out and held it up.

"They are absolutely gorgeous. I can't imagine where you

found them." I ran my hands over a purple and gray floral print silk which had its own petticoat. The full skirt would swish when I walked.

"It wasn't easy, Gloriana. I raided the closets of some serious collectors. There is one in Barcelona who will die if she discovers that iridescent number is missing." She laughed. "Foolish woman. She'll never know. She has all these amazing clothes in storage and never even looks at them."

I pulled out the dress she was talking about. The fabric actually changed colors, from pink to red to coral, when the light hit it.

"I saved the best for last, darling. What do you think?" She pulled one more dress from the rack. "This is the one I had to rescue from the clutches of that grasping creature currently shut inside the bathroom." My mother draped the dress over the worktable. "You're a vampire, Gloriana. Don't you think it's time you put those fangs to work? Kill the bitch. Or at least suck out so much of her blood that she's a prune, too ugly to step foot outside of these walls."

"Mother! For wearing a dress?" I glanced at Rafe. He just stuck his hands in his pockets, not saying yea or nay. I had a feeling he wouldn't stop me if I decided to go for it. "I don't kill mortals. Not unless I'm defending myself."

"Look at this dress and tell me you weren't attacked." My mother slammed her fist on the table. "It was perfect and that, that *thing* had the nerve to come into your private quarters and put this on her disgusting body. It didn't even fit her. So she pinned it. Pinned it! See the holes on the sides?" I swear my mother was going to stroke out. "I wanted to strike her dead but that might draw attention from someone upstairs." She sat down, her hands shaking as she straightened one of her ropes of pearls. "I swear, Gloriana, I am quite beside myself."

"I can see that." I patted her shoulder then finally took a good look at the dress that had her so upset. This was the best of the lot. White velvet. Sticking holes in a vintage masterpiece like this was the equivalent of tossing paint thinner on a Picasso.

"It's beautiful, Mother." The full circle skirt was trimmed in—brace yourself—white fox. There was a fitted waist with a wide belt featuring a sparkling buckle. "Are they—"

"Real diamonds?" My mother's laugh bordered on hysteria. "Of course they are. This dress once belonged to a Scandinavian princess. She wore it to a winter solstice ball and then it was archived. I managed to get it from a museum storeroom." She fanned her face with a hanky. "Honestly, Gloriana, the idea of that creature putting it against her sallow scaly skin . . . Well, she must pay. And this isn't the first time she's abused your hospitality. Think it over. Are you really such a doormat that you'll let her get away with this too?"

Think it over. It didn't take long. The list of abuses was pretty long: Aggie wasting all my hot water while she took endless baths. Aggie lounging around on my couch complaining because I hadn't forked over enough of my hard-earned cash to buy her food *I* sure couldn't eat. Aggie making mess after mess that she couldn't be bothered to clean up, including that disaster in Ian's lab.

I examined the beautiful white dress closely. If she'd managed to ruin this fabulous piece . . . Of course. Her favorite red lipstick smeared on the neckline.

I stalked over to jerk open the bathroom door. Aggie sat on the closed toilet lid wearing only a bra, panties and her last pair of Manolos.

"Come here." I could barely spit out the words.

"What?" She tried to look innocent. "The dress was here. You said I could shop. I shopped."

I grabbed her arm and dragged her out of the bathroom, ignoring her yelp of pain. "You've shopped here for the last time." I opened the back door and threw her into the alley. She stumbled but didn't fall. "You will never come into my shop again. Never step a foot into my apartment again. Whatever shit you left there will be dropped into the alley later tonight. I don't care where you sleep, where you live or if you live at all." I took a breath.

"Whoa. Cool your jets, Glory. I made an honest mistake." Aggie looked past me at my mother. "Come on, lady. I didn't mean anything by it. How was I to know it was a present for Glory?"

"You have taken advantage of my daughter's generous nature for the last time. She's done with you. Don't push your luck, Agony. If it were up to me, you'd be dead on the ground right now." My mother slipped her arm around my waist. "Take her down, Gloriana. She doesn't deserve to live."

Aggie backed up, shivering, tears running down her cheeks. "You can't do this. I'm standing here in my underwear. It's cold."

"Who the hell cares? I sure don't." I slammed the door in her face. My heart pounded. I really hoped I never saw her again. First my apartment, now my shop. Aggie acted like they were hers. Because I'd let her. I needed to reread some of my self-help books on assertiveness. My mother was right. Doormat. When had I turned into one? But I was sure of one thing. Aggie had wiped her feet on me for the last time.

"Wow. I don't think I've ever seen you this mad, Glory." Rafe picked up the dress from the table. "Well, maybe I have. A time or two." He grinned and winked at me. "Anyway, this would look great on you. You'd be like a snow princess." He flushed.

"That was a nice compliment." My mother looked him over. "You may not be as disgusting as I thought, Valdez. Shift out of here and I might start to like you."

"Mother, please. Don't ruin this." I refused to spare Aggie another thought, though she was beating on the back door and calling my name. Finally she stopped. "I can't wait to try all of these on. We'll have a little fashion show. Wouldn't you like that?" I took the white dress from Rafe and hung it back on the rack. With luck, the lipstick wouldn't show. I'd save it for last.

"Love it. Valdez, perhaps you should make sure that female outside can't get into my daughter's apartment. A little bird told me she was busy at that doctor's place today. Sabotage. I wouldn't be surprised if she tried to do something like that to Gloriana." My mother seemed determined to get Rafe out of the room. I didn't argue. Checking on my place was a good idea.

"You're right. I'm on it. I can start tossing her clothes out the back window. You two will be busy here awhile, won't you?" Rafe pulled open the back door. "No sign of her. Which makes me wonder where she went."

"We'll be here. Go. Maybe the zombies got her. But if they were looking for brains to eat, they'd go hungry. I don't think Aggie has any." I bit my lip. *Suck it up, Glory. You are not worried about her.* But old habits die hard. I had to wonder where she'd gone without a purse or, um, clothes. Aggie was always enterprising. I tried to put her out of my mind as Rafe took off, making me promise to lock the door behind him. I stepped into the bathroom with the first dress. Beautiful clothes. Surely I could enjoy a few minutes with some of my favorite things.

I came out in the blue. My mother was zipping me up and exclaiming about the sad state of my underwear when the door from the shop banged open.

"Listen, lady. I don't care if you're the freakin' queen of the Nile. Aggie and I are going to be late for rehearsal." Sienna stopped when she saw me. "Glory. When did you get here? And wow. Love that dress." She saw the rack and her mouth fell open. "So this is where you keep the good stuff."

"It's not for you." My mother inserted herself between Sienna and the clothes. "They are my gift to my daughter and wouldn't fit you anyway."

"Fine. Whatever. Where's Aggie? You dragged her back here a while ago." She glanced into the bathroom. "I have her purse so she can't have gone far. And her clothes are in the dressing room out here. Surely she didn't take off in that fabulous dress. She was supposed to save it for Halloween."

My mother's smile gave me chills. "Aggie's gone. Gloriana threw her out. She never should have touched that dress. It was not for her either."

"What do you mean?" Sienna turned to me. "You tossed her out? Without her clothes?"

"Yes, I did. You have no idea the crap she's pulled. The dress thing was the final straw. I've had it with her." I refused to feel guilty. "Rafe checked the alley. She's not there so I assume she got help."

"I hope like hell you're right." Sienna stared at me like she didn't know me. I just stared back. I wasn't backing down or apologizing.

"Gloriana could and should have done much worse, Miss Starkowski." My mother held on to my arm, in protective mode. "I'd recommend you watch yourself around that agitator. The woman is not to be trusted."

"Okay, point taken. And it's Star. I left Starkowski behind a long time ago." Sienna moved to the back door. "Is she in the apartment? Like her or not, she's my backup singer and we really need to get going. Ray's already called me twice."

"No, I'm not letting her back in there. Rafe's upstairs getting her things together. He'll be putting them in the alley as soon as he can." I slipped on the bolero jacket that matched the dress.

"I love that color on you, Gloriana." My mother held the matching hat in her hand. "But hats can be a pain. What to do about your hair?"

"You two are just going to stand there talking fashion when Aggie is out in the night, in her underwear?" Sienna's voice rose. "What the hell is wrong with you, Glory? I thought you were a nice person."

"Even nice people can be pushed too far, Sienna." I faced her. "My mother's right. Aggie's a user. She's reckless and will stab you in the back if she gets a chance. And she just made a very dangerous enemy in Ian MacDonald." Not that Aggie cared. She'd been eager to hurt Ian. My own anger was wearing off and I couldn't help worrying about the woman. A mortal in her underwear in an alley that had had more than its share of bad happenings?

"She and Ian were already enemies. She told me the whole story." Sienna gestured to Danny, who'd been right behind her since she'd stepped into the room. He'd been the one to shut the door into the shop. Smart, since we didn't want my customers to hear this conversation. "Will you at least help me look for her?"

"Yes." I stepped back into the bathroom. "Wait a minute. I have to change clothes."

"Gloriana, don't be foolish. You don't care what happens to that woman." My mother tried to keep me from closing the door. "We were having fun together."

"I can try on the rest of the dresses another time, Mother. No one else will disturb them. I'll leave instructions with the clerks." I patted her shoulder before gently easing the door shut. Maybe Aggie deserved to be tossed out on her fanny, but I didn't want to become just like her, treating others with callous disregard. I threw on my clothes and led the group out to the alley. Rafe was already there, setting boxes of Aggie's things next to the back door.

"Any sign of her?"

"No, she didn't show up at the apartment." Rafe joined us. "You decided to help her now?"

I stopped next to my car, glad it was still there. "I don't know. She is just a mortal." I turned to Sienna. "Do you have her purse with you?"

"Yes, here." She handed it over.

I took out my extra set of car keys. I'd let Aggie drive my car to Ian's. Had even paid for the extra gas. Doormat didn't begin to cover it. I didn't owe her all that help. But still a niggling worry about what would become of her now wouldn't go away.

"All right. I get it. We'll look around. But if we find her, it will just be to hand her a coat from one of her boxes." Rafe bumped against my shoulder. "Right?"

"Right. I'm not backing down. She's out for good."

Sienna just walked off, calling Aggie's name as she headed toward one end of the alley and looked between cars. I stood where I was and sniffed the air.

"Rafe. Do you smell what I smell?"

"Vampire? Yes. It's familiar but I can't place it." He started toward the other end of the alley. "Stay here."

"Not on your life. You're right. Familiar and unique. I met

the guy once. He's a rogue. Just the kind of vampire who'd be happy to turn Aggie if she could come up with enough cash."

"Surely she wouldn't have arranged to meet him already. He charges big bucks and Aggie just started the band gig. What she gets for giving Sienna blood wouldn't cover a down payment." Rafe stopped at the entrance to the alley. "Hard to tell which way they went but I think Aggie must have been with him."

Sienna came running up behind us. "Did you find her?"

"Not exactly. But we have a lead. Did you give Aggie some money, Sin?" I saw her face. Of course she had.

"She needed an advance. For something really important to her. I knew we could work out her musical issues so she'd be able to stay with the band. I wanted to help her." Sienna frowned. "You don't know my real history, Glory, though obviously your mother has done some snooping. When I landed in L.A. as a teenager, I could have been in big trouble and, yeah, I was messed up for a while. But then I got lucky and met a musician who helped me out, kept me safe and got me started. Aggie just needed someone to believe in her. I figured it was my turn to give back."

"I'm sorry you had it rough, Sienna." I really was. "But Aggie's not you. She didn't tell you what she wanted the money for?"

"No. It was a big secret. A surprise, she said. I made her swear she wasn't on drugs." Sienna bit her lip. "You think she made a fool of me, don't you? Damn it!"

"It's not for drugs, if that makes you feel better." I glanced at Danny. He'd been a silent witness to this. But it wasn't his job to interfere. As usual, his face didn't give anything away as to what he was thinking.

Sienna looked down the alley, staring into the darkness.

"Just tell me, what did she want the money for? Will I ever see her again?"

"This is just a guess, but here's what we think happened." I glanced at Rafe and he nodded. "We recognized a scent back here. It's a vamp who will do just about anything for money. I have a feeling Aggie had arranged to meet him to pay this guy to make her a vampire."

"What?" Sienna's jaw dropped. "She's already found one of those rogue vampires?"

"Yes, but it's illegal according to our local vampire council." I saw Danny nod. Guess he'd brushed up on our vampire rules. Good for him. "You know how desperate Aggie was to become vampire. I bet when she got you alone she mentioned it."

"Sure. She wanted me to turn her. Of course I didn't take her seriously. Talk is cheap, and what do I know about that stuff anyway?" Sienna stroked a fang. "I can't imagine . . ."

"Remember how crazed she was about gaining immortality again? Tonight she trashed Ian's lab. One reason was because she's still furious that Ian reneged on his promise to turn her. She's been in a hurry to become vampire ever since she dropped out of the Siren system. So as soon as you gave her some cash, she must have arranged a meet for tonight."

"How much do you think this guy charges? I didn't give her *that* much." Sienna looked around wildly. "And what's she thinking? You don't recover from the change overnight. I can attest to that. We have obligations. Commitments. Shit!"

"His fee will be pretty high. I have a feeling Aggie probably thought she could give him a down payment and he'd go ahead and make the change. Then she'd work off the rest with her usual fast talking and"—I glanced at the guys—"you know."

"Rogues don't take sex in payment, Glory." Rafe shook his head. "Aggie may be in trouble. If she did meet Miguel, I'm pretty sure of it. He was in N-V the other night. I warned him not to hang around. He's bad news. He's working for Lucky Carver now, collecting debts. When some of my paranormal customers or work crew see him, they take off. You don't want to mess with Miguel. He's a heavy-duty enforcer."

"You think he'll hurt her? When he realizes she can't pay the whole freight?" Sienna dug in her purse when her phone blasted out a shrill tune. "Maybe this is her. I really am an easy touch. I bought her a phone too. She had it stuck in her bra. Said you do that sometimes, Glory."

"When I shape-shift. Not all the time." I listened while Sienna answered. Obviously it was Ray again. Sienna told him she was on her way and didn't mention that Aggie would be a no-show. "Call her now. See if she answers," I said when Sienna hung up.

"Good idea." She hit speed dial. "Aggie! Where are you? We're worried sick." She listened for a while. "Yes, her too." She handed the phone to me.

"This is Glory. Where are you, Aggie?"

"Like you care." Her voice was hard. "I'm fine. Thanks for asking. Are my things in the alley?"

"Yes, Rafe stuck everything in boxes. They're by the back door. He was going to toss them out the window, but took pity on you. I'll let him know you appreciate that."

"Like hell. You both will pay for being so mean to me. Count on it."

"I know who you're with, Aggie. Not a good idea."

"Fuck you. I can hang out with whoever I want to. Miguel and I have worked out a deal. None of your business, that's for sure. I'll send someone to pick up my stuff. There'd better not be anything missing. Tell Sienna I'll meet her at N-V in a few minutes." She ended the call.

"Well, I guess Aggie's not a vampire yet. She's meeting you at the club, Sienna. Let's go." Then I noticed my mother still by the door into the shop. Pouting. "I'll meet you there."

"No need to hurry. Ray and I are going to practice first. You can work with him after that." Sienna sighed. "Aggie really was using me, wasn't she?"

"Afraid so. She's pretty clever about figuring out angles. Just be on your guard. If she doesn't work out singing backup, fire her. She's not your responsibility and she does have a good voice. I'm sure she can find other work."

"You're right. I'm not thinking straight, being a vampire now and all. It's a weird deal. Having to keep so many things secret. I hate it." She glanced at Danny. "He had to step between me and a couple of your customers tonight. My fangs were shooting down, sticking right out of my mouth. Embarrassing. But, God, their blood smelled so fine." She clutched my hand. "What would it hurt to drink from one now and then?"

"Sienna, think. They'd freak if you came at them, fangs down. You and I need to get together and I'll teach you how to wipe their minds. So if they do catch a glimpse of your vamp bloodlust, you can make them forget it." I smiled at Danny. "Good job, Danny. You saved her butt." He just shrugged, his own smile barely a grimace.

"Yeah, we do need time together. Tonight was horrible. There's so much I haven't learned yet. The mirror thing." Sienna brushed at her hair. "Shit. It was insane the way I had to hop around your store to avoid the mirrors once I realized I didn't show up. At. All. If a mortal had seen that . . ." She swiped at a tear that ran down her cheek. "I'm a freak, Glory. How do you stand it?"

"A freak who'll live forever and look hot and young while

doing it." I gave her a quick hug. "Come on, Sienna, look at the positives. Or try to anyway. Don't most mortals have trouble with their singing voices when they get older? I know Ray worried about his. The weather affected it, smoke, lots of stuff. Not anymore."

"You're right. That part's totally cool. But then I can't stay in the spotlight like that indefinitely, can I? Not without telling the world what I am." She frowned when she pushed away from me. "If I could just come out of the closet, I'd be so on board with this." She squared her shoulders.

"Coming out of the closet is never happening. You know that, don't you?" I stared into her eyes, willing her to take me seriously.

"Yeah, yeah. I know. The big bad council wouldn't like it." She tossed her hair and, for a moment, looked just like Aggie at her defiant worst. "Well, I've got to run. Did I tell you Danny's teaching me how to shape-shift? We've already done it a few times. It's *majorly* cool. We're going to fly to N-V right now. See ya there later." She smiled. "Watch." She shifted into a bat. Cliché. Danny, in sympathy I guess, did the same and they took off.

"I need to spend more time with her. Her attitude needs adjusting." I sighed and glanced at my mother again.

"Yeah, I noticed that." Rafe followed me to the back door. "But, as usual, you've got a lot going on. Like this."

"You're too softhearted, Gloriana." My mother took me by the shoulders. "What do you care if that Aggravation lives or dies, freezes in her underpants or gets drained dry? Toughen up, darling."

"I know, Mother. I'm a disgrace to a goddess from Olympus. Perhaps you should just wash your hands of me." I kissed her cheek. This made her gasp and her eyes watered.

"Darling! Come inside. Try on just one more dress. I must see you in the black velvet."

"All right. Just one more." I stroked it with a fingertip. "You know, Mother, if there's one thing I've learned about men in my years on Earth, it's that they love to feel something soft. Pushes their 'on' button."

"Ah, my dear, you *are* my daughter, aren't you?" She actually pulled a hanky out of her clutch. "That dress just might be the one. Try it and see. I have the most cunning shoe and handbag collection too. I'll fetch it while you get dressed."

Rafe stepped closer as soon as my mother disappeared. "You're right. We're suckers for anything soft. Soft material, soft skin." He touched my cheek. "Soft heart. Total turn-ons. But be careful, Blondie. Aggie isn't to be trusted and I'm afraid I put your mother in the same category as that Siren. Manipulators. Beware. That's all I'm sayin'."

"Yeah, I hear you." I sighed and leaned against his hand for just a moment. Tempting. And off-limits. I took the dress into the bathroom and pulled it on. Perfect. Yes, the others were spectacular in their own ways, but this dress fit the mood for the songs I'd chosen. I imagined myself onstage, spotlight hitting the black velvet, beads sparkling and Ray at the keyboard. It would be a night I'd never forget.

I shivered. What did they say? Like someone had walked over my grave.

When I got to N-V, the first person I saw, leaning against the bar, was Miguel. My memory of him was pretty vivid. For one thing, he'd been one of the most powerful vamps I'd ever met. I'd just learned how to freeze people when I'd run up against him. He'd assured me he knew how to thaw them out. Which made me wonder exactly what else he could be besides a vampire. Demon? Or, now that I knew that gods and goddesses had "accidents" aka children, could he have a little Olympus blood in him like I did?

Rafe was furious and went toward Miguel ready for a confrontation. I stopped him with a hand on his back.

"Stop and think. If he's with Aggie, I want to find out what their deal is. You throw him out and we'll learn zilch."

"I told him to stay out of here." Rafe nodded toward the bathrooms. Sure enough, one of his waiters was headed for the break room, his head turned so Miguel couldn't see it. Debt issues? "He's bad for business."

"Let me talk to him." I rubbed Rafe's back. "Maybe he'll agree to wait in the practice room."

"This is *my* place, Glory. And he's dangerous. I don't want you anywhere near him." Rafe grabbed my hand. "Why don't *you* wait in the practice room?"

"I can handle him, Rafe. Let me do this. You can watch us from over here. If he does something you don't like, come help me. And he's drinking, running up a bar tab. Can you really afford to turn away another paying customer?" I saw Miguel smiling at us from across the room. Obviously he had heard every word and thought we were hilarious. For thinking that I could handle him or that either of us could? I didn't wait for Rafe to answer me, just headed over. The music was loud and had a sexy beat. I found myself strutting to it, shoulders back, hips swaying. Miguel's smile got broader and he raised his glass to me then downed his drink in a single swallow.

"*Chica.* Looking good. Can I buy you a drink?" He pulled out the bar stool next to him.

"Sure. I'll have whatever you're having." I settled on the stool. I still wore all black under my red leather jacket. I slipped off the leather and let Miguel see that my black sweater had a low neckline. He noticed with a slow smile.

"Two top shelf tequila shots." He gestured to the bartender. "Are you sure you can handle that, Gloriana?"

"If you can, I can." I lifted the small glass when it was set down next to me, determined to prove I was his equal or better. Stupid? Maybe. Time would tell. "What shall we drink to? Powers?"

"Ah, I like that." He grinned and clinked his glass against mine. "Powers. Yours, mine. May we never have to test them against each other." He tossed back his drink then watched me.

I downed mine then gasped. Ooookay. I'd never had one of those before. I didn't dare try to talk. I had a feeling I'd just burned out my throat lining. I managed a grin, glad breathing was optional. My eyes watered and Miguel laughed.

"Lightweight." Miguel gestured and two more shots were set down on the bar.

"That's enough." Rafe was between us. "You trying to get her drunk? Glory, you trying to kill yourself?"

"You trying to piss me off?" Miguel lost his smile.

"Stop. Rafe, I'm fine." I picked up the tequila, said a quick prayer and tossed it off again. "See? Nothing to it. Now go away. I want to talk business with Miguel. Take care of your own. I see one of your guys waving at you from the stairs." I hadn't made that up. Rafe was always on call once he got to N-V. As for me, I was trying to act okay when I most definitely was not. My throat was on fire and the flames had spread to parts south. The warmth was welcome. The numbness that was taking over my face? Not so much.

"Business, *chiquita*? I can't wait." Miguel stared at Rafe. "You heard the lady. She is perfectly safe with me, shifter. Yes, I can read your mind. I have a woman to warm my bed later right upstairs. I think I can resist adding Gloriana to my little black book for now." He saluted Rafe with his glass then drank. "Adios."

"Call me if you need me, Glory. Someone will be watching you every minute." Rafe touched my cheek then strode off.

"He is very protective." Miguel stood. "Shall we get a table? More private and more . . . comfortable."

"Yes. Rafe's always taken good care of me." I followed Miguel to a table in the balcony. There wasn't a band tonight, just a disc jockey, and the place wasn't too crowded. We had our pick of tables and he chose one in a dark corner, away from mortals. He pulled out a chair for me and I collapsed into it.

He settled into a chair close by, his knee brushing mine under the table. "Now what is this business you wish to discuss? See? I'm being polite and not reading your mind."

"You said once you could read past my blocks. Was that true?" I leaned my face on my hand. It slipped off. Uh-oh. I was really not used to tequila.

"Want to test me? Go ahead. Think something and block your thoughts. Then we'll see if I can get it right." He leaned closer. "I love games like this."

"Me too." I realized I was leaning toward him and jerked upright. "I mean, here goes." I thought about Mel the voodoo woman and how much I hated her. "Okay, what did I think about?"

"Who is Mel? Voodoo? I can help you if this woman is troubling you." Miguel picked up my hand. "I have some experience with the dark arts. They are very dangerous in the wrong hands."

"Wow. That was good. Let me try to break your block." I wiggled my fingers free. "Go." I stared at him. My thoughts were fuzzy. Damned tequila. Suddenly I had a picture of him in a bed stretched out on top of white cotton sheets. He was naked and touching himself. "Hey! That's unnecessary."

"Did you like what you saw?" His grin was wicked.

"I saw way too much." My head wobbled. "Israel Caine has a piercing there too. Does that prove I got through your block?"

His grin was my answer. "So, you and Caine?"

"We have a history. And it's none of your business." I shook my head and the room did a three-sixty. "Can we stop with the games now?"

"Of course, but I must say I'm most impressed. Where did you get your powers?" He stared into my eyes for a long moment then moved his dark gaze down to where my top stretched low over my breasts. "They are amazing."

"I assume we're still talking about my powers." I pulled up my top, suddenly self-conscious. "My mother is a goddess from Olympus. Hebe. I just found that out recently. Discovered my powers too." I sighed. "She dumped me into the Siren system when I was a baby. It's a long story but I was a mere mortal when Jerry found me and turned me vampire a little more than four hundred years ago." Why was I blabbing my life story to this guy?

"Fascinating. We are much alike, with powerful parents." He traced a pattern on the back of my hand. "I'm descended from Mayan priests who were connected to gods that many claim may have come from Olympus too. You must ask your mother. Since we have some of the same powers, it might be so."

"Mayans. About that end of the world thing . . ."

He frowned. "Please. Are you disappointed it didn't end?" He squeezed my fingers. "I am not and I've heard enough of that prediction to last me three lifetimes. We are here now. You wanted to ask me something?"

"About Aggie. What are you going to do with her? Besides use her to warm your bed. You going to turn her vampire?" I snatched back my hand.

"I'm in the loan business. She wants to borrow a considerable sum. She had a small down payment, but it wasn't nearly enough. She needed collateral. Becoming a vampire is an expensive proposition. I don't take making a vampire child lightly, and I charge accordingly." He leaned back in his chair and crossed his long legs. He was tall, lean, and I flashed on that spectacular body I'd glimpsed in his thoughts. Mayan. No wonder his looks were dark and exotic.

"Collateral. What the hell does Aggie have for collateral, Miguel?"

"Her body, *mi vida*. What else?" Miguel leaned forward, his dark eyes intense, the table practically vibrating between us. "She explained that she is a former Siren. I see value there. She wants the loan to pay me. It's a win/win." His grin was a slash of white in his dark face. "I will be her sire. As my child, she can become an earner for me if I so desire." He laughed at what I was sure was my look of revulsion.

"Gloriana, you are too easy. You think I'm a pimp?" He stood and held out his hand. "Perhaps I am. But let's go to this practice room and see how Aggie is doing, shall we?" He pulled me out of my chair. I wobbled. "No more tequila for you, *chica*. You can't hold your liquor worth a damn."

"No, I can't." I followed him to the practice room. It wasn't easy. My steps weren't steady and my mind was spinning. How much of what Miguel had said was the truth and how much of it was just for shock value? I was afraid to find out.

Thirteen

Aggie was actually doing a decent job when we arrived at the practice room. She was singing harmony, quietly enough that Ray ignored her and Sienna threw her a smile over her shoulder. Rafe was waiting for us, his eyes on Miguel when we walked in.

"Are you all right?" Rafe grabbed my arm.

"Sure. Mickey and I had a little chat." The room was swaying to the music. No, maybe I was.

"Sit down, you're loaded." Rafe shoved me into a chair. "What did you do, Miguel, buy her another round?"

"She likes tequila, Valdez. But I would think a descendent of a goddess could hold her liquor. *Es verdad?*" Miguel's smile didn't reach his eyes. "This music isn't what I expected. Loud rock and roll?"

"You think Aggie was backing up chamber music, Miguel?" I giggled at the thought. Oops, Rafe was right. I was more than a little tipsy. I'd enjoyed another couple of tequila shots at the table. It had been a novelty and the liquor had quit burning my throat, the heat in my stomach welcome.

"She has a beautiful voice, *chica*. But you can barely hear her for the noise of the band and those other two singers." Miguel was frowning. "This isn't the best use of her talent."

"She's being paid well, man. Besides working to pay her debt to MacDonald, it's the first money she's ever earned that didn't end with a kill." Rafe pulled up another chair. "Those other two singers are the stars who sign her paycheck. We should shut up and let them finish rehearsal before they kick us out of here."

"Where'd she get the clothes?" I couldn't stay quiet, still focused on Aggie. The last time I'd seen her she'd been in her underwear. "You keep stuff like that in your closet, Miguel?" I wagged a finger at him. "Do a little cross-dressing?"

"Do you think they would fit me, *chica*?" He pulled up a chair too. When he sat his knees brushed mine.

"No." I looked him up and down, almost falling over. I steadied myself with a hand on his hard thigh. "You're way bigger than she is."

"Glory, get hold of yourself." Rafe jerked my chair closer to his and whispered in my ear. "Damn it, if we weren't surrounded by Ray's mortal band members, I'd make you drink from my wrist just to sober you up."

"Mmmm. Hot shifter blood. Yummy." I licked my lips, the very idea sending my fangs down. "Gimme."

"Shit. I'm taking you out of here." Rafe jerked me up out of my chair.

"Stop. That hurt." I rubbed my wrist when he let me go. He was right, I was bombed and out of control. I glanced at the band. They couldn't hear us over the song they were about to finish. Good thing.

I put my hand over my mouth. Two reasons: One, my fangs just wouldn't retract. Two, I thought I was about to hurl.

"Yes, take her away and hurry. She's going to be sick." Miguel laughed. "Not a drinker, are you, Gloriana?"

"No, she's not." Rafe put his arm around me. "There's a bathroom around the corner. Come on, sweetheart."

"I'm not your sweetheart." To my horror, tears filled my eyes. "You've moved on. I'm g-g-glad." I sniffled and wiped my cheeks with a shaky hand. "Oh, run, I'm going to throw up."

"I'm running." Rafe hustled me to the unisex bathroom, threw open the door and held me while I barfed up my toe-nails. When there wasn't anything left in my stomach, I stood and wobbled over to the sink. Rafe wet a paper towel and I wiped my face. Then he waited patiently for me to rinse out my mouth.

"I'm sorry, Rafe. That was disgusting." I leaned against the counter, trying to wipe away more of what I was sure was the mess I'd made of my makeup.

"It's okay. I blame Miguel. What's the bastard's last name anyway?" He took the paper towel from me and cleaned off mascara from under my eyes. "There. Can't have you running around with raccoon eyes."

"Thanks." I sighed. "If he has a last name, he hasn't shared it with me. Where's my purse?"

"Here." Miguel stood in the doorway. "And my last name is Cisneros this century. Not that my name will help you in an Internet search. We're off the grid, all of us, are we not?"

"Yes, sure." I took my purse and pulled out a hairbrush. I went to work, finding my lipstick and compact too. "But thanks for telling us."

"We'll be working together. It's a courtesy." He walked away.

"Working together? What the hell does that mean?" Rafe snatched the lipstick out of my hand. "Did you agree to something, Glory? With this guy?"

I pressed a hand to my forehead. Had I? The tequila haze was gone but I had a blank spot from my time with Miguel. I remembered that he'd asked me to check Olympus for his possible parentage. Was that it?

"I don't know, Rafe. I can't remember."

"Are you two through in here? Mortals actually use a bathroom." Aggie stood in the doorway, tapping her foot. New shoes. Not Manolos but good quality. Miguel was really investing in her. Why? I didn't trust him. Rafe and I agreed on that.

"Get in here." I stepped out of the way and Aggie hurried inside.

"Uh, privacy?" She hesitated before she closed the door on my foot.

Rafe and I exchanged glances. I moved so she could shut the door and lock it.

"Humility? I don't believe it." He leaned a shoulder against the wall. "Are we waiting for her?"

"Yeah. I want to ask her a few questions." I dropped my purse on the floor, suddenly too weak to carry it. "I feel like shit."

"Stay away from tequila. I can't believe you even went there." Rafe shook his head. "You think Miguel did some kind of mind control on you? If he did, I'm taking that bastard apart."

I rubbed my forehead, a memory teasingly close. "He didn't have to, Rafe. I was just too wrecked to remember. Let's see what he says. Business. He did ask me to check with Mother about something. That could be all he meant." I jumped when I heard the lock turn. "Here she comes. Let me handle this."

"What do you want?" Aggie came out ready for a confrontation. The humility had been a temporary thing.

"What do you have going with Miguel? He buy you that dress, those shoes?" I blocked her with my arm when she started to flounce off without answering. "Spill, Aggie."

"I don't owe you any explanations. You tossed me out like so much garbage. If he hadn't happened along, I'd be sick with pneumonia or worse from exposure. And I don't heal in my sleep like *some* people. Yet." She tried to move around me. Rafe stepped in front of her.

"Answer her, Aggie. Glory took you in when nobody else would. You do owe her. Maybe it's stupid, but Glory's worried about you. Miguel's a dangerous character. And we know he didn't just 'happen' along." Rafe smiled at me. "Glo's got a soft heart."

"More like a soft head. What's with you, Glory? One minute you're done with me, now you want to check up on me?" Aggie lifted her chin. "Miguel and I made a deal. I'm his blood donor and he's loaning me some cash to get started, before I get paid for this gig." She smoothed down the green wool skirt that matched her sweater. "He even ran out and bought me this to wear tonight. Lucky thing a little boutique was open late. This is new, not used." Her smirk said what she thought of my shop.

I looked her over. "Yeah, lucky. An expensive boutique that also carried shoes. Just wait till you get the bill." I wanted to shake her, standing there so clueless. "You have any idea what his interest rates are? He works for one of the worst loan sharks in the paranormal world."

Aggie smiled, suddenly worldly wise in a way I never would be. "Maybe I've got my own way of paying off the interest, Glo." She laughed when Rafe made a noise which I took for disgust. "Look at her, Rafe. She's blushing. You forget, Glory, I'm used to trading my body for what I want. It's no big deal. The man's hot too. That's a bonus."

"Aggie, where's your self-respect?" I had to say it.

"I can't afford that kind of high and mighty crap. Besides, Miguel's going to turn me vampire. His price for that is way more than I can come up with, but somehow I'm going to make it happen." She tossed her hair, still sure she was a sex symbol. And maybe most men agreed. I didn't see it.

"Earth to Aggie. Never trust a rogue vampire. You're over your head here." I wanted to slap some sense into her. Of course slapping Aggie would be fun anyway. She was getting on my last tequila-soaked nerve, especially when my head ached and her blood smelled like heaven on the hoof.

"Not even close." Aggie stepped back from me. Obviously she'd learned to recognize the signs of hunger in a vampire. "I'm pretty sure the more I please him, the better deal he'll give me. Or, here's a thought, maybe he'll get carried away some night. Then he'll have no choice but to turn me. How's that for a plan?" She smiled, sure of her sexual prowess. And why wouldn't she be? The woman had thousands of years of experience. My stomach cramped but I was too empty to throw up again.

Rafe had heard enough. "He'd have a choice, you idiot. He could let you die. Sorry if this hurts you, Glory, but I've known too many vampires who'd suck her dry and not give a rat's ass about it."

"No, you're right, Rafe. I've known plenty like that too.

And I have a feeling Miguel is one of them. He has two jobs, Aggie. The other is hit man. He snuffs out life without a qualm. Kind of like you used to do." I tried to catch Aggie's eye but she was too smart for that. She'd been mesmerized before and was obviously afraid that was my intention.

"Yeah, well. Maybe that makes him the perfect man for me." She smiled, completely immune to our warnings.

"Just be careful, Aggie. Being a vampire's blood slave—and that's what you are, make no mistake about it—is dangerous. If Miguel accidentally lets you bleed out, he'll dump you like trash, for real this time." I let the wall hold me up, truly queasy again.

"Gloriana, you wound me." Miguel suddenly appeared in the hallway. "I'm very careful with my, as you crudely call them, blood slaves." His smile was pure predator. "It's so difficult to find a donor who is healthy, willing and beautiful." He pulled Aggie to him. "Aggie is exceptional." He frowned. "Aggie. I do not like this name. It's ugly. We will pick a new one for her. A stage name. Stay tuned."

Aggie leaned against him, practically purring. "See? Miguel appreciates me. I can spare a little of my juice and he treats me well. Buys me decent clothes and he has a nice house in the hills. Right, baby?"

Miguel brushed back her hair, then tightened his hand in the strands so that we could see he was exerting pressure. "I am nobody's baby. Respect, remember?"

"Oh, yeah, sure." Aggie's eyes widened and we saw her swallow. "I'm sorry, Miguel. Rehearsal's over. If I'm going to feed you later, I need to eat now. Okay?" Her voice trembled.

"Fine. Red meat and perhaps a glass of red wine. There's a nice restaurant down the street that serves a late dinner." He released her hair, smoothing it down over her shoulder. "Adios, Gloriana, Valdez. I will speak to you tomorrow night, Gloriana, about our deal. We can meet here again, I suppose. These rehearsals continue." His glance at the practice room made me wonder for how long.

"It'll have to be late. I have an appointment early in the evening. Make it after midnight." I saw him nod. Then he pushed Aggie ahead of him down the hall, his hand firmly on her elbow. "I hope Aggie knows what she's doing."

"She's probably happier with him than scrubbing Ian's toilets. Let it go, Glory." Rafe pointed toward the practice room. "I think Ray's ready for you. Sienna's just come out and is gesturing at us."

"Oh, right." I really shouldn't have tried the tequila. Now I'd have to sing with a raw throat. Plus the liquor was still buzzing around inside my brain and doing cartwheels in my stomach. I hoped I remembered the words to the two songs I'd picked.

Rafe and I passed the band on our way into the practice room. They'd packed up and were heading out. The guys wished me luck and promised to stay for the next rehearsal so they could hear me sing. Sienna grinned and handed me sheet music.

"I love your song choices. Perfect. Especially this last one. This is going to be a Halloween hit! I could even imagine hearing it on the radio." She hugged me. "Is Blade going to be back by then?"

"I certainly hope so." I glanced down at the music. "I'm glad the words are here. I'm a little under the weather tonight."

"You'll be fine. I wish I could stay but I have a radio interview scheduled. Good thing it was a late night show. I'll see you at home later." She waved then left.

Feeling like a condemned woman, I walked up onto the stage, where Ray was running through the first song. I pasted on a smile and fought back my nerves.

"Hey, Ray. What do you think of my song choices?"

"Love 'em, babe. Let's work out your key first." He jumped up and kissed my cheek then we got down to business.

Business. Yes, that's what this was. I'd done a lot of stage work in the past but always in the chorus as a dancer or as part of a band. Now the spotlight would be on me. And singing. At least Ray was so utterly professional that he calmed me down. By the time we'd run through one song a few times, I began to feel comfortable and it helped that Ray was full of compliments.

"You really think this will work? The song's pretty old-fashioned. N-V attracts a young, hip crowd." I still had some doubts about my choices.

"Retro is in. Sienna was right about that. The college kids will get it and I think this vibe suits you. I just wish we could do a duet. Let's add a third number, something upbeat to start. Maybe a song you and I can sing to each other." He thought for a minute then played a tune that I recognized.

"Ray! That's perfect. I like the retro thing but it's good to mix in something more contemporary like that. You're a genius." I sat beside him at the piano. "Of course this may get the paparazzi worked up again. Rumors flying that we're back together singing about 'sweet love.'" It might help Jerry convince Mel that he and I were through too. But I wasn't sharing that with Ray.

"I'll take that chance. I can't wait to see the audience reaction." He started the song again and we worked on our harmony. Ray got really excited. "This needs the band behind it. Damn it, I have a notion to keep them onstage. Give you the full treatment."

"I don't know, Ray. That's a big commitment from the guys." I felt embarrassed. My first public performance as a singer. It was one thing to sing to Ray. Now he was talking about fronting the band. I still hadn't wrapped my head around that live audience, and it would be big with Israel Caine and Sienna Star on the bill.

"You'll kill it, Glory. Never doubt it." He jumped up and hugged me. "I wish your mother was here. I want to thank her. Damn, I can't believe she gave you your voice back! It's amazing." I swear he was about to tear up.

"At last someone appreciates me." My mother shimmered into view.

"For God's sake, Mother. Be careful. Did you check to see if any of the mortals were still around?" I scanned the large room.

"Of course, darling. All clear. Relax. I believe this handsome man is going to hug me." She laughed when Ray lunged off the stage and grabbed her, twirling her around the room.

"Damn right, I am. Glory has a tremendous voice and you gave her back her instrument. I, for one, owe you a debt. Anything you want, lady, anytime." He set her down on her feet.

"Ray, be careful. Mother can use that statement against you." I stepped off the stage. "It was just an expression, Mother, not a vow."

"Oh, I don't know. Your Israel Caine sounded very serious just then. Call me Hebe, Ray. That is what you said I should call you. I may hold you to that promise. If things need doing and you're the best man for the job." She smiled and patted his cheek. "You never know what might come up someday."

"Glory, I meant it. This lady worked a miracle for you. Where's your gratitude?" Ray picked up my hand. "Did you hear her, Hebe? Her voice is incredible. I know it doesn't call men to her, like it did when she was a Siren, but it still stirs something in me. I said it before. She puts her heart into the music. Sienna and I see a real future for Glory on the stage."

"Is that what you want, Gloriana? A stage career?" My mother pursed her lips. Tonight they wore a luscious shade of pink to compliment a deep purple velvet dress.

"I'm not sure yet. Let me survive my first performance and then ask that question." I rubbed my damp palms on my black jeans. I'd shed my jacket and was all in black now. Purple. I should wear that color more often myself. It looked good on blondes.

"You'll be fine. But I haven't forgotten my quest to get you in front of Zeus. Not sure how that will work if you pursue a public singing career." Mother tapped her chin. I'd noticed it was a habit with her when she was thinking.

"Just calm down. I'm not going up to Olympus anytime soon. I have my own stuff going on down here now that I'm not about to leave." I saw Rafe waving from the doorway with my purse in his hand. He held out my phone. "Look. I have a phone call. I hope it's Jerry. Remember, he's my priority now." I saw my mother exchange looks with Ray. "No, you will not ask Ray to interfere in that relationship. No, no, no." I turned to Ray. "Jerry and I are solid. You do know that, right?"

"Sure. Sorry, Hebe. I can't get into the middle of Glory's love life much as I'd like to." Ray's smile was full of his usual charm. "Ask me to do something else."

"Did I ask you to do anything at all yet?" Mother held out her hands, the picture of innocence. "Really, Gloriana, para-noia is very unbecoming. Go answer your phone."

"Fine." I hurried across the hall. Rafe hadn't answered my phone but he must have heard it ring. I saw that I had voice mail. Two messages. One from Jerry and one from his sister. I listened to Cait's first. She and Bart were at Ian's helping him restart some of his research. Good. I felt guilty that I hadn't spared them a thought. Especially since I'd promised Jerry I would keep his sister and her boyfriend entertained while he was gone. I called her back and made sure they were still occupied.

"We're fine. Bart is in his element, helping Ian with these experiments. I *would* like to see you sometime though, Glory. Tomorrow night?" Caitlin sounded distracted. "Oh, good grief. Those two men are arguing about an experiment. I'll be glad to get away from here for a while."

"I understand. But I've got a pretty full night tomorrow. How about Sunday? And next weekend, if you two are still here, is Halloween. That's a big deal in Austin. Lots of fun on Sixth Street. I'll, uh . . ." I felt shy suddenly but plunged ahead. "I'll be making my singing debut at N-V, a club here."

"What?" Cait was surprised and I didn't blame her. For all she knew I still sang like I'd been shocked with high voltage.

"Don't worry, I've got a new voice, courtesy of my mother. It's the singing voice I had as a Siren. Pretty awesome actually. I won't disgrace Jerry." I laughed. "Seriously, I'd love for you and Bart to come. The club owner is a friend and he can make sure you have good seats. He caters to vamps."

"Well, that sounds great. Costumes?" Cait laughed this time. "You had me going, chum. I was trying to figure out how to be diplomatic and beg you not to publicly humiliate yourself."

"I can imagine. Good. I'll set you up. You remember Florence da Vinci?"

"Sure. Is she going to be there?"

I realized I hadn't clued my best bud in on this new development. "I bet she wouldn't miss it. I'll set all of you up in a big table on the balcony. Best seats in the house." I was aware that

Rafe was within earshot. "More details later. Come by the shop on Sunday and we'll find you a cool costume. Call first because we're closed. But I'll meet you and open so we can pick out something. Think Bart will want one too?"

"Knowing him, he'll wear his plaid. The man doesn't travel without it." She said something to those quarreling men in the room with her. "Ian wants me to remind you that you already invited him to come too. Can you squeeze him in at our table?"

"Why not?" I could see this becoming a huge deal and my stomach turned. "And Bart's plaid is perfect. Nothing sexier than a man in a kilt in my opinion."

"Guess my brother will be back by then and probably wear his as well."

"I hope so." I said something else, whatever was necessary to get off the phone, then ended the call.

"Sounds like we'll have every vampire in Austin on the balcony for your big debut." Rafe grinned at me. "Is that nerves I'm seeing?"

"What? Just because my hands are shaking and I've gnawed off half my cuticles, doesn't mean I'm nervous." I paced the room, glancing back to where my mother and Ray were getting way too cozy. "I'm not sure I can do this, Rafe. Sing in front of all those people."

"Sure you can. Now go out in the hall and call Blade back. You'll feel better once you talk to him. Won't you?" He smiled and gently pushed me out the door.

"Yes, I hope so. Especially if he says he's on the way home with some solutions to our problem." I smiled at Rafe. "Thanks. You've gone above and beyond, as usual."

"Happy to help. I'm keeping an eye on your mother. You think she has the hots for Caine?"

"Eww. Now I have that picture in my head." I slapped his

arm then stepped into the hall and shut the door. I listened to the voice mail from Jerry first. He was clearly tired but excited when he said to call him as soon as I got the message. I hit speed dial and he answered on the second ring.

"Glory. What are you doing?" He sounded winded.

"I'm at rehearsals. I'm going to sing, Jer. In public on Halloween. Can you believe it?" I sat on the floor across from the door. It was so good to hear his voice. "What did you find out? Where are you?"

"I'm on my way home. I have a plan, Glory. What's this about singing? At N-V?"

"Where else? You mean you were flying when I called? Be careful answering so fast. You must have hit the ground hard." I pictured him shifting and answering in one swift motion. It was dangerous, out there in the dark, God knows where.

"I'm okay, Gloriana. I just wanted to tell you what I found out."

"So tell me." I gripped the phone, praying he had a solution to get rid of Mel once and for all.

"Well, her sister was a big help. Seems she disapproves of Mel's voodoo tricks. Is a little jealous of her success too, the whole inspirational talk thing, though I had to read her mind to get that from her. Anyway, she said Melisandra has a pattern with men. She gets tired of them quickly once she knows they are hers." I heard him swear.

"Where are you? Did you fall? Hurt yourself?"

"No, just landed in some thorny bushes. I'm fine. Did you hear what I said? Do you get the implications?"

"So Mel likes the chase, but once she catches a guy she loses interest." I stared up at the ceiling. "What's your plan? To come back and turn into her love slave?" My phone cracked and I wiggled my fingers to loosen my grip. I couldn't afford a new phone right now.

"Now, Gloriana, calm down. I can hear the tension in your voice." He coughed. "Damn, I dropped into a swamp. Hang on." I heard water sloshing. "There, I'm on dry land now."

"Jerry, maybe you should call me back." I was trying not to dwell on the whole idea of Jerry convincing Mel he was hers.

"No, let me tell you what I want to do. I'll come back and throw myself at Mel's feet. Tell her how desperately I missed her when I was in Miami." He slapped something. "Damned mosquitos. And people call us bloodsuckers."

"Will you have sex with her? Seems like that would be the best way to convince her." The ceiling blurred but I blinked it into focus again.

"No. Absolutely not. I intend to mesmerize her, Gloriana. I know she's got powers, but her sister thinks that I can do it."

"Then mesmerize the bitch to quit loving you, Jer. That would solve all our problems." I was so frustrated I wanted to scream. A quick look around convinced me that wasn't a good idea. A waiter hurried into the practice room with a glass of synthetic for Ray. He glanced at me curiously.

"You know I can't do that. That's not how it works. We can mesmerize someone to forget they ate a piece of chocolate, but not that they love chocolate. Trust me, I've tried with Mel already. She's wary of me. It's going to take some doing on my part. Alexandra gave me a potion to help get Mel to let down her guard with me."

"So this sister's a voodoo priestess too?" What a family. "Why not a potion to get Mel to hate you?"

"Trust me, I asked. No go. They're Haitian. But Alex practices voodoo in what she calls its pure form. None of the dark arts. Or so she says." More rustling. "Damn that's a big snake. Not poisonous though. Anyway, she was sure that I could plant a suggestion in Mel's mind that we had sex when we didn't, especially if I could slip this potion into her meal beforehand."

"Oh, kind of like how she drugged you, had her way with you and you didn't remember only in reverse?" I was on my feet now. He sounded way too cozy with this Alex. Was she as beautiful as Mel? I wasn't about to ask. My black boots already had one scuff on the toe, another one wouldn't matter. I kicked the hell out of the wall. Too bad for the Sheetrock.

"Gloriana, that doesn't even make sense. There will be no sex. I swear it. I'll leave her in bed with false memories. She'll think I'm her willing sex slave."

"Leave her in bed, Jerry. Oh, yeah. I'm loving that picture." I had a feeling my phone was a goner. The floor was littered with pink rhinestones and I'd lost a piece of plastic.

"My love, I swear nothing will happen. I'll tear out her throat first."

"Really? Because I couldn't get near the bitch." I swallowed, my urge to cry about to take over.

"She didn't trust you. She lets me close, maybe because she wants to believe I return her feelings. If I declare my undying love . . . Hell, if I can't mesmerize her, I'll kill her and damn the consequences." His voice was firm.

"She's famous. The consequences will be many and messy." I was calming down.

"That's why it's my last resort. Are you with me on this plan?"

"The plan sucks swamp water. But I guess it's all we have. I just want you safe, Jer. And back here with me." I heard my voice wobble. Shit.

"That's all I want too. Now about Halloween. You say that's when you're singing?"

"Yes. Whoopee. Good to have something to look forward to. Caitie and Bart will be there. Maybe you can have Mel drag you along as her slave. Meet your sister. Hell, announce your engagement." Okay, so I was still mad about the whole thing. I kept picturing Jerry crawling into bed with that viper. He'd have to kiss her, touch her or she wouldn't believe him. My stomach churned again. Tequila was off my menu forever.

"Calm down, Gloriana. You know you're the only woman I love. But I'll do what it takes to end this and keep you safe. If I'd so demean myself as to literally become her love slave, do you think Mel would still want me?" His voice was low and determined.

"I would. I'd want you any way I could get you." I slid down the wall again. "I don't like it, Jerry. You and that woman, together. She has all these tricks and potions. She could drug you again. Do . . . anything to you."

"Yes, she could. But I plan to beat her to it. And why would she have to if I'm offering myself to her willingly? Especially if she thinks you and I are through, Gloriana. She still thinks that, doesn't she?"

"I hope so. I'll keep doing what I can on this end to make sure of it. It's the only thing I can do to help you now." I pressed a hand to my eyes. "Damn it, Jerry. You'd better sneak over to see me as soon as you get back. Any idea when that will be?"

"Late tomorrow night. I have to stop soon for the sunrise and I'm in Louisiana now. I have a safe house a couple of hours from here." He cleared his throat. "Are you okay, Gloriana?"

"Yeah, sure. Just trying to process this stupid plan. You have to know how much I hate it." I sighed.

"I love you, Gloriana." His voice became husky. "Believe that, if you believe nothing else."

"Stay safe, Jer." I ended the call then barely restrained myself from throwing the phone across the hall. Playing as Mel's love slave? I sure as hell did hate the idea. This could not end well. The woman was too powerful.

At least tomorrow night I'd have a chance to see if she truly believed Jerry and I were done. I struggled to my feet. Through the almost soundproof door, I heard Ray at the piano. Singing to my mother? I needed to get in there and break up that twosome.

Time to practice another song. I didn't have the heart for it. But if everything hinged on Halloween night, I'd do it and make it the show of my long lifetime. For Jerry.

Fourteen

Saturday night Sienna, Rafe and I headed for the large auditorium, tickets in hand. I was ready to see Mel in her natural
habitat as an inspirational speaker. Own the world. Really?
Why not the universe?

"Glory, you look a little tense. If I understand this situation
correctly, you want this woman to believe you and Rafe are
a couple. If so, then you'd better loosen up a little instead of the
current touch-me-and-die vibe you've got going on." Sienna
reached forward from the backseat of the SUV and tapped me
lightly on the shoulder.

I laughed, caught out. She was right. I had to lighten up.
Rafe was driving and I had my fists clenched in my lap. I'd
barely spoken since we'd gotten in the car.

"I'm sorry, guys. I haven't told you Jerry's plan yet. He's
getting back tonight." I told them his idea for getting Mel to
dump him.

"That's crazy. He's taking a big chance that she'll follow her
usual pattern. What if she decides he's the one man who could

be a keeper?" Rafe steered into the parking lot and into a vacant spot. We were early because I wanted to get a good seat, but the lot was already half-full.

"I don't need you to bring me down, Rafe. I've got enough doubts of my own." I unbuckled my seat belt. "This might work. It's all we've got for now anyway. What else can we do? Aggie destroyed Ian's lab. He was planning to work on making a potion to use against Mel. I doubt he'll come through with that now." I needed to check on the status of that. It still might come in handy if Mel did react differently than Jerry expected.

"Hey, I've known women who just like the chase. I say it's worth a shot. Some people just want the unattainable. Then once they've got it, they move on. Kind of like I've seen your friend Flo do with clothes, Glory. I swear she wears something once and then that's it for her." Sienna leaned between the seats again.

"Yes, that's about right." I turned to Rafe. "See? It's possible that's the way Mel is about men."

"I get it. But is Blade really going to be able to keep from having sex with her?" He touched my hand. "Sorry, Glory, but you know he may have to go all the way to be convincing."

"He's right. If this woman's as powerful as you guys say she is, I don't see how he can avoid it." Sienna just had to add her two cents.

I jerked open my car door. "I think we've talked about this enough. Don't forget, Mel's mortal and Jerry's a powerful vampire. I trust him to make this work without sleeping with her. Okay?" I wouldn't look at them, just hopped out of the SUV. "Coming?"

"Sure." Sienna opened her own door. "I'm sorry. It's not my business anyway."

"No, I get it. You were just trying to help." I felt Rafe at my elbow.

"Come on, we need to hear what the woman has to say. Glory claims she wants to become more ambitious. I say it's high time." He slammed my car door, then smiled. "Can you look a little more excited, Glory? Tonight, you and I are a couple. Let's see if you can play that part with conviction."

"I think I can manage." I twined my arms around his neck but stopped with just a kiss on his cheek. "Thanks, Rafe. You know just how to keep me on track."

"I guess so after all these years. Come on, ladies. I may learn something in there too." Rafe offered both elbows and we walked into the building like we were off to see the wizard. Inside, I slipped into an aisle seat not too far back with Rafe between Sienna and me.

There was a large stage up front as well as a podium. A picture of a spinning world, as taken from space, was showing on a big screen with Mel's catchphrase, "Own the World," printed in scarlet letters across it. We had a brochure on our seats which offered private sessions with Mel at a thousand bucks an hour. Or we could buy packages with tapes of different sessions she'd conducted in the past. She even had a series on building a business from the ground up.

"She must have a personal fortune. Look at these prices." Sienna stuffed the brochure in her purse. "I would have to be really impressed to spring for any of this at that cost."

"No kidding." I saw the auditorium was filling rapidly. There were several people in dark blue blazers with the world logo on the pocket—who obviously worked for Mel—helping people find seats. They were also doing sound checks and setting up some equipment on the stage. No sign of her zombie pals. I guess she kept her creepy creatures away from her regular business. Music played softly as the lights began to dim. It was a haunting tune, the kind you expected in an ashram or Indian temple.

"Excuse me." A woman in her forties or fifties pushed her way into our row and plopped down on the other side of Sienna. "Oh, I'm so excited. Have you been to one of Ms. Du Monde's lectures before?"

"Um, no." I answered since no else seemed to be interested in picking up the conversation.

"This is my fifth one. Ms. Du Monde is so inspiring. I've actually taken my business nationally now. I had a little start-up coffee bar before. Nothing great." She smiled at Rafe, who was suddenly paying attention. "Well, after the first lecture, I got focused. Realized I was wasting my time, what with a Starbucks on every corner, you know?"

"Yes, you're right about that. So what did you do?" Rafe looked her over. She was attractive and he didn't mind the age thing, though, as an immortal, he'd always look early thirties. I gave him an elbow and rubbed his thigh, reminding him we were supposed to be a couple.

"I sprang for one of the private sessions with Ms. Du Monde. It was so enlightening!" The woman lit up like a cheerleader at the playoff game. She dug in her purse and pressed business cards into Sienna's hand, Rafe's, and even stretched over to give one to me. "She helped me see what I really wanted to do."

I looked down. "You're in scrapbooking?" The card was cute, eye-catching and a good advertisement for that kind of shop.

"Yes! It was my passion, you see. I did it all the time and had a great network of contacts in that world, online and locally. I knew what people wanted and it's a multimillion-dollar industry. Can actually bring in billions over time. There were no specialty shops meeting our needs. You have to go into the big box stores and dig for what you want. So frustrating. I started with one shop in a strip center in my hometown and I hit at just the right time." She giggled. "I have twenty stores now in some of the biggest cities in the southwest. I'm looking to expand east now."

"That's amazing. And Mel, I mean, Ms. Du Monde helped you figure that out?" I noticed that the woman's outfit was expensive, her hair expertly colored and cut. Her watch was a Rolex and her purse one I would have killed for. Okay, I believed she was doing extremely well.

"She made me realize I hadn't tapped into my potential, or my true passion. It was what I needed to hear at the right time. And there's the fear, honey. It's so easy to let that hold you back. I dumped that naysayer I was married to. Boy, did that help me grow and change!" The lights flickered. "Oh, we're going to start." She laughed. "Brace yourselves. You're in for a life changing event. Good luck to you!"

"Thanks." Rafe picked up my hand which I'd forgotten was clutching his thigh. "We're looking forward to it."

Sure enough, at the exact starting time, the massive doors at the back closed with a loud click and the lights went out completely.

Then the spotlight came on. There she was, Melisandra Du Monde standing center stage. She wore one of her expensive business suits, this one gray silk, with a microphone clipped to the lapel. She had a strand of pearls around her neck and small pearl studs in her ears. Her dark hair was swept back from her face and done up in a French twist. She looked calmly over the packed house.

"Are you ready to own the world?" She sounded like an evangelist at a prayer meeting. The audience shouted "Yes!"

and the place erupted into applause. We all joined in. If nothing else, we appreciated the drama.

"I hope you're ready to open your minds and your hearts to a new way of thinking. Some of you have been content to live small lives. Is that you? Have you been limiting yourself? Telling yourself this is all you deserve? That to seek more would make you grasping or perhaps even, dare I say it, greedy?" She leaned toward us, resting her elbows on the wooden podium. Her dark eyes raked the room, seeking out the weak. I wanted to shrink down in my seat. Guilty as charged.

"Why? Why are you content to be less than you can be? Why do you let others walk on you as if it is their right to be better, greater, have more, be more? How many of you have stood by and watched someone else take what you wanted and done nothing? Raise your hands. Come on. Hold them high. No, I can't see you. The room is too dark, but your neighbor can. Are you ashamed?" She shook her head. "You should be. How can you be so spineless?" There was a murmur of outrage in the room.

I was a charter member of Doormats Anonymous. That had become clear to me lately. I wondered if she could see my hand in the air. I stared right at her. But I was pretty sure she was on a roll, her speech canned, and we were just a faceless crowd.

"Oh, have I hurt your feelings? Too bad. Put your hands down. I don't want to see cowards here. That's over. I spit on that." To our shock she did just that. Elegant, ladylike Melisandra leaned over and spit on the hardwood floor. We all reared back in our seats and gasped.

"Ah, I've shocked you. Good. I'm acting out. Aggressive women are called bitches. Men are hardasses. Ladies don't spit on polished floors. Neither do gentlemen. Why not? Because society doesn't like it?" She strode out from behind her podium.

"What if I tell you I don't give a damn what society thinks?" She pointed a silver-painted nail around the room. "Who is society? You? You? Or perhaps *you* are the one who decides what is acceptable." She stabbed the air in my direction. "I don't accept your rules. Your restrictions. If I think I'm capable of something, if I want it badly enough, then I will do it, get it, have it. I will find a way. And I sure as hell won't allow you to take what I want away from me."

I had chills. Jerry. She'd wanted him and now she was getting him. He thought he could play her. Could he? She seemed so determined, so in control. Not the wild-eyed voodoo woman I'd seen before at all.

She began to pace the front edge of the stage. "Find a way. Did I tell you to break laws? No. But you say you can't get what you want. There are blocks, people, problems in your way. Are there really? Or is it just your fear holding you back?" Her eyes were bright as she stabbed the air. "You build your own roadblocks, my friends. With your fears, your imagined inadequacies. Oh, poor me. I cannot do it. I am weak. I'm afraid I will fail." She stopped in the center of the stage. "Yes, you will fail. If that is the tape running in your head. Failure breeds failure. Fear breeds failure. Stop it!" Her voice rang out in the silent hall. "Get off the pity train right now!"

I was pretty sure it wasn't only the vampires here who had stopped breathing.

"Today is a fresh start for you. There are no failures here. You have arrived at a new beginning. That pitiful person who let everyone else walk all over them is gone and you will never go back there again. It's time to decide. What do you want? Have you even dared name it to claim it?" She gestured with her hands. "Bring up the lights. Now!" she commanded her unseen minions.

"Now look under your seats, all of you. You have paper and pens. Pick them up and write down one thing you want. Must have. Think hard. Don't write down something trivial like a new house or car. Those are things, people. Things you will buy when your success comes to you. I don't want to see a feeling like success either. That's too vague. We must define it to see what it means to you, no one else." She paused, her eyes scanning the crowd, looking for something.

"And you'd better not put a sappy thing like love." Her laugh haunted me. I'd heard that creepy cackle before. "Please. That won't get you what you want. That's the reward you get once you've made it, reached the brass ring and turned it into gold. Love can slow you down, make you weak. Unless it's your love for the work you do and is part of your passionate drive to the top. I see your faces. Some of you want to argue. Then why are you here? If you want to own the world, focus!" She slammed her fist into her palm.

I shifted in my seat. Of course I'd gone to love first.

"I'm talking about a deeply desired something that will make you feel whole again. Change you from the sad sack who never has the best, the promotion, the money to do what your friends or coworkers do. What will make you into the take-charge person who everyone looks up to, the guy or gal who makes a difference, turns the ordinary into the extraordinary." She paused for breath and we all did the same.

"Are you thinking? Maybe it's a business, an idea for an invention you've never had the nerve to pursue, a book you want to write, the job you've always dreamed about. What do you want? It should be something concrete that you can get if you set goals and realize there are logical steps to achieving them. Come on. You're here because you needed me. Something was clawing at your gut, aching inside you and it has to come out. You have a hole that must be filled." She paused, staring around the room one more time, as if searching out the weak so she could shore us up. The woman next to Sienna was practically vibrating with excitement.

"I'm going to help you find ultimate fulfillment and happiness. Aim you toward your greater good and get you moving in the right direction. You're going to take control of your life and make it become what you want it to be. Better, greater. With the world at your feet." She paused and I could see her gathering energy from the crowd that was absolutely mesmerized by her. Hey, even me. I couldn't look away.

"So think, people. Dig deep and find the truth. What do you want? This is the first step. I give you ten minutes. This is *your* idea. Don't talk to your neighbor, friend, lover or whoever came with you. This is *your* deepest desire, not theirs. Go!" She waved her hands then we all dove under our seats for our pads and pens.

My hand shook as I stared down at the paper with her logo on it. The pen had the same. My deepest desire? I had to think about it. Love? No, not allowed. Money? I always needed it. But that was too abstract. I could get it if I went to Olympus. I needed a way to earn it myself without nasty strings attached. I'd never been afraid to work for what I wanted. Security. My heart thumped. Oh, boy, did that resonate. I could have had it with Jerry centuries ago, but at a price. Okay. Independence and security. Bingo.

Work that I enjoyed could get me that. Was it a singing career? Somehow I didn't think so. I hadn't really missed singing that much through the centuries. Probably because my subconscious associated it with murder. The idea of being in the spotlight, the focus of the crowd, wasn't thrilling me either. I'd spent centuries in the shadows, blending. I couldn't bear the thought of changing that much. True entertainers like Ray and Sienna got off to the attention and they'd had it prefangs. Me? I just couldn't see it.

But I did love my little shop. I'd always wanted to make it more successful, to have more capital to spend and to grow the business. Kind of like the scrapbooking lady. I'd seen her excitement at taking a hobby and making it into a moneymaking success. Yes! I wanted a thriving business, the best vintage clothing shop in Austin, hey, maybe in Texas. Successful enough that I wouldn't have to worry about paying the bills at the end of every month like I did now.

I was getting excited, sure I was on to something. My mother had shown me high-quality vintage things. I'd never been able to afford to travel and acquire that kind of merchandise. I would love to be able to do that. The hunt was the thrill I was looking for. I was tired of being looked down on by my friends who wore only the very best of everything. I liked vintage. Why not specialize in buying and selling the best of it?

I got busy writing. I glanced right. Rafe was writing, so was Sienna. Then I looked up. Mel was standing a few feet away. She smiled, a cold smile that sent shivers up my spine. I nodded, then casually rested my hand on Rafe's thigh, making it clear who I'd come with to her program. He glanced at me and smiled, then covered my hand with his. Mel moved closer. Anyone watching would think she was pausing to help me.

She bent down to whisper in my ear. "You aren't fooling me. Why are you here?"

I felt a chill brush past my face. One of her ghouls? I showed her my paper, full of notes. "I saw your Web site, I'm here for help." I tightened my grip on Rafe's leg. "We both are."

She smiled tightly. "A wise decision. Focus on a new beginning. Because your old life is behind you." She flicked her fingers so near my face that I flinched before I could stop myself. Rafe was halfway out of his seat when I pulled myself together enough to hold him back.

"No, Rafe, I'm fine." I kept my eyes on her as she moved on down the aisle. She stopped to speak to a woman who seemed frozen over her pad of paper. Mel was calm and acting totally professional. But then this was her business. I doubted she'd jeopardize it over a personal matter. But I hadn't imagined the threat or warning in her voice.

Still, three hours later I knew Mel was on to something. Despite my resistance, I'd learned from her and I felt drained but exhilarated. I wanted a thriving vintage clothing business and it was time to take it seriously. It seemed like everything and everyone else had come first lately. I was easily distracted. Because I'd never really nailed down my goals. Now I had a list. My pad was full of the insights Mel's program had helped me figure out.

I'd had offers before to get my inventory on computer and I hadn't followed through with them. I'd turned down his help when Jerry had wanted to help me with a business plan. Stupid. The man was a genius with stuff like that. I had a great manager in Lacy but I was underutilizing her talents. My list was loaded with things like that. By the time we headed to the car, I was bursting to share. I could tell Sienna and Rafe had also gotten a lot out of the session.

"I hate to admit it, but the woman has something to sell. She may be weird off the stage, but her seminars are powerful." Rafe started the car. "I'm seriously jazzed about some things I can do with N-V. What about you, Sienna?"

"I got a lot out of it." She clutched her pad. "Tell you later. I want to think it through. Glory? What was your big revelation? Is it a singing career?"

"No. Sorry to disappoint you, but I'm really focusing on my shop." I smiled at Rafe. "Vintage Vamp's. I think Halloween will be a one-shot wonder with the singing."

"You're kidding. With your talent?" Sienna kicked the back of the seat. "I had high hopes for you."

"It's not my thing, Sienna. Truly? The singing is a gift I didn't earn. Making a success of the shop is a real challenge. I started it from practically nothing and it's lasted longer than some shops on Sixth Street. It feels good to be able to say that. I want to make it bigger and better." I leaned back and stared out at the night. "Are we headed to N-V? I have rehearsals. Ray wants to use the band with my set and he was going to tell them about it tonight."

"Well, I guess if it's your one shot, it might as well be a good one." Sienna sighed. "Damn, I wanted to produce your first record."

"Being in the public eye is tricky for a vampire. I'd rather not deal with it, Sienna." I glanced at Rafe. "So. Big plans for the club?"

"I want to get in name bands more often. Maybe try to attract an older crowd. College kids don't spend much money. I want to expand the cocktail menu, do some specialty food items. I really haven't explored that side of the business." He talked on about his plans as he drove down Sixth Street. "Okay, we're here. Didn't you tell Miguel you'd meet him here? You ever figure out what you two have going?"

"No. I'm definitely off tequila forever. I can't figure out how, but I'm going to make it clear to him that I have no business with him. Unless it's to my benefit." I got out of the car when he stopped. Sienna was right behind me.

"Wait. What do you mean?" Rafe leaned over the console. "Glory, don't start something with Miguel."

"Rafe, I know what I'm doing. I'll see you inside. There's Danny, waiting for you, Sienna."

"Good. I called him when we left the auditorium. He made me promise. He's a great guy." She waved when Rafe took off to park his car around back in the alley behind the club. "Rafe's still acting as your bodyguard?"

"Sort of. If things work out as we hope, I won't need one much longer. But hold on a minute. I realize I haven't done my job as your mentor. When the craziness of Halloween dies down we need to talk. I haven't taught you all the stuff you should know as a newbie." I walked into the club beside her.

"No kidding." Sienna frowned at me. "If it weren't for Danny, I'd have been in trouble several times. I'm holding you to that, Glory. Mesmerizing, maybe some other vamp stuff I should have learned by now is important, and I'm clueless."

"I'm sorry. We'll get to it, I promise." Then I saw Miguel at the bar. "Oh, there's trouble. One thing is for sure. I'm not doing tequila shots again. Not recommended for vamps, Sienna. Trust me on that."

Ray came up behind me. "You drank tequila, Glory? I thought we couldn't touch alcohol."

I wanted to vanish. Unfortunately there were mortals all around who would wonder about that. "We can. I just found that out. But in limited quantities. I had a blackout after a few tequila shots last night. It's dangerous, Ray. And, as an alcoholic, I know you're not going to try it."

His smile didn't reassure me. "As an alcoholic, all I can say is, I hope not. I'm heading upstairs to give the boys your songs. You coming?"

"In a little while. I've got to meet with someone first." I rubbed his shoulder. "That hope is good enough for me. I'm proud of you."

"Knock it off, Glo. I'm doing the best I can. I don't need your pity." He shook off my touch and headed up the stairs.

"Touchy." Sienna frowned. "Too bad. He's got few enough friends as it is. I still won't forgive him for what he did to me. I'll tell him to practice with me first, then you can take your time with Mr. Tall, Dark and Dangerous over there." She licked her lips. "He has a certain appeal. I always did like a bad boy."

"He is that. He's using Aggie now for his dining companion so I guess your arrangement with her is off. I'd stay as far away from that scene as I could get if I were you." I smiled. "Fair warning."

"Aggie. Figures. And I'm fine without her. Except she *is* supposed to sing with us. I guess she's upstairs. Might as well get this over with then." Sienna headed up the stairs herself with one last look over her shoulder at Miguel. He caught her eye and nodded. I walked over to join him.

"She's a young one. Has barely broken in her teeth, I would say." Miguel met me halfway across the room. "Shall we go up to a table? I'll have them bring you straight synthetic this time. So you can't claim I got you drunk."

"Yes, she's young. Made only a week ago. I need to do something about training her. All I've done so far is taught her to drink synthetic." I let him lead me up the stairs to a table far away from any occupied ones on the balcony.

"You must pay attention, Gloriana. I believe her shifter bodyguard is giving her his blood. Much as your guard once gave some to you. *Verdad?*"

"What?" I saw Danny follow Sienna closely up the stairs, his hand on her waist. Thinking back, I realized her cheeks *had* been flushed from recent feeding when we'd picked her up earlier to go to the auditorium, a deeper flush than a mere synthetic would have given her. Danny had been with her, of course. I'd smelled shifter on her but figured it was just because he'd been guarding her during her death sleep.

"They seem very close. As you and Valdez are." Miguel just wouldn't let it go.

"I never used Rafe as my blood slave, Miguel. I rarely drank from him. Only in emergencies or when . . . Never mind."

"Ah, I see." He winked. "I can read your mind, you know. There is no better time to feed than after making love." He laughed at what must have been my furious expression.

"Stay out of my mind. I mean it." I sat down, spreading my skirt over my knees. I'd dressed carefully for my excursion to see Mel. I had on a red and black print wrap dress that was as slenderizing as anything I owned. My black heels made me taller than usual but I still felt small next to big, muscular Miguel. I shrugged off my black jacket that had given me a professional touch and set my clutch on the table.

"You are so easy. I didn't even have to read your thoughts. Your facial expressions give you away, Gloriana. But enough play, we are here to do business." He nodded to a waitress who brought over our drinks, slipping her a large bill for her trouble. She blushed and backed away.

"What business? I have no business with you. I don't need a loan and that's all the business I know that you conduct in Austin." I picked up my drink and took a cautious sip. My favorite flavor and nonalcoholic. I took another drink.

"Gloriana, relax. We were talking about a simple exchange of information. You seem to run with what is considered the legitimate crowd of vampires in Austin."

"Legitimate? You mean the law-abiding citizens? Then, yes, I do. While you are one of the illegitimate." I smiled. "Oops, I didn't just call you a bastard, did I?" I couldn't resist. The man had deliberately gotten me drunk and continued to flaunt powers he considered superior to mine.

"You wouldn't be wrong." His smile was tight. "I want to break away from Lucky Carver and her operation. It has a stench that taints everyone who comes in contact with it."

"You mean the stench of sleazy, ill-gotten gains." I set down my drink. "She's not my favorite person, obviously. When she turned Ray vampire against his will, I became sorry I ever saved her life. She loans money to desperate people at an exorbitant rate of interest. When they can't pay, she threatens them, sometimes hiring hit men to make a statement about what happens to deadbeats. You know anything about that?" I was glad we were in a public place. I'd met him in a dark alley once and hadn't doubted he could have killed me if he'd wanted to. But Miguel had let me go. Yes, he could be bad, but even then I'd sensed a better man somewhere inside his hard exterior.

"Of course. You know I do. But I'm through with her. I want to settle down, become an honest man. I need your help with that." He signaled the waitress for another round. "You promised last night to assist me."

"Why should I?" What the hell had we talked about when I'd been in my tequila tailspin? "I can't imagine promising you anything." I picked up my drink.

"You've had too many threats to your shop and you want them to stop. The latest one is by that voodoo woman your lover Blade hooked up with." Miguel put a hand over his heart. "Surely you remember this conversation. You told me everything. How you hate this Mel person."

"So? I've handled threats in the past and I'll handle her too. I'm sorry I unloaded on you. Won't happen again." I drained my first glass just as the second one landed on the table. I was never touching tequila again.

"I was happy to listen. But you confided in me that you are tired of the men in your life running to your rescue. You need someone who's not emotionally involved with you to provide protection for your place. Right?" He'd barely touched his first glass. Now he drank it down while he waited for me to process this bombshell.

Why had I told him all this? Yes, I hated that Jerry, Rafe, even Ray were always coming to my defense. It not only made me feel obligated, it pushed me into the role of helpless female. But the worst thing was that it put the men I loved into harm's way. I looked Miguel over. If there was ever a man who could take whatever crap came at him and survive unscathed, it was this guy. Not only would he survive, but whoever dared mess with him would regret it if they lived long enough. I'd love to see how he handled Mel and her zombie bookends.

"My blessing with the good guys in exchange for your protection?" I traced a circle in the moisture on the table. I'd just written down my future goals. If I'd added protect the business, things could not have fallen into place more perfectly. Mel would have said it was the universe providing what I needed. I just had to pay attention. Too bad I knew this guy for a loose cannon of the most dangerous variety. How confident was I that I could handle him?

"That's the deal." He wouldn't look away when I finally met his gaze.

"What if nothing I do can get you the sweet smell of legitimacy?"

"I have faith in you, Gloriana. And if you can find out from your mother that I might be descended from the gods . . ." He raised his hands in an almost Italian gesture. "Well, we know that kind of pedigree goes a long way toward buying forgiveness for past sins with the upright citizens of the world."

"Having Aggie around you isn't going to add any luster to your image." I had to say it.

"Her name is now Angel. I'm hoping she will start acting more like her new name. And she's disposable." He leaned back like he hadn't just hauled Aggie to the dump.

"Nice name. Good luck with that. But rethink disposing of her. Your new image demands a kinder solution. Maybe you can find her a new sucker, uh, I mean protector."

"So you'll do it?" He leaned forward, elbows on the table. "I want to start immediately."

"Then prove you know something about voodoo. This woman Melisandra Du Monde wants my boyfriend Jerry for herself. Can you check on her? See what she's got going? I don't want her to hurt him or to get a chance to drug him again. She did that once and it almost destroyed him."

"I can do that." He reached across the table.

I stared down at his outstretched hand. "What? You want to shake on the deal?"

"Oh, yes. You've not agreed formally. I insist on it, Gloriana. I know if you give your word, you will keep it. In my business, I've learned how to read people and I've done my homework. You do have integrity, do you not?"

"Unfortunately. It hasn't always been my friend." I remembered Mel exhorting us to do whatever it took to get what we wanted. I'd never been ruthless. Mel would see it as a weakness. I looked into Miguel's deep brown, almost black eyes. He wouldn't hesitate to do what needed doing. Right now, that was an asset I could use.

"Do you swear you will honor your half of our bargain, Gloriana?" He just kept staring.

I swallowed then glanced down at his hand again, dark, big

and calloused from years of handling weapons. I laid my hand in his and felt a shock of power bind us together.

"Deal. Don't make me regret this, Miguel." I glanced up in time to see a satisfied smile soften his harsh but handsome features.

"And don't let me down either, Gloriana." He raised my hand to his lips, then lightly dragged a fang over it. "I don't take disappointment well."

Fifteen

I headed upstairs slightly light-headed from all the power exchange. I wasn't sure what I'd done but, with Miguel checking out Mel, at least I'd done something. Ray was waiting for me and the band clapped when I entered the room.

"Oh, wow. Thanks. But you haven't heard me sing yet."

"If Ray says you're good, that's enough for us." The drummer gave me a cymbal crash. "Hop up here and let's see what you've got." The rest of the band echoed the sentiment.

Aggie aka Angel made a noise as she walked out of the room. Sienna stopped her and spoke to her quietly. They both left, I guess to hash out the right attitude. I couldn't worry about it now. I had to prove myself to seasoned musicians.

When Ray and I were ready, the band started the music, an eighties hit. We looked at each other and smiled. It was fun and the beat with the drums became irresistible. When we finished, the band made appreciative sounds with their instruments.

"Stop! You're embarrassing me. But I had no idea we could sound so good." I hugged Ray. "Thanks for doing this, Ray."

"No problem. Now we'll run through the other two songs. You ready?" He sat down at the piano. We'd talked about how it would go, but now he included the band on these numbers too. I knew it would sound better and it did. By the time we were done, going through the songs time and time again, I was exhausted but elated. We'd rehearse a few more times but basically we'd gotten the songs worked out.

"Thanks, guys." I gave each band member a hug and made sure we were all happy with how it went. I didn't tell them this was the one and only time I'd sing in public. I had a feeling it would take the edge off the performance. But I owed it to Ray to let him know. I was surprised Sienna hadn't told him. But then Sienna probably didn't say a whole lot to Ray anyway.

"You were awesome. What's next?"

I stretched. "I'm going home. Jerry may be back late tonight. I want to meet him. The shop closes at midnight on Saturdays so I don't have to worry about stopping by there for a change."

"You going to give it up? For a music career?" Ray stacked his music on top of the piano.

"No, the opposite. Music isn't my passion. Sorry if that disappoints you, Ray."

"What? With all that talent you're going to just walk away from it? After one gig?" He helped me down from the stage. "I don't get it, Glory. You could have an amazing career."

"Is it? Amazing?" I let go of his hand. "I've seen the strain you're under, balancing a successful career with a vampire's schedule. And I know how the paparazzi hound you. I really don't want to be that public. I had a taste of it when we were supposedly engaged and I hated it."

"Yeah, they weren't too kind to you. You wore a blue dress and they called you a blueberry." He grinned. "I think blueberries are delicious." He grabbed at me playfully.

"Thanks for reminding me." I walked to the door and checked my phone. "Oh, a message from Jerry. Sorry."

"No, I get it. He's won." Ray made a face. "But this singing thing. I'm not giving up on you, Glory. You should sing. Share the gift. You owe it to the world."

"No, I owe it to myself to do what I really want and need. Believe it or not, I learned that tonight from a voodoo priestess." I kissed his cheek. "Now I've got to go. Rafe's waiting for me downstairs. See you Tuesday for practice."

"Fine. See you." Ray had decided to pout. I left him to it while I listened to Jerry's voice mail. He'd stopped at home to shower and change clothes. He would see me on the roof of my building.

By the time I got home, which was still Lily's apartment, I was pretty tired. I left Rafe watching a sports show on TV while I showered and changed into a gown and robe. Then I headed for the roof. Rafe left me to it. He could certainly hear if anyone entered the building and tried to go past him to the roof.

I settled on a lawn chair someone had left out to watch the stars and had just dozed off when I sensed movement above me. A familiar black bird drifted down from the sky. Then the man I loved shifted in front of me.

"Jerry!" I jumped up and ran into his arms. "I'm so glad you're back."

"That's the kind of welcome a man dreams about." He pulled me close and kissed me. When he finally let me go, he ran his hands down my body. "Hmm. What's this? Ready for bed? Rafe around?"

"I'll call him. You can stay with me. Mel probably thinks you're still in Miami anyway." I pulled my phone out of my robe pocket and gave Rafe instructions. "All clear."

"You're still in Lily's apartment?" He followed me down-stairs.

"Yes, I love it." I unlocked the door. When we were both inside, I threw off my robe. "But not as much as I love you."

"I don't deserve this." He brushed my hair back from my face. "Gloriana, you're so beautiful. When am I going to hear you sing?"

"Forget singing." I pulled his hand to my breast. "Make love to me, Jerry. Show me that you're mine, all mine. And that Mel doesn't have any part of you."

"Don't speak that woman's name in this place. I won't have her here." He pulled me roughly to him, his mouth on mine. He swept me into his arms and carried me into the bedroom, where he laid me gently on the bed. He threw off his clothes until he was naked.

I gazed up at his strong male body, the muscles, the scars, every inch of him so dear to me. He reached down and slid my nightgown up and off over my head. Then he began a leisurely exploration, kissing a path up one of my legs and down the other. He stroked my breasts and slipped his tongue around each nipple until he sucked one into his warm mouth. I gripped his hair and urged him on, begging him to take me sooner, harder.

God, but he was being patient. I wanted to flip him over and force him to finish this. No. Why the rush? I bit my lip and let him continue his erotic torture as he kissed his way down to the pleasure point between my thighs. He pulled my legs up and over his shoulders, grinning at me wickedly before he licked inside, his tongue toying with me and bringing me to a screaming peak that had me twisting his ears.

"Bastard! I'll make you pay for that." I shuddered on the bed, beside myself with pleasure.

"Oh, will you?" He leaned back enough for me to see the light in his eyes while he slid his hand down to squeeze my buttocks. Then he ran his fingers inside to tease me mercilessly. "Do you hate this? Or this?"

"Yes!" I panted. "Oh, God, but I hate that even more." I writhed on the bed as the sensations spiraled out of control again. He knew what he was doing to me and laughed before sliding me down his body to plunge inside. This was what I'd been craving, needing so desperately. Oh, the way he filled me. I grabbed his arms, my nails biting into his flesh. I smelled his blood and my fangs were down, eager to take his vein.

"Take me, Gloriana. I want you to have all of me." He fell on top of me, his neck just where I needed it.

I gasped as I held him close, my lips on his warm, salty skin, my bite clean and true. His blood flooded my mouth and I filled myself with him even as I felt him come inside me, warm and perfect just as I was clenching around him.

"I love you, Gloriana. No one else. Ever." He whispered in my ear as he thrust one last time.

I wrapped my arms and legs tight around him, afraid to let him go. He was mine. Only mine. I told him that in my thoughts then gave him my vein, offering him strength that I knew he needed after his long trip. Finally we slipped apart, holding each other and falling on our pillows moments before dawn.

I tried not to imagine him in Mel's bed. He'd have to hold her before he looked into her eyes and convinced her that they'd made passionate love even though they hadn't. Would it work? Were we crazy to even try to fool a voodoo priestess?

I lay dry-eyed, his arm heavy around me, and prayed we wouldn't regret this plan just as dawn began to pull me under. Jerry already snored beside me, exhausted from his shift across country.

Then I heard the hall door open. Rafe. We'd arranged for him to slip back inside the apartment to keep us both safe during the daylight hours. I inhaled once, just to be sure. Yes, it was him. I relaxed and turned to kiss Jerry's bare chest, then his sleepy smile. It couldn't be our last time together. I'd know it, surely. Then the sun rose and I knew nothing at all.

Jerry was about to sneak out after sunset when I took a call from Caitlin and arranged to meet her at the shop. He decided to go down and wait for her with me.

"You actually went to one of Mel's seminars?" Jerry stood beside me while I unlocked the door. "She can be impressive, can't she?"

"Yes, though I hate to admit it. She got me fired up to get serious about the shop. Focus my energy. I guess I can see why you might, might have been attracted to her in the first place."

Jerry leaned against the door before I could open it. "I'll always regret it, Gloriana." He rubbed my cheek with his thumb. "I hope it's taught me to control my bloodlust from now on."

"Come on, Jer. It wasn't just bloodlust at work. She's a beautiful, intelligent, dynamic—"

"Hush." He pressed that thumb over my lips. "You're all the woman I want or need. No more time-outs, Gloriana. Promise me. When we're apart, I obviously go mad."

I reached for his hand. "Poor Jerry. Do you get lonely without me?"

"God, yes." He pulled me to him, kissing me hard, then just as suddenly pulled back. "Do you smell blood?" He reached behind me and threw open the door.

I froze and grabbed his arm. "Yes. It smells like something died in there."

"Stay here and I'll check it out." He had on his warrior face.

"Jer, we go together. This is my place of business." Dreading what I would find, I flipped on the lights and proceeded with caution, trailing behind him since he wasn't about to let me go first. Was this Mel's doing? Who else? I thought we'd resolved our issues. I'd shown up with Rafe, clearly moving on from Jerry. Hadn't I been convincing enough? What did she want? For us to rip off our clothes and get busy in the aisle during her brief intermission?

"Well, shit." He stopped in his tracks. "There's a dead goat lying on your counter."

"Damn her! You know who has to be behind this, Jer. What do you bet she's done some kind of voodoo spell work here." The gutted animal was spread out on top of my fine jewelry case. Thank God the lock wasn't broken so the gold and silver trinkets weren't harmed. But there was blood everywhere, ruining any paperwork left lying around and spreading to the edge of a display of silk scarves. I snatched them back, relieved that they weren't touched.

"That crazy bitch." Jerry strode around the shop. "And look at this. Dead chickens. She's done one of her ceremonies all right."

"Come here." A symbol was drawn in blood on the floor in front of the entrance to my shop. It didn't take a voodoo dictionary to know that Mel was trying to keep customers from entering.

"Guess she wants to ruin your business." Jerry walked over and dropped to his knees to examine a circle of dead chickens. "I'd say Mel's trying to put some kind of spell on you. How do you feel? Any weird aches or pains?" He was up and by my side in an instant.

"No, don't be ridiculous. Are you telling me you believe in

that stuff? I'm, uh, fine." But my throat tightened and I panicked. Could I talk, sing? I swallowed and cleared my throat. Of course I was all right. Mind games. The blood, the dead animals. It was all designed to freak me out. Too bad it was working. I shivered and grabbed a shawl from a display to wrap around me.

"Believe in it? Just the evidence that I've seen with my own eyes that she's got some kind of power. In Miami, I saw her stare at people until they sickened. And you and I have seen her ghosts and her zombie-like creatures. Hell, I don't know what I believe anymore." He kept his arm around me. "You look pale, Gloriana. Sit down and I'll clean up this mess."

"No, seriously, I'm just disgusted, horrified and trying to figure out what that bitch will do next. You know Mel's determined to have you and now we've decided to let her think she's got you." I held on to him and couldn't seem to let go. "God, Jerry. I don't think I can stand the thought of you that close to a crazy woman."

"She's never going to have me, Gloriana." He brushed the hair back from my face. "I can kill her tonight and make sure no one ever finds her body."

"No! I won't have that on your conscience. You're not a stone cold killer."

"To protect the woman I love—"

"I said no, Jer. So far she's done nothing but a little vandalism. I'm not even going to call the police about this."

"Perhaps you should. If she left fingerprints . . ." He let me go and walked over to the dead chickens. "Look here. She obviously wrung their necks then sliced them open and drained their blood into a goblet. She shattered the goblet when she was done. See? There's a piece of the pedestal and the rest rolled under the dress rack. Bet the cops could get a fingerprint off the glass."

"Forget it. The police already think this shop is strange with the vamp mural and some of the reports we've put in. Remember when we were firebombed? All reporting this would do is make Mel mad at me. Do we really want that?"

"No. But she picked your lock." He'd walked over to the back door. "What happened to your security system? Cameras?"

"I couldn't afford to keep them, Jerry. We're rarely closed anyway. Sunday and Monday are the only times someone's not here twenty-four hours a day."

"False economy, Gloriana, but too late to think about that now." He grabbed a garbage bag and began picking up chickens and dumping them in the bag like it was no big deal. I didn't want to touch one. "I tell you this. If you won't let me kill her, I'm making damn sure she doesn't spend a moment out of my sight until that potion is ready. Any word on that?"

"There's been a setback." I told him about Ian's break-in. "But Cait should be able to tell us more when she gets here." I grabbed a bucket and mop. I had to get rid of every sign of Mel's intrusion. What kind of spell had she cast? I looked over the setup she'd used. I'd get on my computer and see if I could find out anything with Google.

"What about during the day?" I stopped next to Jerry. He'd just knocked the goat into another garbage bag.

"I'll keep Rafe watching you and I'll hire a shifter to follow Mel. It's the best I can do."

"But what about *you*, Jerry?" I clutched his arm. "When you're in your death sleep, she could do anything to you."

"I know that." He stared at the smear of blood on my counter. "Do you trust me, Gloriana?"

"Yes, but—"

"No buts. Trust me to do whatever I must to keep you safe. Mel won't hurt me as long as she thinks I'm in love with her. I'll mesmerize her if I can to convince her of that."

I swallowed, the determination in the set of his jaw scaring me. "And if you can't?"

"I'll do whatever it takes."

T**WO** hours later I was on my way to N-V. I'd found Caitlin a costume after she and Jerry had gotten together about that potion. Ian hadn't shared his progress with her, but she knew he *was* working on it. Since he wasn't answering my calls, that would have to satisfy us. I didn't dare call Rafe and tell him that Mel apparently still considered me a threat to her happiness. Otherwise Rafe would never have let me take the ten-minute walk to his club alone. He was at the door when I got there though.

"You okay?" He kept me from going inside. "You look upset."

I unloaded on him. Jerry had made me promise to tell Rafe about Mel's mess in the shop. "So Mel must have been asking her gods or whatever about her future. I guess she's still not sure if it's with Jerry. Or if I'm going to get him. That's what we got when we checked the Internet. She examined goat's entrails. Drank chicken blood too. My shop got her action so she could hurt me, I'm sure. She's still jealous. Can you believe it?"

"Son of a bitch. I thought we'd solved at least one problem." Rafe peered down the street. "Now we've got a new one."

"What do you mean?"

"Have you seen Sienna tonight?" He finally moved aside to let me into the club.

"No, I didn't think to stop by my apartment. I assumed she would have rehearsed first tonight and had already left. Why?" I stepped inside. Miguel was at what I was starting to think of as his usual bar stool and he nodded in my direction.

"Ray's been trying to reach her. She's not answering her cell and hasn't shown up for rehearsal. Then there's this." He handed me a paper. It was a tabloid, one of the same ones that had labeled me a chubby blueberry. I hated those gossipy rags.

"What?" I didn't want to touch it.

"Read the headline, Glory." Rafe held it up so I couldn't avoid seeing it.

"'Rock star claims she's a vampire. Drug meltdown on the air.' What the hell?" I knew my mouth was hanging open. I closed it with a snap. "Summarize the article."

"You'll love it. The only thing missing is a picture of Sienna with her fangs down." Rafe pulled me toward his office. "That's because this all came out when your girl did a radio interview the other night."

"She told me she had one scheduled but not that she planned to say anything like this." I snatched the paper and read through the article. Yes, it was all there. Sienna's claim that she'd become a vampire. She'd bragged about how strong she was and that she would live forever young. Bonus claim? She drank blood now, no more dieting. I moaned. My only hope was that everyone would think she was as crazy as a bedbug with fangs.

"I'm sure she didn't warn you or you'd have gagged her and sat on her to keep her from doing it. It was a nationally syndicated show. Goes to hundreds of stations. There's an audiotape on YouTube. I listened to the whole interview. You won't believe how many downloads it's had already. When Sienna comes clean, she doesn't miss a trick. Apparently she even showed her fangs to the deejay. Volunteered to take him down a pint if he was interested too."

"Oh. My. God." I collapsed in a chair inside his office. Nate was there, his ear to his phone. When he saw us, I heard him say something about rehab before he ended his call.

"You told her." Nate's phone buzzed. He glanced at it then turned it off. "Sienna's manager and agent are forwarding all inquiries to me. And, trust me, there are plenty. You heard what I just said."

"You going along with blaming it on drugs? Sending her to rehab? Or pretending to."

"What else can I say, Glory? That she's telling the truth?" Nate rubbed his eyes. "I can't imagine the fallout if this goes any further. I'm sticking with the drug story. Hoping this blows over fast."

"She's going to hate that. You know how proud she is of her sobriety." My own phone vibrated in my jeans pocket. I looked at the caller ID. "Here she is. Let's see what she has to say for herself."

"Sienna, where are you?"

"I'm at Danny's place. Um, did you hear what I told the deejay last night? Isn't that amazing?" She sounded tentative, despite her brave words. I hoped that meant she was getting a clue.

"Yes, I heard about it. Saw the tabloids." I'd managed to stay calm so far. Then I lost it. "Are you freaking nuts? We do not tell the world we exist, much less offer to drink from a mortal on national radio." I was yelling. Okay, maybe I should stop and take a breath. Rafe and Nate just sat back and watched.

"I listened to Mel last night, Glory, just like you did. I thought about what was holding me back from being the best

I could be. It's all this secrecy. I can't stand to sneak around. It was keeping me from reaching my potential. I have power now. Why can't I use it to show the world what I am? Fans will love it. I'll be breaking new ground. Can you imagine? The first vampire rock star!" She sounded excited now.

"No, that's not going to happen. And Ray has that honor, if you want to call it that. Not you." I said it as firmly as I could. "Listen to me. Going public isn't in your best interests. There are powerful vampires out there who will make sure that no one believes you. They will take you out before they let you spread the word like you tried to do last night."

"Take me out? What the hell does that mean? Don't be ridiculous. What I did was great. People are fascinated by us. Look at the books and movies out there. Vampires are cool. And mortals don't know what we can really do. All they know is just fantasy." Sienna wasn't paying attention. "I've come out of the closet and I'm staying out."

"Listen to me, Sienna. I'm not kidding. People aren't fascinated by vampires, they're scared of them. When they see the reality of what we are, they want to kill us. Face a vampire hunter with a stake in his hand and then tell me coming out is cool."

"No, you're wrong. Once they see how normal we are—"

"Normal! Are you freaking kidding me? You drink blood. Have fangs. Are dead all day. Are you saying that's normal?" I was yelling again. I tried to calm down. Counted to three. "Please. We have a small window of opportunity to fix this. We can put out that you were high. That you were tripping and made up this vampire nonsense. We'll send you to rehab. Not really but you'll have to lie low for a while. Until the talk dies down and some other star jumps the shark."

"No! I'm clean. I won't have my fans think—"

"Your fans know addiction is a struggle. They'll feel for you. Understand that you're trying but are only human. Ray can tell you that they stick by you when you relapse." I heard her curse Ray. Nothing new there.

"Look. This will give me time to work with you, teach you what you need to know to be a successful vampire. I can introduce you to some experienced vamps who can help you deal with the daily grind of keeping a low profile. Some people who will be better mentors than I've been." I glanced at Rafe. "I know I've let you down or you never would have done something so stupid."

"Stupid? I don't appreciate that, Glory."

I stared at my phone. "Shit. She just hung up on me." I slid the phone back into my pocket. "She's at Danny's. I think we'd better go over there."

"Will it do any good?" Rafe jumped to his feet.

"You'd better try something. Her career is circling the drain right now. Reps from her label have called me twice, wondering if she's stable enough to make the next record. They have grounds for canceling her contract." Nate pulled out his phone again. "If I can assure them she's on her way to rehab, we might have a shot at fixing this."

"Okay, I'll tell her that." I turned to Rafe. "Did you know she's using Danny as her blood donor?"

"No. That's not good. I thought he knew better." Rafe jerked open the office door. "It can make him too weak to do his job."

"They may be sleeping together too. I got a bit of a vibe about that before." I followed him out of the office.

"Wouldn't be the first time a guard and his employer got involved. Remember?" Rafe stalked across the dance floor. It was crowded and he had to weave around the dancers.

"What's going to happen if Sienna has to disappear right away?" I stopped him next to the bar.

"You lose one of your lead singers? I have a suggestion." Miguel was right there, his smile predatory. "I saw the tabloids."

"Not now, Cisneros." Rafe clearly wasn't in the mood.

"Just keep in mind, amigo, that you have a big night coming. Israel Caine singing alone? Okay. Maybe. But with a new singer? Even better. Gloriana has her little set, yes. But what if Angel were to step in for Sienna? She knows the songs and her voice is certainly up to the task."

"Angel?" Rafe looked clueless.

"Aggie." I had to give Miguel credit. He knew how to take advantage of a situation.

"Talk to Caine about that. I'm going with Glory now to see what we can do about Sienna." Rafe took my elbow and marched me to the door. "Wait here. I'm pulling the car around." He strode off.

"Too bad about the rock star. Can't keep her mouth shut." Miguel stayed close while I waited by the door.

"Yes, well, I'm going to set her straight on that." I didn't like the way Miguel was almost enjoying this crisis.

"You'd better. I've already had three calls, requesting hits on her. There is no wish among powerful vampires for our world to be exposed." He leaned against the brick wall, looking totally at ease discussing murder. "I told the clients I'd have to get back to them." His smile gave me chills. "It would be smart to wait anyway. There may be more. So far the contracts were from people who don't speak to each other. I could accept them all and get paid for each one. I like that."

"You wouldn't." I hated how calm he was about this.

"Why not? It's a simple business deal. And this woman is endangering all of us. I might even be tempted to do it for free, except I won't have to." His smile widened. "I think this vampire council the A-list here in Austin thinks so highly of would be quite happy if Ms. Star were to simply disappear one night. Don't you? I'm sure they hate troublemakers."

"*I* wouldn't be happy. Leave her alone, Miguel." I poked him in his powerful chest. "She's my responsibility. Let me handle her."

"Seems to me you failed. She's out of control." He grabbed my hand, squeezing just enough to make me bite my lip. "Shut her up, Glory, or I will. And I'll make it look like an overdose. *Entiendes?*"

"Yeah, I get you. Let me go or Rafe will jump out of that SUV that just pulled up and go shifter all over you." I jerked my hand away.

"I'd like to see him try. I really would." Miguel stepped back inside the club.

"What was that about?" Rafe asked as I slid into his car.

"Nothing. Let's go. I assume you know where Danny lives."

"Yep, got it off his employee records. I accessed it and Google Maps from my phone." He gunned his motor. "I don't like seeing you with Cisneros."

"Too bad. He's useful. I'm using him." I looked out at the passing houses. "Is it far?"

"Not too. What's with the attitude?" Rafe glanced at me.

"No attitude, I'm just taking Mel's advice. Focusing on my goals. Miguel's a scary dude. Sometimes it's handy to have one on call, that's all. You have your own business to run, Rafe. You don't have to always be available to take care of mine." I realized we were stopping already. "He lives here?" It was a nice home, almost an estate with the size of the grounds around it.

"In an apartment over the garage out back. We'll leave the

car on the street. I'm afraid if we let them hear us coming they might take off. Danny's no fool, though he certainly acted like one when he let Sienna shoot off her mouth on the radio. By now he'll have realized we'll try to shut Sienna down." Rafe pocketed his keys and helped me out of the car.

"You think he knew what she was going to say during the interview?"

"I hope not. Surely he would have told you or me what was coming or stopped her himself. Shifters also fly under the radar you know. This isn't cool for any of us." Rafe led the way toward a stone three-car garage with a second-story apartment above it. "Looked like there's an entrance on the right."

We slipped quietly up the stairs then listened. There was a TV going and the murmur of voices. Finally, I just knocked. Someone immediately cut off the television and there was complete silence.

Sixteen

"Come on, Sienna, Danny. We know you're in there. Answer the door." I knew I sounded insistent. "Please? We just want to talk."

"Who's with you?" Sienna's voice.

"Just Rafe. Can we come in?" I jiggled the doorknob. Locked of course. "You know either of us could break the door down. Don't make it come to that. I'm sure Danny has a security deposit he doesn't want to lose."

Finally we heard the door unlock. Sienna opened it, Danny's arm around her. "What do you want? I said all I'm going to on the phone."

"Can we sit down and you listen to me for a few minutes?" I didn't wait for permission, just stepped inside. Rafe stood in front of the door. I guess he wanted to make sure they didn't make a break for it. Smart.

"If you're going to call me stupid again, save it." Sienna glared at me.

"I'm sorry. I was upset. But I don't think you realize what

danger you're in." I walked over and sat on the couch. "Sit and let me explain."

"I'll stand. I told you, I'm not pretending I'm back on drugs. I worked too hard to get clean." She crossed her arms over her chest and leaned back against Danny. Clearly their relationship was more intimate than just a bodyguard and his client. Fast work.

"How else are you going to explain that what you said to the deejay wasn't true?" I leaned forward, totally serious. "Because you have to retract your statements, Sin. Your life depends on it."

"You're exaggerating. No one would try to kill me over this." She looked away, unwilling to meet my eyes.

"Yes, they would. I talked to a hit man tonight. He's already received calls. Requests to take you out. You'll be dead in days unless you make sure no one believes your tales of fangs and blood drinking."

"You know a hit man?" Sienna looked bewildered as she finally sat beside me.

"Is that all you got out of that? I'm serious, Sienna. Your record label is ready to dump you. Ranting about vampires to the media on a national broadcast made you a liability." I grabbed her arm. "And I'm going to tell you something and trust you will not repeat it. There's an executive with your label who's a vamp. He could very well be one of the clients that hit man heard from. When people start looking for vampires? They find them. He's an important man who can't afford close scrutiny. Threaten his business and you're expendable, Sienna."

"What? Someone from my label? Who?" Sienna couldn't have looked more startled.

"You think I'd trust you with that information?" I laughed. I guess it was a good thing Sienna and Ray weren't on speaking terms or she'd already know who it was. "Honey, you've gone way past getting me to share any more confidences with you. Now assure me that you're ready to check yourself into the vampire version of rehab. Nate can handle a public statement for you. It's the only way to keep that career you're so proud of. And your life."

To my complete astonishment, she didn't even take time to think about it. Instead she got a mulish look on her face that I'd never seen before. Didn't she believe me?

"No. Figure out something else. I simply can't say I'm doing drugs again." She reached out and Danny moved close to take her hand. "And there's the concert on Halloween. I won't miss it. I honor my commitments."

"Oh, yeah? I guess your commitment to keep vampires a secret doesn't count. Since you never wanted to go there in the first place."

"You got that right." She held my gaze, obviously deadly serious.

"And you'll just let your singing career go down in flames?"

"I don't believe it will. It's a bluff by the label. There's no such thing as bad publicity. Wait and see. I'll attract new fans. Pick up some Goth bodyguards to go along with the new image. I've got it all worked out." She smiled up at Danny before aiming a defiant look at me. "Screw your fake rehab."

I fumed for a minute. Clueless newbie. But the set of her jaw convinced me she wasn't budging. Finally I thought of something.

"Trust me that this isn't the right time for your, um, coming out. Maybe later." Like never. "When you're more used to our ways, you can consider alternatives, not be so impulsive." I at least had her attention.

"You're right. I would have liked to have been on national

television. At least *TMZ*. Showing off the fangs loses its punch on radio." Sienna laughed.

Oh, boy, did I want to smack some sense into her. Instead I plowed ahead with my diversion tactic.

"There you go. Now, the Halloween gig gives me an idea of how we can at least put this one fire out. To delay things." I caught Rafe's eye. He obviously wanted a private word with Danny. "I need to teach you something first. Danny, I believe Rafe needs to speak to you outside." I sent Rafe a mental message to be sure to let Danny know that he'd dropped the ball with Sienna. She wasn't out of the woods by any means, especially if what I had in mind didn't work.

"What are you going to teach me?" Sienna stood and paced the floor. By the time I'd outlined my plan, she was excited. "This is perfect! Even my publicist will love it."

"We'll see. Now, you sure you can do it?"

"I think so. Call in the guys and let me practice." She grinned.

"Shifters aren't as easy as mortals, Sienna. But you can try."

When Danny and Rafe came back inside, both of them were pretty grim. There'd obviously been a scuffle. Danny had a scrape under one eye.

"We're all set. You figure out what to do?" Rafe still wasn't smiling and kept flexing his right hand.

"I hope so. Danny, would you look at Sienna?" I was anxious to see if my fledgling could carry this off.

"Sure. Honey, I need to apologize. I let you down. Rafe explained the danger I've put you—" He stopped. "What the hell are you doing? Trying to mesmerize me?" He pulled her to him. "Sweetheart, that's never going to happen."

"Damn it. Then this plan won't work." She turned to me. "Glory, you're going to have to come along. I keep getting distracted. I was thinking about how serious Danny looked instead of the whole whammy thing. I know once we get there I'll be nervous too. I won't be able to concentrate."

"I was afraid of that, and we don't have time to find anyone else for you to practice on." I glanced at my watch. "Call the deejay and find out if he can see you tonight. We have to do this now. On top of everything else, you know Ray is probably throwing fits, don't you? Because you didn't show up for rehearsal."

"Let him." She brushed Danny's cheek with a fingertip. "Baby, are you all right? Rafe didn't hurt you, did he?"

"I can take care of myself, Sin. Rafe pointed out that I should have done a better job of watching you. Letting you shoot off your mouth last night wasn't smart. It's on me. From now on, you've got to let me take the lead and you should talk over your plans with me first. I do have years of experience in this world." He pulled her to him.

"So I've found out. Lots of experience in everything." She sighed then ran her fingertip down his chest. "I'm sorry too. I got you in trouble, didn't I? But I'm still not convinced outing vampires isn't a good idea." She stared at me. "I mean it, Glory. You may have talked me down this time, but I'm coming out someday. Wait and see."

"Sienna . . ." I was beginning to think I should mesmerize her and see if I could change her whole attitude. Would it work? Probably not. To paraphrase what Jerry had said, you could make someone forget breaking a particular rule, but not that they loved breaking rules in general. Damn it.

"I'm not talking about this anymore. Ray's called so many times that I turned off my phone." She pulled it out of her purse. "Oh. I've got three missed calls from a Damian Sabatini. Who's that, Glory? Do you know him?"

"You bet I do. He's the head of the vampire council. Call him back. You'll see that I'm not exaggerating your problems if you persist in trying to make the vampire thing public."

"I'll take your word for it." She stared down at her phone.

"No, you can't ignore him. Hand me that phone." I hit the button to call Damian back. "Damian? It's Glory. I'm mentoring Sienna Star."

"Well, you're doing a piss-poor job, I must say. What the hell is going on, Gloriana?"

"I guess you read the tabloids?"

"Of course not. But I've received plenty of irate calls and been directed to a YouTube audiotape. Your fledgling is out of control. What are you doing about it, *signorina*? Eh?" His Italian accent was coming out, a sure sign of agitation.

"It's under control. She's recanting. But maybe you should hear her say that." I passed the phone back to Sienna.

"Hello." She listened to what had to be a long speech about the importance of vampire secrecy. "Yes, sir. I'm going back on the radio tonight." Another long pause. "Yes. I'll call Marvin now. He's the deejay. I'm sure he'll be all over this. It's a scoop he can't resist." Tears in her eyes. "No, sir. I don't want that." Her eyes widened. "No! I don't!" She hit the end button with a shaky fingertip. "Wow!"

"What did he say?" I knew Damian had a temper but he must have pulled out some big threats to make her go pale and turn her face into Danny's chest.

"Never mind. I'm going to call. Give me a minute." She took a breath then began scrolling through her contact list.

Rafe pulled me outside. "What's the plan?"

"Wait and see. You're not going to want to miss this if we can pull it off."

Sienna and Danny met us on the porch. "Let's go. Marvin's eager to talk. This whole kerfuffle has given him great ratings. I think it's going to work, Glory. It *has* to work." Sienna ran down the stairs.

"The radio station is on I-35, Rafe. You want to drive?" Danny ran after Sienna.

"Guess I'd better." Rafe shrugged as we followed them. "I hope you know what you're doing, Glo. Putting that loose cannon on the radio again."

"I hope so too." By the time we arrived at the station, Sienna and I had worked out her spiel. We were met at the door by the night manager and ushered into the booth during a commercial break.

"Didn't expect to see you again so soon, Sienna." The deejay was a middle-aged man who'd obviously been in the business quite a while. "Here to add to that rant last night? Let me see those fangs again."

I leaned forward and looked into his eyes. "You never saw any fangs, Marvin. Sienna doesn't do drugs anymore. You and Sienna were playing a little trick on your listeners, but especially on the tabloids. It was to promote her Halloween gig. Do you understand?" He nodded, definitely mesmerized.

Sienna's mouth was open. "You make it look so easy."

"You'll get the hang of it." I noticed Rafe and Danny had just brought the technician back to the control room since the commercial break was about over. The men had been our necessary distraction during this part of the process. "Okay, Marvin, looks like you're on with Sienna Star."

"Welcome back to *Marvin at Midnight*, America. Have I got a surprise for you. Guess who's with me here in the booth again? It's the lovely Sienna Star. Yes, you heard me. She's here and she's just as sober as she was last night. Yes, I said it. Stone-cold sober." Marvin laughed. "Shall we let them in on the joke, Sienna?"

"Sure, Marvin. Did you see the headlines today? I don't know about you, but those tabloids make me crazy. How many alien babies have I had this month?"

"Right. And there was that time you and Israel Caine supposedly got married in Tahiti."

"Exactly. I've never been to Tahiti and I sure haven't married Ray. Though we make some great music together." Sienna chuckled. "How about that vampire joke? They jumped on that fast enough. Like I'd have fangs. And ruin these pearly whites?"

"No kidding. I can't believe the tabloids fell for it."

"Hook, line and blood bag. You and I know it was all to promote the fantastic gig Israel Caine and I have coming up here in Austin on Halloween night at Club N-V. Two shows, one at midnight. And for a special treat, my pal here, Gloriana St. Clair, will be making her singing debut." She grabbed my arm and pulled me toward a microphone. "Say hi to the folks, Glory."

I stammered out something, suddenly tongue-tied.

"A new rocker, Sienna?" Marvin looked me over with interest. "I have to tell the crowd out there that she's a blond bombshell. A real looker."

"You're making her blush, Marvin." Sienna laughed. "Glory has a retro style fans will love. Think Michael Bublé only in a miniskirt. Totally hot." She went on to talk about her upcoming album. I relaxed back in my chair, glad to be done.

Rafe winked at me through the glass and I figured Sienna had redeemed herself. Now I had to get us all back to the club and settle things with Ray. I bet he was unhappy that we'd never called him back. A glance at my phone let me know he'd tried to get me a half dozen times. I was late for our rehearsal too.

Back at the club, I hurried up to the practice room. I could hear Ray and Aggie singing when I got to the door. So he'd really agreed to give her a chance to take Sienna's place. Had Miguel used some kind of persuasion technique on him? Ray was still a relatively new vamp. I bet Miguel could mesmerize him and Ray wouldn't even know it.

"Ah, Gloriana. What do you think?" Miguel stood by the doorway, listening. "Pretty good for an early run-through. Of course Caine is being hard on her. He's disappointed that Ms. Star let him down."

"I'm not letting anyone down. We got it all fixed. Didn't you hear? The vamp thing was a publicity stunt. It'll be all over the regular newspapers tomorrow. I doubt the tabloids will print it." Sienna strolled in. She calmly stood in front of the stage until Aggie noticed her. To her credit, the former Siren finished the song then jumped off the stage.

"Shouldn't you be on your way to rehab?" Aggie put her hands on her hips. "As you can see, I managed to fill your shoes."

"Sorry to disappoint you, but I'm not on drugs and won't ever go there again. Also, my shoes aren't the issue here, chickie, so get out of my way." Sienna brushed past her and took Ray's hand to climb onto the stage. "Sorry, I'm late. I guess you heard I had a kind of meltdown last night. It's all good now. Glory helped me see the light."

Ray stared at me. "Yeah, she's pretty good at that. You okay?" He glanced back at the band. "Sienna looks good, doesn't she, guys?" Their answer was a raucous cacophony of sound and cheers.

Aggie flounced over to Miguel's side. "I quit. If they can't appreciate me, they can do without a backup singer."

"No, you will not quit. There is publicity. Right, Glory?"

"Yes, national publicity after tonight. I wouldn't be surprised if someone from Sienna's label shows up just to make sure she isn't using. A good backup singer won't go unnoticed." I felt kind of sorry for Aggie. She looked pale and had lost weight. The weight thing was a positive, still leaving her far from skinny. However, if it was because Miguel was taking too much of her blood each night, then I had to hate that.

"But they keep disrespecting me." Aggie was in a full pout now.

"Earn their respect. Be a professional. Now get back on the stage and do what you're paid to do." Miguel swatted her bottom. "Do you hear me?"

"Yes." Her lower lip quivered but she did what he said.

"Wow. You've got her trained." Bully. Aggie wasn't a friend, but no one deserved to be brought so low.

"She responds to a firm hand." Miguel shook his head. "The rock star managed to clean up her mess?"

"Yes. I can assure you, the contracts for the hits will be withdrawn. Wait and see." I smiled at his look of disappointment.

"Lucky for her." He glanced at the stage. "Because I got two more calls since we talked. I hate to miss such lucrative opportunities. I will leave the clients hanging until we're sure the matter is properly taken care of." He smiled and glanced at his phone like he was waiting for a text.

"I'm sure you can afford the financial loss." I couldn't help noticing that his clothing was of the finest quality. His silk shirt, fine woolen trousers and leather shoes were custom Italian. He was all in black, a habit with him apparently. He seemed to like to disappear into dark corners and alleys.

"Glory! Here you are. Rafael sent us up." Flo tugged on my arm. "Come out here and talk to us. Richard had a friend call him. He heard on the radio that you're singing here on Halloween. I couldn't believe it. First, because he has a friend who actually listens to the radio, and second, that you would do such a thing and not tell me."

I began to explain the strange happenings that had led to my performing on the N-V stage. I found myself pouring out the entire Mel situation too. Even Jerry's plan to make her dump him.

"No! I can't imagine Jeremiah loving anyone but you. I don't think he'll be able to fake it and make her believe him." Flo hugged me. "And how will you stand seeing him pretend to adore the woman you hate?"

"I'll just have to suck it up. If they do come here on Halloween." It would be a great way to prove to Mel that she could have Jerry. But could I calmly sing my songs while Mel watched and gloated?

"Have you seen him? Talked to him lately?" Flo's look of sympathy just about broke the layer of calm I kept covering the worry that was eating a hole in my heart.

"No, he's committed to staying with her every waking moment until she tosses him aside." I flashed back to that gutted goat. A woman who had such disregard for life . . . I had no idea what more she was capable of. No idea at all. And Jerry was with her. At her mercy.

Halloween night already. I'd agreed to let my staff close the shop at eleven so they could come to the show. Had even arranged tickets for them. Hey, if I was going to humiliate myself, might as well have a full house with plenty of friendly faces.

"Glory, I guess I'd better tell you about the table I booked last week in the center of the balcony." Rafe had come backstage to make sure I had everything I needed. We'd laughed when I'd asked for a one-way ticket to anywhere else.

"The vampires? I know about Flo, Richard, Cait and Bart. Oh, and they're dragging along Ian." I added some more dramatic eye makeup. Sienna had warned me that the spotlight would wash me out otherwise.

"Damian too. He's bringing Diana. But that's not the one I mean." Rafe pulled up a stool. "Your mother booked a table, a big one."

"Why am I not surprised? But I wonder who she'll bring? Not Zeus. She's still trying to figure out how to break the news that she has a daughter. I can't imagine that he comes down to Earth on a regular basis anyway." I gave up on more eyeliner. My hand was shaking too badly.

"I hope to hell not Zeus. If he gets pissed off, I imagine everything around him takes a hard hit." Rafe picked up a blush brush and grabbed my chin. "I've worked too hard to make this club a success. I won't see it go down now. Hold still. You look even paler than usual. Nerves?" He expertly stroked blush over my nonexistent cheekbones. I guess he'd watched me do it enough over the years to get the hang of it.

"I'm terrified. There's so much riding on this. Not that I want a music career. I think I've finally convinced Ray and Sienna that this is a one-time thing. But what if Mel and Jerry come? The idea of that bitch watching me . . . She could shoot one of her creepy creatures at me when I'm in the middle of a song!"

"Oh, they'll be here. Blade called in a favor and asked me to book a table for two next to the dance floor. As for Mel, I'm sure she's way too aware of her professional reputation to pull a stunt like that." Rafe frowned at me when I handed him my eyebrow pencil. "What?"

"I think I made a mess of my eyebrows." I should have brought along my computer mirror setup.

"Pretty much. Unless you *want* to look surprised." He wiped them off and started over. "Blade sounded like shit, Glory. I actually feel sorry for him." He laid down the pencil.

"I'm sure he's going through hell." I shuddered. "It freaks me out that he spends his death sleep in her bed."

"That's not good. If she decides he's playing her, she could just stake him in his sleep." Rafe stood. "Shouldn't have said that. I'm sorry. You have enough on your mind tonight."

"Believe me, I think about that constantly." I sighed. "Guess you'd better get out there and take care of business."

"Yep. The first show was packed. Then we had to empty the place to get ready for this midnight gig." He was trying not to let me see how happy this made him but I'd known him too long not to pick up on it.

"Sounds like it's a success. I'm glad for your sake." I took his hand. "Thanks for everything, Rafe. Lacy okay that I'm your date tonight?"

"Yep. It's tough though. You should see her in a mermaid costume Aggie would kill for. I'd like to be out there right now beating off the single guys." He frowned. "I guess she's punishing me. This better be over soon."

"It's got to be. I can't thank you enough for what you've done. As usual." I managed a smile and let him go. "All we have to do is get through tonight, get rid of Mel, and maybe we can both have what we want. If I survive this performance."

"Cheer up, Glo. I've heard you practice. You'll be dynamite." He stopped at the door, suddenly very serious. "Now about this deal with Blade. I know you're trying to trick Mel into thinking you two are through. But as a man who has loved you, I've got to tell you, that last song of yours is going to make it impossible for Blade not to show how he really feels."

"Don't say that! We need for her to think he's over me, Rafe. What was I thinking?" I dropped my face into my hands.

"You were thinking that you don't give in to any woman. You want Blade, you go after him. Voodoo? Forget about it. In a face-off, I'm betting on you." Rafe leaned against the door.

"This is so screwed up." I raised my head. He was right. I'd never wanted to meekly hand Jerry over to Mel without a fight.

"Pull yourself together, Blondie. You look beautiful. Knock 'em dead. I'll help both of you, any way I can." He opened the door before I could say another word. "You have company. I'll leave you to it."

"Thanks, Rafe. For everything. It means . . . so much." I would always love him, as a friend. I pasted on a smile when Flo, Richard next to her, waved at me from the doorway. "Come in, guys. Rafe was just leaving. He's the one who makes this place run smoothly, you know."

"It looks like tonight's a big success, Valdez. The place is packed. We gave up on parking and shifted here. Congratulations." Richard shook Rafe's hand then Flo hugged him.

"Yes! I can't wait to hear our Glory sing. She is good, no?" Flo glanced at me, clearly anxious.

"Oh, she's great. Just wait till you hear her." Rafe winked and left, closing the door behind him.

"We have a message from Jeremiah, Glory." Flo sat on the stool Rafe had vacated. "Love the dress. Designer?" She smiled. "Of course it is. You look perfect except for that lipstick. Here, let me put my new shade on you, Scarlet Woman. It will be amazing under the lights."

"Flo, what message?" I could have cared less about lipstick right then.

"Hold still. Ricardo, you tell her." Flo carefully wiped away my old lipstick and pulled out liner and a black and gold tube.

"Blade called me. Said he couldn't phone you directly." Richard looked serious.

"I know. That bitch has him on a short leash." I wanted to slap Flo's hand away but finally just let her line my lips.

"Anyway, he'll be here with her tonight. They've been together almost every moment since he got back from Miami and he's finally seen signs that she's getting tired of him."

I had a break while Flo switched to the lipstick. "What signs? Did he, um, say how things were going?" I blinked, refusing to cry, but I kept seeing Jerry in that woman's bed. "If he and Mel . . ." I couldn't say it.

"You want details? You know he wouldn't tell me and I certainly wouldn't ask. It's better you don't know, Gloriana." Richard moved closer and put a hand on my shoulder. "Blade said she asked the spirits for guidance, that kind of nonsense." If Richard ever rolled his eyes, this would have been the time. Instead, he got very serious. "Anyway, she got a message from the spirit world—her words—that she would get what she deserved. She took it to mean that she would win Blade and triumph over you. You'd think that would make her happy, but Blade read her mind. She's not satisfied and has started to criticize him constantly."

"Arrogant *puttana*!" Flo had finished with my lipstick and stabbed the tube back into her silver evening bag. "I have a message for her. She deserves to burn in hell!" She gripped my hand so hard I gasped. "Sorry, *mia cara amica*."

I felt a tear roll down my cheek and Flo exclaimed.

"Glory! Don't cry and ruin this makeup. That bitch is not worth it. You know Jeremiah's heart is yours. *Sì?*" She hurriedly blotted my cheeks when I nodded.

"Thank God you used waterproof mascara. There now. Tonight that *brutta cagna* will see that you and Jeremiah are done. She will let the man go and move on. Am I right? That is the plan. *Sì?*" She looked at Richard then slid her arms around me when I nodded dumbly again, afraid if I tried to speak, I'd break down. "Come now. You mustn't be upset like this right before your big performance. Promise me."

I closed my eyes and pulled on reserves of strength I hadn't known I had. Yes, I knew I had Jerry's heart no matter what that *cagna*, whatever that meant, had done to him in the meantime. We would settle this tonight, even if one of us had to do something we might regret.

"I hate this, Flo. Having to go onstage, smile and sing while Jerry is forced to serve that woman and take her abuse." I shuddered but took comfort from Flo's gentle touch as she leaned back and patted my shoulder. "But you're right. I can handle it. I'll do what I have to do."

"It will all be over soon, *amica*. You have never looked better and I can't wait to hear you sing." Flo stood and reached for her purse again. "Forget the woman and enjoy your night."

"Thank you. No one could have a better friend." I took a hanky from her and touched it to my nose. The linen was exquisite, trimmed in lace with her initials embroidered on it in silver thread. It had a faint scent of jasmine that made me smile. Richard had forbidden Flo to wear perfume because the smell interfered with his defense but she had put a little of her favorite scent on this wisp of perfection.

I realized I hadn't even complimented Flo yet and she looked wonderful, dressed in a vintage costume to look like Marie

Antoinette. She'd skipped the wig but, knowing Flo, she'd actually worn that very dress to the queen's court back in the day.

"Look at me now." She raised my chin. "*Perfetto*. Black is your color. Am I right, Ricardo?"

"Yes, you look wonderful, Gloriana. Blade will have quite a job keeping his heart from showing in his eyes. But he's the man who can do it." He helped Flo to her feet. "We must go, darling. Gloriana will have things to do before she goes onstage. Everyone at our table wishes you well, my dear. You'll hear us cheering for you." He leaned down to lightly kiss my cheek. He'd been trained by Flo not to smudge my makeup. "Break a leg."

"Ricardo! What a mean thing to say." Flo looked indignant.

"It's traditional, Flo. It means good luck in the theater. Thanks, Richard. And, Flo, you look spectacular. I meant to say that when you walked in." I stood and shook out my dress.

"This old thing." But she looked pleased. "You should see Diana. She's trotted out her same old southern belle costume. The woman still thinks the south will rise again. I swear she's going to burst into one of Scarlett O'Hara's famous speeches from *Gone With the Wind* any minute now and 'frankly, my dear, I don't give a damn.'"

We laughed and I finally relaxed. What else could I do? How the night would end was anyone's guess.

Seventeen

Flo and Richard left. A few minutes later the door opened again.

"Ian! You should have knocked." I wasn't sure if I was glad to see him or not. It depended on the reason for his visit.

"I was hoping to catch you with your pants down, so to speak." His grin was wicked. "Guess it's not my lucky night."

I ignored that, not in the mood for his flirting. "Have you brought me a potion Jerry can use against Mel?" I sat down to slip on my black velvet heels.

"I managed to come up with something. I followed the recipe you gave me." He moved closer and rubbed my shoulder. "Like the dress. Velvet. Feels good." He smiled and handed me a small vial. "You want this now?"

"I could have used it days ago. Couldn't you at least have answered my calls? What took you so long to get it to me?" I knew my nerves were making me short with him, but he was cutting things awfully close.

"You know what. My lab was decimated. I had to

start many vital experiments over. Thank God Bartholomew O'Connor is almost as smart as I am. He's been a great help. I've persuaded him to stay on for a while."

"Well, at least it's here now, and thanks. But I'm not who needs it. Jerry should have it. He's the one stuck next to the voodoo priestess." I gave the vial back to Ian. "Will you find him in the crowd and slip it to him? Maybe you can arrange to meet him in the men's room or something."

"What's in it for me?" Ian looked me over. "You know I don't do favors without expecting something in return."

"What do you want?" I was distracted or I never would have used Ian for anything. Now I saw that calculating look in his eyes that I hated.

"The rest of that voodoo book. You have no use for it and I want to study it." He grinned. "I enjoyed making this potion. If Blade does use it tonight, I hope I'm around to see if it works."

"Are you telling me you didn't test it? That's not like you." I was thinking fast. Give Ian a potentially harmful book? I couldn't like the idea. But I had, gulp, less than five minutes before I had to go onstage.

"I wanted to test it, but this recipe made precious little after it was distilled and decanted. Look. This is all I've got." He held the glass container up to the light. I could see that it was a shade of mustard yellow and there wasn't very much of it. "What's it to be, Glory?"

"Maybe I'll find someone else to take it to Jerry. I really don't trust you with the book."

"Did you know I have a photographic memory? I saw the cover and the title. I'll troll the Internet, work my connections, call in favors, but I *will* get a copy. Eventually. And you might miss your chance to get this vial where it needs to be in time to help Blade." He tucked it into his pocket. "I warn you, I'm like a dog with a bone when I want something badly enough."

"Ian, you've just insulted dogs everywhere." I frowned. "Promise you won't use any of those potions on me or the ones I love."

"You can't be serious. What would be the fun of that?" He glanced at his watch. "Don't you go onstage in a few minutes?"

"Damn you! Fine. I'll give you the book. After this is all over and the woman is gone. Okay?" I pushed him toward the door. "Take it to Jerry now."

"I don't like those terms. The book is mine no matter how this goes." He stopped in the doorway. "Deal?"

"Only if you agree that I'm off-limits and so are my people. And don't pretend you don't know who I mean. I can play hardball too, Ian." I snatched the vial from his pocket. "Decide. How badly do you want my copy of the book? It could take you a long time or you might never find one of your own."

"Damn it, Gloriana. You are most appealing when you negotiate." He smiled and held out his hand. "Deal."

"Good." I laid the vial in his palm. "Now find Jerry and slip that to him. Give him instructions. I'm sure you have some."

"Yes, of course. He should toss it in her face if he can manage it while she's looking directly at him. Once I got the text translated from the Creole language, that's what it said to do. It should make her hate the sight of him. Not exactly the repellent we thought it would be but I think it will do the trick." Ian stared down at the potion.

"Yes, that should be perfect." I could tell from the way Ian kept glancing from the potion to me that he'd had another idea. A quick peek into his mind made me sure of it. "Stop thinking, Ian. Right now. This is only to be used when Jerry is face-to-face with Mel. No one else is going to use it. Are we clear?" I could see his usual scheming brain at work. "If anything goes wrong and I hear it was your doing, I'll burn that book before I give it to you. Or maybe Bart O'Connor would like it. I'm sure he could make a fortune selling potions from it to paranormals around here. Fancy some competition?"

"Settle down, Gloriana. What did I say? Of course I'll hand it off to Blade." Ian tried to look innocent. It wasn't a look he wore well.

"I'll count on that. If this potion works, it'll solve our problem."

Ian tucked the vial into his jacket pocket. He wasn't in costume, of course. I couldn't imagine him relaxing his image enough to play a part other than brainiac doctor. Tonight he had on a black velvet blazer and white silk shirt. The look suited him and women would notice him in a crowd anyway. He stepped into the hall but stopped so abruptly that I bumped into his back.

"Aggie!" I jumped in front of Ian as soon as I saw her. She'd just come out of her dressing room. "Uh, you're not on yet."

"Hey, Glory. Good luck tonight." She smiled, a really fake effort. "Ian. I see you came dressed as yourself, the devil." She literally ran back down the hall toward the restroom before Ian could react.

"Bitch. What's she doing here?" He was tense where I held his arm.

"She's the backup singer for Ray and Sienna's set. Remember? I told you. Trust me, she hates that I'll be in the spotlight and she's not." I saw Miguel come out of Aggie's dressing room and look down the hall. "You'd better go. Please? Get to Jerry before the lights go down."

"Fine. At least she wished you luck. I do as well." He kissed my cheek before I could stop him then took off, fortunately away from Miguel.

"That's the man Angel hates so much?" Miguel was beside me in moments.

"Yes. Ian MacDonald. I'm surprised you haven't crossed paths before."

"He's used my services. We just haven't met face-to-face. I recognize him from Angel's description." He looked me over. "You are beautiful tonight, Glory. I'm looking forward to seeing and hearing your performance."

"Thank you." I gripped the doorjamb. "I just want to get this over with."

"You might be interested to know that Jeremy Blade has arrived here with that voodoo woman you asked me to check out. She's a minor talent in the dark arts. Yes, she could do you harm. But your powers should be much stronger. Don't let her intimidate you with her tricks and evil spirits." He studied his perfectly manicured fingernails.

"It's Jerry I'm worried about." I did enjoy hearing that Miguel thought my powers were stronger. So why had I failed to overpower her before? Mind games. I had to be more confident if I got the chance to confront her again.

"You should be. He's dressed as her slave." He glanced up and his face was grim. "He allowed her to lead him into the club in shackles. She was pulling him by a chain around his neck. The man has lost his pride, Glory. I would kill a woman who treated me so disrespectfully."

"I'm sure you would. But it's an act, Miguel. We're trying to get her to lose interest in him. Jerry learned that it's her pattern. She doesn't want what she thinks she's captured." I hated that Jerry had let people—our friends, my mother—see him like that.

"That plan sucks." Miguel turned and walked away.

I wanted to call him back, say something to defend Jerry,

but Ray emerged from the dressing room across from me, all smiles.

"Hey, it's time, Glory girl. You ready?"

"Not in a million years." I took his hand though and walked with him toward the stage. I could hear the band playing the intro to the song we'd arranged to start the set with. The drums were sounding out a great beat and I could feel it from my toes to my tummy. I had to do this. I *wanted* to do it. Ray and I hurried up onto the stage to thunderous applause, screams and cheers. It had started. There was no turning back now.

The lights were still bright enough in the club that I could see the audience from the stage. I knew it would be darker as soon as I started my second song. I was singing my duet with Ray before I knew it, all that practice making it easier than I'd thought it would be. I could even scan the room while we sang.

There was the group of my friends on the balcony. Flo grinned and waved. As one, the gang raised their glasses full of a ruby liquid that I knew was blood and sent me a silent toast. I licked my lips while Ray took his turn in the song. I really should have fed or at least finished my glass of synthetic before coming onstage.

"Whenever I call you friend . . ." Ray and I sang together. The song was full of meaning for both of us. Yes, we were friends and would always love each other on some level. The fast beat made it a fun way to start the set and the packed crowd on the dance floor moved to the music, everyone smiling and seeming to enjoy themselves.

I grinned, jazzed by their reaction. I hadn't spotted Jerry yet but another glance at the balcony made it impossible to miss my mother's table. She was reigning like a queen over her court. A queen of Olympus. My God, they'd all come dressed in their togas. All except Mom's date for the evening. Mars was in full battle regalia. At least he'd taken off his helmet with the red plume and it was sitting on the table. I recognized Circe, the goddess who'd made sure Jerry had found me back in London centuries ago so that he'd give me immortality. Apparently that had earned her a seat at the table. She and Mom hadn't always been friends, but they'd forged a bond over their mutual hatred of Achelous the Storm God.

Ray and I leaned in. We were coming close to the end of our song when I saw Jerry. He and Mel were at the edge of the dance floor. Damn, but Mel *was* leading him around by a chain. His buff body couldn't have looked better in what was little more than a leather loin cloth belted at the waist with a wide studded belt. With his powerful chest and legs bare, he drew eyes in a crowd where more than one person had gone for a skimpy look. Then I saw the choke collar around his neck.

My proud Highlander wore a choke collar. I wanted to cry or scream or throw up. What I didn't want to do was sing. Good thing I was on autopilot by now.

When she caught my eye Mel smiled and gave the chain a tug. I looked away from Jerry, trying not to add to his humiliation, but I couldn't help myself. One more glance. How was he taking this? He wouldn't look up at me, just kept staring at the woman in front of him. Oh, God, Jerry. My heart was breaking for him.

Ray nudged me with an arm around my waist and I realized I'd dropped the ball, forgotten to come in when it was my turn in the song. I quickly focused again as we came to the final chorus.

"I know forever we'll be doin' it right." I looked into Ray's eyes and saw sympathy. It was almost my undoing. Of course he'd noticed Jerry and Mel. *Sing, Glory.* We harmonized, in sync, as we sang the final notes. Friends. Thank God for them.

Ray had his arm around me, supporting me in more ways than one, as we took a bow.

The applause was deafening and the building shook with the sound of stomping feet. Then the lights went out for mere seconds. It was enough to quiet the crowd before twin spotlights hit me and Ray, who was now sitting at his piano. He nodded and the band started my first solo. I wasn't about to sing to Jerry, though in my heart this song was for him. So I leaned on the piano for the opening notes, deliberately sultry as I sang to Ray.

"You give me fever."

The crowd went wild. I'm sure they thought that meant Ray and I were an item again. Whatever. Ray certainly knew we weren't. Working together had been fun, but he realized there was no romantic future for us. I sashayed around the stage, putting a wiggle into my walk and holding the microphone like Ray had taught me. He'd been a wonderful musical mentor.

"Fever all through the night." Oh, yeah. I was selling that song. It was an oldie, but had a timeless message. I thought about Jerry and the first time we'd been together. We'd been so hot for each other. Ridiculous but we were still that way. He could touch me and I'd go up in flames. I put that feeling into the song and became almost breathless.

I could feel hundreds, maybe a thousand pairs of eyes on me. It was a heady experience. The room was silent except for the band and my voice. This was a new kind of power. I should be getting off to it. But I'd had too many years of trying not to be noticed. All this attention and a roomful of mortals only a few feet away . . .

My fangs started to come down and I fought them back. No, no, no. With the spotlight in my eyes, I couldn't see anyone out there but they sure as hell could see me. Jerry, my friends and my mother who was either proud or horrified, take your pick, they were all out there watching my every move.

That rush of power suddenly evaporated and I wanted to run and hide. I couldn't. The only thing I *could* do was stroll over to Ray again and touch his shoulder. Get strength from him. His smile encouraged me and he sent me a mental message to just sing. That I had the audience in the palm of my hand. I squeezed his shoulder, trusting him, and kept going.

By the time I came to the end of the song, I knew Ray was right. I'd made it through and no one had a clue I'd been close to a meltdown. Ray's grin as he played the final notes said it all. He was proud of me. I was Gloriana the Siren as I worked my hips and stood behind him at the piano to sing that last line, twining my fingers in his hair. Finally, I leaned forward and blew in his ear. I was an actress and I'd played my part. It hadn't been comfortable, but I'd survived.

The crowd loved it, especially when he jumped up, grabbed me and gave me one of those big fake Hollywood kisses that leaned me back over his arm. We hadn't rehearsed it but the moment was right. We both came up laughing, Ray fanning himself like he did have a fever. The applause was deafening as the lights came up briefly.

"Ladies and gentlemen, Gloriana St. Clair!" Ray held my hand while I took a bow. He let the applause roll over us for a few moments then held up his hand for quiet.

"Now for her final number, if you've got a light on your phone or a lighter, let's see it. I think you're going to get a kick out of this. It's a special song for Halloween. Are you ready?"

There was a howl of agreement as hundreds of lights came on until the room looked like a mass of twinkling stars when the overhead dimmed again. I had enough light to see Jerry's reaction to this song, if I could still find him in the crowd. I waved at the audience then nodded to the band. Ray sat back at the piano, all of us waiting for the mood to hit the room as the drums throbbed and the music started. It was a really old song but perfect for the night.

"I put a spell on you . . ." I wanted to sing straight to Jerry, but didn't dare. Not when the next line made it clear I considered him "mine." I put everything I had into the song. I wanted Mel to think that, despite my act with Rafe, I was pining for Jerry. She could kill chickens in my shop and examine the insides of a thousand goats, but she'd never deserve Jerry. I'd cast my own spell on him centuries ago. A love spell. He'd been mine first, would always be mine. Mel had come way too late to the party.

"I ain't goin' to take none of your foolin' around." Was Mel laughing at that? Sure of herself and her ritual sacrifice? Was she gloating and tugging on Jerry's chain? If I could have reached her, I would have wrapped that chain around her neck and squeezed the life out of her. What would her ghosts and ghouls think about that?

I forced myself to slink over to Ray and aim some of my smolder at him. I could probably still put a spell on him and end up in his bed tonight. His bright blue eyes telegraphed that message loud and clear. I shook my head as I fell back across the piano like I was making love to it, just short of giving Ray a glimpse down my vee-neck. Too much of that wouldn't be fair to the man. On the next line I was up again and making love to the audience instead.

I noticed couples entwined, dancing to the slow pulsing beat. Ray's lead guitarist had fallen in love with the song and had worked up a fantastic solo that showed off his skill. He sounded great and I stood aside, swaying as he worked the electric guitar strings.

It gave me a chance to scan the audience again. What I saw made me swallow. No! This couldn't be happening. Jerry was pushing his way toward the stage, carefully moving aside dancing couples as he strode closer and closer, his eyes on me now. The chain Mel had been flaunting earlier was wrapped around his fist. Mel stumbled along behind him, trying not to trip because the cuff at her wrist was connected to the other end of that chain. Was he crazy? This wasn't the plan.

I realized my cue was coming. I had to sing again and I knew what I had to do. Okay, change of plans. I'd sing to the man I loved and put my trust in Jerry and that potion I hoped to hell he had handy.

"Because you're mine." I couldn't have made it any clearer as I sang straight to him. Jerry was close to the stage now. He took the chain in both hands and broke it like it was a toy made of plastic. I'm sure that's what the mortals close by thought. I could see Mel's face clearly now. She was livid. So much for showing off her love slave. The last note lingered in the air, the lights went out and I gasped when Jerry leaped up onto the stage and swept me into his arms.

"Damn right, I'm yours and nobody else's." He kissed me and kept kissing me, even when the lights came on and the audience went into a frenzy.

I didn't push him away. Couldn't. His strong arms were my safe haven. His mouth on mine gave me the very air I didn't have to breathe but yearned for anyway. When Jerry finally pulled back, he glanced at the audience and seemed to realize that he was stealing my big moment.

"Take a bow, Gloriana. You were incredible."

"Damn right, she was." Ray stood on my other side. "Get off my stage, Blade."

"Calm down. The audience loved it. They thought it was

part of the show." I said this as an aside to Ray, bowing as the audience cheered, whistled and stomped their feet. I gestured toward the guitarist and he took his own bow. Then I held up Ray's hand and kissed his cheek.

Before Ray could say another word, I dropped his hand and dragged Jerry off the stage, toward the dressing rooms. We paused next to Aggie and Sienna, who stood waiting in the wings, ready to go onstage to do their set. Aggie ignored me.

"Great job, Glory." Sienna grinned and gave me a thumbs-up. "Blade, that was some surprise at the end. Good showmanship."

"I may regret it." He looked down at me. "But I couldn't help myself. I had to follow my heart."

"Jerry." I brushed his cheek. "What about Mel?"

"I'm sick to death of that woman and that charade. We'll deal with the fallout together." He pulled the vial from his belt where he'd had it tucked next to his skin. "I'm sure I'll see her again before the night is out. If this works, problem solved."

"Can you two move out of the way? Miguel says there's a big producer in the audience." Aggie had on a costume that hadn't come from my shop. It was an expensive harem outfit that complemented Sienna's but was in the green that Aggie loved. It revealed more than it concealed and had enough jewels in the trim to catch the spotlight. She was sure to be noticed.

"Relax, Aggie. Ray has a solo first, remember?" Sienna frowned at her. "I thought I told you to lose the headband. I'm the star here. You're background." She reached out and snatched a jeweled piece off Aggie's hair. "Now, don't screw around up there. The producer will ask me if I think you'll be easy to work with. *If* he's interested. You want a good recommendation, do as we've practiced."

"I get it, Sienna. I'm sorry. Miguel made me wear that

thing." Aggie looked anxiously down the hall. "I do what he tells me."

"What's this?" Jerry kept his arm around me and I leaned into him. "You and Miguel, Aggie? Isn't he that hit man, Glory? The one who works for Lucky Carver?"

"Yes. Let it go, Jer. Aggie has made it clear that she doesn't want or need our help. Right?"

"Right. I'm fine. After tonight, I might even be on the fast track to a record deal." She cocked her head. "There's our cue, Sienna." She followed Sienna to the stage. "Wish us luck."

"Good luck." I turned to Jerry. "I'd like to see her get a record deal. Maybe head to Hollywood to record it. Far away sounds good to me." I pulled him toward my dressing room. I wanted some alone time with my guy.

"You want to stay out here and listen to the music?" Jerry offered. I knew he could care less about it.

"I've heard it all week during rehearsals. Come into my dressing room. Tell me about your week." I followed him into the room and shut the door.

"I don't want to talk about it. I'm done with that woman now, whether she wants me or not." He looked away, not meeting my eyes.

"I'm sorry you had to go through that." I slid my arms around him. We obviously weren't going to touch the subject of whether or not he'd had sex with Mel. Did I want to know? Could I handle the truth if it wasn't what I wanted to hear? Maybe not knowing was for the best. I was dropping it. And I sure wasn't going to read his mind.

He rested his cheek on my hair. "God, it feels good just to hold you."

"Why'd you do it, Jer? Why'd you come up onstage when we'd planned . . ." I studied his dear face. He looked tired.

Vampires weren't supposed to have circles under their eyes. It made me wonder if Mel had tampered with his blood again.

"Simple. You must have known it when you picked that song. You did put a spell on me. Centuries ago, Gloriana. Seeing you up there, looking so beautiful. Hearing your voice, golden and pure. It was like falling in love all over again. How could I just stand there, shackled to that insane creature when the woman I really wanted was just feet away? I moved before I could stop myself." He ran his thumb across my lips. "God, how I've missed you." He leaned down and kissed me, his mouth moving over mine for endless moments.

I sighed into his mouth, reveling in his taste again and having him this close. When we finally parted, I stared into his eyes. "You took a big chance, Jer. I expected to see ghosts and ghouls any moment when you jumped on that stage."

"You missed them? They were there. I guess the spotlight blinded you." He grinned. "When I started dragging her toward the stage, Mel went into her usual death-will-get-you mode. I felt the cold fingers of her familiars all around me. The crowd loved it. They thought they were special effects Valdez had managed to produce. Part of your song."

"You're kidding. But you kept coming." I held him close, listening to the slow thump of his barely beating heart as I pressed my cheek to his chest.

"Not even Viking berserkers could have held me back, Gloriana." He rubbed my back. "You're everything to me. I had to get closer."

"I hope you, we, don't regret it."

"So do I," he said as the dressing room door flew open.

Eighteen

"**You'd** better get out here, Blade. That woman is a nightmare." Rafe actually looked frazzled. I don't think I'd ever seen him that way.

"What's she doing?" I didn't want Jerry anywhere near her, though he'd started toward the door anyway. "Stop. Wait, Jer. Please."

"She's unleashed what I'm thinking are the hounds of hell. And she's got two creepy people with her who I swear are zombies. Ray and Sienna are in the middle of their set and Mel is disturbing the crowd. At least on her side of the stage. When I sent some of my bigger guys over there to move her, they couldn't even touch her. She froze them out somehow." Rafe moved when Jerry pushed past him.

"I've seen her do this. I hope your customers are still thinking it's a light show you put on as part of the entertainment. As for the zombies? Mel won't let them act out in public. Trouble will start if anyone tries to push her around." Jerry shoved aside a curtain and looked out at the crowd.

I peered around him. Sure enough, we could see Mel waving her arms. She totally ignored the music, the singers on the stage and the hundreds of dancers milling around her. She was obviously trying to find Jerry. She must have sensed him because she whipped her head around and glared in our direction. When she pointed at us, I felt an immediate chill.

"Get back here, Jerry. Please. We can't have a confrontation in the middle of that crowd." I grabbed his arm. "And you can't toss the potion at her there and take a chance that your arm will be jostled and you'll miss."

"Glory's right. We need to take this outside." Rafe pulled the curtain closed. "Come on. Go out the side door. Mel will just have to follow you there."

"Yes, and I'm sure she will." Jerry glanced back at the drawn curtain. "I'm sorry, Valdez. This night is important to you and my problems are ruining it." I could tell he meant it.

"Not at all. You saw the crowd. The people closest to her were a little freaked out, but then they just moved away and kept dancing to the music." He glanced at the stage. "Ray and Sienna are pros. They're ignoring the disturbance and have never missed a note. Those creepy apparitions floating over Mel's head look like a cool lighting effect if you don't know that they're the real deal. Even the zombies could be bankers who've marinated too long."

Jerry put his arm around me. "No kidding. Their blood smells fermented. Nasty. And those ghouls are certainly real to Mel. The woman speaks to them constantly. Right now she's probably getting ready to make me pay for leaving her like I did. And she's going to want to hurt Gloriana too." He stopped at my dressing room door. "Lock yourself in here, my love. I'll be back once I've taken care of her."

"Are you kidding me? Don't you know me better than that

by now, Jer?" I poked him in his bare chest. "I'd never let you face her alone. We're going out to the alley together." I turned to Rafe. "If she comes through here, tell her that's where we'll be. We need to get her away from the show." We'd kept our voices down but I didn't want to take a chance that we'd disturb the performers onstage.

"The alley, Gloriana? Why are you going there? You should come up to the balcony. Meet my handmaidens." My mother had appeared in the hallway. "Darling, you were absolutely brilliant." She dabbed at her eyes with a handkerchief. "I was so proud."

"Thank you, Mother. Later. After I deal with a little problem, I'll come up and meet everyone. Say hi to Mars for me." I tugged Jerry toward the exit. "Quiet. Remember, there's still a show going on."

"What's this? Introduce me to this fellow, Gloriana." Mars suddenly stood behind my mother. "I must judge if he's worthy of you. Since you have no father to vet your suitors."

"Don't you think I'm old enough to skip such customs?" I smiled though as I finally got the group outside. "I'm touched at your concern. Mars, this is Jeremiah Campbell, currently known as Jeremy Blade. He and I are a couple. With or without your approval I'm afraid."

"Gloriana! It would be wise of you to indulge us. Mars could certainly give you good advice and is an excellent judge of men." My mother looked Jerry over from his head down to his toes which looked nicely masculine in leather sandals. "So am I. He does cut a fine figure."

"The physical form is the least important aspect of a man, my dear Hebe. It's his substance that must be of worth." Mars studied Jerry from beneath lowered brows. "I did like the way he charged the stage. Broke that chain and went right up to Gloriana. Took her away from that singer who struck me as a lightweight. Glad you're not taking him as your lover, Gloriana." Mars patted my shoulder. "But coming in on a leash, as it were, Campbell. Not well done of you, my man. Not at all."

"If it helps my cause, I hated every minute of it." Jerry's shoulders were back, his jaw stiff. "It was part of a scheme Gloriana and I'd set up. Stupid now that I think back on it. If you'll excuse us, we were about to finish things with that bitch who led me in." He nodded as if he'd dismissed the god. Mars stopped him with a hand on his shoulder.

"Hold. I didn't say I don't like you for Gloriana. Of course I know you're vampire. But so's the girl. Damnable thing, but she seems used to the blood drinking." Mars took my hand in his other one. "Perhaps you two *are* well suited. You strike me as a warrior."

"I am. Was. When it meant something to be handy with a weapon." Jerry shrugged away from Mars's touch. I was surprised the god let him. "These days I have little use for the old ways. It's more important to be clever. This mess with the voodoo woman should have been resolved long ago. Somehow we weren't clever enough for her."

"Then, by Zeus's right hand, I say we all stay out here and have a little fun with her. I'd like to see her fight all of us with her dark powers." Mars linked arms with my mother. "What do you say, Hebe? Are you up for a little witch hunt?" He finally let go of my hand. I felt released in more ways than one. His touch had paralyzed my body and my tongue. Now I shook my head.

"I'm not sure . . ."

"We'll take all the help we can get," Jerry said when the back door opened and Rafe signaled before going back inside.

"I think she's coming." He scanned the alley, shoving aside a pile of wooden crates and positioning himself with his back to a Dumpster.

"What's the plan?" Mars was suddenly wearing his helmet, the red plume waving above us all.

"I have a potion that's supposed to make her hate me on sight. As soon as I'm sure I have an open shot at tossing it in her face, I'm taking it." Jerry held the vial in his hand. "Gloriana, I wish you'd stay behind those crates since you insist on being here for this."

"My daughter isn't one to cower in the shadows, Blade." My mother stood proudly next to Mars. "Why does everyone here on Earth have such absurd names?"

"Get over it, Mother. Are you just here to fuss about trivialities?" I touched her hand. "Sorry, I'm stressed. Thanks for the compliments. About the singing and not cowering. You're right. I guess I do have a little goddess in me."

"More than a little, darling." She looked very pleased then wrinkled her nose. "Oh, what have we here? Zombies? Honestly, Blade, Gloriana should have dismissed you just for consorting with such disgusting creatures."

"Mother!" I had to admit, the reek warned us that Mel was getting closer and she hadn't even emerged from the building yet.

"She doesn't have them with her during her seminars," Jerry grumbled.

"Well, they're here now. And your friend that shifter is here too, Gloriana. You do inspire loyalty, don't you?" My mother smiled at me proudly. "Say the word if you want me to use a lightning bolt on the woman. It would be my pleasure."

"I'll keep that in mind." I braced myself, startled when Jerry swept me behind him despite my protests. The exit door crashed back when Mel charged out, surrounded by screaming banshees, her two zombies shuffling along behind her. They had deteriorated badly since the last time I'd seen them. It made me wonder what their shelf life was.

"There you are. What in the hell do you think you're doing?" She stopped inches from Jerry.

I waited for him to toss the potion then and there. Instead he seemed frozen in place.

"How dare you embarrass me by running away!" She swept her arm in a circle. He shuddered and fell to his knees.

"Jerry!" I dropped down beside him. "What have you done to him?"

"Let me incinerate her, Gloriana. I can blast her to ashes right now." Mars grinned and stepped forward. "Voodoo. Child's games."

Mel's eyes widened. "I don't know who or what you are, but I wouldn't taunt the spirits if I were you."

I stood when it became obvious that Jerry couldn't move or speak. "I asked what you did to Jerry."

"It's a little spell I put on him." She laughed, the cackle of a crazy woman. "I took his blood while he slept. Used it to make a powerful conjure. You and your song. Pathetic. How you wish you had my kind of power."

"My 'spell' is love, freely given. Something you will never understand. What you do is evil." I quit breathing when her zombies lumbered closer. I avoided their dead eyes. My mother watched them closely and I had a feeling if one of them had reached for me, she would have zapped it with a few thousand watts of lightning.

Mel screeched and her ghostly minions flew about my head, making a mess of my hair and hitting my arms. My mother shouted and would have jumped into the fray but I signaled her to stay out of it.

"Jerry doesn't love you, Melisandra. Let him go." I made myself say that calmly even though all the dead things whirling around me were seriously freaking me out.

"Never." She smiled, obviously proud of herself. "While Jeremiah slept, dead to the world, I spoke to Loa and used my most powerful charms to bind this man to me. Yes, I used his true name. Jeremiah Campbell. He gave it to me. That's how much he loves me. See? You are wrong." She swept me aside and knelt in front of Jerry, running her fingers through his hair.

"Don't touch him." I wanted to jerk her back, make her scream in pain. But her sharp red nails were inches from his eyes. Would she hurt him to hurt me? I couldn't take that chance.

"My love. I've done much more than touch him, vampire. He craves me and my hot blood, pulsing with life. That's something you can't give him, can you?" She gazed at me triumphantly. "No, I'm sure your blood is cold and dead."

I just stared at her. What could I say? Jerry had admitted he liked hot mortal blood. But from her? I doubted he could stand the taste of it anymore. I didn't dare provoke her so I stayed silent.

"I see you don't deny it. And just look at what he gave me." She held out her left hand and I gasped. It was the engagement ring Jerry had offered me months before.

"He didn't give you that. You stole it." I remembered what Miguel had said. I had the power. I read her mind. Of course she'd stolen it. She'd crept into Jerry's house during the day while everyone staying there, all vampires, had been in their death sleep. Thank God she'd left without hurting any of them.

"I don't see you wearing his ring, do I, Gloriana?" Mel shot a triumphant look around the alley. "No! He hasn't claimed her as his woman. I've claimed *him* now. Jeremiah Campbell is *mine*. And he's just where I want him." She backed up and pointed a bloodred fingernail at me. "You, Gloriana, you have nothing."

"You want him helpless?" Tears stung my eyes just before I threw myself at her. I had surprise on my side and she didn't have time to protect herself. She fell back, her dead spirits vanishing when I wrapped my hands around her throat and began to squeeze. "Take it off, take off this horrible spell you've put on him."

"Why should I?" She wheezed, the life draining out of her. I didn't care if she was dying or not. I couldn't ease up on her throat, not even when her face turned red. "K-k-kill me and he'll never be yours again." She glanced at her zombies. "Attack! Take her out!"

There was a sizzle and a pop and the smell of something nasty burning. My mother blew on her gold-lacquered fingernail as if it were a gun barrel.

"They aren't going to be attacking anyone. Get her, Gloriana."

I didn't have time to see what Mother had done because I was too busy trying to squeeze answers out of Mel. I kept holding her throat but let up enough to shake her, knocking her head against the concrete.

"Why not? Tell me why he won't be mine."

"I'm not telling you anything." She gasped and waved her arms wildly, trying to summon her spirits. I trapped one arm under each knee, straddling her.

"Stop it. Now tell me what you've done to him."

"He'll always belong to me, heart and soul. There are words

that must be spoken or he won't ever love another." Her eyes were wild, her smile triumphant. "You'd better believe *I* won't speak them."

"He wasn't yours a few minutes ago. He came to me on the stage. He said he loved me." I snarled, let her see my fangs and the urge to kill in my eyes.

"That's because I'd failed to mark him. But I did just now. Look and see. He carries my mark and will be mine forever or until my mark is removed." She was still defiant, even though I could almost see the life draining out of her with each gasp as I tightened my grip on her throat.

"Go, Gloriana. See if she's telling the truth. I've got this." My mother touched Mel and she was instantly paralyzed. "See if you can find this mark she's bragging about. We will make her take it off. No matter what we have to do to her." Mother's smile was cold and determined.

I couldn't have a better ally. I glanced at the zombies. Or what used to be the walking dead. Now they were two piles of ashes.

"What can I do to help?" Rafe was there beside my mother.

"Don't let anyone come into the alley. Can you stay by the door?" I'd been worried about that. This bizarre scene didn't need any spectators or distractions.

Rafe helped me to my feet. "You can count on me." He squeezed my shoulder then rushed to stand against the door.

I ran back to Jerry. Mark. I hadn't seen her touch him but maybe she could have thrown something or her spirits might have been capable of carrying it. Did I even believe her? But she'd done something to make him first freeze, then fall unconscious to the ground. Then I looked closer. He wasn't unconscious. He stared at nothing, now just like one of her walking dead. Oh, God.

"Gloriana, let me help." Mars stood next to me.

"How? Do you know anything about these voodoo curses?" I ran my hands over Jerry's shoulders and back. I knew his body so well. If there was anything new here, I wasn't finding it.

"Loa. Melisandra claims she talked to Loa. Believe it or not, that's one of my other names. This religion is one of my minor ones. I *am* a god, you know. Some people choose to worship me. Gods of war are popular. We have power and that appeals to people. But I don't like it when their worship is twisted like this." He frowned at Mel where Mother stood guard over her.

"Yes, I'd say Mel's gone off the deep end." I still hadn't found a mark. Where could it be?

"This woman has invoked my power and abused it in a way that displeases me." He lifted Jerry to his feet, making it look effortless. "Check out his upper right thigh, under that loin cloth. That's where such marks are usually found."

"I can't believe . . ." I shook my head. "Never mind. I don't think I'll ever figure out Olympus and all the bizarre happenings there." I sank down to study Jerry's thigh, tracing an old scar. He'd won it in a battle centuries ago, before he'd been turned. There, just inches above the edge of that skimpy leather, was a small black mark like a brand. It looked like an *x*, with the bottom turned into an upside down heart. I rubbed my finger over it and it throbbed, hot to the touch.

"This must be it. Can you take it off?" I wished Jerry would moan, something. Instead, when Mars let him go, he just slumped in place, like a puppet left to hang from a hook by its strings.

"I'm afraid, my dear, that only the one who puts on the mark can remove it." He stalked over to Mel. "Let her up, Hebe." He stood glowering down at the priestess.

"Are you sure?" My mother frowned down at the frozen woman. "I could end her here and now."

"And leave Jerry like this? I don't think so. Thaw her out, Mother, and back off. Please?" I stood next to Mars.

"I hope you know what you're doing, both of you." She tapped Mel then moved back. Mel jumped up, wild-eyed.

"What have you done?" She raised her arms, ready to bring in the ghouls.

"Stop." Mars fixed her with a commanding gaze. "I am Loa, the god to whom you pray. Do you know me, my child?" His voice had gone deep and guttural. It made my insides quiver.

Mel fell to her knees. "My lord Loa. You honor me." She bowed until her forehead touched the rough pavement. "How can I serve you?"

"Remove your mark from this man, daughter. Set him free. Your attachment to a blood drinker does not please me. Have you not learned that we despise such creatures?" Mars stalked around Mel in a circle.

"How can that be your wish when you helped me gain his love in the first place?" Mel hadn't looked up, and said this to the pavement.

Mars sighed. He touched the top of her head and she froze again. "This is what comes from having so many supplicants. I should listen more closely to their pleas. Get a few more assistants to handle incoming calls. If I'd known it concerned you, Gloriana . . ." He shrugged. "Well, this is a tough one. I'm not supposed to intervene once I've given the green light."

"Let me talk to her. Like Jerry said, we have this potion. If he can thaw out and then toss it at her, it's supposed to make Mel hate him."

"What's it called?" Mars gestured. "Let me look at it."

"I can't pronounce the name but here it is." I slipped it out from behind Jerry's belt.

Mars opened the vial and sniffed. "Good news. This will work. Talk her into thawing out the man and then, if he throws it in her face while she's looking straight into his eyes, it *will* make her despise him. She'll take off the mark willingly, unable to bear the sight of him carrying it." He glanced at my mother. "Hebe, we need to get out of here. The woman will be insufferable if she remembers Loa himself deigned to speak to her. I think Gloriana can handle things from here."

"Can you, dear?" My mother glared at Mel. "I don't like leaving you with that woman. She means you harm. And of course she's taken her religion to a very dark place. Sorry, Mars." She linked her arm through his. "Perhaps I can comfort you later."

"I wouldn't mind that at all. But we must go back inside. I saw someone I think I recognize. You must tell me if I am right or not." He smiled at her. "Gloriana? I'll erase her memory of ever meeting me. Are you happy with this plan? Sure you can carry it off?"

"Yes. I'll do whatever it takes to get her to thaw him out. Jerry knows what to do with the potion. Unless what she's done to him will erase that memory."

Mars walked over to Jerry and stared at him intently. "I think he'll be fine. Inside his muddled brain he knows two things. He loves you and hates that bitch. I take that to mean this Melisandra." He swept his gaze over her one more time. "Good thing Hebe didn't incinerate her. She's one of my priestesses. From now on, I'll pay closer attention to what's going on down here. In the future, this woman will have a rude awakening. Loa will come to her in her dreams and she'll see the light, so to speak. Voodoo is a fine religion when practiced properly."

"Glad to hear it. Now please go. I can't stand to see Jerry like this." I brushed my lover's cheek but he didn't move a muscle. Finally I tucked the open vial into his hand and sent him a mental message, reminding him what it was for. I tried to read his mind but I wasn't as powerful as Mars because I couldn't make the connection. "Ready."

"Fine. I'll release her, and your mother and I will vanish at the same time. Good luck, Gloriana." He touched Mel and, true to his word, he and Mother disappeared.

"How do you like Jeremiah now, Gloriana?" Mel was back in her usual bitingly sarcastic form.

"You can have him. When I think of all the nights you two were together it makes me sick. Yes, it was cool that he came up onstage like that. I couldn't have planned it better myself. It made for great theater. But, honestly? Why would I want your leftovers?" I shrugged and started toward the exit door where Rafe had been a silent observer. "Here's my guy. Rafe, baby, can you take me somewhere not polluted by evil spirits and crazy women?"

"Sure, Glo." Rafe pulled me close. "Mel, enjoyed the pep talk the other night. Gave me lots to think about. Big plans for the club here for instance. Glory and I may come to another one of your seminars. You give great advice. We left there totally inspired, didn't we, baby?" He kissed my cheek.

"I admit it. I want to own the world." I patted Rafe's butt. "I hear the music's still going. Let's go inside and dance."

"Fine. I'll take your money." Mel turned to Jerry and waved her hands again. "Jeremiah, lover. Are you ready to go?" She stared into his eyes.

"More than ready." He tossed the liquid in the vial into her face.

"What have you done?" Mel's screech would have been heard inside except Ray's band was loud enough to hear through the closed door. She wiped away the liquid, which looked like egg yolk, from her eyes and face. "This burns! What the hell is it?"

"A little something a doctor I know whipped up in his lab. It's supposed to be a love potion. What have I done? I've shown you just how I feel about you." Jerry watched her closely as she pulled a black handkerchief from between her breasts. She'd worn what I'm sure the audience had thought was a costume but were probably her work clothes when she was talking to Loa. The floor-length black caftan plunged low in front and her headscarf had symbols in gold around the edge.

"Leave the potions to the experts, Jeremiah. Clearly you were tricked." She looked him over, her lips curling. "How pathetic. What did I ever see in you? A bloodsucker." She shuddered.

"You said you liked for me to drink your blood, Mel." Jerry smiled, showing every inch of his very long fangs.

"No! I seem to remember . . ." She put a shaky hand to her forehead. "By Loa's light, what was I thinking? I don't know why I wasted my time with you. You'll not wear my mark another moment!" She swept her arms around in a circle, murmuring words that I certainly couldn't understand. Then her whole body jerked as if she'd pulled something out of Jerry. I hoped that meant what I thought it did.

"Are we done then?" Jerry crossed his arms over his chest. "You're leaving me? Just like that?"

"Oh, we're done. Do not cross my path again." She snarled, while spirits came howling out of her fingertips to circle her in a frenzy before finally disappearing like they'd gone down a drain. She faced Rafe and me and, eerily, there was no sign of crazy Melisandra.

"My next seminar is in Dallas, next weekend. I'm sure you signed up for my e-mail list. Perhaps I'll see you there." She looked down at the two heaps of ashes. If she had any regrets for her two minions, she didn't waste time sharing them. Instead, she swept down the alley, her head held high.

We all stared after her, frozen in place, as if afraid that wasn't the end of it. But she finally turned the corner and walked out of sight. Then I ran to Jerry.

"It worked! You're free." I held on to him then smiled at Rafe. "Thanks for helping. I didn't think this would ever be over."

He laughed. "Can you believe she plugged her business at the end? That woman is a trip." He leaned against the door. "And don't you have friends in high places. Mars. Wow." He shook his head. "Glad it worked out." He disappeared inside.

"She *is* a trip. And I'll believe she's gone when I get the e-mail that she's in Dallas and ready to do her seminar." I sighed, still afraid to relax.

Jerry kissed me, taking a good long time with it. "At least Ian's potion worked as promised."

"I was worried about it. And what about Mars? Could you hear everything when you were in that weird state Mel put you in?" I couldn't let go of him.

"Oh, yeah. Mars/Loa. Whatever you call him, he seems a true warrior. And very fond of you. Did something go on with him I should know about?" Jerry raised an eyebrow.

"Are you kidding? You heard him make a date with my mother. Olympus is hinky with lots of inbreeding, but I think I'll leave him to her." I shivered in the cold night air. I knew Jerry had to feel the chill in his next-to-nothing outfit. "Hey, you promised me a turn with this sex slave thing. You still will-ing?" I really wasn't so sure I wanted to go there. I'd hated the way Mel had treated him and he still had the collar around his neck. Part of a chain dangled down his chest.

"Glory, I've always been your sex slave. The clothes or lack of have nothing to do with it." He kissed my sudden smile. "You want to head to my place and pull my chain, let's go."

I ran my hands over his back then patted his butt. "One thing first. Let me see your right thigh."

"You can see more than that at my place." He kept touching my velvet dress. "Did I tell you how beautiful you looked on that stage?"

"Thanks. Really. Now hold still. I need to make sure Mel's mark is gone. Humor me." I pulled back. "Okay?"

"Fine. Whatever. I don't remember any silly mark. But she could have done anything during my death sleep. And don't think that wasn't hell. Hitting the sheets at sunrise and not knowing what would happen while I slept." He looked grim.

"God, Jerry, I'm sorry." I dropped to my knees and studied his thigh, going past the scar to the place where the mark had been. Then I spotted it. Oh no. The x was still there. The only thing that had changed was that the heart at the bottom was missing and it was cool, not hot, to the touch. What did it mean? Was he still in danger?

"See anything there that interests you?" He was smiling because of where I had my fingertips.

"Of course. But I'm not taking this further in a dirty alley." I stood and looked into his eyes. He seemed fine so I wasn't going to share my concerns. The mark wasn't in a place where he'd notice it, especially since we couldn't see our reflection in mirrors.

"Then let's head to my place and my king-size bed. Unless

you're determined to go inside and speak to your adoring fans."
He took my hand.

"I can live without that. Let's do it." I held on tight. "Shall
we shift?"

He grinned and we did just that. Love slave. I felt like one
too. Jerry's love slave. If there was more to worry about, I'd let
it go till later. Tonight was for celebrating. And that's what
we'd do.

Nineteen

The next night Ray asked me to meet him at N-V. I felt I owed him that much, since he'd let me have my moments in the spotlight. Jerry and I arrived about an hour after sunset, too early for much of a crowd. Rafe met us at the door.

"They're upstairs in the practice room. Go on up." He nodded toward the bar. "Miguel wants to talk to you too. I'd ignore that one."

"Give me a minute." I turned to Jerry. "Do you mind? Miguel helped me last night. Gave me a pep talk when I needed it."

Jerry studied the man sipping tequila at the bar. "Really? I can't imagine what he could say or do that would be helpful. I'll stay close. I can't like the guy or his reputation."

"Fine. I'll just be a minute." I walked over to the bar. "Hey." I smiled at Miguel. "You know what you said last night? About my power? It helped me get through things."

"And did you vanquish the evil woman?" He nodded toward Jerry and then downed his drink. "I see your man has left his chains at home."

"Yes, Mel's gone and we're all good." I sat down on the bar stool next to him and shook my head when he offered to buy me a drink. "No tequila. I know I can't handle it."

"No, you can't." He put down his empty glass. "I have a question for you. Your mother. She is a goddess from Olympus. How did you find this out?"

"She claimed me. One of the other goddesses saw our resemblance and alerted her." I frowned at him. "I haven't had time to ask her about you yet. Sorry."

"Don't forget. It is important to me." He picked up his fresh drink and studied it. "I have wondered if I could be . . ." He shook his head. "Mayans have many myths and legends." His grin was startling, the more attractive because I'd so rarely seen his smile. "Okay, so the world didn't end. But we have many other prophecies that are more correct."

"Okay. You told me before that you think maybe you have a god or goddess in your background too, because we share some of the same powers. Is that one of the prophecies you're talking about? You descended from some Mayan god who'll raise the tribe to new heights or something?"

"Don't mock, Glory. I'm serious. It's not that simple. And you don't need to know what I'm talking about. But I saw you go out to the alley with a man dressed as a warrior. A man who sat at your mother's table full of toga-wearing women. Is he a god?"

"That was Mars." I studied Miguel's face. Could there be a slight resemblance? The coloring was different. Miguel definitely had the Indian black hair and eyes. But the shape of the nose and chin . . . It was possible. And Mars had said something to Mother about recognizing someone. How funny if he'd left some offspring in Mayan territory. Maybe that was another place where he was worshipped.

"You're going to think I'm crazy." Miguel looked away, pretending to examine the dance floor.

"No, I think you might be on to something. We do have the same superpowers." I touched his hand. "Reading thoughts through blocks, paralyzing people. With time we could probably figure out some more. I remember you can dematerialize too. I just learned that one."

"Right." He gripped my hand. "So you'll follow up on this for me?"

"Next time I see her, I'll ask my mother to check on it for you." I saw Jerry heading our way. "I don't think my lover is too happy that we're holding hands, Miguel. Listen, she never comes when I call. It's a control thing with her. But I'll be in touch as soon as I find out anything."

"Thanks, I'll owe you."

"Good to know." I got up and he dropped my hand just as Jerry reached my side.

"Ready to go, Gloriana?" Jerry didn't acknowledge Miguel.

"Jerry, you know Miguel Cisneros, don't you?" I wouldn't let him play that game. "He and I might be working together so I hope you'll be civil to each other." I had noticed Miguel wasn't bothering to get up or even pretend to care that Jerry had an attitude where he was concerned.

"Working together? On what?" Jerry narrowed his gaze. "I know what you do, Cisneros. Ugly business."

"Loan sharking? Or murder? I'm planning to get out of both occupations. Gloriana and I won't be involved in either, I can assure you." He tipped his glass and then finished his drink. "Excuse me. I have an appointment." He got up, dropped cash on the bar and walked away.

"Tell me that was a joke of some kind." Jerry frowned at me.

"No joke. But let's go on upstairs. I'll tell you later." I pulled him toward the stairs.

"You certainly will. The man is bad news." Jerry dropped my hand. "Don't drag me, Gloriana."

"Sorry." I looked at his set face. I was pretty sure just being here after last night wasn't exactly a treat for him. We were silent as we headed up to the practice room.

Inside, Ray, Nate and Sienna were sitting at a table with a couple of men I didn't recognize. Ray jumped up immediately with a smile.

"Here she is. Glory, this is Steve Jessup, producer from our label. He was very impressed with your performance last night. Sit down and listen to what he has to say."

I shook hands with him and was introduced to Steve's assistant who was taking notes on a tablet computer. "What is this, Ray? I told you that was a one-shot deal."

"Now, Ms. St. Clair, or may I call you Glory?" Steve was determined to start the ball rolling.

"Glory is fine." I gave Ray a look that meant I'd talk to him later.

"Glory, Ray here didn't do a thing. I was here to make sure Sienna was feeling well. And weren't we thrilled with the work she and Ray did last night." He and his assistant were beaming and high-fiving all around.

Sienna's smile looked strained. She knew now that I hadn't been bluffing about her career being in jeopardy with her vamp announcement. Seems some publicity *was* bad publicity. At least at her label.

"Anyway, then you get up there and just knock my socks off. I mean, look!" He actually pulled up his pants and showed me he didn't have on socks with his loafers. Oh, big laugh for that one.

"Thanks, Steve, but—"

"Now, hear me out. I'm telling you this is a fresh sound. I know, I know, the songs have been around for a while. More than a while. But look at what singing standards has done for Rod Stewart. Tony Bennett is still crooning just like he did back in the fifties. There's a hot market for that retro sound." He beamed at Sienna. "I know Sienna spotted the potential right away, didn't you?"

Sienna smiled at me and started talking about how we'd come up with the songs and costume. She was in her element, eager to produce a record and eager to smooth things over with the record execs. I really hated to burst her bubble but I'd already made my decision.

"I'm sorry." I stood and looked around at the group. "You are very kind. I'm flattered. But I have a business to run. One that I love. I'm not interested in a singing career. It's not for me. Aggie, the backup singer, is eager to make a name for herself. Please consider working with her. She's beautiful and has a wonderful voice." I started to say more, but bit my tongue. Hey, she could get it or not on her own.

"Now, don't be hasty. Did you know you were taped last night by at least three cell phones? You're up on YouTube already. Over ten thousand hits and climbing hourly. You looked good, sounded good. Ours won't be the only offer you receive, but remember we were first. And you'd have your friends here to work with." Steve was serious now. "Think it over. We'll be in town for a few days. Contract talks with Sienna and Ray. Here's my card. You can call me anytime."

I took it. It would have been rude not to. "Thanks, now good night." I turned and almost ran out of the room, Jerry right behind me. He hadn't said a word the entire time.

"That sounded like a great opportunity." He caught me at the bottom of the stairs.

"I don't want it." I kept going. "I enjoy my shop. I want to spend more time making it a success. Maybe you can help me draw up a business plan."

"Really?" He stayed next to me as we walked down the street toward the shop. "And all this talent you have? The singing? It will just go to waste?"

"I can sing to you, if you like. 'Loch Lomond.' And now I won't drive you to earplugs. How's that?" I stopped in front of the shop. I noticed Megan was taking down the Halloween decorations. Good. Time for turkeys and then Christmas. I loved the holidays. We usually did a good business.

"It sounds great. I'd much rather you sing a duet with me than with Caine, any night." Jerry pulled me close for a long kiss.

"Jerry, we're in public. But I'm not complaining." I laughed and kissed *him* this time. "Mel's gone and I got an e-mail tonight confirming that the Dallas seminar is filling up. She also posted a list of even more dates in cities farther north—Kansas City, Chicago, then on to New York. I think we can take it as a sign that she's moving on from her obsession with you."

"Right. I sure haven't heard from her." He kissed me again.

"There you go. I'm as happy as I've been in a long time." I sighed and leaned against him.

"Me too. There's just one thing that would make this night better. Perfect." Jerry pulled away then dropped to one knee and dragged a Tiffany's blue box out of his pocket. "This one was in a safe-deposit box." He snapped it open and the streetlight hit it, dazzling me. "Gloriana St. Clair, will you marry me?"

I blinked, totally shocked that he'd do that here and now. Megan had dropped a fake pumpkin and stared out at us. She must have signaled Lacy because she was suddenly at the window too, pushing aside spiderwebs to gawk at us. People walking down the sidewalk stopped in their tracks. Everyone knew what the down-on-one-knee thing meant. Jerry had done this before. How many times? I'd lost count.

But this time it was different. I'd finally figured out what I wanted in my life. For my life. Forever.

"Yes."

Glory's Playlist

"Whenever I Call You 'Friend,'" a great duet by Kenny Loggins and Stevie Nicks, tells a story of friendship that becomes love, but it's the other way around for Glory and Ray.

"Fever," sung by Peggy Lee, is a great vintage song that is timeless. Glory sings it in her fifties black velvet dress and pretends it's for Ray, but we know better.

"I Put a Spell on You" was performed as a sultry duet by Joss Stone on vocals and Jeff Beck on guitar. That version inspired Glory's rendition, but the song was also made popular by Creedence Clearwater Revival.